Immortality

Dee Henderson

Contact the author/publisher:
Dee Henderson
P.O. Box 13086
Springfield, IL 62791
dee@deehenderson.com
www.deehenderson.com

current printing revision: October 8, 2018

****

If you had a free summer, how would you fill it? Chemistry Professor Emily Worth is working with friends at Bishop Space Repair, Inc who are repairing satellites in space via repair robots. She's finishing a design for a new type of battery. And she's also doing some traveling to explore the Rocky Mountains. It's going to be an enjoyable three months. A relatively new Christian, she wants to know God better than she does now and that, too, is part of her summer plans. What she hadn't considered was a summer romance, but walks into one compliments of God who has been richly blessing her. This is the story of Emily Worth and Noah Shepherd. It's also a story of God's romance with us through Jesus for God has purposed in His heart to love us forever.

****

*

Good News

How beautiful upon the mountains
are the feet of him who brings good tidings,
who publishes peace,
who brings good tidings of good,
who publishes salvation,
who says to Zion, "Your God reigns."
Isaiah 52:7

*

1

"When we come back from this brief commercial break, we'll be joined by retired Astronaut Jim Bishop. Bundle up Chicago, it's a brisk 51 degrees out today with gusty winds and steady rain showers."

Always interested to hear what Jim had to say, Professor Emily Worth paused her breakfast preparations and reached for the television remote to turn up the volume for the Chicago Morning Show. She broke eggs into a skillet, put the lid on to slow cook them hard for a breakfast sandwich and opened the bread drawer to make toast. The month of May was going out the way it had come in, with days of dreary cold rain. She so missed Texas in the spring. May should be warm and filled with bike rides, street art fairs and outdoor music festivals, good barbeque and graduation celebrations, not spent reaching for jackets and umbrellas, dashing inside and forever fighting chilled hands. The last three years had been an uncomfortable reminder she had fallen in love with Texas. Being back home in Chicago was nice, but it wasn't entirely lovely.

The Chicago Morning Show came back from commercial break. "Welcome, Jim."

"It's good to be here, Allison."

"You've made quite a name for yourself in the years since you retired."

"The Space Shuttle flying its last mission rather forced that early retirement. I needed something to do, so BSR was born. Bishop Space Repairs, Inc has the capability to repair satellites while they are in orbit. We replace failing parts, reload fuel, upgrade instruments, and extend the useful life of what are very expensive pieces of technology.

"I like to say I'm a mechanic who does his best work in space. That's still the case even though I'm now on the ground working in space via repair bots, which are spider-like lobster-size robots that can move around, grip objects, use tools, and perform tasks. We will send up between 8 and 16 of the repair bots on any particular satellite repair mission along with the necessary replacement parts."

"We've all seen the rocket launches from Florida. There have been nine over the last year. You've brought video of a recent launch that we'll roll now for our viewers as we talk. Tell us about the rocket. I understand it's a breakthrough in rocket science."

"The rocket we fly is called a BBR, a Bishop Bottle Rocket. It was designed by Gina Bishop in model form nearly fifteen years ago. When I retired, that model came off the shelf, was scaled up, engineered and wind tested. Gina has figured out how to keep a rocket stable in flight without the need for adjusting engines. She has basically designed a bottle rocket that can carry a payload and hit a precise spot in space."

Emily turned to watch the rocket fly. It ignited with a spiraling ripcord of explosives around its base circumference and surged upward from the launch pad, beginning to spin even as it lifted away from the tower. Spun by the powerful unseen hand of physics, the rocket climbed into the deep blue sky leaving a sparkling glitter of burning flakes trailing in its wake like a living firework tail. It was a beautiful sight. She had that video on her phone, her laptop, on CD in very high-definition video taken by the Navy. She knew how that rocket was designed and why it flew so precisely. Gina's design was brilliant. And that rocket had been created with a touch of her own chemistry. It was a confidence booster just to watch that video. She did excellent work.

"You are 3-D printing these rockets. And isn't that an amazing statement? I don't understand the science but I can see the results of it. These rockets are flying with precision."

"We are indeed 3-D printing them near the launch site under a production agreement with the Navy," Jim replied. "They are providing us security for the process and use of the launch platform in return for the Navy now flying this rocket design for their own small scientific payloads. This type of rocket costs only a fraction of a conventional rocket and production takes only a matter of days."

"The next launch to repair a satellite is scheduled for Monday, June 17th?"

"It is. We will launch from Florida just after 8 p.m. CST to repair a communication satellite. The launch will be streaming live for anyone who would like to watch it with us. It will then take three days of orbits to intersect with the satellite in question. Repairs will begin around 10 a.m. on the 21st and will also be streaming live as you would see the video in mission control."

Emily had that date starred in her calendar. She'd been training to do the intricate maneuvers assigned to repair bot 7 for the last three months. It would be her first assist in a satellite repair and was going to be the highlight of her summer.

"We wish you every success with those satellite repairs," Allison said. "I can't leave a conversation with you, Jim, without asking the obvious question. Are you yourself planning to return to space atop one of those rockets?"

"An astronaut always dreams of being in space. Are we working toward that day? Absolutely. But for now I'm keeping my attention fixed on these repair flights, as satellite repairs will fund whatever we do in the future at BSR."

"Thank you, Jim. We appreciate you stopping by the studio today."

He did a nice job with the interview. Emily reached over for the television remote and shut off the set as the program went to another commercial break. Over the last year, Jim had been having variations of that conversation with reporters and those touring Bishop Space Repair, Inc. Only someone comfortable with both their subject and being in front of a camera could calmly deal with the fact upwards of half a million people might be watching the broadcast. The firework patents and licensing, the accompanying press conference, had hopefully been the first and final time she would ever be in front of television cameras herself. She'd been highly nervous for something not nearly as significant. She picked up her phone and sent Jim a congratulations text.

BSR was indeed working toward that day Jim could return to space, but it was still very much a work in progress. The latest simulation had been predictable in its outcome – the scaled up rocket simply exploded in a more graceful fashion than the last iteration. The Bishop Bottle Rocket had been designed with the thermodynamics of a tilting rocket in mind so it could precisely maintain vertical flight. The design worked because the fuels involved, the circumference of the rocket, the total weight and distance the rocket needed to traverse, were within a narrow functional band. The rocket used simple physics and chemistry to achieve what appeared impossible to do. But scaling the rocket to lift the larger and heavier payload of a manned capsule simply sent the rocket toppling end over end as it reached the upper atmosphere. And the production problems inherent with a heavier rocket were immense on the chemistry side of the equation.

It was going to be easier and cheaper to send Jim back to space as a tourist than it was to build a rocket capable of lifting a rugged and affordable capsule into space. Given the progress others are making with privately launched rocket and capsule designs, Jim would likely be back in space within two to five years. The satellite repairs are generating the profits necessary to secure a seat on one of those other private flights. It wasn't ideal, but it was better than there being no viable path. They'd get Jim back into space one way or another, of that Emily was certain. When the Bishop family focused on something, mountains tended to move. Going up as a tourist wouldn't be such a bad thing, given how much Jim loved space. He'd done the repair flights via the space shuttle. It was time for him to have some fun in zero gravity and just enjoy the trip.

The timer chirped for her eggs and she lifted the lid

from the skillet. She slid them onto the toast, added bacon she'd fixed in the microwave, cheese, then folded three paper towels around her breakfast sandwich. She headed to the bench in the hall to put on her shoes. She had two chemistry classes to teach and lab hours to cover. It was Tuesday. Friday was the end of the semester. She liked teaching. She also shared the joy of being done with classes just as much as her university students did. Her anticipation was exceedingly high this year. In four days her first sabbatical began. For the first time in ten years she was not teaching a summer class.

Out of habit, Emily looked at the multi-month wall calendar. This Friday night was the Chicago University faculty gathering marking both the end of the term and end of the school year. It was considered bad form to not attend when you were a tenured professor, so she'd be there. It wasn't as though there was a Friday night date vying for her time. And rather sad to say, her Saturday night was also still free. When she'd been in Austin, filling the weekend with activities had been simple as her friends had been mostly single. Here in Chicago, it was the opposite. Her friends were mostly married couples without kids who still went out on dates on Friday and Saturday nights. Even when invited to join them, she was loath to say yes and be the third at the table.

In June she had the BSR rocket launch party on the evening of the 17th and the satellite repairs on the 21st. Her birthday fell in-between on the 19th which would make that a really good full week. The rest of June and July were still mostly blank by design. She wanted to be intentional about how she spent these next three months.

She would be helping at BSR and she had work to do on her own projects. Those were two core decisions already made. Being a tenured research professor at Chicago University came with enormous freedom to explore whatever question interested her on university time and with their budget for the chemistry laboratory. She liked making use of that agreement. It had made the creation of the fireworks and now exploration of a new battery design part of her work day.

She'd be traveling this summer. She wanted to explore the Rocky Mountains and Washington State, Idaho, Colorado. She planned to take a flight west, rent a car, sightsee for a few days, then fly back, letting the weather and her mood determine when and where she went. Thanks to the firework patents and licensing she had significant additional money to work with this year. She'd decided to "waste" part of it by not trying to create a travel schedule ahead of time. She'd pay more for the plane tickets and hotel rooms, but she'd keep her summer calendar flexible and that was worth the price.

"What do you think, Jesus? What would make a really good summer?" Emily asked the question aloud knowing sometime in the next couple days a plan would formulate with the peace she'd come to recognize as God's way of saying 'let's do this'. She was learning how to interact with God. She wanted to know Him better than she did now and that was something to ponder for her summer plan too. Unscheduled time gave her options, she simply had to make decisions and then enjoy the choices she made. It was going to be a fun summer. She picked up her breakfast sandwich and headed to the university to finish out the semester on a good note.

2

Emily recorded the grade for the last student and drew a line in her official grade book. She needed to do a better job of teaching why hot plus cold equaled warm, why heat moved the way it did. It had been the common weakness in her first year student's final exams. She'd turned the knowledge of how heat moved around into a new type of battery design so it wasn't as though she didn't understand the concept. She just needed to figure out how to better present the information.

She printed the class sheet with the exam grades to post on the board in the morning. Choosing two of the color dye experiments in her freshman folder, she sent them to the printer for those who wished to raise their grade or who just wanted to tinker in the laboratory for the final class hours. She had a few students who enjoyed chemistry with the same passion she did. They weren't necessarily the top students in her grade book, but they would get there if they came back for another semester or two with her. She'd already graded the second, third and fourth year chemistry exams. Her marathon of paperwork was finally done. Emily capped her pen with relief. No students had failed this semester. Even Jason, Benjamin and Stacey, whom she had spotted early as needing extra help this semester, had managed to pass the exams.

Emily slid the graded papers into a manila folder, wrote the date of the exam and class period on the outside, then added it to the storage box destined for the archives. In three years the university would shred the papers if no one had raised a concern about some irregularity with her grading or with a particular student. The large table she had chosen over a desk for her office was finally clear of paper. She was in good shape for a Wednesday evening. Her Thursday and Friday would be marathon days of another kind as she completed the inventory of the chemistry laboratory around the final class sessions.

The leather chair she'd hauled into her office for the comfort of its big size faced the rolling whiteboard and the flat screen television. She moved over to sit there, tucked her sock feet under her and turned her attention to her latest research project. She opened the ceramic burn box beside the chair and picked up the older model phone inside, confirmed it was still on. She surfed the internet looking for podcasts about the bible she might want to listen to over the summer. It had been four years of gifts from God since becoming a Christian, one after the other, so lavish in their beauty she often found the experiences overwhelming. God had just gifted her with another one, potentially bigger than those which had already arrived, in what she was now holding.

Emily heard a light tap on the frosted glass of the chemistry lab room door and then the lock turn with a key. There were nine people with keys – a janitor, four grad students, herself, two other chemistry professors and Gina Bishop. If it had been an undergraduate student needing access after hours they would have pressed the admit button which caused the blue light here in her office to blink.

Motion sensors turned on lights in Chemistry Lab Four as her guest walked through the spacious room. Emily had chosen this office in the northeast corner of the lab so she could remain accessible to her students needing help. Hearing two sets of footsteps and guessing Gina Bishop had just arrived, Emily reached over to the small refrigerator and pulled out two cold Diet Cokes.

One of the security officers who traveled everywhere with Gina appeared in the doorway first to confirm she was alone in the office, nodded hello, and then Gina appeared as he headed back to the hall.

"You look…joyful or at least very pleased," Gina offered, after a pause to consider the right word.

"I am so glad you were still on campus," Emily replied, holding out a Diet Coke to her friend. Gina was teaching a course on Solar Weather and Upper Atmosphere Dynamics this semester.

"I wasn't, but your text message sounded interesting enough I made the short trek back from home to see you. Mark says 'hi' and you're to keep me busy for an hour. Reading the clues, I think we're going to Niagara Falls for a few days as a surprise trip."

"The power of that waterfall you would enjoy calculating. And if that is where you're going, bring me a thermos of the water so I can analyze what's in the river."

A couch was shoved up against the locked hallway door no one ever used. Gina took a seat there, put her feet up on the oversized ottoman students often sat on. "So what's going on?" Gina asked.

With Gina she didn't have to lead into the interesting science. Her friend was smarter than she was and had been breaking scientific ground since her first Ph.D. thesis on sonar. So Emily simply offered the reason for her text message. "What if you could recharge a battery with heat?"

Gina choked on the drink she had just taken and coughed to clear her windpipe. When she could breathe again, she just laughed. "Can you?"

Emily held up the older model phone. "Apparently. I've been thinking about it for a few years, but could never finish the design. God suggested a way to do so last year. This is prototype number 17 and so-far its stable. The phone has been in use for three weeks now mostly doing internet searches, never shut off, nor plugged into a charger. The battery still shows a full charge."

"Okay, wow. Your days are coming to look more and more like mine. One interesting discovery follows another."

"As long as I never need to rate the security, I'd be fine with that."

Gina shrugged, having grown philosophical about it after a few years of permanent security. "I work on topics where the Navy likes to promptly classify what I develop. You're going to have the opposite problem—first the fireworks, now this—in a few years people are going to know your name for your useful science."

"May I remind you those fireworks were mostly your doing? I helped you figure out the chemistry for your rocket design and how to 3-D print it, so give me about twenty percent of the credit for that interesting science. I came up with the new class of fireworks because the Navy wanted a false flag to lead away from your work. Mine only looks like a miniature version of your rocket."

"The best false flags have enough truth in them they appear to be the real answers. You were perfect in how that played out by the way, the patents, the licensing, the university involvement, the press conference. The way the Navy immediately scrambled in reaction, it appeared to every interested foreign intelligence service that you'd accidentally breached the line of saying too much when revealing that miniature rocket design and how the rocket and fireworks are 3-D printed. We'll have Iran, North Korea and a few other hostile governments devoting considerable time by their scientists scaling up your rocket, only to have it blow apart when carrying payloads. Which was the whole point of the endeavor. It looks like it should work, yet it never will."

"It still feels wrong, that I'm the one earning the licensing money, have my name on the patents, when the idea was both our creation," Emily mentioned.

"You did the chemistry work and fireworks are mostly chemistry," Gina pointed out. "The miniature launch rocket was simply a fun design challenge for me. You are like a decoy so I need less security around me than I otherwise might. And since I'm a principal in BSR, the real rockets are generating plenty of profit for me. Besides, consider it this way, we are both saving more than a few lives around the world by making fireworks considerably safer and cheaper to manufacture. And at the same time, the number of firework patterns and colors have spiked with the 3-D printing precision. This year's Fourth of July celebrations across the country are going to be truly new and beautiful.

Tens of millions of people are going to see your new fireworks light up the sky."

"Those are very nice fringe benefits," Emily agreed. "And won't that be a sight?"

"I predict you're about to become the new poster girl for what women can do in science," Gina mentioned with a smile. "You're good at developing new science, you've proven that over the last few years." She nodded to the phone. "And I'm already fascinated by this one."

Emily slid off the back of the phone to show the battery prototype and passed the phone over to her friend.

"It looks like a fried jelly-filled donut," Gina decided.

Emily laughed. "I'm thinking about naming it exactly that. The forever on donut battery."

"Catchy names work for a reason." Gina cautiously touched it. "It's cold, rather than hot."

"An unexpected bonus. It pulls in any heat that comes near it."

"This is fascinating. Are you willing to share the internals?"

"That's why I sent you the text. I was hoping that would be your reaction as I need help on the math for the physics going on. The chemistry I've got nailed down, but the physics is mostly intuitive guesswork. It's experimentally working, but now I need the theory to back it up. After another few months of safety work, I'll be ready to take this to patent."

"I would love to help."

Emily got up and crossed to the whiteboard, flipped it on the center axis pins to show the other side she'd filled with notes before she sent the text. "I've recreated this board so many times searching for the answer to how to make this device work that I can do it from memory. The answer for how to build it turned out to be deceptively simple."

"The best discoveries often are."

Emily took her seat again and walked Gina through the internals of the device. "All electronics generate heat, it's a waste product designers have to work around so equipment doesn't overheat and fail. If that heat could be made useful it would be a significant improvement. Hence my question – what if you could recharge a battery with heat?"

She shot a rubber band at the board and hit the starred note. "Heat causes elements to melt. That's the key to making this useful science. That part of the answer showed up early on. Positive and negative charges easily move around in liquids. Take away the heat, the elements go back to a solid state, but with polarity of charge locked in. That has always felt like the basic design.

"The problem was how to separate the charges and hold them apart as the elements solidify again. That answer fell about ten months ago – magnetism solves what I needed and can be built in by the choice of metals for the casing of the battery.

"That left solving the more minor problem of heat transportation, what brings the heat to this new battery. The overriding source of heat in most electronics is from their present battery, so with that heat source gone, I'm left with the ambient heat circuits themselves generate from power flowing around. It turns out most modern electronics have a heat conducting layer already built into the circuit board so all I needed was a snap-in design that would create a snug contact with the heat layer.

"This battery design is mostly passive chemistry, you add heat and stuff happens. Which is really useful when it comes to crafting the prototypes. I needed a device where the internal elements go from solid to liquid back to solid again without having it gunk up inside when that sequence is repeated hundreds of times. What works best looks like this jelly filled donut design. My math says these batteries should last five years under steady use. They recharge themselves with even low levels of heat. And price wise they should be cheaper than today's batteries as there is nothing particularly exotic in the chemical formula. If you run into a pinch, you can set the battery on a fifty-cent hand warmer, or out in direct sunlight on a hot summer day, and it will be fully charged in about five minutes."

"Nice. When the day comes, Bryce can help you again with the patents and licensing, the university coordination, the inevitable money management as you become not just rich but very rich."

"I like your optimism."

Gina smiled. "There's not an electronics company in the world that isn't going to be interested in this discovery. Or power company, if you can turn sunlight into direct battery charge – just think of the ways they could scale this concept up."

"I'm hopeful that's true. What I've got on paper is the design specs for this latest prototype and the power readings the device is measuring for amount of heat absorbed." She passed over the folder of paperwork to her friend.

Gina studied the pages with interest, then picked up a dry-erase marker and pointed to the whiteboard. "May I?"

"Have at it."

"I want one of these batteries. The thought of not having to find a battery charger appeals to me." Gina turned the board over to the blank side. "Why don't you order yourself in some dinner while I start sketching in some physics? That can of cashews makes for a woefully inadequate meal."

Emily reached for the basket with menus from area restaurants which delivered. "Will you split dessert with me?"

"Something chocolate would be nice."

Emily ordered a pastrami sandwich from The Chef's Corner Grill and two desserts to share and thought if the coming summer had a few dozen days in it like this one it would be fine with her. A good friend to work with, an interesting problem to complete, no particular schedule or time constraints, just a hoped for successful outcome to reach. She was living her childhood dream, for as far back as grade school she had answered the question of 'who am

I?' with 'I'm a scientist" or 'I'm a chemist' depending on the person asking. She liked this life a great deal.

The whiteboard filled in as Gina began constructing the physics that modeled the battery design. Emily watched, fascinated. She could do chemistry with that ease, but not physics. To Gina the math of physics was a language she was fluent in.

When the meal arrived, Emily settled back at the large table she used in place of a desk and unpacked the sack. Gina set down the dry-erase marker and came to the table to share dessert.

"Thanks for that math," Emily said.

"It's a good beginning," Gina assessed, considering the board. "I'll take a photo of that work and spend a couple weeks developing the rest of it." Gina unwrapped the plastic around a napkin and fork. "Have you settled on your sabbatical plans?" she asked, curious.

"For travel, its going to be the Rocky Mountains, Washington State, Idaho, Colorado. I've decided to paint some rooms in the house, shop for furniture for the guest bedroom, that kind of thing."

"That's a useful plan. I meant to ask. Have you heard from Austin University?"

Emily shook her head. "No and I don't expect them to call. They've got internal candidates who would be the safe pick."

"You would be an equally solid pick," Gina replied.

Bradley Reinhart was retiring as Dean of the Chemistry Department at Austin University. He'd been a teacher, mentor and remained a friend. Emily knew her name was on the list of individuals being considered to replace him as Dean. She'd taught at Austin University for seven years and liked the campus and the faculty. She would be faced with a difficult decision if offered his job. She had a good life in Chicago, this was home. She missed Texas. Both were equally true. She wasn't going to let herself ponder the question while it was simply theoretical, nor pray for one outcome over the other. She had no idea which would be the best location for her five years from now. "I enjoy being a tenured research professor. I like this job. I just hate the snow and cold wet springs. I miss Texas weather. I miss being able to reach the ocean whenever I want to take off for a three-day weekend and spend it on the sand and sea."

"Born in Chicago and doesn't like snow – it's a bit unexpected. For the record, I don't want you heading back to Texas."

Emily smiled. "I appreciate that, since I mainly moved back to Chicago because of you and that rocket."

"I like having you only twenty minutes away. If you want company this summer, just give me a call. Mark can handle me being gone for a few days if you want a travel buddy. And I'm always good with a paintbrush."

"Thanks, I'll likely take you up on both offers."

"You want to plan a late lunch for next week and start this vacation off right? Say Monday, 1:30? We'll talk physics, Washington State since Mark and I know it well, whatever else comes to mind, then spend a couple hours painting or shopping for furniture."

"That sounds perfect." Emily added the date and time to her calendar. A summer of afternoons like that would be ideal. She had needed this sabbatical break in so many ways. And in two days, it would officially begin.

*

3

As the faculty event concluded Friday night, Emily gathered up her jacket and the award she'd received and said goodnight to those she had met for the first time this evening. She had chosen to join the table of creative arts professors – imaging, ceramics, paint, fashion design – to change up who she sat with and add another few names to the faculty she passed on campus.

She looked around for Professor Shepherd. She had been introduced to him at one of the meet and greet gatherings three years ago when she arrived on campus. His photo on the university staff webpage had refreshed her memory of a tall gentleman and their brief casual exchange. She didn't see him in the Great Hall but there were over three hundred in attendance this evening. She could easily be overlooking him for most of the gentlemen were in suits and ties. It had been an occasion for her to bring a nice dress out of the closet and a matching jacket.

She might have better luck spotting him near the main entrance and moved that direction. The Great Hall of the Performing Arts Building where the faculty gathering had been held led out to curved sweeping steps designed by the architect to reflect the curving lines of the orchestra and theater auditoriums inside. Emily knew Professor Shepherd favored a long black coat for she would occasionally see him walking the campus in the evening even in winter. It was cool enough this evening he might have worn it. He was one of only a handful of professors who had attended this university as an undergraduate, taken his bachelors, masters and Ph.D. degrees here, then remained at the university to teach. She'd calculated he'd been on this campus eighteen years now. That was a lot of faculty gatherings and President of the University speeches to hear.

She had made one decision last night as she locked up her office and the chemistry lab to head home. It had been four years of gifts from God since she had become a Christian, one after the other, so lavish in their beauty she often found the experiences overwhelming. The rocket work, the firework designs, now a new type of battery. If God was going to gift her with chemistry ideas on that scale simply because he liked to delight her, she was going to find a way to structure her summer to get to know Him better. She learned best by going to an expert and asking questions.

"Professor Shepherd, may I have a moment?" She caught up with him on the front steps near the marble swan statute, delighted to have spotted him. "I'm professor Emily Worth. I teach chemistry, mostly to undergrads."

He had paused at his name and now smiled at her introduction. "I know who you are, Emily. Your fireworks have made you rather famous on campus."

"Oh. I suppose they have." He slowed to match her steps and she felt honor-bound to clarify matters to the extent she could. "It wasn't all it seems, all that publicity the university did when the patents were filed and the licenses were signed. They made quite a big deal of something which is rather routine."

"Your fireworks needed to garner that public attention because they were a false flag for the Navy to help obscure Gina's rocket design. I know." He shrugged at her surprise. "Gina and I were undergrads together on this campus many, many years ago. And I'm good friends with Bryce Bishop, I have him as an occasional guest lecturer. Once you've gotten that far into the family, the rest of the Bishop family rather absorbs you in."

"I've experienced the same through Gina and Jim."

He nodded toward the east parking lot as the direction he was heading. "I heard you and Gina had settled on fireworks as a direction to explore. That seemed like a novel idea to a serious problem. 3-D printing the fireworks, launching them by miniature rocket rather than lobbed shells, it will save lives during manufacturing while providing an extraordinary variety of colors and patterns.

It's a novel false flag. I'm glad you were successful."

"I wish Gina's name was also on the patents."

"There are plenty which do have her name and I predict there will be many more. Your fireworks are good science in their own right. The university is certainly benefiting financially. And from tonight's award, I'd say you are doing equally well as a teacher."

She'd received the chemistry department's Most Helpful Teacher Award as voted upon by students. "My parents were both teachers. I learned by watching them what it took to be good at this job and I've been trying to do the same."

"Tenured Research Professor of Chemistry. It speaks to the work you've invested to know your field. They'd be proud of you."

"I hope so; I wish they'd lived to see the award." She had been able to fulfill one of her parent's desires for her tonight, to be honored by her students for her dedication to teaching with excellence.

"What can I do for you tonight, Emily?"

He was younger than she had remembered, better looking, his voice deeper, and as tall, a few inches over six feet, as she recalled. She pulled together her courage to ask the favor she wanted. He hadn't brought someone with him tonight, he wasn't wearing a ring, and this could be construed as an indirect way to be seeking his time for personal reasons. In his place, she wasn't sure how she would react to this request. "I hoped to audit your course on Jesus this semester but had a chemistry class overlap. I was wondering, do you take private students? I want my life with God to have equal time with my other plans this summer. I need someone to point the direction. I'm new to being a Christian. I don't know what I don't know. I've been trying to study on my own. I've got lots of notes, but even more questions."

He stopped walking at her question, clearly surprised by the request. "I'm around campus this summer as I'm teaching a course and developing the curriculum for another two. Find my office and stop by when you like. I'll make time for you."

"Thanks. I appreciate that."

"I always enjoy a good question. And Emily? It's Noah."

"Okay, Noah." She didn't want to take up more of his time tonight, so nodded her thanks and parted ways. She felt a deep sense of relief at not having been politely dismissed. Professor Noah Shepherd had just given her permission to show up with questions. She sincerely hoped he didn't come to regret the offer. She learned best by asking questions. And if the questions were easy to answer, she would have already figured them out.

If he had said no, she would have next asked Bryce Bishop. He was as gifted a teacher of the bible as any she knew. She just preferred someone who might have already heard from other students some of the questions she wanted to ask and the campus was a convenient location. Another major decision had just been made for her summer and it felt like a good one.

"Thanks, Jesus," she said softly as she walked to her car. It was Friday night. She was already upscale dressed. The meal served with the evening program had been fine; but she was on the edge of hungry again and wouldn't mind a second good dessert. She made a call. "Jackie, can you fit me in for dessert? A table for one?"

"Come. I don't have a table for one, but Ann and Paul are in the kitchen at the chef's table and you can join them. There is a Chocolate Cherry Cheesecake coming out of the oven in ten minutes."

"Thanks. I'll be there in fifteen."

Emily hung up the phone and unlocked her car. She was crashing another couple's night. It had become the reality of her world. At least with Ann and Paul they'd been married long enough she considered it more intruding on good friends who would pick up their date night on either side of her drop-by appearance without skipping a beat.

She should have gotten married while in Austin when

she had the chance, but she'd chosen to part ways with the one guy who had wanted to take their dating relationship to that serious consideration of forever. She'd been young, not ready to mix marriage and a career, enjoying teaching and being carefree in her plans. That had been ten years ago. And no one else had appeared in those intervening years to even warrant the thought of marriage. She'd become content with being single, but on Friday nights she felt that impact more than other days.

She felt a peace settle upon her and smiled. "You're my date tonight, aren't you Jesus?" There was a tangible quality to their relationship that on nights like this was very personal. She was learning to abide in his love and let it fill up every corner of her heart. Jesus considered her his date. That was good enough for tonight in an overwhelming way.

*

4

Noah paused the high-definition video Gina had sent him as the rocket cleared the tower, beginning to spin, its base full of fire. The beauty of the image was breathtaking. The rocket wasn't a shiny white metal, but a dust gray-black, with the faintest lines of white and red flowing upward through its composite substance in apparent random fashion. They were 3-D printing rockets. And wasn't that a fascinating fact? He'd been looking for the perfect birthday gift for his brother Frank. This was the image. He'd arrange a print and get it framed in matte black.

The week before summer classes began was his favorite week of the year. Spring was in bloom. Graduation was behind him. The summer session brought students who were ambitious and students who had to catch up on a few more credit hours and area residents taking a course for personal enjoyment. They would all be attending his class at least in part by choice.

He'd spent the weekend clearing his office of one semester and setting up for the upcoming one. His summer class materials were neatly printed and ready to highlight. The coffee beans ready to grind were new and expensive. The order-in menus were updated and the petty cash tin refilled. Even the office plant was new. When he was in this office this summer, it was going to be an enjoyable experience.

This week was basically prep for the months ahead with birthday gifts, travel arrangements, errands and routine appointments to get cleared off his list. Nine weekend speaking engagements and two conferences where he was presenting three and four sessions respectively were on his calendar for June, July and August. That busy calendar suited him.

Noah reached for the phone and hit speed dial four which would ring on Gina's desk at BSR. The Bishop

family were lined up in a row in his speed dials, Bryce
Bishop being the one he spoke with most often.

"Hey, Noah," Gina answered.

"I'm thinking 17:21 in the video for a still would be
perfect."

"Hold on. I'll bring it up," Gina said. "Oh, yeah.
That's beautiful."

"Now the hard question. What size works best?" Noah
asked.

"Long and narrow conveys the scale best. And bigger
is better. The print in my office is 24 x 48. The ones in the
lobby are all 48 x 96."

"I love those lobby prints, but I'm thinking Frank
might want to hang it in the restaurant."

"Go with 24 x 48. Do you want Jim to sign it with any
particular inscription?"

"Happy Birthday, Frank."

"I'll call in the order today and have the print for you
next week."

"Thanks, Gina."

"I like small favors. It lets me hit you up with one of
my own."

Noah grinned. "Ask it."

"Bryce is working the grill for the Bishop Fourth of
July party and he needs meat, a lot of it. Do you think
Frank would be willing to put in a good word for us with
his butcher? And could you handle the pickup and
delivery? We'll feed you well, I can promise you that. I'm
not even going to ask if you're coming because you have to
be—Emily's fireworks are going to be public for the first
time and I plan to hand you a video camera so you can help
me get crowd reactions as they see her fireworks for the
first time. I want to do a video montage as a record of that
night for her."

"To the first part, no problem, that's easier than being
asked to source the sodas. To the second part, I'll be glad to
help, as it will make a nice gift." He didn't have to look at
his calendar to check if the holiday was free. His travel

schedule had stepped on too many of the Bishop gatherings in prior years. He'd been declining invitations this year to keep some launch dates and the major holidays open.

Catching motion in the corner of his eye, Noah glanced over and realized the woman in question was standing in his office doorway. "Hold on a sec, Gina." He moved the phone to the side. "Gina Bishop. Want to talk to her while I have her on the line?"

"We're having lunch at one thirty," Emily Worth replied.

He nodded toward the couches in his office for her to have a seat. "Gina, Emily just walked in. I'll see you next week. Thanks again for the favor."

"Anytime."

He hung up the phone.

"Welcome to the Bright-Wells Building, Emily." Out of politeness he moved from behind his desk to the second couch set at a facing angle. He spent most of his days in conversation with students and faculty alike and had arranged his office accordingly. Emily had come and found him mid-morning on Monday, he found that useful information. It told him her request of Friday night mattered to her. "I hope the signs have been restored so you didn't wander down too many wrong hallways."

She smiled at his comment. "I was warned before I set out this direction. Signs being swapped is a rather tame last day of class prank. In the chemistry building you watch out for novel shades of dyes on doorknobs, sodas which foam and the occasional stink-bomb."

He chuckled at her description; he'd heard rumors which were apparently birthed in fact. "You trained them well, so they have a built-in need to impress their teacher with a bit of showing off."

Her phone chimed and he nodded to it so she wouldn't feel obligated to ignore it for courtesy sake. Adapting to technology and multiple conversations was a fact of life for a professor. Emily pulled out her phone to scan the message.

"Excuse me, Noah, this one does need an answer."

"Sure."

She quickly typed a reply.

The Bright-Wells Building was the most historic of the campus buildings. The most beautiful in Noah's estimation, but also the most remote, tucked between the equipment garage used by the maintenance staff and what had once been the President's House which now served as both the University Museum and the Library Archive. You didn't happen to pass by the Bright-Wells Building, it was your destination.

Emily's reply triggered another incoming message. "Do you know what time it would be in Japan?" she asked, typing again. "I normally wear a watch set to Tokyo time but forgot to pick it up this morning."

"I can look it up."

"That's okay. My grad student is an excellent chemist but English is still difficult for him. I use his sister who still lives in Japan to have three-way conversations on important matters. He was just selected for a research position in Boston, he'll have a full-ride scholarship to his Ph.D. They made a great choice."

"Congratulations are in order."

"They certainly are. I'm going to miss him."

"Your first major placement of someone you've taught here?" He'd looked up her bio in the faculty database and knew she had been teaching here three years, had been teaching at Austin University in Texas for the seven years prior.

"Third, but yes. Everyone has landed somewhere interesting, either in job offers or continuing on in graduate school. Some will be here a few more years, but there are always a few standouts in each class. I've been watching what unfolds with four students in particular."

It spoke well of her that she'd been making that effort to know what was going on with students she had taught. This was a university that excelled nationally in the physical sciences, in medical sciences, and to a lesser degree in architecture and business. Philosophy and Languages, World History, Political Science were here as well, if of lesser importance in the curriculum.

Noah knew he was well liked among the student body, but his lectures would never be widely sought after. He taught theology at a secular university. Religious studies were the university's way of saying we're inclusive. You could take a class on Religious World History. You could elect to take a class on Hinduism, Islam, or Christianity. You could take Comparative Religions. He had classes full of skeptical students needing to mark a humanity elective off their degree requirements who had decided listening to him was better than their other options. He considered it an opportunity to present Christianity in a way most of them had never heard before.

He enjoyed teaching. He hadn't wanted to become a pastor. He'd wanted to teach what the bible said in a way that challenged people to think. Teaching theology at a secular university was a perfect fit. It was why he had taken his bachelors, masters and Ph.D. degrees here. A former professor and mentor whose office he now occupied had been integral in helping him achieve his goal to remain and teach here.

Emily smiled, sent a single emoji reply and shut off her phone. "Sorry, I should have done that before I walked into your office. Thanks for giving me the minutes to handle that."

"It's no problem." Noah noticed a subtle shift as she put away her phone. Now that the student matter was addressed, it returned to being why she had come to see him. She no longer looked nearly as at ease. Noah leaned over and opened the half size refrigerator, the top of which served as a makeshift stacking place for books being loaned out or returned by students. "I've got orange juice, sodas and water, if anything appeals."

"I'm good for now, thanks."

He retrieved an orange juice for himself. The faculty who came to see him with a question most often were leading into asking for advice about a student who was a concern or about a personal matter, the addiction of a family member, marriage troubles. He had become something of a chaplain by virtue of what he taught. Conversations which began as questions often turned into counseling sessions. Noah wasn't sure what to predict with Emily given the way she'd phrased her request Friday.

Emily's remark she was a new Christian had caught his interest. He'd like to know if that decision had come before or after her move to Chicago. The odds were good it was just before and a relationship in Austin had ended because of that difference on religion, with Emily moving to Chicago in the breakup aftermath. Emily was going to be interesting to get to know, if only because she was a shared mutual friend of the Bishop family and he already liked what he knew of her science. Not knowing what to expect, Noah relaxed against the couch and let Emily open the conversation wherever she liked.

"Am I intruding on your preparation time? Summer classes begin next Monday. I always needed the week before to prepare for the longer, more intense, class periods."

Noah knew what Emily meant by intense. His summer class met for three hours each Tuesday and Thursday morning. "Thanks for asking, but I'm in good shape. I'm refreshing my own recollection of the material this week, but the course is one I've taught several times."

To give her time to become at ease again, Noah gave her the brief overview of what he expected to be his summer. "A course on Biblical Prophecy attracts the spiritually curious. If history is a guide, I'll have in attendance self-professed psychics and witches and fanatical Christians—a description used not as a put-down but simply for accuracy. Fanatical fans of a sports team see all the games, quote all the stats, know every player and remember all the team history. Christians coming to a Biblical Prophecy class have typically memorized everything the bible says about the last days and have deciphered what date they think best fits when the world will end. I like choosing to teach a fun class for my summer."

"It sounds like you enjoy that diversity."

"I do. I first teach how to evaluate prophecy by discussing fulfilled prophecies we can verify. I then show that Jesus statistically is himself a unique fulfillment of prophecy. Jesus is the prophesied Messiah. Then I take the statements Jesus makes about the end times, the prophecies in Daniel and Revelation, to present the descriptions of hell and the Throne of Judgment. If the prophecies in a book which can be verified are true, they gives weight to the reasoned conclusion that the prophecies in the book which are describing future events will also prove true. Biblical Prophecy is actually a course about Jesus without the weight of that name in the course title."

"That sounds intense and answers one of my questions. I wondered how specific you could be in presenting the bible when it is a secular university."

Noah smiled at her statement for it showed both a common and rather naïve understanding of tenure. "I'm a tenured professor of theology teaching elective classes on Christianity. I have more freedom to discuss the bible than most preachers do within their denominational boundaries. What I don't do is ask students 'would you like to believe in Jesus?' in a classroom setting. Nor do I grade based on a student's beliefs. I grade based on participation, knowledge of the presented material, reading assignments, open book tests and typically two papers they write. I ask students to answer questions based on what I said in class or assigned in reading and to put an X at the end of an answer if they personally disagree with it. After the X, they have the option to add what they would consider to be the correct answer. I'm not looking for uniformity of beliefs, but for students to be students. I'm asking them to think. We read the bible in class and outside of it just as students would do with any other course textbook."

Emily considered that reply and nodded when she

grasped what he had said. "The basic chemistry textbook I use is filled with details students need to grasp to be able to understand the concepts coming in the next chapters. I think I'm here because I need a textbook for Christianity. Something that can orderly fill in a foundation of what I should know and then build on it. I know Jesus, but not as well as I would like. I'm learning my way around the bible, but it is still fitting together for me. I don't understand what God is saying in many passages. While that doesn't make me feel stupid, it does make me feel frustrated that I'm not seeing what I should be by now. I want to be making better progress in knowing this God who loves me, who has astonished me the last four years with his incredible goodness."

Noah knew the feeling she was expressing about God's goodness from personal experience. He didn't bother to glance at the floor to ceiling bookshelves that ran the length of his office's east wall. There were books, if chosen wisely, that could be that systematic guide. But Christianity wasn't a set of facts like chemistry, it was a relationship with Jesus. Time spent with Jesus asking questions about those scriptures would bring Emily that understanding she was after as well as deepen their personal connection. Jesus and the Holy Spirit both loved to teach and would often use scriptures to explain another scripture, or would bring a specific answer via a specific book. So Noah chose to set aside the suggestion of a foundation book for now to come back to the subject later. He offered instead the best analogy he had for what she was experiencing.

"Studying scripture is rather like learning a new language. The bible has sections which are history, others of poetry and songs rich with emotional words, portions that are instructions, fascinating passages of God speaking in first person, chapters of prophecy which are filled with visual language discussing coming events, teaching passages filled with details about God and the invisible spiritual world around us. All of scripture has one outcome – you are learning to hear God's voice. He authored the bible using people he chose as his secretaries. He wrote it to be understood. But some scripture is like milk and some like meat, some is easier and some more advanced. I can teach you how to see the arc that runs across all of scripture which will help you fit the narrative together. I can show you how the first use of a term can help bring clarity to understanding later passages. And I can give you some practical suggestions for how to let the Holy Spirit guide your study and help you. But first," Noah nodded to what she had brought, knowing it was important to her and thus to this conversation, "what did you bring with you?"

Emily opened the lid on an inch-high box that had once held mailing labels. "I brought some of my notes and questions. I keep a ream of paper available as I study so I can write down verses and useful passages I read in books. I circle questions as I have them. Some questions I've found the answer to by further study, many of the questions remain open. I've got a lot of paper on bible related studies, not nearly as much as I do on chemistry, because I've loved chemistry for decades, but a lot of notes."

Noah leaned over to the table with the lamp, opened the cabinet door below, took the first inch of loose paper off the stack and held it up. "Look familiar? Notes like this?"

Emily tilted her head slightly as she smiled. "Your handwriting is considerably neater than mine."

He nodded and put the pages back. "You either think in your mind, think on paper, or do a combination of both. If you think on paper you can go back and see how you arrived somewhere. I have questions in my stacks of paper which go back to my undergraduate days."

"How much paper do you have after all these years?"

"A spare room full. The shelves are neatly labeled by year. I pare it down frequently, but those accumulating pages produce what I teach on now and what I have published."

The fact she was a note taker by her own choice, a reader, told him how she best learned information. He'd be offering her books knowing she would read them. For those who learned best by hearing, he had a vast archive of sermons and teaching sessions to share as resources. He'd give her a few audios, but they wouldn't be his main contribution as a way to help her. Noah nodded to her box. "So what kind of questions are you wresting with?"

Emily picked up the pages from the box. "I pulled together a random assortment just to give you a sense of what I would like to ask you. Do you mind if I just read you some of these questions / topics? They aren't in any particular order of importance."

"Sure, that's fine with me." Noah thought about getting a legal size pad of paper off his desk to make a list of them but set aside the thought in favor of just listening to how she presented the questions. She'd chosen questions and topics to bring with her, which told him they wouldn't be as random as she thought. She would have subconsciously rejected bringing questions which sounded overly basic and thus be embarrassing to ask him. The number of people who wanted to ask him 'Who is Jesus?' but who didn't have the nerve to ask that basic of a question was so prevalent among those he spoke with he would often simply give that answer as though they had asked the question. Emily had also likely stacked that box in an order that obscured the question that most mattered to her. It probably wouldn't be the first question or the last. But there was a reason she had decided to track him down and ask for his time now versus a year ago. She had a question she deeply wanted to find the answer to and he'd likely hear it in this first conversation.

"This first one is showing my chemistry background. God made every living thing to replicate through seeds. An apple tree produces apples which have seeds for more apple trees. A grain of corn planted grows a stalk with several ears of corn. Plants multiply through producing seeds in abundance. Fish, animals, mankind, have sperm, seed, that create babies after their own kind. Living things multiply in abundance. So my question is this. Can matter replicate?

Does matter also have a seed nature?

"I read two accounts in the Old Testament that were intriguing. In the first, oil in a jar continued to pour until the widow had no more empty jugs to pour the oil into, then the oil stopped flowing. In the second, flour and oil never ran out, they continued to be present in jars to feed a widow, her son and Elijah the prophet, while a famine was in the land. Oil was producing more oil. Flour more flour. Do those two examples point to the existence of a law of multiplication for matter which we haven't discovered yet?

"For example, gravity – things fall down – has been understood by experience since Adam and Eve. The law of lift overcomes the law of gravity. But we didn't understand the law of lift and didn't develop airplanes until the 1900s. God, who understands the law of lift, created birds which fly. So in these Old Testament examples, was God using a law of multiplication for matter which He understands and which anyone could use today, if we simply understood how it worked?"

Noah rarely got surprised by a question, but she had just stunned him. "I love that question, Emily. Even God's word is described by Jesus as being a seed which produces what it says. I'm curious to see what the bible has to say on the topic of matter and will do some research for you. There is logic to your question and the intriguing possibility there might be something there waiting to be discovered. It's certainly worth the time to think about the question and investigate what clues scripture gives us."

"Thanks." Emily looked clearly relieved he hadn't dismissed that question as fanciful or out-of-bounds and turned pages to offer another one.

"Another science type question. There are detailed lists for the years people lived and when their children were born. Are the lists complete? Do the genealogy records give a date for when Adam and Eve lived? Genesis says Adam and Eve were created on the sixth day of creation. Do we know how old the earth is? The stars and galaxies?"

Noah nodded his approval of that question. He spent a

good deal of time talking about God as the Creator and the timeline of history with those who were scientists or who were studying the sciences as part of their education.

"A question about prayer. What does it mean to ask something in Jesus' name? What does the phrase 'in my name' mean? The way Jesus brought up the subject suggests there is enormous authority and power conveyed in doing so. But I don't understand that phrase and what Jesus was granting to us."

Emily was asking the right questions. Noah looked to his bookshelf to see if any of the Jack R. Taylor books had been returned, in particular the one on the kingdom of God. He didn't see it and made a mental note to buy another copy. It was a useful title and one he was frequently loaning out.

Emily moved several pages to the back of the stack and then stopped and fanned out three pages. "I have an involved question about the timing of things. Jesus took all my sins on himself and was punished for all my sins on the cross. That is why God can forgive me. Jesus exchanges my sins for his righteousness.

"Jesus on the cross is in the year A.D. 33.

"I wasn't born yet.

"I know God operates outside of time, but can you help me understand this better? Salvation was finished for me before I was born. But it is when I repent, believe and am baptized that I receive my salvation. Are all God's gifts to me like this? God has already done them for me before I was born and they are now mine to receive in the present day? Is this why Jesus said on the cross 'it is finished'?"

"It is," Noah replied, intrigued that she was already exploring how the timeline worked. "A brief answer for now?"

"Sure." Emily reached for a pen and turned to a blank piece of paper to make notes.

Noah chose to begin his answer with a question. "Who would you say most believes God the Father keeps his word? It's not a trick question."

Emily thought for a moment and replied, "Jesus."

Noah smiled as he nodded. "Exactly. Everything Jesus does hinges on the fact he trusts his Father to keep His word.

"God sends His Son Jesus to be the Savior of mankind, to save us from the mess our sins have made, to save us from death followed by eternal hell. But before Jesus comes, God writes down what salvation for mankind will look like and what will be required of the Savior. The details are described in the bible in many places, one of the most well known passages being Isaiah 53. The Old Testament is the record of God's words to mankind before Jesus comes as the Savior and it contains numerous references to his coming.

"Jesus is born in the land of Israel in the town of Bethlehem and dies on a cross outside Jerusalem in A.D. 33. We mark our modern calendar as starting at his birth. During those 33 years, Jesus pays the price to be the Savior of all mankind. That price was a sinless life and his death on a cross. At the cross he took upon himself all of mankind's sins and diseases, was cursed, and bore our punishment from a righteous God. Jesus tastes death for all mankind. Jesus is resurrected from the dead three days later. What we call the New Testament are accounts written by the witnesses to Jesus' life and resurrection and their letters to the first century churches.

"Jesus inaugurated the church ten days after his ascension back to heaven. Some of the New Testament is written by the men closest to Jesus like Peter, Matthew and John. About a third is written by Paul, who at first persecuted Jesus, only to later have an encounter with the risen Jesus and realize Jesus was in fact the Son of God. Paul would be used by God to take the good news about Jesus to the entire Gentile (non-Jewish) world. The last accounts included in the New Testament were written around the years A.D. 70 to A.D. 95."

Noah paused there so Emily could catch up on her notes. With that information as the backdrop, the answer to her question was straightforward. He wanted to present it in a way that conveyed the beauty of what God had done without making too many assumptions regarding what she already knew. The good news of Jesus was so vast he had come to think of it as ever expanding good news. Time spent with Jesus, reading the scriptures and listening to good teaching continually brought more understanding of what was included in the good news. Emily nodded she was ready and Noah offered the best answer he had for her question.

"Think of Jesus as a man who wrote a will. He died and the terms of his will are now in effect. A man can leave gifts in his will to future generations not yet born. That is, in effect, what Jesus did for you. A new will, what the bible calls the new covenant, is now in effect.

"It's a beautiful agreement. Under the terms of the new covenant, God not only forgives our sins, God agrees He will not even remember our sins and misdeeds anymore. When we accept Jesus, God changes us from being sinners into saints. All the gifts Jesus secured for us by being our Savior – forgiveness, righteousness, peace with God, adoption as a child of God, healing, deliverance, riches, the gift of the Holy Spirit, eternal life, heaven – are listed in God's word. We receive these gifts because of the agreement God made with Jesus our Savior. Their agreement has been written down, fulfilled, finished. We aren't actors in the agreement, but recipients of it. We are the beneficiaries."

He paused there as he saw her smile.

"Oh, that's perfect, Noah. A.D. 33 to today – there's still a will in effect leaving gifts to me."

Emily's joy was apparent in her voice. It really was good news. "When Jesus rose from the dead, he became what is called the Mediator of this new covenant. God raised Jesus from the dead, exalted His Son to sit at His right hand in heaven and gave Jesus all authority in heaven and earth. Jesus is now like the executor of his own will, as his death is what put this agreement into effect. Jesus' blood secures it. Every good and perfect gift that God desires to give us flows to us through Jesus and this new covenant. Every request we make of God flows to God's throne through Jesus and this new covenant. Jesus is the Mediator, the one whose blood made peace between God and man.

"God's gifts to you in the present day depend only on what Jesus has already done for you. You can't be too bad in character or conduct to disqualify yourself from being eligible. If God waited to act until after you were showing yourself good or bad, righteous or evil, you might in error think his gifts had something to do with you. God gives us grace, something which is unearned, when He gives us salvation. These gifts were determined before you were born and they are the same for every man, woman and child of every nationality. As John 3:17b says, 'God sent the Son into the world, not to condemn the world, but that the world might be saved through him.' Your choice is do you want to accept Jesus and what he has done for you. God will honor your decision because He always honors free will.

"There is only one way to become a beneficiary of this new covenant. That annoys many who think it is wrong to say there is only one way to God. But their annoyance doesn't change the truth. God sent only one Savior to help mankind. Jesus says of himself, 'I am the way, and the truth, and the life; no one comes to the Father, but by me.' (John 14:6). Jesus is our Savior and way back to God. In John 8:24b Jesus says, 'you will die in your sins unless you believe that I am he [the Savior].'

"These gifts from Jesus are free because they aren't earned by our own works. But the acceptance price is following Jesus and that is a lifetime decision. Following Jesus is a choice that comes from your heart. Jesus becomes your lover and you are choosing him, and your relationship with him, over everything else in life. You are committing to his agenda, his thoughts and his directions. He laid down his life to save yours; you now lay down your life and accept his. That's the decision that brings you into this new covenant."

Noah fleetingly saw intense discomfort cross Emily's expression as he finished his answer. He didn't have to ask its cause. She was a new Christian. She had used the past tense in reference to her parents Friday night. Either her parents hadn't believed or a sibling in the present didn't and that was a tough reality to live with. He suspected the chief reason she had come to see him was ultimately going to be found in a question she had about her family. And that was likely to be a very difficult conversation for both of them.

Emily quietly finished her notes and nodded. Noah saw when she chose not to ask about her family, a peace returned to her expression as she refused to follow that train of thought. She instead tapped the third page she had fanned out. "That answer takes me directly into this related question. How do we receive the things God has given us? How do they become our experience? Is it as simple as they just happen or do we need to do something in particular to receive them?

"For example: Jesus said I give you my peace. (John 14:27). He said come to me and I will give you rest. (Matthew 11:28). Peter writes God has given us all things which pertain to life and godliness. (2 Peter 1:3). In Corinthians it says we have received the Spirit from God that we may know the things freely given to us by God. (1 Corinthians 2:12). To know something is more than mental knowledge about something. To know something is to experience it. Is it by the Holy Spirit that we experience these gifts God has given us?"

"The short answer is yes," Noah replied. "It's summed up in Deuteronomy 28:2b 'all these blessings shall come upon you and overtake you because you obey the voice of the Lord your God.'

"We have a personal Father, we are now children of God and He's written down what He desires to give us in the scriptures. This is a relationship where the Father respects what we desire and gives what we ask. If we don't ask, we won't receive. Jesus says, 'Ask, and it will be given you; seek, and you will find; knock, and it will be opened to you. For every one who asks receives, and he who seeks finds, and to him who knocks it will be opened.' (Matthew 7:7-8) Our Father invites to come have a conversation with him about life and what we need.

"Gifts originate with God the Father and with Jesus in the invisible heavenly realm and it is The Holy Spirit, God now on earth, who makes these gifts visible to us in the physical realm. Faith is our confidence in God, the Word of God and Jesus during the window of time between when we ask and when we have. Once we have seen in the Word of God what God wants to give us, we ask for it, we keep a steady faith knowing the Word is true and God fulfills His Word, and we will have what we have asked."

Emily nodded, writing down that answer. "That's very helpful."

She sorted through the pages she had brought with her. "There's a related question I had about the Holy Spirit. Jesus sends the Holy Spirit to us from God the Father. The Holy Spirit dwells in us. Scripture says we are to be led by the spirit, walk with the spirit, be filled with the spirit, pray in the spirit. We are told not to quench the spirit and not to grieve the spirit. What does that look like in a typical day? I'm not sure I understand how I am to interact with God the Holy Spirit."

"We'll enjoy that conversation. We interact with the Holy Spirit as we do with other people – we talk with Him and He with us. He does things by His power, just as we do things by our own muscle power, only the Holy Spirit's power is immeasurably greater in its force. The Holy Spirit applies his power to things in the invisible world as well as the physical visible world. Every healing recorded in the scriptures is the Holy Spirit applying his power to destroy a disease or restore a body."

He paused the conversation for a moment. "I'm not asking for a label – Catholic, Baptist, Methodist, Presbyterian, Evangelical, Charismatic, Pentecostal – rather the comfort level you have with conversations about the Holy Spirit. How would you describe your background?"

"I don't know enough to tell you what the differences are between those groups of Christians," Emily replied. "My grandmother's Bible with her underlined verses is my primary church background. I was attending a campus church in Austin for just over a year before I moved to Chicago. I was baptized there. The pastor's background was Baptist, but the church gathering of students was diverse and my teachers had a variety of backgrounds. I've been attending Lake Christian Church since moving here.

"I like to talk about the Holy Spirit. I know He's God. I know He's the Spirit of Truth. I know he's a Teacher who loves to teach, as that's the primary way I know Him thus far. And I often feel him as the Spirit of Peace, the Comforter with me. I know He dwells in me and is with me. I'm simply not sure how I'm suppose to be interacting with Him, what I'm doing that He likes and what I'm doing that is causing Him grief. Our relationship is still mostly a mystery to me."

Noah wanted to hear her history of coming to Jesus in more depth but for now she had given him enough to have a sense of what she was looking for with her question. "We'll spend some time talking about that relationship." Noah nodded to the papers she held. "Tell me more. You've brought good material."

Emily turned pages and pulled out one. "Isaiah 53 is Isaiah prophesying about Jesus on the cross. Matthew quotes from it when he writes, 'when Jesus entered Peter's house, he saw his mother-in-law lying sick with a fever; he touched her hand, and the fever left her, and she rose and served him. That evening they brought to him many who were possessed with demons; and he cast out the spirits with a word, and healed all who were sick. This was to fulfil what was spoken by the prophet Isaiah, "He took our infirmities and bore our diseases."' (Matthew 8:14b-17) Matthew is quoting Isaiah 53:4. Peter also quotes that verse when he writes, 'He himself [Jesus] bore our sins in his body on the tree, that we might die to sin and live to righteousness. By his wounds you have been healed.' (1 Peter 2:24) It's a past tense statement. What Jesus did gives us physical healing. So my question is, are Christians never to get sick?"

Noah smiled. "It's a great question. If you haven't listened to the conversational tapes between Connie August and Ryan Cooper on the topic, remind me to get you a set." Connie August had been a combat medic for eight years and had experienced healings and miracles on the battlefield similar to those in scripture. She taught on the subject in a practical way. Emily would know her at least by sight, as Connie was engaged to Jason Lasting, the worship leader at Lake Christian Church.

"I've met Connie, but haven't heard the audios," Emily mentioned, making a note of the names.

"I'll get you a set." Noah had a couple brief answers regarding the topic and offered the first. "Isaiah 53:4-6 are pivotal verses to understanding the agreement God made with his Son. I'll quote the Young's Literal Translation of the Hebrew as its shows the verb tense of what Isaiah wrote:

Surely our sicknesses he [Jesus] hath borne, And our pains -- he hath carried them, And we -- we have esteemed him plagued, Smitten of God, and afflicted. And he is pierced for our transgressions, Bruised for our iniquities, The chastisement of our peace [is] on him, And by his bruise there is healing to us. All of us like sheep have wandered, Each to his own way we have turned, And Jehovah hath caused to meet on him, The punishment of us all. (Isaiah 53:4-6 YLT)

"Isaiah is seeing something 700 years in the future as already fulfilled and finished, that's how emphatic God was about what would happen on the cross. God has healed me because of His agreement with His Son. We were healed in A.D. 33 by Jesus on the cross. It's done. No matter the

disease, Jesus has taken it from me and given me health in
its place. Jesus took everyone's sin, sickness, pains and
punishment on himself. We receive forgiveness, peace, and
healing. That's the new covenant.

"We receive that gift of healing by faith, just as we do
every gift Jesus offers us. Hebrews says 'without faith it is
impossible to please him [God]. For whoever would draw
near to God must believe that he exists and that he rewards
those who seek him.' (Hebrews 11:6b) What rewards does
God give? Forgiveness, healing, redemption, love. The
word translated benefits in Psalm 103 is the Hebrew word
for rewards.

Bless the LORD, O my soul,
and forget not all his benefits [rewards],
who forgives all your iniquity,
who heals all your diseases,
who redeems your life from the Pit,
who crowns you with steadfast love and mercy,
who satisfies you with good as long as you live
so that your youth is renewed like the eagle's.
Psalm 103:2-5

"Like Isaiah 53, Psalm 103:2-5 is another description
of what Jesus does for us on the cross. God gives those who
seek Him these rewards. Which is why we are charged not
to forget any of them. You won't have faith to receive a
particular reward if you don't know, or you've forgotten,
that gift is yours.

"Believe Jesus on the cross healed you, have faith in
what the Word of God says, ask God to give you that
reward, and your body will heal. Physical healing is a free
gift from God just like forgiveness of our sins."

"Wow." Emily stopped her notes simply to take that
answer in.

"Wow indeed," Noah agreed, having felt the same
when the truth had registered with him. "How healing
becomes mine as a Christian is elegant. Life is the source of

health. Jesus says about himself, 'I am the way, and the truth, and the life'. (John 14:6b) He's being literal. Jesus is the way to the Father. Jesus is *the truth*. Jesus embodies truth in everything he says and does. What he says is the truth, nothing he says is shaded by a lie. And Jesus is *the life*. Jesus abiding in us is literally the life in us. Jesus was never sick during his years on earth and that's the kind of healthy vibrant life we now have abiding in us. In Romans it says the Holy Spirit dwelling in us gives life to our mortal bodies. The Holy Spirit is also called the Spirit of Jesus. Paul describes it as the life of Jesus being manifest (made visible) in our mortal bodies."

"That's very useful. The references?"

"The Holy Spirit gives life to our mortal bodies – Romans 8:11, The Holy Spirit also being called the Spirit of Jesus is Philippians 1:19 and 1 Peter 1:11, the life of Jesus being manifest in our mortal bodies – 2 Corinthians 4:10-11."

Emily wrote down the references. "Do you have most of the New Testament memorized? You quote verses and their locations with ease."

"I was studying and teaching in this field before apps on phones made it simple to look up verses so the verses I studied the most often ended up memorized."

"You didn't just start one day and decide I'm going to memorize the book of Philippians?"

"I wasn't that studious about it," Noah replied with a smile. "Christians are sick because they don't know they have life abiding in them and have already been healed. There is no disease or death in life. Our salvation includes healing. But until you believe that and say thanks, take communion knowing what Jesus has done for you, the Holy Spirit can't show the life of Jesus in your mortal body. You're quenching what the Holy Spirit freely does."

"Ouch."

"People need taught," Noah replied, understanding her sentiment, but already knowing its answer. "Life is like blue eyes to Jesus. Jesus has life as an intrinsic characteristic of his being. Jesus doesn't have to do anything in particular to heal us. Jesus is the life. He just needs to abide in us. It is his presence in us via the Holy Spirit which heals us and keeps us in health.

"Jesus left us one thing to do. Jesus gave us communion. In John 6:56-57 Jesus says, 'He who eats my flesh [the bread] and drinks my blood [the juice] abides in me, and I in him. As the living Father sent me, and I live because of the Father, so he who eats me will live because of me.' Jesus is describing communion.

"God's gift to us is life. Jesus abiding in us is how God gives us that life. Romans 5:17b says, 'those who receive the abundance of grace and the free gift of righteousness [will] reign in life through the one man Jesus Christ.' My healing happens because Jesus – life – now abides in me. Life is the source of health. The truth is elegant." Noah chose to pause there, aware he'd begun expressing the same truth in different ways.

"I feel like everything I knew just slid into the trash as overcomplicated," Emily remarked. "I am already healed because I have Jesus abiding in me right now. I just didn't know it, so I couldn't express faith in that fact."

"That's it," Noah agreed. "The most powerful medicine in the world is the word of God. Jesus healed us at the cross in A.D. 33. God healed every disease, no matter how progressed or debilitating.

"God wrote to us his children through Solomon, 'My son, be attentive to my words; incline your ear to my sayings. Let them not escape from your sight; keep them within your heart. For they are life to him who finds them, and healing to all his flesh.' (Proverbs 4:20-22) The Hebrew word also translates as 'medicine' to all flesh. If we get sick, God's word will powerfully bring us back to health if we're attentive to it and we get those promises regarding healing into our hearts so the Word can produce what it says. Our side is faith in what the Word says and obedience to the Holy Spirit.

"You take communion with faith, abiding with Jesus

who is your life. Then you do whatever else the Holy Spirit directs. God may heal us without a doctor, with the help of one, we may be healed immediately or gradually, when we seek God for healing in agreement with other Christians or privately on our own – our experiences will vary but the outcome is assured. At its core, life and health comes down to one exchange. When we have faith that we were healed at the cross, God promises to freely give us that reward."

Emily finished her notes. "Thanks. I want to come back to this answer after I think on it for a while."

"Sure. It's a topic which gets ever richer the more you think about it."

Emily thumbed through the rest of the papers she held, then stopped and tapped them lightly against the box lid to straighten the pages. "There are more questions, some harder than others, but that's a good sample." She put the pages back into the box.

"Thanks for sharing them."

She'd given him 7 questions and topics. The range of them showed she liked to think about what Christianity was and how it functioned. They were all interesting questions and topics in different ways. But which had been her big question that brought her to his office now?

Noah considered them and surprisingly thought she hadn't asked it. She'd given him well thought out questions and topics as a good student would, she was trying to learn and understand the truth scripture presented. But none of them felt like what would have triggered her to seek him out now. He'd learned to trust that internal impression for what hadn't been said in a conversation. He hoped she'd come to trust him enough to ask it.

They had been talking about forty minutes. It felt like a logical place to conclude given she had lunch plans with Gina. "Those are all good questions. Let's talk about them, and others you have, as you have time this month. We'll simply start a conversation at one of those points and see where it goes. In the meantime, a few resources do come to mind." Noah walked over to his bookshelf, found the book

Foundational Truths by Derek Prince and scanned the index. "Add this one to your reading list. And this one." He selected a book titled Understanding Genesis by Dr. Jason Lisle, for it was a useful guide for understanding basic analysis of scripture texts. He added Transformed for Life by Derek Prince as the thinner volume of the three and probably the most helpful to her today.

Emily accepted the books. "Thanks. May I come by again this week? This conversation was very helpful."

"Come by daily if you like. I'm fine with drop in visits, it's how my days are designed. If I need to pause a conversation to assist a student, I'll do so. You can't interrupt me at an inconvenient time. If I don't want to be interrupted, I'm simply not on campus. I've got an equally comfortable office at home when I want a few quiet hours to work on something."

"That's easy enough." She gathered her things. "Thanks, Noah."

"You're welcome."

He paused her when she reached the door. "One comment before you go?" She turned back with an inquiring look.

"You've been astonished at what God has done the last four years. He's just begun what he has planned. God would like to do even more good things for you. Just keep walking the way you have been and enjoy what He brings into your life. He'll lead the way."

Emily looked startled, then smiled. "Thanks, Noah."

She left, but her footsteps only went so far before they paused and she came back to the doorway. "Was that prophesy? What you just said? It edified, exhorted and encouraged, to use Paul's definition."

Noah thought about the comment and realized it wasn't what he had been thinking about to say, nor was it phrased as he would have normally expressed a thought. "Not consciously, but probably. Jesus is in love with you. The words were likely a reflection of what He was thinking. When I get nudged to say a parting comment, it's often his words."

"I liked them a great deal." Emily left a second time.

Noah pulled out a cold soda, took a seat at his desk and felt a peace settle deep inside. "I handled that conversation okay?" he asked Jesus.

He made it a policy not to replay conversations after the fact, not to spend time sorting out how he could have said things differently with a person. But this conversation felt different. Every year he found in a few students a curiosity that was a clue to where they were going with God. He had just found that curiosity in a chemistry professor. Jesus seemed as pleased with the conversation as he was.

*

5

Emily felt like hugging her box of notes. She had known it would be a good idea to ask questions of someone knowledgeable about God, but she hadn't imagined this.

"You saved your best summer gift as one you just slid in, didn't you God?" She hadn't had a particular nudge to choose Noah Shepherd over someone else to go see to ask her questions. But it was clear after one conversation he had been the right choice.

That answer on healing was elegant and immediately useful. And the timeline of events, Jesus was like a man who had left in his will gifts for future generations not yet born, had resolved a lot of her confusion. She was the direct recipient of gifts from Jesus which he'd given to her in A.D. 33.

If conversations with Noah could settle questions in her notes at this pace she would have no questions left by the end of the summer. "Did you decide I was learning too slowly, God? Did you just drop me in an advanced class with a tutor, someone you've already been teaching for years?" She directed the question to the Holy Spirit, certain their relationship was solid enough to do some teasing and felt His good humor in return and a steady certainty He was enjoying this walk as much as she was.

"You like Noah, don't you?" she offered, curious if the Holy Spirit would say something specific in reply. She was certain the Holy Spirit had used Noah to prophesy in those parting words which had been so delightful to hear. Noah was going to be an interesting guy to get to know for so many reasons. She needed to look up what papers he had written and published, see if he had published any book length works. The Ph.D. thesis he'd written would likely be interesting to read and would be worth tracking down if only because doing so would show respect to its author.

Gina and Noah had been undergrads together on this

campus, so their friendship went back 18 years. Emily doubted the two had ever dated given the age difference, Gina had started college at 14 and been doing graduate work at 20, but Gina would have a unique perspective on Noah. Emily would like to know more about his history. Going to a secular college to major in theology was an odd path to have taken. She was benefiting, but it stirred her curiosity. She could steer the conversation to Noah for a few minutes over lunch and see what Gina might be willing in share.

Emily was surprised she hadn't crossed paths with Noah at Bishop Space Repair, Inc. while working on the rocket design, given he was also friends with Bryce Bishop and Bryce was serving as the acting CFO of BSR. It was likely she had passed Noah in the building, or coming or going in the parking lot, but hadn't recognized him as university faculty. Had assumed he was one of the engineers who populated BSR, the majority of them volunteers involved in the work because they loved space. She hadn't made all the recent launch parties, but she had been there for several of them. Their lives would have inevitably eventually overlapped. That Gina hadn't introduced her to Noah in the last three years wasn't a surprise. She had a 'no introductions unless asked' agreement in place with her friends when it came to single guys. But it was easier, Emily thought, that these conversations had begun as they had today, rather than arise from a friendship first. She wanted Noah to talk about what he knew, to teach, rather than calibrate what he said because they were friends. If an answer hit a nerve, as the topic of salvation had given her family history, she would still rather have the answer than have him trying to skirt around how to say the truth he knew.

Christian friends in Austin hadn't talked to her about God in part because of her parents who had been on the vocal side of believing science precluded there being a God. It had taken her grandmother who had become a Christian in her sixties to be the source of her hearing the good news about Jesus. Emily had already concluded her parents were wrong, the study of chemistry itself had convinced her she was looking at something created by a beautiful mind at work. She'd known there was a God. She'd just needed someone willing to risk comments being said to talk to her about Jesus. Her grandmother, their Saturday morning walks, had become the best two hours of her week. When her parents had died in a car crash, it had created a deep ache inside and also been the push she'd needed to intensify those conversations with her grandmother. She couldn't have changed her parents, her grandmother had tried and been politely rebuffed, but Emily was willing to change herself. Accepting Jesus had been the best decision of her life. She'd discovered a joy that didn't have words to express its depth. And she lived with a sadness she still was struggling to face regarding her parents.

After her grandmother's death, she'd begun to see God move in her life in a broader way. God had offered through Gina a change from Austin to Chicago. Returning to her family roots in Chicago had been a gift from God. Emily had known it when Gina made the offer. The last four years had been an outpouring of goodness from God that she marveled at receiving. She was beginning to understand why now. It was like she was standing under a waterfall of God's love pouring out via Jesus. She was experiencing being loved by one who was truth and grace and entirely good. She was being flooded in good gifts. How anyone could want to live a life without Jesus was hard to fathom now that she'd tasted his goodness.

God was carrying for her the grief over her parents unbelief and her grandmothers belief but passing. Eventually she wanted to talk to Noah about the fact her parents hadn't believed, but she wasn't ready for that conversation yet. She pushed away the sadness which came every time her mind drifted to the topic and instead thought about her plans for the rest of the day. Lunch with Gina was a perfect way to continue the first full day of this summer vacation. 'I'm going to say in advance, God, thanks for the coming lunch and afternoon. I'm enjoying this day immensely and I hope you are, too." She could feel his pleasure in reply. With God being present, this was indeed going to be a good afternoon.

6

Emily sliced her fork into her second enchilada, pleased with the choice she'd made. A carry-out order for dinner tonight would be a smart way to save time and enjoy more of the food this restaurant had to offer. For a random choice of where to try for lunch the Holy Spirit had steered them to a gem.

"It was probably my sophomore year," Gina decided, continuing her answer about college after setting down her ice water, "because I'm getting buffeted by the attention, the youngest person in the room, a deer-in-the-headlights kind of effect going on. I loved college and the joy of so many branches of science to explore. But these weren't my peers. They were nineteen to twenty-four year-olds, in the tangle of relationships and freedom from parents and the stress of making grades. I didn't have my driver's license yet, my mother would drop me off and my father pick me up from campus. I'm wondering what color nail polish I have the nerve to try as I'm just beginning to decide makeup looks okay on me. The classes were a breeze and I'm leading the grade curve. It's the rest of the experience that is making my speech occasionally freeze."

Emily smiled because Gina was delivering the story with her typical humorous look back. Those college years at a young age hadn't been easy for Gina. But asking about her friendship with Noah had opened a door to some of the better memories and it was turning into a very nice lunch just listening to Gina reminisce.

"The only saving grace of those days is my brother Jeff," Gina continued as she picked up one of her fish tacos, "who doesn't mind the fact I'm genius smart. He expects me to take out the trash when its my turn and say nice things about his date. To call him when someone makes a stupid comment so he can come do whatever big brothers do. Jeff is heading to the Navy as his choice of career, heading toward being a submariner.

"Noah was like Jeff's fallback guy when I needed a friendly face on campus. Noah was the reader with a stack of books and the quiet table in the cafeteria and the guy easy to find in the library. I could plop down my backpack beside him and pull out a book and sometime in the first half hour he'd put something cold to drink beside me, but he didn't require conversations unless I wanted to interrupt him and chat. We were reading buddies. He was deep into studying Greek and Hebrew and Ancient World History and the Bible and I was diving into Math and Physics and some Astronomy. We didn't try to connect on topics other than the occasional shared smile when I'd mention Jesus or he would. Noah and I shared Jesus and that was a big deal in a secular campus setting. We had a relationship in common. We were friends because of it. And Noah genuinely liked me. I could always tell the difference even back then, between who was humoring me for what I knew or might one day do and who was really seeing me for me.

"It was my brother Jeff and I who were more attuned to Jesus than our parents. They had the language and the occasional church attendance but not the love affair with Jesus we did. Noah was one of us and Jeff and I instinctively gravitated to his company. Noah treated my smarts much like Jeff did, as just part of the package of me. When I'm sixteen and driving, he offers me keys to his car so I can practice, when I'm eighteen and pining for a date, he's good for a Friday night movie to keep me company. When I'm twenty and working on sonar math until my eyes are crossing, he pulls me outdoors to get some sun. Noah was the backdrop of the university for me. He was there the first day and there the last day and every day in-between like a german shepherd God had assigned to watch over me."

Emily laughed at that image, for it felt true to Gina's memory of those days and now that image was rather stuck in her mind too. Noah Shepherd struck her as a conscientious kind of guy, attentive to details.

"I adored the fact Jesus was smarter than I was. Everything I explored, it was something God had created. I connected on a personal level with Jesus as a very young girl and I never let go. Jesus was as real to me as anyone else. Noah understood that, shared it. When I'm talking excitedly about how God made light, sound and heat to be interchangeable – they are all different kinds of waves, governed by the same math – Noah is not only listening, he's taking a few notes and saying thanks for the explanation. Noah was as bible smart as any person I knew, yet you never met the smarts first. You met the guy who was nice and cared about what was going on, who knew how to be a friend. He could always give great advice. There was wisdom baking into him from all that bible study, rather than academic skepticism. He loved God first, and from that came the dream of the job he wanted."

Emily found that picture of the early Noah helpful. "It surprised me to realize he's been studying and teaching on a secular college for all these years. He didn't consider attending a bible college?"

Gina shook her head. "I asked him that once," she replied. "Noah said he knew how to read. He could think for himself. And the Holy Spirit was an excellent teacher of the truth and able to cut through whatever he was told which was wrong. A secular university needed light more than a bible college did. If a Christian never showed up on campus interested in studying Jesus, how was there ever going to be light there? So he took his theology degrees and stayed to teach. He's living the tenured professor job he always wanted, teaching theology at a secular university. He is a bright light simply by being unafraid of conversations on the subject of Jesus. Noah is well liked by even those who disagree with him. He speaks with the authority of truth without condemnation being part of it. That's a good fit for his role. He's made it easier for those of faith to join the faculty. The ground has been softened to accept Jesus, at least the mention of him, even in the physical sciences." Gina picked up the last taco from her plate. "How'd we get onto this subject?"

"I was having a conversation with Noah this morning, because I wanted to ask some bible questions which are easier to simply ask of an expert."

Gina nodded. "You made a good choice. You'll like him for the same reasons I do. He's simply a nice guy."

"No wife?" Emily knew the risk of asking Gina that kind of question, but her friend simply smiled as she shook her head.

"No wife, no girlfriend photo on his desk, no comments about having a date on Friday night, other than the occasional remark when he takes out someone I've introduced him to. What you're looking at in Noah is a Christian guy who has always tried to figure out how to be God's man in whatever setting he is in. He's a genuinely nice guy, one who isn't actively looking to get married, so rarely dates so as to not break a girl's heart. I don't know what would be on his marriage list if he has one. I don't think its divorce he's skittish about as his parents were happily married for decades before their passing.

"My dating record was difficult because of the 'who's going to want a smart wife?' problem. Mark solved that for me. Submarine Commander of the ballistic missile submarine *USS Nevada* puts his smarts in a very interesting category. My husband was one of 28 men entrusted with half the US deployed nuclear arsenal. He can handle me and being my husband. Sonar discoveries, rocket designs, they don't phase him. He retired from the Navy and stepped into being President of Bishop Space Repairs, Inc. and never missed a beat. He's coordinating with the Navy 3-D printing rockets now and will one day oversee putting his brother Jim safely back in space. I found my answer for 'who's going to want a smart wife?' and his name was Mark Bishop. It was the right answer for me.

"Noah may be having a subtly similar problem to mine with 'who's going to want a theology professor as a husband?' It's not like he's asking someone to be a pastor's wife where the role is mostly people skills. Noah reads. He hangs out with God. He can help with questions. He travels and speaks on weekends presenting shorter variations of what he teaches. He doesn't have a lot of what you would call hobbies. He simply loves hanging out with God and talking about Him. And spending time with his brother – those two are close.

"His brother Frank is an older gruffer version of Noah. Frank reminds me of a seaman who would have worked the Navy boats in WW II crossing the Atlantic in all kinds of weather. Stocky, solid, unshakeable. A salt-of-the-earth kind of guy. He's an incredibly good cook who will put a plate of food in front of you with a smile and say maybe ten words as the entire conversation. They are unique guys and maybe that is why they are both still single," Gina offered.

Emily considered that answer and slowly nodded. She shared something she'd been considering. "I think I'm not married because God was protecting me. If I'd married in the past I would have married someone who wasn't a Christian because I had no idea yet it was an important consideration. God wasn't part of my life yet. Maybe no one ever asked me the marriage question because God was keeping me out of a mismatched relationship. God knew I would find Jesus. I find Jesus, fall in love with him and move here. Those steps probably wouldn't have happened if I were married."

Gina nodded as she reached for her napkin. "I like that thought as it makes sense to me. God had to bust up a relationship I had in Colorado and send me to Washington State to introduce me to Mark. Maybe God brought you to Chicago to meet someone. Or he brought you to Chicago to give you a few years to get your feet under you as a Christian so he can then introduce you to someone back in Texas. I know you miss Austin. The cowboy boots come out on occasion, as does that cowboy hat, and you are always on the lookout for barbeque that does justice to what you call good cooking. Maybe God is preparing to send you back there to meet the right guy. Maybe you do get offered the job as Dean of Austin University's

Chemistry Department as that open door."

Emily felt that statement click as possibly a comment from God. Maybe she did get that call. And there were major universities around the greater Texas area where she could find work teaching chemistry beyond just returning to Austin University. Old friends would appear in a different light now that she knew she was looking for the solid Christian in the group. She'd been a Christian for only a year before she left Austin for Chicago. How many people in her personal history had even heard she had made that decision? For all she knew the owner of her favorite restaurant in Austin was a Christian and he just hadn't asked her out on a date because he had known she wasn't one. She'd had a serious crush on him ages ago. "Is there like a dress code to say I'm a Christian now? Is wearing one of those T-shirt scripture verse decal prints going overboard?"

Gina laughed until she had to put a hand to her ribs to ease the ache. "Try one of those cross necklaces or carry a bible and journal into the coffee shop to put on the table. You can be a bit more subtle and still make the point. Or you can just skip subtle and show up at his church and sit in the row in front of him. That always works."

"A useful suggestion. Jewelry is a bad idea in a chemistry lab. So I got in the habit I rarely wear necklaces, bracelets or rings."

"Necklaces are to play with when you're bored, to catch attention when you want him to notice you've painted your nails and to make a statement that they are a safe gift. When a guy wants to say he likes you in a more personal way than flowers but without having to spend more than fifty dollars, seeing the type of necklaces you like is helpful."

Emily considered that and chuckled. "Thanks. I think I'm glad I've not been dating all that much recently."

"Food, flowers, fun, those are first tier gifts," Gina replied, ticking them off on her fingers. "The necklace, bracelet, upscale restaurant, travel destination, meeting family, those are moving matters into serious interest. You get a ring, you simply be as kind as you can in wisely saying yes or no from your heart. I about really blew that with Mark because I was so deathly afraid of the question and what it might mean to be married to him. It didn't help that I was caught between two guys liking me and I was having to make a decision about each of them."

Emily nodded in sympathy for that was a girl's night out story that Gina had told in-depth one evening. Gina ending up with Mark had been a good outcome, but the road there had taken several detours. "I want simple," Emily decided and punctuated it with an air stroke of her fork. "The 'this is so obvious we should have become a couple years ago' obvious."

Gina and Mark Bishop were the kind of couple she liked hanging out with and thought of as an example of a good marriage. Ann and Paul Falcon were another. They suited each other and fit together as a couple. She didn't see two individuals when she thought about them. She saw Gina and Mark. Ann and Paul. They had made a life together. If she were married, she wanted that kind of life, that picture of being well fit together.

"You can pray for simple and obvious and let God make the arrangements," Gina suggested.

Emily shook her head. "If I start praying about it in earnest I have to want to get married and I'm not sure if I do yet. I'm in that in-between kind of stage, mostly content with being single and having the occasional thought maybe I'd be okay with being married, too. I like the idea of being married in Texas. If I get married in Chicago I am never going to get out of these winters."

Gina laughed. "I can't believe you don't like snow."

Emily shuddered at just the memory of this last winter. "I'm made for a different climate. I'm like a lost parrot or whatever would be the inverse of a snowbird." She turned the subject toward their afternoon plans. "I've got some ideas on paint colors and the flyer for a furniture sale. Let's hit shops for both. I'm ready to spend some money."

"I'm game." Gina reached for the check. "I'm getting the check for this lunch since you bought last time."

"Sure." Emily was fine with that, they were both flush with extra cash these days. "Double it so there is a nice tip and we'll both kick in the check price. They deserve it for the good food coming out of that kitchen. And I need an order of sweet-and-sour soup to go. I'm planning the stress tests for the battery prototype tonight and putting in order the early design paperwork for the patent process. Good food will make that detailed work go down easier."

"You know you're only doing it because you love it. You are now officially on vacation."

Emily grinned. "I am indeed. And I'm thinking I'll spend this coming weekend looking at some mountains out a hotel window."

"Starting it in style; I like that plan," Gina replied with a laugh. "I'd head to the continental divide as a place to start, that or the Teton Mountains."

Emily finished her drink and gathered up her purse as Gina went to pay for their meal. This had been as enjoyable a lunch as she could have hoped for and perfectly suited the first day of vacation.

****

Back at her university office shortly before five, now the proud owner of two gallons of paint for the dining room and a bedroom furniture set being delivered tomorrow afternoon, Emily found a brief email from Noah in her inbox with an attached document. *You might find these verses helpful. Noah.* She opened the document, scanned its content and sent it to the printer, grateful he'd thought to send it. She was going to enjoy their conversations this summer.

God is not man, that he should lie,
or a son of man, that he should repent.
Has he said and will he not do it?

Or has he spoken, and will he not fulfil it?
(Numbers 23:19)

Surely our sicknesses he [Jesus] hath borne, And our pains
-- he hath carried them, And we -- we have esteemed him
plagued, Smitten of God, and afflicted. And he is pierced
for our transgressions, Bruised for our iniquities, The
chastisement of our peace [is] on him, And by his bruise
there is healing to us. All of us like sheep have wandered,
Each to his own way we have turned, And Jehovah hath
caused to meet on him, The punishment of us all. (Isaiah
53:4-6 YLT)

the word of the cross is folly to those who are perishing,
but to us who are being saved it is the power of God. (1
Corinthians 1:18b)

And without faith it is impossible to please him. For
whoever would draw near to God must believe that he
exists and that he rewards those who seek him. (Hebrews
11:6)

Bless the LORD, O my soul;
and all that is within me, bless his holy name!
Bless the LORD, O my soul,
and forget not all his benefits [rewards],
who forgives all your iniquity,
who heals all your diseases,
who redeems your life from the Pit,
who crowns you with steadfast love and mercy,
who satisfies you with good as long as you live
so that your youth is renewed like the eagle's.
(Psalms 103:1-5)

He himself [Jesus] bore our sins in his body on the tree,
that we might die to sin and live to righteousness. By his
wounds you have been healed. (1 Peter 2:24)

If the Spirit of him who raised Jesus from the dead dwells in you, he who raised Christ Jesus from the dead will give life to your mortal bodies also through his Spirit which dwells in you. (Romans 8:11)

I [Jesus] am the bread of life. (John 6:48)

He who eats my flesh and drinks my blood abides in me and I in him. (John 6:56)

As the living Father sent me and I [Jesus] live because of the Father, so he who eats me will live because of me. (John 6:57)

7

Noah liked walking the university campus in the evening, praying for the students and professors who studied and taught here. He knew the grounds as only an inquisitive freshman and now a tenured professor could. He held keys to some of the more obscure nooks and crannies where historical treasures were stored. He had his favorite places to sit and watch a sunset or end his evening star gazing.

The university had been founded in 1827. It had grown in size and national prominence, but it was still a college where young men and women were experiencing independence from home for the first time. There were societies and clubs and traditions to maintain as well as friendships to solidify and romances to search out. He had been here eighteen years and each entering freshman class brought new technology, but the same timeless quests for professions and relationships.

He'd looked up Emily's location after she left his office. The lights were on in what he thought was the chemistry lab where she held reign, so she was still on campus, or a janitor was at work. On a whim he diverted to the Physical Sciences Building. He might as well locate her office this evening and say hello on her own territory. And if it suited the flow of the conversation, ask her a question that had been on his mind this afternoon.

Noah knew the Physical Sciences Building had been renovated at least twice during the university expansions and its square footage increased. Once inside, he realized how much it had changed since his own student days. The departments for the Environment and Climate were new, joining Chemistry, Physics, and Geology. The directory and map for the building presented a zigzag of connecting hallways, long stretches of laboratories, multi-level theater-seat classrooms and offices tucked sporadically in between. Professor Emily Worth was listed for chem. lab 4 and office 4-C, which turned out to be adjacent spaces located on the first floor, hallway four, in the first phase expansion. He'd been looking at the right windows, he thought. Noah followed well marked signs through the brightly lit hallways, occasionally passing a student, but mostly passing empty rooms and offices.

The Chemistry Lab Four door was propped open by a chair and the sweet smell of honey with a bit of burnt undertones drifted out into the hall. Noah couldn't help but smile as he stepped into the doorway to find Emily watching a smoking beaker in a sink cool off. She hadn't bothered to turn on the fume hood, so he took a guess it was something edible she had been trying to concoct. "Would this be a photo titled failed chef at work?"

Emily glanced back and laughed. "Hi, Noah. On the contrary, it is one of my better successes. I'm making bird bark, it's like jerky, only for Cardinals, which flakes off when they nibble on it. It needs to cool to putty consistency before you dip it out onto popsicle sticks. I'd make it at home but you need precise temperatures and a clothesline to dry the sticks." She nodded to the wire strung between cabinet posts.

She tested the beaker content with a long stick. "Sorry for the smell. The fan on this exhaust hood is temporarily unwired as maintenance is putting me in an industrial one with an attached condenser I can control. I started working at this station before I realized it wasn't already back together. I'm melting element this summer for one of my own research projects and that is going to be smelly work. This smell I'd classify as just a nuisance."

"It's not so bad. It smells like my own kitchen has at times."

Noah slid over a stool and took a seat.

Other than the three feet of counter space she had cluttered with her project, it was presently the most pristinely lab he'd ever seen, everything wiped clean and floor tiles gleaming. The room was four open rows of shining black work surfaces with cabinets beneath. He recognized microscopes, scales, spinning centrifuges, computer keyboards and screens and what he thought was a light source, amongst equipment he couldn't hope to name. There were sinks and fume hoods and gas burners. In frosted front cabinets he could see the silhouette forms of beakers, test tubes and pipettes neatly stored in various sizes and quantities. The periodic table on the wall he recognized, though it had more elements than when he had taken high school chemistry. "Where are all the chemicals you work with?"

Emily nodded to her left. "There are pharmacy grade controls for access to that room so as to lessen the odds someone wants to make off with my chemical budget. You can break my glassware and cause my equipment to need repairs, but they are all insured. My supplies, that's another matter."

"That makes sense."

There was an emergency first aid station for washing out your eyes, a pull cord for an emergency showerhead and four fire extinguishers that were colored coded for chemical safety. Emily had developed fireworks here, so he wasn't surprised to see the black boxes for combustible chemical waste products or the explosive box that still had a police department property tag on the side. The biohazard containers did surprise him, as he normally saw them only in the medical sciences building. The most common items he saw in the room were the student lab coats neatly hung on a row of hooks and the bins of safety glasses.

Emily was more watching her project cool off than actively working so he asked what else he was curious about. "Let me take a guess, the row of lockers outside are so students aren't searching for somewhere to set their backpacks and laptops, not to mention their coats, gloves, and boots in winter."

"Socks in my lab are encouraged," Emily confirmed with a smile.

He glanced down and realized she was wearing socks with baseballs on them, one sock in Cardinals red and the other in Cubs blue. They suited her. She was the type of professor who would set the example for students and have some fun while doing so.

Emily poked at her creation with the long stick again. "This is ready. You want to try your hand at this? You want a lot of it on each popsicle stick, and then you press it flat against the wax paper into a wedge shape. Think caramel bars." She did one to demonstrate, then clipped it to the line, hanging the stick upside down to dry.

"Why don't I just source you the popsicle sticks instead?" Noah offered, picking up the box of them and offering her the next one.

Emily took it. "Gina would have jumped at the offer to take over the hands-on task." She coated the stick, pressed it flat, hung it up to dry.

He handed her another popsicle stick. "I am well acquainted with Gina and her love of playing with science and making models. She would treat this room as her own kitchen and go exploring. You like to tinker here?"

"Sure. Think of a chemist as a chef with a set number of ingredients to work with. I can create all kinds of interesting things in this lab. I love to cook at home for the same reason. The right ingredients, temperature, time – if mixed properly, you get something tasty."

"You would like my brother Frank. He opened a restaurant so he would have an excuse to be in a kitchen full time."

"My second choice of career would have been chef."

Emily moved through her project with the speed that told Noah she had done this many times. She liked feeding birds, which meant she likely had a feeder she could watch out of a window at home. His dad had always kept one filled so he could bird watch as the seasons changed.

"Last one." She hung up the popsicle stick, then picked up heat retardant gloves and moved the beaker from the sink. "I'm going to cheat on the cleanup and freeze this. The remaining honey mixture flakes off like snowflakes once the glass is chilled."

She opened one of the pieces of equipment he didn't know the name for and set the beaker inside, then punched in numbers on a control panel. "This is like a refrigerator, only I can tell it what temperature to go to over what period of time. That's handy when you don't want to crack glass by a quick temperature change."

"Got it."

She threw away trash, wiped clear the counter and put the box of popsicle sticks back into a cupboard. The drying popsicle sticks were soon the only evidence of her project.

"Do you keep everything in your life as neat as you do this lab?"

She laughed at the suggestion. "Absolutely not." She pulled off her latex gloves as a final step and washed her hands. "Did you come find me for a reason, Noah?"

"I saw the lights were on and thought this lab might be yours. I wanted to see if I was right. And tangentially, I thought I'd see if you wanted to take a walk."

"Sure, I'll take a walk with you, Noah. The textbooks have already come out on the current research project so it's going to be a long night. The bird bark was a distraction so I could take a break from the reading and planning. I could use a longer pause. But I need a water bottle to go with me." She stepped into her office to retrieve one. "Gina and I had Mexican for lunch and I had carryout Mexican for dinner. Can I get you something?"

He stepped to her office door to see what she had to offer. "What's that green stripped can on the lower shelf?" Her personal refrigerator was, like his, within reach of comfortable seating. A pile of professional Chemistry Journals rested atop hers.

"Try it at your own peril. It's called lime lemonade."

"I'm the adventurous sort."

She offered him the can and took a water bottle for herself.

She'd ditched a desk in favor of a large table with rolling chairs so students could join her. Technical papers and chemistry books were open on the table alongside pages of chemical equations and hand-drawn designs. She had clearly been working on something of her own. The couch and leather chair looked comfortable. The facing wall was filled with snapped photos of various colors and forms, microscope images, he thought, jumbled into a huge collage. The whiteboard rolled in really didn't fit, but was obviously the main focus of whatever was happening. What he didn't see were personal pictures, photos of pets, mementos of her years in Austin. This was where she worked, might even be where she relaxed, but it wasn't where she lived.

"What do you think?" she asked, curious.

"It looks like a chemist at work, accustomed to being surrounded by students. You're only missing the clutter and the personal."

"I cleared the clutter out of habit when the semester ended. The personal I like to leave at home. When personal is in the office it soon gets buried under other things and dates so quickly it becomes only a conversation topic for guests rather than something I'm seeing each day for my own enjoyment. Work is thinking about this," she gave a sweep of the table, "while home is about people and relationships and anything but this."

He made an educated guess. "Spend much time at home?"

She smiled at the question. "Not as much as I once did. Austin was home and over a decade of memories. I grew up in Chicago but I'm still finding my footing now that I'm back."

She followed him out. She locked her office door, then moved the chair propping open the chemistry lab door and locked it as well. She opened a locker and retrieved her shoes.

"You'll need the jacket, it's on the cool side tonight."

She nodded and slipped it on.

Outside, he turned the direction of the stadium, as the sidewalks were wide and they could easily walk side-by-side with people still passing by in either direction. He cautiously tasted the cold lime lemonade and was pleasantly surprised. It was refreshing and light in aftertaste. He'd been more thirsty than he realized and was glad for the drink.

"I see you occasionally walking the campus in the evening," Emily mentioned as she opened her water bottle.

"It's a habit that goes back to my undergraduate days. I like to think and walking is the best way I know to have every topic which needs some of my attention drift up to be considered."

She drank deeply, then recapped the bottle. "Gina is helping me on my current research project. It was nice, talking science over lunch with someone who could handle random tangents between chemistry and physics and topics which had nothing to do with it." She glanced at him. "Our conversations are likely going to feel like that. I appreciated today, the comments you made and brief answers you gave, as I spun out an array of subjects."

"Not so brief answers."

She smiled. "Relatively. I've decided when I'm in town, that I'm going to spend my morning on bible questions and afternoons digging into science and the evening on whichever of those has me the most fascinated that day. An equal opportunity busy summer. I shall enjoy it immensely as I'm not teaching."

Noah laughed at the way she said it. "Not teaching is a very different kind of freedom," he agreed. "I've certainly enjoyed the occasional semester sabbatical. But I enjoy teaching, it forces me to pull together what I've learned and get it into a form which I can share. It's how you assess what you yourself have learned."

"I like that about teaching, too. It was good to see Gina teach this last semester," she mentioned, "and do so without any particular speech problems. I sat in on her class a few times. She talked about mapping the ocean floor, doing sonar work, modeling the upper atmosphere, the solar flare research she's doing now. The real-world applications of the large database sets she specializes in."

"Her life has had fascinating chapters to it."

"She only touched briefly on the rocket she designed because there is so much else going on in her life it really was just one of a string of recent accomplishments."

"Yet for you it was one of the most significant."

Emily nodded. "It's what brought me back to Chicago."

"Are you glad you came?"

"I am."

"Still missing Texas?"

"Desperately." Emily glanced his way with a brief smile. "Why did you really come to find me tonight, Noah?"

She was shutting down this conversation going toward her recent personal past and he could understand that. "That obvious?"

"You don't strike me as the wander by kind of guy. You were thinking about something and came to track me down."

He considered how he wanted to ask this. "What would you consider the hardest question you have?"

"Why do you ask?"

"You brought it with you this morning, but decided not to mention it." Her expression told him that remark had hit solid ground. "You don't have to discuss it now, but I find it fascinating that for most of my afternoon the Holy Spirit has been giving a steady nudge inside that you didn't mention the question you think about the most. It must be important to you, which is why it matters to God. He's been persistent with me today for a reason."

"It's simply a puzzle I've been trying to work out, more than a question. But I have been thinking about it for quite awhile."

"Your choice, talk about it tonight, or another day?"

"I'm not sure how you'll take it."

"Try me and find out," he offered.

"There is a verse in second Timothy that says Jesus 'abolished death and brought life and immortality to light through the gospel.' It's 2 Timothy 1:10b. It's a past tense statement. Jesus abolished death."

Noah nodded. "Young's Literal Translation of the Greek phrase reads: 'our Saviour Jesus Christ, who indeed did abolish death, and did enlighten life and immortality through the good news'."

"You know the verse."

"Very well. It's one of the most beautiful treasures in all of scripture."

"I read that verse and it leads me to ask another question. Why do Christians die? It's illogical that we do. It's appointed to man once to die, then the judgment. But Christians have already died and passed out of judgment."

Noah glanced over at her in surprise, not expecting to hear her make that connection. A relatively young Christian realizing the contradiction and proposing the question certainly got his attention.

"Stupid question?"

"On the contrary. It's an elegant and important one," he replied. She was trying to sort out three passages. Noah quoted them to confirm they were talking about the same specifics.

it is appointed for men to die once, and after that comes judgment Hebrews 9:27b

Do you not know that all of us who have been baptized into Christ Jesus were baptized into his death? We were buried therefore with him by baptism into death, so that as Christ was raised from the dead by the glory of the Father, we too might walk in newness of life. Romans 6:3-4

Jesus said… "Truly, truly, I say to you, he who hears my word and believes him who sent me, has eternal life; he does not come into judgment, but has passed from death to life." John 5:24

Emily nodded. "That's my puzzle."

"It's a fascinating one," Noah agreed.

"Is there an answer?"

There was something special going on in how she was thinking, how she was curious. The Holy Spirit was illuminating key connections in scripture for her. Mary, the sister of Lazarus, had been able to perceive Jesus was about to die and had poured expensive perfume out to anoint him for his coming burial. It felt like Emily was listening to the Holy Spirit in the same way. Noah considered how to answer and chose to keep his reply simple. "There is no death in God."

"Why do I get the feeling there are a few more paragraphs behind that brief sentence?"

He smiled. "I know this topic well. The study is a useful one. Answering it forces you to think about important subtopics, like mankind's fall into sin, salvation, resurrection, baptism, life. Your puzzle has a simple answer. But it's counter-intuitive."

"I like hearing there is a way to answer this. I don't mind studying, wondering about questions and talking about them with the Holy Spirit. But it would help to know how to figure this out. I don't want to think as long and as hard as you have Noah."

He smiled at her mild protest. "When a chemistry student asks an important question that is beyond their present year of study, how do you answer them? Do you avoid confusing them, or do you present the answer that may require them to grasp concepts that are of a more advanced level in order to understand your answer?"

"If they were able to figure out the question to ask, I assume they are ready for the answer, no matter how advanced it needs to be. I give the roadmap as best I can from where they are to what they have asked and let them study their way to understanding my answer. It's always easier to swim to a destination, to run a race to a finish line. They are showing me with the question they are ready to think beyond their present year of study."

"You need to be like a child to answer your puzzle,

Emily. Rather than need to grasp something more advanced than where you are, you need to be able to grasp something simpler.

"There is a verse in Proverbs that says 'It is the glory of God to conceal things, but the glory of Kings is to search things out.' Proverbs 25:2. God has filled his word with treasures for us and those who abide in the word find them routinely, like pearls of great price. They are concealed because God wants you to desire them, search them out and then be delighted with your discoveries. Your puzzle is one of those treasures. Why do Christians die? It is indeed illogical. The Holy Spirit will build an answer for you over time, like a master builder upon a foundation, if you want to put in the effort and time and let Him. Just ask Him 'where should I read today?' and see if a book and chapter comes to mind."

"He likes to take me on scavenger hunts," Emily mentioned, "offering the suggestion of a word I should follow through the bible, reading every passage where it appears. Those journeys inevitably take interesting detours."

"I'm glad you're willing to follow those suggestions. You're learning to hear his voice and recognize it," Noah replied.

"I'm doing my best. He's a very creative teacher; I love that about Him." She glanced over. "Can I bounce what I'm thinking off you so you can steer me away from any ditch?"

"Sure."

"I think we've misunderstood the definition of the word eternal," Emily offered. "Eternal means always, so eternal means now. God is eternal."

She looked his way and he simply nodded his agreement. "You're defining it correctly."

"Jesus says he is the life. We always have Jesus abiding in us. So therefore we have eternal life. It's literal. Eternal life has already begun. It isn't something which begins at some time in the future. Jesus is the mechanism, the how, for this gift of eternal life. It's his presence in us. The moment we receive Jesus as our Savior we have received eternal life."

Noah would have given her an A had she handed him only that paragraph as her entire final thesis. She'd already found the key to her puzzle. "Eternal life is something we have now," he agreed. "The verb tense God uses is present tense rather than future. The passage you want is in 1 John 5," he offered and quoted it:

He who does not believe God has made him a liar, because he has not believed in the testimony that God has borne to his Son. And this is the testimony, that God gave us eternal life, and this life is in his Son. He who has the Son has life; he who has not the Son of God has not life. I [John] write this to you who believe in the name of the Son of God, that you may know that you have eternal life. 1 John 5:10b-13

"Oh, that's perfect!" Emily pulled out her phone to note down the reference.

Noah didn't offer another comment, just walked with her enjoying her delight, letting her think after she pocketed her phone. They were coming to the stadium and Noah detoured them toward the side gate for which he had keys. He liked to walk the track and sit in the stadium seats of an evening and watch the first stars appear, to pray for the athletes who spent hours on the field and on the track training as well as the students who would fill the stadium seats to watch them compete.

Emily finished her water bottle and tossed it into a recycling bin beside a trash barrel. "Life and death are contradictory. No matter how many times I circle my question, why do Christians die? it comes back to the fact these are irreconcilable. God has given us eternal life. And eternal means always, means now. So its death which is the illogical fact. What am I not seeing, Noah?"

"You're already seeing it."

As they stepped onto the track to walk its circuit, Noah took a risk and answered Emily's puzzle, putting into words the one step she wasn't yet taking. She wasn't yet willing to trust the truth she had seen when it produced a radically different answer than expected.

"Death is not part of a Christian's life. Eternal life is not a future event. It's a tangible reality within us right now. Jesus is the life. Jesus abides in us. There is no death in life. Jesus has abolished death and brought to light life and immortality in the good news. 2 Timothy 1:10b isn't complicated. A child understands when you abolish death, you have life, and life that never ends is immortality.

"Christians die only because no one has told them they don't need to die. It's like healing, Emily. Christians are only sick because no one has told them they are healed. God has given us eternal life. That life is ours now. It's already begun. Jesus has abolished death. By his wounds we have been healed. What we've been hoping for is already finished for us. It's already ours. God has given us all things pertaining to life and godliness through the knowledge of His Son Jesus. Past tense given.

"It is appointed for men to die once and after that comes judgment. That's true. And we've already died. It wasn't just words, in baptism it was a true death. We've experienced our one death when we were crucified with Jesus. We've been buried. We've been resurrected from the dead. Once means only once. Our one death is in the rear view mirror. We have already passed from death to life. We do not come into judgment because Jesus came into judgment in our place. We have fulfilled this verse – we have died and been judged – Jesus simply stepped in and took the judgment due us upon himself. God poured out love and grace upon us through Jesus and perfectly saved us. It's finished. Our sins are gone. Judgment is over. We have put on Christ and there is no death in God. Death is not part of a Christian's life. We have eternal life now."

Noah watched Emily absorb that answer. She simply smiled when she had it. "Okay. You were willing to say what I was only willing to look at and puzzle over. It is a beautifully elegant answer. Thank you." She grinned. "I love this truth! I wish the second coming of Jesus was not so near. Jesus is going to come back before I've had a chance to live two or three hundred years enjoying this experience of not dying."

She was like a little kid who had just found a new candy store. Noah was inclined to indulge her joy and offered what else he knew about the treasure she'd found. "We still live in mortal bodies made of dust which need to put on immortality. But salvation is designed so we can live and not die in these bodies of dust, just as the original Adam and Eve lived in bodies made of dust which were designed never to die. The Holy Spirit continually gives life to our mortal bodies. The Holy Spirit never leaves us. When Jesus returns for his church we rise to meet him in the air and our mortal bodies of dust change in an instant, in the twinkle of an eye, into heavenly bodies. The mortal will put on immortality."

"We rise again. It's one of Jesus' favorite phrases," Emily remarked.

"It is," Noah agreed. 'There's a related verse in the Old Testament which says, 'in the way of righteousness there is life; along that path is immortality.' It's Proverbs 12:28 quoting the NIV translation. In the Amplified version it reads 'life is in the way of righteousness and in its pathway there is no death but immortality (perpetual, eternal life).' God was thinking about this part of our salvation, writing about it, a thousand years before Jesus came as our Savior to be the source for us of this eternal life. Jesus understood our salvation was this complete. Jesus talked about it several places. One of my favorites is John 8:51, where Jesus remarks, 'Truly, truly, I say to you, if any one keeps my word, he will never see death.' Jesus wasn't hiding this good news."

They took the far turn of the track walking together, Noah content with where the evening had gone and relieved the Holy Spirit had been pushing this afternoon that he should follow up on the question Emily hadn't asked, so this conversation could unfold at the beginning of their summer. The rest of the summer would likely circle around their two conversations of today and that was useful groundwork to have established. A young Christian had puzzled out one of the best treasures of scriptures. Her question confirmed what he'd realized this morning. Emily was curious about the good news in a way God loved.

Emily finished making a note of the verses on her phone. "What a perfect way to wrap up tonight. I've enjoyed this, Noah."

"It was a nice start to my summer as well," Noah assured her, wondering casually if he had just met his future wife.

[If you would like to read the rest of their conversation while on this walk please turn to page 327 in the extra section. Their topics include immortality, the kingdom of God and Jesus' return.]

*

8

Monday evening's conversation was still being mulled over by Noah Tuesday afternoon. He was breaking his own policy and mentally replaying it. It had been an interesting evening on so many levels. Emily had introduced one of his favorite topics and the desire to keep talking about its implications could have taken them to dawn. She had been very gracious with his habit of giving long answers packed with information. But it was the personal question which had appeared as their conversation concluded that had his attention at the moment.

A man planning to live a long life had the luxury of time to sort out matters of the heart. Marriage had always been a someday in the future matter for him, for he was serious about wanting to avoid having his wife die at 85 while he lived considerably longer. Emily had already stepped over the line to realize eternal meant always, meant now. God was going to gift him with a romance if this was the woman God had in mind to be his wife one day. He needed to figure out if she was in a relationship now and how serious it was. Gina was going to have to be his source for that. He wasn't one to step on an existing relationship. But for the sake of thinking about the question, he'd let himself assume for now it wasn't going to be an issue. A year or two of being friends, even a decade or two, suited how this would likely unfold. But common sense said it would be worth the effort to bring a lot more information about Emily to the table sooner rather than later.

He needed to find out who else beside Gina was in Emily's circle of friends so he could find out if they had another natural overlap in friends. BSR was an easy overlap. There would be a launch party for the rocket on the 17th and she'd likely be there. The fourth of July would be a special upcoming evening in Emily's life. Those were two near-term overlaps. Gina could get him Emily's birth date so he could buy a present for her this year. He would want one which was neither expensive nor considered particular personal by others, but that would be intrinsically perfect for Emily. That would take some time to sort out but he'd enjoy doing so. He liked searching to find the right gift.

It shouldn't be hard to ask questions that would begin to fill in who she was and what she liked to do. He had already put her university phone number on speed dial so he could propose lunch at the faculty club or the occasional walk in the evening. He could get their time overlapping on campus easily enough. He had picked up two chemistry books from the used book table at the college campus bookstore to learn some of the language of her professional life. He needed to find out what he could about Austin, Texas where she had taught for seven years so he understood what her recent life had been like and why she still missed Texas. He had the impression her parents as well as her grandmother might have been living in Texas when they passed away. It would be helpful to know how recent those losses had been in her life.

"Are you going to eat that lunch or look at it?"

"I'm thinking Frank," Noah replied mildly to his brother, rather surprised his thoughts had drifted far enough he was ignoring a perfectly stacked cheeseburger with hand-tossed onion rings on the side. He hadn't mentioned Emily to his brother yet and couldn't remember the last time he'd withheld that kind of news. When he met someone interesting, he said so, and within a month or two introduced Frank to the woman he was talking about. 'Frank, I think I may have just met my future wife.' That comment was going to get some attention. He probably would introduce her name precisely that way. No use not being upfront about it with his brother. But it wasn't a conversation for the barstool lunch counter at Frank's restaurant.

Noah considered his brother clearing away dishes from another counter patron. "Are you still planning to take

Friday afternoon off to go riding over on the state park trail?"

"Thought I might."

"I was thinking I would come along," Noah said.

"I'm going to get you up on a horse voluntarily?" Frank asked.

"I don't dislike the experience and I could use the fresh air."

Frank gave him a skeptical look at that answer but didn't challenge it. "I figured I would leave here at two after the lunch crowd clears."

"I'll be here by two if I'm coming," Noah agreed.

Emily had lived in Texas. She would ride, or know someone who did, or have an image of riding as being a common way to fill free time. He could brush up on the details for the stable and trail Frank used regularly. If Emily didn't already have a place to ride figured out for this area the information might come in handy. That was one avenue to investigate. There were other obvious ones. She had been back in the Chicago area three years. If she wanted to renew seeing the sights she had probably already hit the major ones. The art, history and science museums would either be somewhere she enjoyed spending a few hours or she would shrug at the idea – a casual question would let him know that answer.

Fitting her into his social life and introducing her to his friends wouldn't be hard. It was just when and what made sense to offer. Emily was attending Lake Christian Church and the worship leader Jason Lasting's band played in concert most Friday nights. He was rarely in town on Friday nights but when he was, those evenings were an enjoyable time. And he had friends who would take a suggestion of an evening gathering and invite her to join them as one of the faculty coming over.

Having Emily meet his family, namely Frank, was simply a matter of when he suggested lunch here at his brother's place. He needed to look at his summer calendar and think about what made sense. He liked having a plan for relationships so they went somewhere, even if it was simply into the destination of becoming good friends. God had introduced him to Emily at the start of his summer for a reason and Noah was going to enjoy seeing where this went.

"Eat. Or else tell me what is on your mind."

Noah ate another onion ring. "A woman."

"Yeah?" Frank grinned. "About time."

"You'll like her."

"Probably will. She got a name?" Frank took two of the onion rings. "They're getting cold and that's an insult to good onion rings."

Letting food go cold could bring Frank's wrath on an otherwise good day. Noah slid his plate toward his brother. "Then help out. Professor of chemistry, Emily Worth. Four years a Christian. She'd already figured out for herself eternal means always, means now. Her question was 'why do Christian's die? It's illogical.'"

"The holy grail of your wish list."

"I think I just met my future wife."

Frank laughed. "Then you won't be eating all of this." He pulled over the plate and used a knife to slice the cheeseburger, moved half to a napkin for himself. "I'll fix you another one to go so if you also let it grow cold I won't have to watch it happen."

"Works for me." Noah picked up his half because he had come for lunch somewhat hungry. "And I'm changing the subject for now. Gina Bishop could use grilling meat for the Bishop Fourth of July gathering, a lot of it. Can I talk you into tapping your butcher for the meat? I'll handle pickup and delivery. She's thinking a hundred adults plus kids. Bryce wants to slow cook pork the day before for pulled-pork barbeque, smoke some chicken that morning, have those for lunch, do brats and hamburgers at the dinner hour when most of the people will be arriving, with steaks coming off the side burner throughout the day for anyone interested."

"Can he handle refrigerator space for that much meat

or does he need some of it frozen to fast thaw in the microwave?"

"He's already figured out the refrigeration."

"I'll write up an order and make a call, let you know the bill. Back to Emily Worth. When do I get to meet her?"

"Give me some time. I had a brief conversation with her Friday night and a couple conversations yesterday."

"You're worried she's going to like me more than you," Frank assessed.

Noah laughed. "You're more lady cop, restaurant owner, the single mom with three kids, kind of guy," he replied, having watched who caught his brother's attention over the years.

"Any of those would suit me fine," Frank agreed. "Bring your Emily around. I'll serve good food, she'll credit you with having good family. It will help."

"It won't hurt," Noah agreed. Frank was a good plus in his life, a mark of stability and a reassurance that there was a practical side to his life beyond theology. He wasn't so book smart he had forgotten how to bus a table or haul in produce when his brother could use a helping hand here. He'd get the occasional question about God from the regular customers he knew, been asked to talk to family members, to give counsel when there was a crisis, not unlike at the university. But he'd also get the questions about politics and sports and be told to give shorter answers when he started to run long. Noah liked hanging out at this place for a reason. It was home to his brother and a comfortable place for him as well. He'd been a silent partner when the restaurant opened though his brother had long since repaid that gift.

"Eat. You're disappearing into random thoughts on me."

Noah turned his attention to finish the half cheeseburger he held. Next week wasn't going to give the luxury of time for this kind of mental wandering. He'd wait until Emily appeared in his office again rather than follow up with her first, as it was best if she set the pace of what this became. He predicted she would likely go one of two ways when they next spoke. Either she would be bubbling with verses and questions about what they had discussed or she would have packed the topic of eternal life to the side and would move back to her original set of questions to give this subject more think time. Either move would be helpful to him to see as it would give him a look at how she processed complex topics. She struck him as one who pondered on her own for a considerable time before asking questions, but that was a guess based on limited information. He'd learn her rhythm and adapt to it.

A milkshake slid down the bar and stopped an inch from his hand. It looked like vanilla with a hint of chocolate and several cherries, so Noah accepted Frank's suggestion with a nod of thanks. He took the glass with him as he slid off the stool for it was one of three with his name etched on them which rotated between his home, office and the restaurant. He folded a fifty under the corner of his plate, a mild tip compared to some he left, accepted the carry-out sack with another cheeseburger from Frank and headed back to the university.

Getting married would change every corner of his life outside of the lecture hall. If he was in his last years of being single, it would be good to put a list together of what he wanted to do that required being single or at least was best done when single. That question was a good one to ponder but not much came immediately to mind. His speaking schedule would shift depending on her desire to travel with him. The long walks he took of an evening would adapt in part to them walking together. The amount of time he spent reading would change. Friendships would shift to become theirs rather than his and hers. That was the routine of his present life. He hadn't planned on such a settled life but it worked for him. He hung out with God, read books, taught students, spoke at churches and conferences and met up with friends. There wasn't a more vanilla life than his. She didn't strike him as a woman with a vanilla life. The rocket work and the fireworks were good clues she had risk taking as part of her personality. He made a personal decision to say yes whenever she suggested something that pointed toward risk so he could see that part of her life.

He had walked past his car. Noah turned around and backtracked. He dug car keys from his pocket. If he didn't think about something other than Emily for a time he was going to end up driving home rather than to the university out of habit. Bryce had offered to guest lecture when his Biblical Prophecy class talked about the calendar of history, the internal timeline within the bible and the external sources which dated events spoken about within the bible text. They hadn't settled on the date for it, but it suited the first weeks of class. Emily would enjoy that lecture. Noah could invite her to be his guest, to sit with him at the back of the class and enjoy Bryce's presentation. As his thoughts headed straight back to Emily, Noah gave up. "God, am I smitten? Is this what that feels like?"

Jesus laughed. It was such an instant response Noah heard it audibly.

Thinking about the entire topic of dating without calling it that was rattling his brain. He liked what he knew about Emily. And if this wasn't what smitten felt like, he wasn't sure what else to expect. He was building a big house of cards that was easily going to get blown over by reality. He knew practically nothing about Emily beyond comments Gina had made and brief observations of his own. She was probably already comfortably in a serious relationship, with no interest in a guy like him. But for today, it was what was. He might as well enjoy it while he could. In a day or two he was likely to find out she had been dating someone for the last year and they were on the verge of becoming engaged and this flight of fancy would end in a quiet predictable landing. But it was an enjoyable flight just the same. "You just like to rattle my thinking occasionally, don't you God?"

The reassuring smile he got in reply suited matters. He didn't have to figure out his future. Who should be his friends. Who he would enjoy spending time with. Who might one day be his wife. God solved those questions for him and people just showed up in his life. Walking with God was an adventure. Noah had learned to trust that friendship when it came to people. "Thanks for introducing me to Emily, Father." He left it there. He drove back to the university, careful to keep his attention on cars around him rather than let his thoughts drift back to personal matters. It would be a good summer, that much was already clear. And he was looking forward to all of it.

9

Emily was leaning against the wall next to his office door working in a sketchbook Thursday afternoon as Noah arrived back from a faculty meeting. His relief was palpable. He'd begun to think he wasn't going to see her again this week. "Hi, Emily."

"Give me a sec. I've learned to take advantage of brainstorms whenever they come."

"Sure." He had thought artwork but as he drew near he saw the page was covered in chemical equations and when she ran out of room to finish a thought she turned the sketchbook and continued the equation up the side of the page and then added arrows to attach it into prior work. "That looks complicated," he mentioned when she finished writing.

"The language of chemistry makes even simple things look intimidating. I need an adhesive glue that absorbs and transfers heat without drying out or becoming brittle. Nothing on the market right now really fits what I need, so I've been creating my own. This is version 22 of the mix and hopefully an improvement over version 21. It's going to be my evening science project."

He could hear her pleasure as she spoke of that plan and found it reassuring. Enjoyment in work was one of the hallmarks that a person had found God's plan for their life. She was doing chemistry on a sabbatical, so it was definitely something she did for her own enjoyment.

She closed her sketchbook. "Do you have time for one of my questions?"

The rest of his day's schedule was open. "Sure. What would you like to talk about?"

"Mankind got into this mess of sin and death because of a choice Adam made in Eden. I'd like to talk about the first chapters of Genesis and what happened."

"A powerful subject." He unlocked his office and

turned on lights.

"I'm not ignoring our conversation of Monday night, I'm just not sure what I want to ask about it yet in follow up."

"We've got all summer. We can come back to it months from now if you like."

Emily took the same seat on the first couch as her prior visit and set her things beside her.

Noah opened the refrigerator. "Like a drink?"

"That Iced Tea would be good, thanks."

Noah handed her the glass bottle and chose a soda for himself. He settled comfortably on the facing couch. He wanted a casual conversation with Emily about something other than the bible at some point in this visit but patience was a virtue and for now what felt like a plan was to simply offer a couple follow-up questions about the chemistry she was working on before they parted ways. The more involved the subjects she asked, the more likely this was going to become a summer long conversation and she had just offered a huge topic, which suited him fine. "Genesis and Eden. Okay. Do you want to talk about creation as well, or focus on Adam and the fall?"

"Focus on Adam for now, how we got into this mess and how God arranged to get us out of it via Jesus."

Noah mentally sketched an outline of the answer before he began. "The best way to answer that is to present the creation saga as it pertains to Adam and Eve. Pause me as you have questions. I have a habit of falling into teacher mode and giving long answers as you've already experienced."

Emily simply smiled. "That's not even a unique trait on a university campus. I'll pause you when I want to check something."

"Good, thanks." He opened the soda and pulled over a coaster. "Jesus, being a good Jewish boy, would have likely memorized the first five books of the bible by the time he was twelve. I mention that because when I speak from memory on this topic, I'm not trying to show off. Learning scriptures is simply part of my history with God."

Emily laughed. "You're that worried I'll think you're smart? Noah, why do you think I'm asking you the questions rather than someone else?"

"Good point." He settled in to answer her question. "So this is how the bible describes man's story with God:

'When God created man, he made him in the likeness of God. Male and female he created them, and he blessed them and named them Man when they were created.' (Genesis 5:1b-2)

"And I'm going to pause already to make a point off topic. Note God called them both Man. It was Adam who named the female woman (meaning out of man) and who named his wife Eve. In scripture, when God is speaking to Man, he's speaking to both male and female. The context will make clear when God is speaking only to a male man. The scriptures are already 'gender neutral' to use the politically correct term of today. When God says man, He has always meant mankind. Jesus is the Son of Man. It's Jesus' favorite title for himself. He is the son of Mary, a female Man. He was not the Son of Joseph, a male man, even though his hometown thought Joseph was his biological father."

Emily nodded. "That's a great observation."

"It tends to lower the temperature on that gender debate when people realize God was not putting down women in Genesis. God gave His blessing and dominion rule over the earth to Man – to men and women equally. The Son of God title is Jesus' origin from a divine Father. The Son of Man title is Jesus' humanity. Being born of a female and being of male gender Jesus represents all of Mankind. He is both fully God and fully Man. And that brief observation just got a lot more technical than I like."

Emily laughed. "I'll give you a pass."

"Thanks. So back to what you had asked:

'the LORD God formed man of dust from the ground, and breathed into his nostrils the breath of life; and man became a living being. And the LORD God planted a

garden in Eden, in the east; and there he put the man whom
he had formed. And out of the ground the LORD God made
to grow every tree that is pleasant to the sight and good for
food, the tree of life also in the midst of the garden, and the
tree of the knowledge of good and evil.' (Genesis 2:7-9)

The LORD God took the man [Adam] and put him in
the garden of Eden to till it and keep it. And the LORD
God commanded the man, saying, "You may freely eat of
every tree of the garden; but of the tree of the knowledge of
good and evil you shall not eat, for in the day that you eat
of it you shall die." (Genesis 2:15-17)

when the woman [Eve] saw that the tree [of the
knowledge of good and evil] was good for food, and that it
was a delight to the eyes, and that the tree was to be desired
to make one wise, she took of its fruit and ate; and she also
gave some to her husband, and he ate. (Genesis 3:6b)

to Adam he [God] said, "Because you have listened to
the voice of your wife [Eve], and have eaten of the tree of
which I commanded you, `You shall not eat of it,' cursed is
the ground because of you; in toil you shall eat of it all the
days of your life; thorns and thistles it shall bring forth to
you; and you shall eat the plants of the field. In the sweat of
your face you shall eat bread till you return to the ground,
for out of it you were taken; you are dust, and to dust you
shall return." (Genesis 3:17b-19)

Then the LORD God said, "Behold, the man [both
Adam and Eve] has become like one of us, knowing good
and evil; and now, lest he put forth his hand and take also
of the tree of life, and eat, and live for ever [in this fallen
state]" -- therefore the LORD God sent him forth from the
garden of Eden, to till the ground from which he was taken.
(Genesis 3:22-23)

This is the book of the generations of Adam. When

Adam had lived a hundred and thirty years, he became the father of a son in his own likeness, after his image, and named him Seth. The days of Adam after he became the father of Seth were eight hundred years; and he had other sons and daughters. Thus all the days that Adam lived were nine hundred and thirty years; and he died. When Seth had lived a hundred and five years, he became the father of Enosh. Seth lived after the birth of Enosh eight hundred and seven years, and had other sons and daughters. Thus all the days of Seth were nine hundred and twelve years; and he died. (Genesis 5:1a,3-5)

sin came into the world through one man [Adam] and death through sin, and so death spread to all men because all men sinned (Romans 5:12b)

death reigned through that one man [Adam]   (Romans 5:17a)

Noah paused there. "That's how mankind got into this mess and began to die."

"It's a sad sequence of events," Emily said.

Noah nodded. "Mankind paid for it until Jesus came and set us free." There were several observations which might be helpful to her before he turned to how Jesus rescued mankind. Noah chose a few of his favorites to share.

"The first thing I like to mention is that all the universe was created in a functional form. Adam and Eve were created as adults. Animals were not baby animals. The sun was giving heat and light at the right proportion to warm the earth. There was functionality in the original design of the universe, not just the potential for it, but the finished reality of it. Adam was talking with God and naming the animals on the first day of his created life.

"God finished creation in six days. When He was done, God inspected everything and He rendered his judgment and declared it was very good. Look at what was in creation. Free will is a good thing. There was free will because there was a choice to obey God or not – there was one command about a tree. And life is a good thing. There was a tree of life, a way to live forever by something Adam and Eve ate. Adam and Eve were created as righteous beings. They were as clean and pure as God. They were in relationship with God, they walked together in the garden talking with Him. They were holy, set apart to God as a unique part of creation, created in the image and likeness of God. They were made of dust, but also had a soul and spirit, they were a living being.

"When you ask people who Adam was, most people reply Adam was the first created man, and they are accurate, but there's something else scripture says about Adam. In Luke 3 we are given information about Jesus' earthly parents. Listen to how scripture records the genealogy. 'Jesus, when he began his ministry, was about thirty years of age, being the son (as was supposed) of Joseph, the son of Heli, the son of Matthat ... the son of Enos, the son of Seth, the son of Adam, the son of God.' (Luke 3:23,24a,38)

"God considered Adam his son. Most people don't realize the Father's heart toward us began with Adam in Eden. When Jesus shows up and calls God his Father he was perfectly reflecting the fact he was both from God and was also the second Adam. Adam in Eden was made of earth in the likeness and image of God, he was an eternal being created for relationship, to be a son to a Father God. Only the first Adam in Eden fell from that glory he was born with when he sinned.

"Jesus is the second Adam. Jesus comes to earth in the form and likeness of man, as a Son of Man, to restore to us our glory. Jesus came to earth to restore sons and daughters to God the Father. In order to do so, Jesus had to deal with our sin because God is righteous. So Jesus by his death makes us righteous again. Jesus, on the morning of the resurrection, says in John 20:17 'I am ascending to my Father and your Father, to my God and your God.' By His death and resurrection Jesus has completely restored us to God our Father. When we believe in Jesus we become children of God. That's not a concept, but a very personal relationship."

Emily paused making notes. "I had never heard that before about Adam. But as soon as you mentioned it, its like a light bulb went off. The Father's heart. The first Adam was a son. Had man not sinned, God would have had sons and daughters from Eden, a world full of them as children were born, a family that walked in righteousness with God."

"God's purpose with creation was always about having a family for Himself," Noah agreed. "Mankind isn't here on earth because God created a planet and needed people to do the work of managing it. God could have given angels the job of tending to animals and crops. God created mankind for us to be in relationship to Him as sons and daughters of God. That's why in the parables it's a Father looking for his prodigal son, it's a shepherd looking for a lost sheep. That's why Jesus is tender to a woman caught in adultery, it's a daughter being restored to her Father. God's heart is at peace when his kids are back with Him. When we are lost, God's love is on a mission to find us. Mankind is a big deal to God because we are his family. It's why God walked with Adam each day in the garden. That Father-Son relationship *mattered* to God in ways we have only begun to grasp. It matters just as much to Him with us today."

"I've been feeling that kind of pleasure from God when I hang out with Him of a morning," Emily remarked. "He's glad I'm there. He's glad I have my attention turned toward Him."

Noah knew exactly what she was describing. "It gives Him joy when we come to hang out with Him and His pleasure restores something in our hearts that nothing else can."

Noah thought for a moment about where this conversation had begun and turned the topic slightly. "Did you notice what was not in creation? There was no disease and no death. No animals or man died. Plants are considered alive but not living beings. Plants growing, producing seeds, being eaten for food, drying out and returning to the soil to add nutrients back to the ground, they are displaying their created nature. But animals and mankind were created to live and not die. God walked with man in the garden. Mankind talked to God to receive knowledge and wisdom. Mankind ate of the tree of life and by doing so their bodies made of dust lived forever. Adam and Eve were a family and God was their Father. All was very good. It was designed to continue uninterrupted.

"Notice what God called the tree they were not to eat from? The tree of 'the knowledge of good and evil'. How do you really know something? You experience it. We now experience evil because man ate of this tree. That's why bad things happen to people. We are experiencing what this tree Adam chose to eat from brought into the world. God had created the potential for evil when he created free will. Free will is good. But sin is lawlessness; it is acting contrary to the word of God. It was man who brought evil into the world, not God.

"God, in his mercy, cast man out of the garden of Eden so they couldn't eat of the tree of life again and live forever in that fallen state. God did not restore life to us until Jesus came and first restored us back to righteousness.

"Did you notice that this tree of knowledge includes 'good' as well as 'evil'?" Noah mentioned. "There is a 'good' which comes from our own decision and free will that has no origin in God. We can do something 'good' that other men would judge and say 'oh, that's good!' and yet God will say 'that's your own free will creation that is not of me. That 'good' you're doing while ignoring what I did tell you to do? It's sin.' The Pharisees were experts at doing religious 'good deeds'. They were hypocrites who didn't know God, they were in sin and were going to hell. The tree of 'the knowledge of good and evil' is the source of where that kind of 'good' comes from. There's a spirit for 'doing good' but its not of God. It's actually an evil spirit which is putting on the appearance of light."

"That's a powerful distinction," Emily remarked.

"John Bevere wrote a book called Good or God? which is a solid look at the topic. Jesus says you can know a tree by its fruit. If the 'good deeds' you are doing as a Christian are growing a sense of pride in you, a sense of arrogance, 'look at how much good I've done', 'look at how righteous I am compared to others', the odds are high your actions are actually from an evil source. You aren't submitted to God and doing the 'good' that He wants you to do. What you've been doing is creating a 'good church-person persona' because you like the admiration of men. God will send you to hell for it because you're lawless and doing your own thing. Jesus will declare 'I never knew you'. Satan counterfeits what Jesus authentically creates.

"Following Jesus is the good tree. That good tree produces both good works and humility. God will fill your plate with plenty of good things to do. He will also fill your days with time in his Word, and time alone in his presence. The Christian church, in the western world in particular, runs around busy and much of it is works that are not of God, but are works we think would please God. It's fruit of the wrong tree. It's sin. God told us to abide in him, to be people in his Word, and from that abiding to obey his voice. If you are doing so many 'good works' you don't spend your first fruits of time with God during the week, about 17 hours, on a consistent basis, I can pretty easily predict you're not listening to God and doing only his assignments. You're adding in what sounds like a good work which He didn't assign to you to do."

"That's a blunt warning, Noah."

"I wish more Christians would hear it. The only way to stay out of deception is to press into knowing God. He is the light we need so we walk in light. And that tangent is normally a weekend message."

Noah shifted back to the topic of her question. "God knew before the foundation of the world that satan would sin and that satan would then deceive and corrupt mankind, that Adam would also choose sin. But knowing isn't causing.

"God never intended for man to experience evil. God intended mankind to obey Him, to conquer satan by rejecting disobedience. And had we done so, had we not sinned, God would have had the family He desired with the first creation. But instead, we disobeyed and brought death upon ourselves. And because God had given to man the rule over all living things on earth, animals under our rule also began to die, for animals were subjected to death by our death. When we obeyed satan we left the rule of a good God for the rule of an evil angel. The world came under the dominion of satan who is a wicked ruler, one who corrupts and kills what he rules. Creation was corrupted because of our decision to sin."

Emily held up her hand to pause him as she finished a note. "That's very useful Noah, why the animals were also subject to death. We had dominion over them, so what happened to us happened to everything under our care."

Noah nodded. "You see the principle of it all through the bible. When a good king rules, Israel is blessed. When an evil king takes the throne, everyone under him suffers. Adam and Eve were given rule of the earth, they were the first King and Queen, with authority over God's creation. Their sin subjected earth to corruption. Their death subjected the living things under them to death."

Emily finished her note. "Come back to that later and tell me more when we talk about creation."

"Sure." Noah made a mental note to talk about Romans 8:19 as part of that discussion. He pivoted their conversation toward how God rescued mankind via Jesus.

"One of the most beautiful things about God is His faithfulness to how He does things. God speaks what is to come and then that word comes to pass. God doesn't surprise us. God announces events, speaks about them, and then those events come to pass. All the bible is basically God speaking and telling us what is going to happen. God was telling us about Jesus and about grace all through the Old Testament.

"The cross was a military move of God to redeem mankind. Satan is described as a murderer from the beginning. Who did satan murder? Jesus. When mankind sinned and obeyed what satan said to do rather than obey what God had said to do, we gave satan authority over us, we became slaves to sin and satan could make us sick, injure or even kill us as he chose because we were now under his rule and he is a cruel ruler. Jesus never sinned. He was the one man satan had no right to harm or kill. When satan instigated Jesus' crucifixion and murdered an innocent man, satan was judged and condemned as a murderer and stripped of all rule, it cost satan the dominion over the earth he had acquired from mankind. God gave the rule of the earth back to a specific man, to Jesus who is called the Son of Man, the last Adam, the Righteous One.

"Adam shows us the power of free will to produce evil. Jesus shows us the power of free will to produce good. Jesus is able to save the entire world because his free will chooses obedience to God – 'not my will but thine be done.' The first Adam disobeyed God and brings to mankind death. The second Adam is obedient to God and brings back to mankind life.

"In the garden of Eden there was one rule, one choice. Don't eat of the tree of the knowledge of good and evil. Mankind made the wrong choice and satan became our ruler and we suffered death because of sin. Now mankind's salvation has come. Jesus has come as our Savior. There is one rule again. Believe in my Son. We once again have a choice between life or death. Our free will is still free.

"Our choice decides our eternity. Hell was created for the devil and his angels, not mankind. God never wanted mankind to experience sin and evil in the first place. God came and died Himself so that we would never have to experience hell because we had sinned. God will take that kind of very personal step to help us. But what God won't do – God won't remove our free will. He respects our free will at a much deeper level than we do. He will not remove that gift. Rejecting Jesus, not following Jesus, is a devastating eternal decision. Yet God won't stop us from going to hell. God honors us by respecting our right to make our own decision.

"Can you imagine how painful Judgment Day will be for God? Many of His kids, those He created to love for all eternity, the kids He Himself died to save, will be thrown into hell by their own choice. It's agonizing for a parent to lose a child, and on that Judgment Day the Father will lose millions if not billions of his children. We wonder at the patience of God. It's the patience of a Father who will do anything to avoid losing a child. The Father is pouring everything He has into crying out 'accept Jesus and live! Come back home, I love you!' It breaks my heart to know how devastating that day is going to be for our Dad."

Emily nodded. "Until you said that, it had been theory, Noah. I know there are many who reject Jesus. It's when you see that rejection through the Father's heart – no wonder God was willing to send his beloved son Jesus to die for us. To lose sons and daughters by the millions if not billions on Judgment Day – God's heart has to have a breaking point and that sounds like it."

"I think this is why God says He gave all judgment to his Son Jesus. God couldn't face being the one to say to a child, 'You're lawless. You have chosen hell. So I must now send you there.' I think Jesus couldn't face being the one to declare that judgment over a person either, because Jesus in turn gave all judgment to the Word. It will be the Word, the written scriptures, that judges mankind on that last day. God's word is truth. We'll be judged fairly, by truth, without partiality. It will be the question 'did you believe in Jesus, call on Him to be your Savior and follow Him?' The Word is living and powerful, sharper than any two-edged sword, dividing soul and spirit. Every person's heart will be visible. We will have a good heart or an evil one. Those whose name is not in the Book of Life will be sent by the Word to hell. The scriptures warn, there is a 'day of judgment and destruction of ungodly men.' (2 Peter 3:7b). God desires no one to perish and yet many million if not billions will."

"Someone is going to need to wipe God's tears away," Emily said softly.

"There isn't going to be a handkerchief big enough," Noah guessed.

"How can judgment day, and the marriage supper of the lamb, Jesus marrying the bride of Christ the church, be so close together at the end of time? One is pure joy, the other is incredible sadness."

"I am glad I'm not the Father sorting that out," Noah agreed. "God's perspective on creation, on mankind, on who will accept Jesus and who will not, comes with perfect knowledge. God longs to give his children a world without evil in it. Scriptures are pointing to this longing, 'we wait for new heavens and a new earth in which [only] righteousness dwells.' (2 Peter 3:13b)

"For the sake of His kids who have come home, God has set a date the wicked, all causes of sin and satan will be removed from this world forever. I can understand part of the reason that day is coming very soon. Our hearts and spirits are grieving now in ways we can't understand as they endure being in a place where sin abounds around us. We're very much like Lot, a righteous man living in Sodom. 'what that righteous man saw and heard as he lived among them, he was vexed in his righteous soul day after day with their lawless deeds' (2 Peter 2:8b) We've lived in a world dominated by sin for so long that we've never experienced a place which is only righteous. God longs to give us that freedom, to give us back a world in which only righteous dwells. It's not just God who has been suffering because of sin, its us, his kids. And a Father's heart longs to protect His kids.

Jesus said… '[at the close of the age] The Son of man will send his angels, and they will gather out of his kingdom all causes of sin and all evildoers, and throw them into the furnace of fire; there men will weep and gnash their teeth. Then the righteous will shine like the sun in the kingdom of their Father. He who has ears, let him hear.' Matthew 13:41-43

'the creation waits with eager longing for the revealing of the sons of God; ... because the creation itself will be set free from its bondage to decay and obtain the glorious liberty of the children of God. Romans 8:19b,21

"Creation will be set free from bondage. Animals will no longer die. Creation will obtain the glorious liberty that the children of God have already obtained over corruption and death. Because mankind is a mixture right now – some accepting and rejecting Jesus – we are living in the kingdom of God but aren't seeing only righteousness, for the free will of evil men is still causing corruption to flow into creation. When evil men are removed, decay, disorder, corruption and death will no longer flow into creation. The church has authority in Jesus' name to free creation now – we can bless the ground and it will yield good crops for example – we can break droughts by bringing in rain – creation is progressively being freed as Christians declare the good news. Creation has been set free from the bondage of decay and from the curse upon the ground by Jesus at the cross. To bring it into effect, we use the dominion God has given us over the earth to bless and rule the animal kingdom and all the earth itself. The sons of God are revealed – we are revealed by the fact we take the authority and power Jesus has given us and we begin to rule."

Emily nodded as she added to her notes. "Thanks for that, its very helpful."

"Sure. It's like we're looking at two stages of recovery, in the first part God was recovering his kids, and in the second part God is recovering his creation through his kids' rule," Noah replied. "From the beginning, Jesus was God's plan to get us entirely out of the mess we got ourselves in.

one man's act of righteousness [Jesus'] leads to acquittal and life for all men. Romans 5:18b

by one man's obedience [Jesus'] many will be made righteous. Romans 5:19b

those who receive the abundance of grace and the free gift of righteousness [will] reign in life through the one man Jesus Christ. Romans 5:17b

By his [Jesus'] wounds you have been healed. 1 Peter 2:24b

"The first part is huge and it is finished. God has reconciled the whole world to Himself through Jesus. All mankind are forgiven their sins. Jesus has healed every disease of every person. Under the new covenant God has forgotten all our sins and lawless deeds. We are fully redeemed and restored. All a person needs to do is look at Jesus and accept God's grace. The second part is in process as sons of God begin to reveal themselves by ruling."

Noah reflected for a moment. "Mankind delays deciding for Jesus and following him because lawlessness seems like fun – doing your own thing, partying, being your own boss – sin seems on the surface desirable and enticing and pleasurable. People think they can change their mind at a later time because we live a world where everything is temporal and changeable. We are warned Jesus is coming soon. But people show by their actions they don't believe that day is coming soon. We are warned it's a permanent decision. But people show by their actions they think we can decide to change their minds at a later date and they will be able to do so. God says now, today, is the day of salvation, because tomorrow that door may no longer be open to us. We are flippant about important decisions. We are deceiving ourselves. That arrogance will cost many eternity in hell if they delay a moment too long.

And the hardest thing to do is get someone to slow down their life long enough to listen to the fact there is a judgment day coming soon." He chose to end his answer there.

"Thank you, Noah."

"That went a lot darker at the end than I intended."

"There's an urgency to you when you talk about the end of times. I think the Holy Spirit is prophesying through you about just how urgent this rescue mission is to share the good news with the world."

"I live very aware time is short. Still, it would be helpful if I gave you room to talk occasionally, to ask questions."

Emily laughed. "Wait until we land on subjects where I'm the expert. For now, this is exactly what I desired, Noah. You're giving me the framework to help me place what I already know into the overall content of scripture, to see God's plan unfolding. That's very helpful." She slid her notes back into her bag. "I've been studying the verse list you sent me and that is what raised the question about Eden."

"As I've mentioned before, I like a good question. Do you have plans for your weekend?" he asked, curious, shifting the conversation to another topic while he had the opportunity.

"I'm leaving for Washington State in the morning to do some sightseeing. I've always wanted to get up close and personal with the Rocky Mountains and this is the summer to make that happen."

That news wasn't entirely unexpected given what he knew about her thus far. "You'll enjoy that a great deal."

"What about you, Noah? Any plans?"

"I'm normally speaking somewhere on weekends, but this is a rare weekend in town. I'll do the routine of paying bills, grocery shopping, cleaning house. I may go see Jason Lasting in concert tomorrow night. Those are always good Friday evenings."

"I agree with that."

"I hope your adhesive formula gives you the qualities you are after." He wondered what she was currently working on that needed it. Tenured research professor carried with it an expectation of discoveries and she'd produced some fascinating ones thus far.

"Thanks. So do I." Emily gathered her things together and rose. "I appreciate your time."

He rose out of politeness to say goodbye. "Anytime, Emily. I look forward to seeing photos of your travels when you get back."

"I'll bring a few," she promised with a smile and departed.

Noah picked up her empty glass bottle and his soda can and put them in the recycling box. "What do you think, Father? Jesus?"

The impression which settled on him was one of heaviness. "Yeah. We think our family histories get dysfunctional, it's nothing like your story with your kids. Your story with us is not a particularly light one. For the record, I love you, Dad. I love you, Jesus. I wish everyone I met would say the same." It wasn't only the Father who was grieving what Judgment Day was going to be. Noah knew he was going to lose those who could have been his brothers and sisters for eternity to their decision not to know Jesus. And that train of thought just led to more hurt. Understanding that God knew who would accept Jesus and who would not didn't make this pain less. It just meant God had been living with that awareness and weight for all eternity. God, for the sake of those who would accept Jesus, had considered this creation and its unfolding journey worth all its costs. God passionately wanted a family. God was the one who had paid the heaviest cost of all to have that family. Trying to live as a good son or daughter during these final days of earth struck Noah as the kindest thing Christians could do for God right now. God knew how many kids He would lose to hell on Judgment Day, knew the exact number, knew every one of those individuals names. That grief had to be overwhelming.

Noah deliberately shifted his thoughts away from the subject. "Emily surprised me with her question again. She seems to be thinking more about the story of You, God, than anyone else I'm currently talking with."

He smiled at the thought which came to mind. "She does indeed like to learn. And if I don't figure out how to hang around her in settings other than these question and answer conversations I'm never going to make progress with her in a way that personally matters. It would be nice if you'd set us up for a casual conversation next week."

Noah left his request there knowing they would likely return to the topic of Emily during their evening walk. He hadn't intentionally taken from Eden's story the habit of walking with God of an evening, but after a couple years of doing so he had realized why it mattered so much to both of them and it was now a permanent part of his life. Walking together was sharing life together. He liked walking and talking with God. And since Emily had arrived in his life, there had been more to talk about than usual.

10

Emily had never before been speechless, but she was right now. This was the most spectacular sight she had ever experienced. Around her seven mountain peaks rose majestically into the sky. The sunset was casting warm light on three peaks and shrouding in silhouette the other four peaks. There wasn't snow on the mountain tops but they were so raw with rock and jutting peaks it was as if the snow had melted the day before. The life vest she wore for safety was both comforting and an extra source of warmth over her layers of shirt and sweatshirt. With the setting of the sun the temperature was dropping. Her guide paddled them deeper out into the still lake. The colors of the sunset reflected in the water and danced in the wake of their small motion. At the center of the small lake they drifted quietly, a gentle wind stirring the top branches of the mostly fir trees surrounding them.

They remained motionless on the water as the sky unfolded above them, stars appearing by the thousands.

"You were right, George."

It was the first words she'd spoken in nearly an hour. Her guide smiled and tapped his heart in agreement. He'd been right in his counsel to leave the camera behind, to simply experience this the first night. Tomorrow she'd try to capture the beauty so she could show others this place. It had been a recommendation of a friend of Gina's made over coffee the day she arrived in Washington State. 'You should let George and Caroline take you up to seven peaks lake.' And God had walked her into this. The beauty of this place was redefining for her the word glory.

She'd thought the hike to this majestic spot couldn't be surpassed. She had forgotten God's handiwork that lasted only for a changing hour every evening. God had painted His sunset and then unfolded a night sky as only God could do. "Thanks, Dad," she whispered. There was such vastness to the night sky it made her feel very small and very much seen as well. God had arranged all of this experience. There were tents and a comfortable air mattress and a campfire and fresh caught fish from this mountain lake that had been their dinner. And all she'd had to do was follow the desire in her heart to see the Rocky Mountains.

George, relaxing against cushions opposite her, equally enjoying the view, mentioned softly, "When you think of relaxing with God the best place to meet Him is where it is his home. Caroline and I come up here every month during the summer. God is wild. God is majestic. God is like a lion, not tame, but good. He invites his kids to come get to know Him. He didn't ask man should I make stars, should I make sunsets, should I make water you can swim in and drink and boat on. God does His own thing. And when we let God do what He would like in our own lives, they turn out like this place. Wild and beautiful and yet orderly in their own way."

"You're a poet."

George smiled. "If you don't find what you were looking for on this trip, come back again. You can practically reach out and touch Him on nights like this."

"I'll likely take you up on that having seen this place." Emily felt a deep contentment. Life was good right now. This sabbatical felt like a season to absorb that goodness, to rest in the peace of what life was. Life would inevitably change, she knew that, but the day to day of this summer was going to be like this. She'd needed the rest. And she was wisely going to take it.

They drifted for another half hour. "Ready to go in?" George asked softly.

"Ready for the hot chocolate and the marshmallows," Emily agreed, the cool of the night having finally penetrated through the layers she wore.

He picked up the oars and moved them slowly back toward shore. "You can have a couple hot cherry pie sandwiches tonight with a bit of practice, they cook nicely in the fire coals in those sandwich tongs."

"I'm game to try. Your kitchen up here is remarkable."

"Years of bringing the one thing we don't have stored here has filled out the basics in our storage box. If its cast iron the weather and the animals don't bother it much."

"I deeply appreciate you both sharing this place with me."

"We enjoy the occasional company."

＊＊＊＊

The fire was down to red hot embers under the last of the wood chunks. The roasting stick for marshmallows rested against the log Emily sat on. She'd just heard what she thought was her fourth owl and her first distant coyote call. George and Caroline had turned in for the night. Emily opened her bible and clicked on her travel flashlight. "What do you want to talk about tonight, God?"

She felt like she had stepped into the presence of God in this place. It was so unlike Chicago or Austin. She didn't want this night to end. They would be here two more days, she could sleep in as long as she desired in the morning. Right now she wanted to talk to God about profound stuff and small stuff – whatever was on his mind.

Psalm 18 came to mind and she turned there, curious what God wanted to say. It was David's song when God had delivered him from his enemies. Emily read aloud the verses the Holy Spirit highlighted.

[1] I love thee, O LORD, my strength.

[19] He brought me forth into a broad place;
he delivered me, because he delighted in me.

[35] Thou hast given me the shield of thy salvation,
and thy right hand supported me,
and thy help made me great.

[46] The LORD lives; and blessed be my rock,

and exalted be the God of my salvation,

[50] Great triumphs he gives to his king,
and shows steadfast love to his anointed,
to David and his descendants for ever.

As she read the last verse, she realized why God had
taken her to this Psalm. She was a descendant of David
through Jesus. She was one anointed now by God. The
success of the last few years, the rocket design, the
fireworks, the battery she hoped to bring to completion this
summer – God wasn't doing a new thing. He was fulfilling
to her a very old promise.

"I come from a lineage that through Jesus goes back to
David. I've been grafted into this family, this promise.
You're giving me great triumphs because you promised
David this is what you would do for his descendants for
ever. You recorded it for me when you had David write
these words. Your steadfast love is mine, you will
constantly show me your steadfast love." Emily stopped
speaking, overwhelmed. God's steadfast love was going to
be hers for ever, what she had been tasting for the last four
years was never going to end. She didn't deserve this. She
looked up at the night sky, the stars spread out in glorious
numbers. "I'm glad you made me worth this again, I'm
glad you restored me to being your daughter, Dad. I want to
know you, not just sort of know about you. I want you.
How do we connect so well I can finish your thought and
you can finish mine?"

She needed this relationship with God. It wasn't just a
desire anymore, it was such a deep need she wished she
could see heaven and hug him and not let go. Her
biological parents had loved her, but not like this. They had
dreams for her and hopes and had given her a safe home to
grow up. But they hadn't understood who she really was,
hadn't understood she had been created to be God's
daughter. They hadn't known how to introduce her to her
real Father God. She was home with God. She belonged

with God. She could feel that certainty. She just didn't know how to build this relationship she so desired to have.

I want it too.

The thought crossed her mind so swiftly and softly it was an answer in the same breath as her thought. She felt a deep breath rise in her and exhaled, felt a rest settle gently on her emotions. God was abiding in her, seated in this place with her, enjoying the fire, enjoying the quiet night. There wasn't a thought she had that He wasn't tuned in to hear. He was listening to her. "What else do I need to know Dad?"

She sat listening, watching the fire, the lake, the sky and slowly formed the realization she worried too much about tomorrow. If they were going to form memories together, it would be because they walked together every day. She'd be able to remind God of this place and their conversation around the fire. She'd be able to remind Him of the first rocket launch and the joy of the day the phone had stayed on with her new battery. They were building memories of being together and from that was going to come relationship. She was worrying unnecessarily about how to build relationship, it would happen because they lived life together.

She accepted that thought as being God's view on matters, considered it and decided to tell him about her summer from her perspective. "So my summer thus far is the battery design you gave me which is way cool and elegant, and travel like this, and talking with Noah which has been wonderful because he's been able to give me the picture for how what you've been teaching me fits together. Coming up soon it's the satellite repair. I'm controlling repair robot 7. If ever you gave me success in something Dad, there's my big request for the summer. It's a seventy million dollar satellite and I'm going to be holding the wiring harness that lets it communicate with earth. I have to be perfect in every movement of that repair bot, and I need you to help me with that. And enough about that subject or I'll just get frozen with nerves. In smaller matters, I really like the bedroom furniture Gina helped me pick out and when I get home I'm painting the dining room. If that goes well, I'll consider moving on to do the kitchen." She picked up the stick and the bag of marshmallows and fixed herself another one. "So what's on your summer plans?"

She listened to see if God wanted to bring something to her mind. He probably wasn't going to tell her if Jesus was returning this summer, but it would be a busy calendar for God if this were the last months before Jesus return. The words of Psalm 18 came again to mind, so she finished her toasted marshmallow and picked up her bible to read the song again.

Her Dad liked to write down his plans and then do them. She'd learned that about Him in a fresh way on this trip. She'd also learned her Dad knew where the most spectacular scenery was to be found and how to connect her to people who could take her there. She wouldn't be stressing about the rest of her summer travel plans. She'd just follow the desires of her heart and expect God to have made arrangements ahead of her. What else had her Dad written down for her? She wanted to spend this summer on that treasure hunt. She moved on to Psalm 19 and instantly grinned.

[1] The heavens are telling the glory of God;
and the firmament proclaims his handiwork.

"Oh, very nice, Dad. You set that one up perfectly when you ordered the Psalms, knowing I'd be reading 18 and then 19 tonight." Emily read through Psalm 19 with joy bubbling up inside. She might not be able to see her Dad with her, but He was here. She was reading his words.

This summer sabbatical itself was feeling arranged by God. Ten years of teaching and this was the year she'd desired not to teach over the summer, something she'd never felt before. God had been planning something and needed her free to be places like this. She was beginning to realize the entire summer was going to be like this, filled with surprises and joy, walking with God who had prepared the days for her. The battery design, talking with Noah, this travel. This was God's choice of where they should spend three days together and it was an incredible place.

"Thanks for pouring out love upon me, for filling up my heart's need to be seen and loved. It's nice, Dad. And I really needed this." She was barely past the first week. There would be more of these moments over the course of the summer, God had been preparing 90 days worth of blessings. "I want it all, Dad. I want a full summer of walking with you."

She could feel His pleasure. She stayed up watching the stars until the moon passed behind a mountain top and then turned in, finishing a perfect day.

*

11

Noah knew what a bountiful blessing felt like, it was having a summer class filled with sixty-five students. Having Emily show up slightly sunburned, with photos of a gorgeous lake and mountain peaks, bubbling with delight over what God had arranged for her first trip, was another blessing in its own right. She loved the outdoors, that was useful both to see and hear firsthand. His Wednesday evening walk had changed focus when Emily tapped on his office door and asked if she could join him.

"Let's talk about something easy tonight," Emily suggested.

"You're going to need to give me more definition than that," Noah replied, amused with her request.

"Prayer."

Noah didn't consider that an easy topic, but it would go interesting directions. He was glad to have the conversation, to see her again. Letting this friendship develop however it wanted to flow had become his only personal priority for the summer. They skirted around students making their way to evening classes and walked toward the south entrance of the university where the food trucks set up. He was going to buy her dinner tonight and ask more about her trip while they ate. Their walk itself, the subject they discussed, suited whatever question she desired to ask and the topic of prayer was an interesting one. It would make a nice evening.

"Prayer is a conversation with God, just like the one you're now having with me. Prayer is much more intimate than people realize. God is three persons, Father, Son and Holy Spirit. When we are speaking to one, all are listening. Jesus modeled that we pray to our Father. We ask the Father for what we need in Jesus' name. And when we aren't sure what to pray for or how to pray, the Holy Spirit steps in to help us.

"In prayer we're talking to God and building a relationship with Him. We're having a conversation with Him about life. We're also learning how to bring the kingdom of God to bear on concerns and needs. 'God says by Jesus' stripes I am healed, so headache, in the name of Jesus, I command you to leave right now' and that headache leaves. Where do we learn how to say that with faith? In prayer. Think of prayer as God teaching us like a Father would a son or daughter how to do things in the kingdom. Why are we kind to people? Because our Father is kind. Why do we love our enemies? Because our Father loves like that. When you spend time talking with God and listening to Him what you are learning is how to be like Him. God does everything he does by speaking. So do we in the kingdom. Jesus modeled that for us, what a son of God is like."

"Prayer is like the family dinner table. 'Here's what's going on Dad. What would you do?'" Emily suggested.

Noah nodded. "That's very much what's happening. We honor God when we ask 'what should I do in this situation?' and take serious His counsel. Jesus spent significant hours alone with his Father. He was being taught and counseled and loved by his Father. Because we have a heart-to-heart conversation with God, its not just our own life which will change. Nations and businesses, families and churches, will also change. The power we have within prayer is something very few Christians have grasped."

Noah paused for a moment, thinking about how to present what he understood. "Let me go back to our prior conversation for a moment, to Adam and Eve in the garden."

"Sure," Emily agreed.

"When Adam and Even were in the garden of Eden, Adam did not labor for life. He simply ate from the tree of life. Adam did not labor for food. He had only to reach out his hand and pick whichever fruit appealed to him to eat, there was always a vast array of fruit ripe and in season.

Adam likewise did not labor for authority or power. God gave Adam dominion, rule, authority and power, over the animals, birds, fish and all the earth. In Eden, life, food, power and authority – rule – were gifts from God the Father to Adam his son.

"For six days God formed creation and everything man would need, then God made man on day six and placed man in the garden. God blessed Adam and gave him dominion. God then rested on the seventh day and blessed it. Adam's first full day of life was day seven, a blessed day and a Sabbath rest, it was a perpetual Sabbath, it continued on all the days of Adam's life until he sinned.

"Adam's mandate from God was to subdue the earth. As Adam and Eve had family and multiplied, mankind were to extend Eden outward until it encompassed all the earth. Adam's assignment was to bring the kingdom of God to all the earth. Adam did not labor with sweat and struggle. He spoke and what he said happened. He ruled in the same way as his Father, he spoke and creation obeyed what he said. The Sabbath rest Adam lived in was a life without labor, sweat or effort. Adam had life, food, power and authority, as gifts from God so he could spend his time doing his assignment.

"Then Adam fell and Adam lost authority and power in his words, he had to now work the earth and take from the ground his food by his labor, toil and sweat. And the ground was cursed so that it could not produce its abundance, but would instead be producing thorns and thistles. Adam now had to live by a self-effort struggle to provide for himself. When Adam sinned, the result was Adam walked away from the life, food, power and authority, that was God's constant provision for him. Adam's life became trying to provide for himself. The assignment God had given him to subdue the earth – there was no capacity or authority left to pursue that any longer. Both mankind and creation came under the rule of satan when man sinned. Man had authority over the earth and when man sinned all he was responsible for was likewise subject to satan.

"Jesus came as the Second Adam. Jesus took away from us the first Adam's act of sin. John the Baptist's introduction of Jesus – 'Behold, the Lamb of God, who takes away the sin of the world!' (John 1:29b) Jesus made us righteous again, saints instead of sinners. Jesus restored us to being right with God. Galatians 3:13 says Jesus also became a curse for us. Jesus not only redeemed us from sin, Jesus redeemed us from the curse of labor and toil and sweat. Jesus bore a crown of thorns, he died on a tree, he was made a curse for us. In doing so, Jesus redeemed our life. Jesus took away from us not only Adam's sin but the effects Adam's sin caused in how we live on earth.

"A Christian does not struggle for life, for necessities (food, drink, clothing), nor does a Christian struggle for authority and power. We have been given all these back by God through Jesus. We have been restored to the life God intended for mankind, for the children of God, to have on earth.

"We do not struggle for life – we now eat of the new tree of life during communion. We have Jesus – the life – abiding in us, we are healed by his stripes, we have eternal life again as a gift from the Father. We do not struggle for necessities (food, drink, clothing) – as we seek first the kingdom of God and God's righteousness all these things are added to us by the Father. (Matthew 6:33). God now supplies all our needs. We do not struggle for authority and power – God has returned authority and power to us through Jesus. We have been given the right to speak in the name of the King.

"In Matthew 17:20b Jesus says to his disciples, "if you have faith as a grain of mustard seed, you will say to this mountain, 'Move from here to there,' and it will move; and nothing will be impossible to you." Notice *it* will move – creation itself will again respond to our words. If its made of earth and water you can tell it what to do and it will obey you. God has also given us authority over all the power of the enemy. In Jesus' name we cast out demons. Rather than satan rule us, we now rule over his kingdom. (Luke 10:19) When Jesus says 'all authority in heaven and earth has been given me. Go therefore…' Jesus was reaffirming that power and authority is back in the hands of mankind. What we speak in Jesus' name has the authority and power of God behind it.

"What is happening? We are re-entering the Sabbath rest that God prepared for his kids. There is a rest that comes from God that is available to the children of God today which looks very much like Eden did for Adam. God has prepared all the provisions we need for life and as his children we again are given rest from labor. We are given back rule as Kings over this earth. Having restored us to the Father's care, Jesus promptly restores to us our assignment as well. 'Go and make disciples…' Our assignment is to preach the good news of the grace of Jesus, to preach the good news of the kingdom of God, to all the nations. Our assignment to once again bring the kingdom of God to all the earth.

"Hebrews chapters 3 and 4 talks about this Sabbath rest that now exists for the children of God.

So then, there remains a sabbath rest for the people of God; for whoever enters God's rest also ceases from his labors as God did from his. Hebrews 4:9-10

Therefore, while the promise of entering his rest remains, let us fear lest any of you be judged to have failed to reach it. For good news came to us just as to them; but the message which they heard did not benefit them, because it did not meet with faith in the hearers. Hebrews 4:1-2

And to whom did he swear that they should never enter his rest, but to those who were disobedient? So we see that they were unable to enter because of unbelief. Hebrews 3:18-19

we who have believed enter that rest Hebrews 4:3

"This is the rest Jesus' spoke of in Matthew 11:28 'Come to me, all who labor and are heavy laden, and I will give you rest.' This rest is a ceasing of the sweat, toil and labor mankind has endured because of sin. This rest is beautiful. When we enter the kingdom of God, we step back into a reality where life, food, authority and power over creation, are once again provided for us by the Father. They are provided so we can then be about our assignment on earth.

"Jesus walked in this rest. He told the weather what to do, he stilled storms, he multiplied food, he healed bodies. 'Go and tell John what you hear and see: the blind receive their sight and the lame walk, lepers are cleansed and the deaf hear, and the dead are raised up, and the poor have good news preached to them.' (Matthew 11:4-5). Jesus was using authority and power and ruling creation.

"Jesus in the gospels never prayed for someone to be healed, he simply healed them. Why the distinction? Jesus understood the Father had given man authority over creation. If its made of earth and water, tell it what to do and it will obey you. Jesus was modeling what that rule looks like so we could see it in action. Through Jesus the Father was giving mankind back rule.

"The Kingdom rests upon authority. When you want something done on earth, you don't speak in your own authority. You speak in Jesus' authority. What you say has the same impact as if Jesus spoke those words. Our source of authority over creation is Jesus' name. Jesus has given us the right to speak in his own name.

Whatever you ask in my name, I will do it, that the Father may be glorified in the Son; if you ask anything in my name, I will do it. (John 14:13-14)

"Jesus came to restore us to relationship with our Father and to restore to mankind rule over the earth. When we speak in Jesus' name our words are backed up with the power and authority of God. We have been restored to being children of God with authority and power in our words. 'whatever you ask in my name, I will do it.' Jesus is being literal. He's inviting us into a relationship of being under authority and with authority. Jesus is inviting us to be a King under the King of Kings.

"Ruling is speaking with authority what is to be done. You don't know how much authority and power you have on earth until you begin to speak with authority in line with God's kingdom. You can tell a plant that is dead on Friday to 'wake up in Jesus' name' and come back on Monday and find the plant is thriving. You can tell a rain shower to come when the land is suffering drought and tell hot humid air to cool off when it is miserable out. The kingdom is about people, but its also about growing abundant crops and putting out wildfires. God is practical. If you need to talk to someone, ask Jesus to have them call you when they have a free moment. Ruling is coming to realize that with Jesus, you obtain what you ask from him. Jesus expects you will do what he asks you to do; and Jesus returns the favor. If we ask him for something, he'll do it. It's friendship. It's rule. It's a big deal, but its also not. That kind of life together is what ruling actually is. Jesus is the King of Kings, and you're an appointed King ruling under him. Jesus knows your name. Jesus has the Holy Spirit at your side to help you rule well. This was always intended to be a partnership, we are co-laboring with Jesus to bring about the Father's will on earth."

Noah paused the conversation there as they reached the university entrance. There were four food trucks set up along the boulevard. "Your choice."

Emily considered options and pointed to the Chili Den truck. "I'm in the mood to eat hot and spicy and then regret it. I'll take the 5-alarm bowl and a cherry coke."

Noah smiled at her remark and scanned the menu on the chalkboard. The 5-way Cincinnati chili suited him.

They settled at a picnic table with big bowls of chili and super-sized soft drinks.

"I love what you've been describing, Noah. That return to who we're intended to be."

"Christianity isn't about something for the future, its about the present. We will enjoy heaven but what Jesus came and did for us – it has always been about restoring us here on earth back to what we were created to do.

"Prayer sits at the intersection of relationship with God, God's kingdom, and ruling in Jesus' name. Jesus would spend the night with his Father in prayer. Then Jesus would walk into his day and spend his time teaching, preaching the good news of the kingdom of God, and healing people. The power for the events of the day came because he was hanging out with His Father before it began. Jesus was listening to His Father then doing His Father's works. That is why prayer is so important to us. We rule earth by what we speak. We tell creation what to do. How do we know what to do and when to do it? We hang out with God first. The Holy Spirit helps us in our weaknesses. According to Romans 8:26 our primary weakness is the fact we often don't know what to pray for and how to pray for it. One of the chief things the Holy Spirit does for us is step in to help us pray."

Emily thought about what he'd offered. "I'm beginning to grasp listening to you Noah, how vast this assignment of being in the kingdom actually is. Christianity is about Jesus, that relationship, but its also much more involved in works, doing good deeds, than I realized. We've been given a lot of authority."

He smiled as he nodded. "God is actually waiting on us most of the time. When the Holy Spirit describes us as co-laboring with God, it wasn't a feel good comment with some exaggeration involved. Jesus is our King. He knows how to rule. And He knows how to teach us to rule. When we hang out with him in prayer asking him questions about matters around us, we see how to bring the kingdom into situations. Jesus brings righteousness into this world by Christians taking authority over problems in Jesus name and solving them. He's given us rule and he won't take that assignment away.

"Jesus is very practical. He knows what he wants done on earth on any particular day. Prayer is for your needs and also for kingdom business. You can have the country of Thailand come to mind and then see a boat catching fish and you'll find yourself praying for their fishing season to be prosperous. If you will linger in prayer with Jesus you'll find yourself involved in matters all around the world. You made yourself available to the King. That's who Jesus uses most in his kingdom – those who are available."

Noah considered how to make it practical and settled on a couple thoughts. "Did you know God has a wish list? He wants to lavish you with blessing right now simply because you're one of his kids. He doesn't need you to be perfect. He will make you perfect as you walk with the Holy Spirit. God needs you to be His kid and want His blessings. God needs your free will to say yes so He can pour love all over you.

"We don't have because we don't ask. That's pretty much the only reason we don't have what we need. God won't override our free will. We need to ask. There are promises from God to us for every area and need of life. God only puts items in his Word that are His own will. Our Dad keeps His promises to us passionately, full steam ahead, with a right now priority. He is not acting reluctantly, sorry He made and wrote down that promise that He's now being asked to keep. He wrote these promises down because He wants to do these things for us. We love God. We love our neighbors. And from that heart position, we just ask Dad for whatever we want. God will gladly provide it to us."

"Wow. That's a nice description of prayer."

Noah laughed. "Scripture says Jesus is the 'Yes' to every promise God has made. When we say 'Amen' and accept what God wants to do we receive those promises happening in our lives."

"God doesn't mind all the requests?"

"He loves them," Noah replied with a smile. "You

should come expecting to receive from your Father with every conversation. All too often we think receiving from Him isn't a good constant thing to do, that our relationship should just be 'I'm good, I just wanted to say hi'. And there is truth in that. We are in relationship with a person and relationships are about fellowship, not just coming to get things. But an equal truth is Jesus' words, 'It is more blessed to give than to receive.' (Acts 20:35) We deny God joy when we try to wave our hands to decline a gift as not necessary. It gives Him joy to meet our needs. God's not into just enough, God's into providing abundance."

Emily finished her bowl of chili and reached for her soda. She drank a good portion of it. Noah didn't comment but he couldn't stop the grin. He'd had the 5-alarm chili once and it wasn't an experience you forgot. The Cincinnati chili, with its base of spaghetti and mild chili topped with a lot of cheese, was more his level of mild spice.

"You pray a lot," Emily mentioned as she dumped a package of the soup crackers into her palm to eat to help cut down the intense spice from the chili. "It's why you walk so often with God in the evening. You're talking with Him."

"I enjoy prayer," Noah agreed. "Most of my life is spent talking to God. I've learned that when I can see something as God does, it is much easier to then do with a willing heart what He asks me. You will leave prayer with things to do, meetings to have, checks to write, phone calls to make. You'll leave prayer with differently arranged priorities, with new assignments. Any good friendship has a cost with it. Jesus is both our older brother and our King. As we are faithful in small things he asks, he entrusts to us more. We learn to be about the King's business on earth. Prayer, speaking to God and Him with us, is the wellspring of how we function as citizens in his kingdom."

Noah paused the conversation there to nod toward the food trucks. "Would you like dessert?"

"I'm thinking something cold. Does the barbeque truck have ice cream bars listed?"

He had better visibility of the board than she did. "It does."

"That suits me."

"Coming up." He gathered up their trash. "I'm surprised you didn't choose barbeque tonight given your love of Texas."

"That's not barbeque. That's Chicago's attempt to call something barbeque."

He laughed at Emily's remark and nodded. "I promise you, the next time I'm traveling in Texas I shall make the effort to understand what good barbeque is."

"Your life would be so much better off if you did."

Noah returned with two ice cream bars and offered her one, along with extra napkins.

"What does it mean to pray in the spirit?" Emily asked, curious.

Noah unwrapped his ice cream bar, glad to get the question. "There are two ways to pray. With our mind or with our spirit. I am a new creation. I now have a spirit and a soul who both use words and language as their primary ways of expressing themselves. They simply speak different languages. As fluently as my mind speaks English, it's still a limited language compared to the heavenly language my spirit speaks. Scripture says 'one who speaks in a tongue speaks not to men but to God; for no one understands him, but he utters mysteries in the Spirit.' (1 Corinthians 14:2b) Praying in the spirit is speaking aloud a prayer in the language your spirit speaks, rather than the language your mind speaks.

"The one who wrote 'I want you all to speak in tongues' (1 Corinthians 14:5b) was the Holy Spirit. God likes this gift. Paul scribed those words, but the author was God. Paul goes on to remark later in that letter, 'I thank God that I speak in tongues more than you all' (1 Corinthians 14:18) If Paul prayed often in the spirit throughout the course of his life, its reasonable to assume much of what we see in his life was in part because of those prayers. He was very useful to God and understood the good news of grace at a very deep level."

"That's a very good point," Emily agreed.

"I can think of three basic reasons the Holy Spirit encourages us to pray in the spirit," Noah offered. "When I pray with my mind, the English words I speak are sincere, it's the best prayer I can make, given what my understanding is of God's plan and the needs around me, but it's probably got a lot of my own ideas within it, making it partly good and partly not. And there are situations and people I would be praying for if I knew about the need but I'm simply in the dark at present as to what is going on.

"My spirit is hanging out with the Holy Spirit. The Holy Spirit knows the thoughts of God. When my spirit talks to God it does so with perfect understanding of God's will. The Holy Spirit knows what I need to pray about and how I need to pray for it. When we pray in the spirit we are praying perfect prayers. Full of thanksgiving and praise, glorifying God for His works. Scripture says we speak mysteries—our spirit is talking to God about things our mind doesn't yet know or understand.

"All my spirit's prayer is good. And my spirit has perfect faith. So I let my spirit talk with God. 'I yield to my spirit, if you'd like to say anything to God,' and I just start talking and it's a language I don't know. It's a beautiful language. When I choose to speak in tongues, I am praying from my spirit and I am choosing to talk to God in His language rather than mine.

"Sometimes its helpful not to know what we're praying about. God knows your son is going to get distracted while driving and be in a car accident. If you knew that, your mind and emotions would be very anxious as you prayed for your son and that intense emotion might interfere with your faith. Your spirit can pray for your son without that stress and God can answer your prayer so the accident is avoided or it becomes only minor.

"Scripture says 'One who speaks in tongues edifies himself.' (1 Corinthians 14:4) Edify is to build up, make stronger, make capable of handling more. In the Greek edify means building a house, building an edifice, a structure. Scripture says our bodies are the temple of the Holy Spirit. The language used for our bodies is that of a structure. Praying in tongues is building up my spirit, soul and body in ways God has designed. Healing is happening in my body. My soul is being restored. Not only are past traumas in my mind being resolved, but things I haven't understood are being fit together. My emotions are being restored to peace. I'm being edified, built up, restored. In my spirit, I'm rejoicing with perfect praise. It's all helpful to me.

"Praying in the Spirit is also part of the armor of God. Praying in the Spirit is our only offensive weapon, the rest of the armor is defensive in nature. 'Put on the whole armor of God, that you may be able to stand against the wiles of the devil. ... take ... the sword of the Spirit, which is the word of God. Pray at all times in the Spirit, with all prayer and supplication.' (Ephesians 6:11,17b-18a) Praying in the Spirit is directly tied to the Word of God, which makes sense, as the Holy Spirit authored the Word of God. Praying in the Spirit is how we swing that sword we just picked up. The Spirit knows exactly what the enemy is doing and defeats the demons every time. God has never ever lost a battle. I wonder how many people have ever paused to consider that victory percentage – it would certainly cut down on the uncertainty and fear that shows up when you're in a struggle with something and wondering if God is going to get you out of it. Even when satan thought he was winning by killing Jesus, he was actually losing everything. God is our Banner, our Victor, its one of the names God gives Himself because He's never lost a battle. Ever. I love that about Him. He's the God who always wins. That's our God. Those are probably the three main reasons God is encouraging us to pray in the spirit."

"I speak in tongues more now than I did a couple years ago," Emily mentioned. "It's helpful when reading the scriptures. It's like the Holy Spirit is acting as a tutor explaining verses as I read. I have a question about a passage I don't understand. When I pray in the spirit and ask for the interpretation, I'll read the same passage again and I'll see what I was missing before. Comprehension comes. I knew the verses, some I had even memorized, but I didn't understand them. It's like the Holy Spirit says, 'would you like me to tell you what it means? Speak in tongues, I'll tell you in my language, and then you can ask me for the interpretation and your mind will understand what I just explained.' I receive the answer in his language, then ask for his language to be put into English for my mind to understand."

"That's one of the most powerful combinations you will ever do," Noah agreed. "God likes faith. You speak in tongues by faith, you ask for the interpretation by faith, and you then find out that unknown language you were speaking is actually the Holy Spirit talking with you via your spirit. The more you speak in tongues and ask for the interpretation the more interactive your relationship with the Holy Spirit becomes. He's got really insightful things to say that explain what you hadn't understood before."

Noah loved this topic and what the Holy Spirit revealed to the children of God. "God's mysteries are fascinating things. They are hidden from our enemies and for us. The fact Jesus was coming as our Savior was there in the Word of God, for God announces what He is going to do and then He does it. How Jesus would redeem mankind was clear in Isaiah 53, but satan couldn't understand that hidden mystery. Satan didn't realize that by murdering Jesus he was going to be stripped of his authority on earth and tossed out as its ruler.

"Satan knew something was afoot, he tried to kill Jesus as a baby through Herod. Satan tried to get the religious leaders to arrest and condemn Jesus. Eventually satan convinced one of those closest to Jesus to betray him. Satan got the religious leaders and the roman ruler Pilate to crucify Jesus. Satan thought he was destroying God's plan while God was actually using satan's actions to accomplish that plan. Everything that happened to Jesus was written beforehand in the scriptures, the death of the infants, the betrayal by Judas, the details of the crucifixion and how it would come about – God tells us what He is going to do and then He does it. God has no problem using wicked men, even satan, to accomplish his own plans. God hid the redemption and restoration of mankind from the eyes of the enemy even as He wrote about it in detail in the scriptures.

"In the same way, the fact God was choosing the nation of Israel to be his people, but was also going to bring the Gentiles in to also be his people wasn't understood until the Holy Spirit was poured out upon Cornelius and his household in Acts 10. God prophesied what would happen, Jesus talked about the other flock of sheep to be brought in, but even the leaders of the church, Jesus' own apostles, didn't understand it was coming until it arrived. It was a hidden mystery of God, present in his Word, but not understood.

"The scripture says we speak mysteries when we pray in the spirit. One of the things which seems to be happening is our prayers are releasing details of God's plans for us and others. God has prepared beforehand good works for us to do. If a meeting needs to happen, if a resource needs to move from here to there, if someone needs healed, if we need to understand a passage of scripture, whatever is necessary for the will of God to be fulfilled upon the earth in our lives and others – those are some of the mysteries we are speaking. It may be that God is speaking directly to the angels and to demons as we pray in the spirit.

"Our biggest problem in accomplishing this task of bringing the kingdom to all the earth is knowing what to do when. Praying in the Spirit solves that problem. We're praying with perfect knowledge of the will of God. And when you then ask God for the interpretation of what your spirit is speaking, you'll receive guidance and understanding in your mind. You'll have a new thought about how to approach something, see a new way to solve a problem, you'll have a plan for what needs done, you'll have a desire to do something new. God leads us. The desires of our heart are being shaped by God to match his plans for us as we pray."

"Some of the chemistry I do, its felt like that. I couldn't figure something out and then I have a thought that solves it. I didn't understand something and then it connects and I do. I comprehend what I didn't before. It's small things too. I've had dinner menu plans pop into my mind when I walk into the grocery store with a comment from Jesus, 'fix this tonight'. He'll mention 'stop for gas' when I'm heading home of an evening. This morning it was 'phone' when I started to step outside having forgotten it. I'm very aware Jesus lives with me."

Noah smiled at her comment. "I think Jesus likes to help us in practical ways just like any good friend would. I don't have to ask if you did as he mentioned, the fact he's offering more comments is because you're paying attention to his voice."

"I'm learning to trust him and his timing for things."

"Jesus likes to provide for us. He's preparing what you need so its there when you need it." Noah went back to a prior thought. "When Satan said to Jesus as a temptation in the wilderness, paraphrasing Matthew 4:3, 'you're hungry. Why don't you speak to these stones and turn them into loaves of bread?' Jesus didn't reply 'I can't do that.' Satan and Jesus both knew he could. But Jesus knew wisdom was to look to his Father for his provision rather than act to provide for himself. Jesus refused to step back into the first Adam's curse of providing for himself.

"When the temptation was over, the scriptures say angels came and ministered to Jesus. The Father sent angels to his son. (Matthew 4:11) Jesus has been fasting for 40 days and he's hungry. I like to think the Father sent Jesus a meal of all his favorite foods over the next unfolding days. God provided for his son. And in a dessert where it is rocks and sand, providing meant angels arrived with the provisions.

"That's a picture in scripture of what our lives are like

with the Father. When we stay with what the Word says, when we obey His voice, when we don't try to make things happen in our own strength, we are the most strong we will ever be for we are trusting the Father to be Our Father. We trust His plan over our own and in that trust, in that obedience, we will obtain the very things we need.

"There is a reason Jesus has been exalted to the right hand of God. Jesus is trustworthy. Jesus was made perfect by that obedience – Jesus showed he was perfect by his actions of obeying his Father even when obedience meant death on the cross. Jesus will faithfully carry out only the will of God the Father for all of eternity. Jesus was trusted to bring God's family back to Him at the price of his own life. That's how valuable the Father sees us. That's how valuable Jesus sees us. Jesus willing gave his own life to save us because Jesus loves us like the Father loves us.

"God has restored us to life in His kingdom. So pray constantly in the spirit and pray with your mind. We command evil to stop and bless what is right. We rule. Jesus calls us his friends. It's because we do life together, one King to another King. Jesus will be your very best friend if you will let Him. God has promised he will never leave us or forsake us. How close of a friend you want to be with Him is a matter of your free will. God is not holding anything back from what our relationship can be. He's desiring that intimacy that only family can have when sons and daughter are at peace with their Father. That's why the Psalms are filled with 'delight yourself in the Lord.' Our relationship lets the Father's blessings pour out on us."

"It's a good life together."

Noah nodded. "Better than we could ever imagine." He chose to end the topic there.

"Thank you, Noah."

"You realize I took your easy topic and turned it into an hour and a half answer."

"You like my company."

Noah grinned. "I'm not saying I don't. Are you going to be in town for a few days, or are you traveling again soon?"

"I'm painting my dining room."

"That's being very practical. I'm in Baltimore Friday afternoon to Monday afternoon. I'm going to speak on the topic of the kingdom of God four times in various venues. You did me the favor of being yet another round of practice for the material."

Emily laughed. "I'm glad to be useful. You like public speaking?"

Noah considered how to answer that. "I don't hate it." He didn't have good words to describe it. "I like talking about Jesus. I love what conversations can accomplish. I'd just rather be doing it one on one like this than before crowds of a few hundred to a few thousand. But it's not practical to speak one on one when so many need to hear the good news, so I've become comfortable speaking to larger audiences."

"Do you think God chose you in advance to know what you do, or did you choose God and because you've hung around Him every day He's kept adding more to what you know, teaching you more depth?"

It was a good question, one he'd pondered at times himself. "God likes availability. Obedience. A willingness to be sent out. The world is too busy for God. Christians for that matter are mostly too busy for God. If you want to be useful to God, slow down and just hang out with Him every daily. You'll end up with a busy plate full of assignments that can get accomplished without sweat, labor and toil. I travel, I speak to crowds, I prepare materials to share, but its not work for me. Jesus gifted to me the ability to do this along with the assignment. I am never more aware of the Holy Spirit with me than I am when I get up to speak on behalf of Jesus. There's a grace to this life that is God's gift to me. It's fun being in the kingdom of God working for Jesus."

Emily smiled at his remark. "I do chemistry with joy, you speak about the kingdom, Gina does science on a scale that is genius level. God didn't create any of us alike."

"I think its because He likes his kids to know they are one of a kind. We've lived with rejection most of our life. With God there is acceptance. He knows us, how he created us, how we think and who we are, but its also deeper than that. He's been involved in our lives, he's watched us grow up, we are His in every sense of that word. We belong to Him. When we show up in prayer to have a conversation with God we get to pick up matters right where we left off before because it's a perpetual conversation. Some concerns have been resolved, new topics have arisen, but the person we are talking with is still the same. God is perfect. There is no shadow or variation of change in God. He's perfectly good and always available to us. The biggest desire of His heart is for us to simply come and see Him, talk with Him and trust His good heart toward us. God likes to walk us into success by preparing all the moving parts of events to come together at the right time. He's preparing us and those we will help. If you can relax knowing God's abundance heart toward you even the impossible will seem easy. Whatever God asks you to do, He's already equipped you to succeed. It's when you take those first steps by faith and do what He has asked that you find out you're standing on rock." He'd gone off topic far enough Noah chose to stop there.

"Thanks, Noah. I appreciate time like this."

"I like the topics, Emily. And the fact you want to hear what I've got piled up to say. You're getting graduate level and first year introduction and some weekend material, all piled together."

Emily laughed. "I admit, you give me a lot of good things to think about and then go study. I like that."

"The fact you like to learn is one of the most interesting facts about you. So have you thought about what topic you want to discuss next?"

"I like surprising you. I get the unfiltered answer that way."

"That's one description of these wandering conversations. I shall look forward to whatever you next ask," he promised. It would likely be next week before he saw her again given his schedule and hers. He'd asked Gina and been given some helpful information, Emily's birthday and the fact she wasn't dating anyone at present, but it was still too early Noah thought to be offering something beyond these conversations. He'd see Emily at the BSR launch party. For now his plans were focused there.

They rose to walk back on campus. This evening hadn't gone as he planned, but he could still make it work for what he had hoped. "Talk to me about your trip. I want to hear the details."

Emily promptly pulled out her phone to show him more pictures. Noah laughed and accepted it.

12

Noah parked at the east end of the BSR parking lot, arriving late to the launch party. The still full parking lot indicated he hadn't missed the main event. He picked up the wrapped gift he'd brought and headed to the main entrance.

Entering Bishop Space Repair, Inc. was always an experience. In the main lobby was a satellite mockup, built to scale, the size of a small city bus with its solar panels and antennas extended. Motion on it caught Noah's attention. He counted eight robot spider-like repair bots working on the satellite. Two side panels had been removed and wiring guts were being maneuvered aside to get at three circuit boards to be replaced. They moved with deliberate grace as though alive, analyzing each move before they made it, always attuned to one another.

He had watched the entire sequence one afternoon. When the circuit boards were replaced, they would close up the satellite, put the removed circuit boards into the adjoining supply box and fold themselves down into pocket-knife sized foam slots in that box, returning themselves to their starting position. Then the program would loop and the robots would wake up, unfold themselves and do the repair again. It took them eighty-three minutes. They were early practice bots for the first satellite repair BSR had done. The demonstration was remarkably close to the actual event which had been done in the weightless of space on the actual satellite.

Tonight a rocket was launching from Florida to intercept a failing communications satellite. From what Gina had told him, when she invited him to the launch party, the satellite needed two new gyroscopes, more fuel, a new hi-band antenna and two circuit boards replaced so it could stay in service for another decade. Noah knew enough to enjoy the launch and watch the people who did understand the science set out to accomplish another remarkable feat.

He touched the Welcome – Begin Here words on the new video screen, interested to see what they had added in the last month. News conferences were becoming a regular event and they were beginning to do tours of BSR for the occasional high school group.

Jim Bishop appeared on video. "Welcome to Bishop Space Repairs, Inc. I'm retired astronaut Jim Bishop, and I lead this largely volunteer endeavor along with several members of the Bishop family. I'd like to begin this welcome message by introducing Kelly Gold. She needs no introduction to those of you who love space as she's the daughter of one of the most beloved astronauts in US history. Her father, Scott Gold, was one of twelve men to walk on the moon. Kelly is a former NASA flight manager for the space shuttle program, a gifted engineer, and was the voice of ground control in my ear during numerous space walks. I'm pleased to have her as the second paid employee of BSR. She serves here in a variety of capacities including Flight Manager and effectively runs day-to-day operations alongside my brother Mark Bishop, the President of BSR. Kelly—the podium is yours."

Kelly Gold stepped onto the platform, a faint blush apparent to those who knew her. "Thank you, Jim. I, too, would like to welcome you to BSR. As some general background, there are now 1,187 satellites in orbit around the earth being used for communications, weather forecasting, military purposes, or study of the earth. Satellites fail for a variety of reasons—instruments cease working; they suffer communication, flight, or guidance system problems; after a certain number of years they run out of fuel onboard and cannot correct their orbit. Once a satellite fails, it drifts in space, being pulled down by gravity, slowing from the drag caused by traveling through the earth's upper atmosphere. When a satellite reaches the critical day in its death spiral, it will begin to tumble and spin and will burn up in the atmosphere as it crashes to earth. A piece or two of debris might make it to the ground as a charred bit of metal the size of a golf ball, but the overall craft will be incinerated during the heat of re-entry.

"We're pleased to announce that Bishop Space Repairs, Inc has the capability to repair satellites while they are in orbit. We will replace failing parts, reload fuel, upgrade instruments, and extend the useful life of what are very expensive pieces of technology.

"The satellite mockup in this lobby is Earth Orbiter 3, the first satellite we went into space to repair as a demonstration of our capabilities. A workhorse for the National Oceanic and Atmospheric Administration for the last eleven years, EO-3 has been studying the oceans and providing real-time data used in modeling earth's weather. With EO-3 running critically low on fuel and no longer able to maintain its orbit, the satellite would have re-entered the earth's atmosphere and been incinerated during its re-entry. BSR sent into space a box of spare parts and eight small robots to remotely repair the satellite. That mission successfully accomplished every objective. EO-3 has been boosted back into normal orbit and given another seven years of effective life. EO-3 marked a solid beginning for BSR.

"As of this month, we have now completed nine satellite repairs and have another seven scheduled for this calendar year, with forty more on the urgent waiting list as BSR expands capacities.

"Engineering of the satellite mock-ups on which we practice and production of the necessary replacement parts is handled by our satellite manufacturer partners. This facility handles mission planning, the repair plan and practice of that mission, configuration of the robotics, and preparation of the supply box which will fly atop the rocket into space. This facility does not have rocket production or launch responsibilities, those are shared with the Navy in exchange for their use of the rocket technology we have developed here.

"The rocket we fly is called a BBR, a Bishop Bottle

Rocket. It was designed by Gina Bishop in model form nearly fifteen years ago. When Jim Bishop retired due to the grounding of the Space Shuttle fleet, that model came off the shelf, was scaled up, engineered and wind tested. Gina has figured out how to keep a rocket stable in flight without the need for adjusting engines. She has basically designed a bottle rocket that can carry a payload and hit a precise spot in space.

"Those rocket specifications, at the request of the government, are not available beyond this description. The repair bots we use, however, are available in schematic form, as is the software we use to control them. We encourage their use in a variety of disciplines to assist with mechanical tasks in dangerous and hard to access locations. The majority of the engineering and mission control software we use has been developed by a team of volunteers, many of whom worked with Jim Bishop at NASA in past years.

"We encourage you to check the BSR website for the latest updates on rocket launch times and repair schedules. Launches and repair missions stream live on the internet with screens as you would see them here in mission control."

"Noah, you made it!"

He missed the final comments from Kelly on the video as he got slammed into for a hug by a girl about ten-years-old. With a laugh Noah knelt to give her a proper hug. "Angel, did you really think I'd miss something you helped with?" Noah knew the twelve bots flying in the supply box for this repair mission had all been named by Angel as they were being built. Angel's mother Grace worked here part-time helping construct those repair bots. "It's good to see you."

"Josh came," she whispered with joy.

"Good," he whispered back, well aware Joshua and Grace were getting close to announcing their engagement. It was no secret this little girl was dreaming of having a father in her life. "Who else is here?"

"Gina and Emily and Charlotte and Bryce and a whole bunch of the engineers I've only met by their screen names before, like cowboy_7, and whitehair_4, and Petras_6. The launch clock is paused at 20 minutes because the winds are gusting. Jim is pacing in mission control. Kelly keeps telling him to find a seat and he mostly ignores her. She's reading poetry, 'cause it takes about a minute per poem and she can look up and decide if anything has changed in that minute before she reads the next one."

Noah grinned. "That sounds like Kelly." She was the BSR flight director because she was superbly qualified for the job. She'd worked in ground control for the space shuttle then as the night shift flight director for the mars rover program before joining BSR. Kelly knew every moving part of what a launch and successful mission needed to be and didn't show stress when things were going wrong. She simply implemented the plans already worked out to deal with the situation.

"How's the food tonight?" Noah asked. A conversation with a faculty member having family trouble had run late enough he hadn't had time yet for dinner.

"Better than launch eight, not as good as nine. It's mostly Mexican, which is wonderful, just messy. Come on," Angel tugged his hand and Noah let her lead him to the launch party, the path marked by balloons and hand-drawn signs she'd made.

The warehouse ceiling was three stories above them. The building was originally designed and built for a crane manufacturing company. They would potentially need that height one day. They had walled the warehouse into functional areas, created some offices, workshops, and left the rest as open work area.

A crowd of about forty people were assembled outside the glassed in mission control. There were tables with food and drinks, tables with festive tablecloths and folding chairs. On the opposite side of the food area was a variety of comfortable seating, mostly acquired couches and wingback chairs volunteer employees used year round.

The rocket on the launch pad was a beautiful sight to behold on a video wall the size of a nearly two story building. Noah was looking at it nearly life-size. When repairs were happening in space, that video wall would divide into the camera views of the various repair bots. Right now the rocket was center screen and they were presently linked into the satellite flight operations center in Houston on the left and the launch operations at NASA's Space Flight Center in Florida on the right.

The full scale mockup of the satellite being repaired on this flight occupied the center of the open room and was larger than the one in the lobby. Practice bots were perched along its upper panel in a row holding a banner that read 'fly!' and doing a thumbs up motion in sequence as a crowd wave. Someone had fit all of them with sunglasses and little ball caps. Noah had to smile at the sight; the engineers were having fun with this launch.

The Mission Control Room with its bank of monitors and glassed in walls curved to Noah's left facing the video wall. The launch clock was indeed paused at 20 minutes. Kelly had her feet up on a worktable, was reading a book and Jim was pacing, just as Angel had described. The four others in mission control were watching the monitors and video feeds and occasionally sharing a comment. The external speakers were on so the assembled crowd could listen in to what was going on in the room.

This location controlled the satellite capture and deployment of the repair bots. They would take over once the rocket had reached the upper atmosphere. Launch control would presently be with Mark Bishop at NASA's Space Flight Center in Florida, where the launch clock was presently being held due to the winds. Noah saw Gina's husband Mark walk by on the video wall. Mark looked as calm as Kelly here. Overseeing the rocket production and now launch would be comfortable terrain for him, given he'd spent a career managing nuclear missiles for the Navy. The mood in the room was good, Noah decided, this was simply a delayed launch but all was going well.

Gina waved him over to the comfortable seating. "Noah, I'm glad you could make it. I was beginning to wonder if I should give you a call." She made room for him at the end of the leather couch.

"I got held up by a faculty member with an urgent question," he replied. He nodded hello to familiar faces among the group. Emily had chosen one of the wingback chairs. "Happy early Birthday, Emily." Noah offered the gift and because he'd chosen well when to give it, she simply smiled and accepted it with a soft thanks.

"What did you get, Emily?"

Angel was eager to see and Emily accepted her plea and opened the package now.

Emily's delight when she saw the contents confirmed he'd made a good choice. "Where did you find this, Noah?"

"Connections in Colorado."

It was a variety of flavored salts from all over the world, each in a test tube of their own, mounted in a display rack with a small spoon dipper to measure out amounts. It wasn't a particularly expensive gift, but he'd seen it and instantly thought of her. She was a chemist by profession and loved to cook. It was a gift that honored both.

"Thank you."

"You're very welcome."

He accepted the soft drink Bryce Bishop brought him and settled in to enjoy the evening. He'd see a rocket launch, enjoy the hand slaps between engineers to the successful beginning of another repair mission and a few days from now watch as the repair bots in the supply box atop that rocket were used to repair a very expensive satellite.

****

They were going to scrub tonight's launch attempt if the winds didn't ease up by eleven p.m. Noah returned to his seat on the couch this time with a piece of cake, having enjoyed a very good dinner over the last two hours. He liked Mexican food.

Most of the crowd had dispersed into clusters around engineering problems for the capsule Jim Bishop still hoped to build, taking the opportunity to work together on the design rather than work remotely as they often did by video. He'd listen to Emily and Gina, along with three of the engineers, have a chemistry and physics discussion about scaling up the rocket to carry a heavier payload, that conversation well above his range of science knowledge. They had headed to Gina's office an hour ago to reconfigure the rocket flight simulation to try out some ideas. It was a typical night for him, a theology professor in a room full of math and science types. The talent here as volunteers rivaled the best paid staff at any company dealing with space flight. If it was possible to get an affordable rocket and capsule built to take Jim to space, they would figure it out.

Emily returned and stopped by the table of food, filled two soft shell tacos. She sat down on the arm of the couch opposite him. "Angel has a favor she wants to ask you, not that she's found the courage to do so yet. Just saying, so you'll know to say yes when she asks."

"I wouldn't likely say no, but thanks for the heads up." He set his plate with cake aside. "I didn't realize you were part of this repair mission. Repair bot number 7. That must be exciting."

Emily smiled as she picked up one of the tacos. "I'm nervous about it but so ready I can do the maneuvers in my sleep. Literally. I've been dreaming about the sequence the last few nights. I'm doing group things like helping hold the satellite panels as they are unbolted and moved aside. And I've got tasks as a transport bot, I help unpack items from the supply box and carry them to the bots that are doing the installations. My unique step comes is the second half of the repair sequence. I'm removing the wiring harness that feeds the antenna bundle so an upgraded hi-band antenna can be installed. There is no part of the mission that isn't critical, but wiring is on the ultra critical list. It becomes fragile and brittle when exposed to the cold of space which is why I have to watch the orientation of how I work. You don't want to cast a shadow blocking what sunlight is present and find yourself holding frozen pieces of wire spaghetti rather than flexible functional wires."

Noah could see that as she described it. "I didn't know that could happen."

"There are all kinds of odd things that can happen. The delay in time between sending an instruction and the bot's movement is the hardest thing to learn, hence all the training sessions on the mockup here. Then there is the lack of gravity and the risk of things detaching and floating away in all directions. When you're not on your task you're on lookout. I have to remember to always hold on to the satellite frame or the supply box line while being on the lookout for anything that starts to float by so I can grab it. Kelly teaches you how to grab hold of another bot, a flat piece of metal, a floating screw. My bot has seven arms so I can do a lot of maneuvers if needed. And you need to always be talking to others so you don't have two of the bots collide like two outfielders trying to catch the same fly ball. Those bots in the lobby make the work look easy only because gravity and the precise knowledge of the mockup and its parts make their sequence predictable and repeatable. In space it is mostly see, study and adapt. No one can tell us in advance how many debris strikes the satellite has suffered over the years in space or what else may have failed that sensors and systems couldn't tell us in advance. This satellite repair flight is going to be the highlight of my summer if we manage to successfully get the job done."

"I have a feeling you were chosen to be part of the team because you've got the skills and just enough nerves you'll be that over prepared for the task."

Emily smiled. "I've certainly got the nerves." She nodded to the present mockup. "I know this satellite like the back of my hand. They don't tell you to memorize the tasks other bots will be doing but I pretty much have by default. I've crawled around with my bot on that satellite for months watching others work and learning from them. Handling connectors and screws, maneuvering bot arms in tight space, it only looks easy. Jim is a true pro at it. How you keep shifting your camera angles really helps with the depth perception." She gave him a considering look and asked, "Would you like to walk a robot through its paces on the practice maze? Angel has been having fun building lego towers with a bot."

"I'm good, but thanks. I enjoy the watching, not so much the doing, when it comes to mechanical things. I successfully used an early robot to carry around a small bucket and trowel to build a sandcastle and mount a flag, that's going to remain my claim to fame."

"That was you?" Emily asked with delight. "There's a picture of it on the wall by the backdoor. You raised a Lion Flag, one of those Great Britain standards."

"That's my handiwork." Noah nodded to the video wall where the rocket was now brightly lit by launch pad spotlights. It was a towering and awesome sight. "It must feel good to see a rocket that's partly your handiwork ready to fly. Are you going to Florida to see a launch in person this summer?"

Emily turned to study the rocket. "I've thought about it, but honestly, this is the best seat to a launch there is. With the volume turned up, we'll be hearing it as if we were in launch control. And the tracking cameras the Navy is using will keep us seeing the rocket up close even as it reaches nearly a mile in the night sky. I love the sight of the rocket. I just have to hold my breath during every launch hoping that it burns with precision and maintains its perfect flight path. Manufacturing is still more art than science even when you are 3-D printing below sand-size grains of material. We're unzipping solid rocket fuels. That still amazes me every time I consider the design. It's simple chemistry, but that rocket is the first time its been done at scale."

Emily turned from the video wall. "I don't know if I'm more nervous about the repair bot tasks or the rocket flight tonight. Either way, it's time to change the subject. It's been an evening of watching rocket simulations virtually blow up, probably not such a good thing to be doing on the night an actual rocket is ready to launch."

"Probably not," Noah agreed with a smile. He'd take the conversation a more personal direction and offer an invitation to go to lunch with him after the satellite repairs were done on Friday, he'd like to introduce her to his brother, but that question would fit only if the rocket successfully launched tonight. "What topic would you like?"

"Those pages I brought to our first conversation, let's finish out one of my first questions. How about creation? That suits this science type evening. How old is the earth?"

Noah did the math in his head to bring it to the current year. "6,146 years old."

Emily bobbled her plate. "You're kidding me."

He smiled, having expected that kind of reaction. "The bible gives us the genealogy record highlighting five key individuals, it flows from Adam to Noah to Abraham to David to Jesus. Adam to Jesus is 4,128 years, from Jesus to today is another 2,018 years, so the earth is 6,146 years old. That answer may be off by a hundred years or so, but not more than that. There's a bit of variability in the math because the genealogy record of the kings may give the age of the son when he began to rule in place of his father, or give his age when he died and how many years he ruled."

Since it was helpful to hear history as an arc, Noah offered Emily some more basic dates. "The earth was created in 4,128 B.C., Noah's flood happened in 2,472 B.C., the Exodus from Egypt was in 1,446 B.C., David's son Solomon reigns as King of Israel in 971 B.C. Jesus was born probably in 2 B.C. rather than zero B.C. but that quibble is not worth rewriting our calendars over. That biblical chronology matches up with non-biblical sources back as far as those other records go. The only record of the earliest earth history prior to the flood is in the biblical record. But genealogy is well understood. Arriving at the years from Adam to Noah is simple addition."

"So how old is the universe, the stars and galaxies?"

"Genesis 1:1, the first verse in the bible, says 'In the beginning God created the heavens and the earth.' The earth was created on day three. The sun, moon and stars on day four. So the universe is a day younger than the earth."

Emily smiled at that equally unexpected answer.

"Genesis' definition of a day is a night and a morning. God defined day and night, our present time periods, on the first day of creation. 'God called the light Day, and the darkness he called Night. And there was evening and there was morning, one day.' (Genesis 1:5) The same word for day is used throughout the creation account. God wasn't using some stretched amount of time early in creation and a smaller amount of time during the fifth and sixth days. Creation took God six days as measured by a night and day, so 144 hours, and then God rested on the seventh day and blessed it. God wasn't tired, there was simply nothing else He could think of to do, creation was perfect down to the smallest detail, so God stopped and enjoyed what He had made. The universe we see is 6,146 years old." Noah concluded his answer there. It was always fascinating to watch someone who had spent a lifetime having been taught differently deal with that answer.

Emily finished her tacos before she offered a comment. "Does science get anything right?"

Noah grinned. "Not much when it comes to the early history of the universe and earth. By denying the global flood and assuming the rates things move today are a constant going back in time, scientists end up with all kinds of wrong conclusions when they try to date things on earth. Whether you try to figure the age of earth and from that the age of the universe, or go the other direction, from the universe to the earth, you need accurate foundations for the calculations to produce sound answers." He offered her some help, for the problem was not in what was seen and observed, but merely in the math that scientists made from faulty assumptions. "Start with the universe. What we see plainly tells us the universe is young. I'll give you five obvious examples."

"Okay."

"The moon is still near the earth. The moon moves away from the earth an inch and a half per year. If the universe were old, the earth would have no moon, it would have drifted away by now. The moon's gravity is always pulling on the earth and water moves easier than dirt. The moon is causing earth's seas to have tides. And because the earth is spinning, the moon is always getting pulled forward by those tides so its orbit moves away from the earth a measurable inch and a half every year.

"Comets exist. You can see them shedding matter as they circle the sun, its why we can see them in the sky, their bright tails are mostly ice and rock chips tumbling away. The fact they exist points to the fact they are newly formed. There are no comets after a maximum of about 100,000 years because they've all come apart.

"The rings around Saturn are clear and clean, like fresh fallen snow. They haven't been made dirty and disrupted by lots of hits of space rocks, hits which we can see occurring, pointing to the fact the rings are newly formed. If those rings were old, they would no long be clear and clean.

"Spiral galaxies are very young. You can tell that just by looking at them. Their arms are stretched out while their centers are spinning faster. It's impossible to have an old spiral galaxy. They would have wrapped themselves into tight balls by now. The outer spinning arms are being pulled in by the more rapidly spinning center. It's like an ice skater spinning with her arms out who pulls her arms in to spin faster. Spiral galaxies are by definition young star formations. There are a lot of spiral galaxies in the universe.

"And a favorite of mine – blue stars. They burn out in X years, its some short number, and blue stars still exist in large numbers. If the universe was old there would be no blue stars."

Noah stopped there and just enjoyed watching Emily's reaction. She wasn't one to ponder what she was thinking aloud, rather the opposite, she appeared to be looking through what was in front of her as she thought about the topic. They were beginning to attract a group to the conversation as people came over and took seats but it was a friendly group who had heard this discussion before who were content to simply listen in.

"That is a very fascinating list," Emily decided.

"Am I convincing you?"

"Keep going. I'm enjoying this topic."

"Astronomy is full of visible evidence that the universe is young. The Big Bang Theory. Evolution. They are man's attempts to explain things without God involved. They all require vast time scales. So Astronomers build theories not based on what they see, but on what they think the answer is and try to fit what they see into those models. It doesn't work in astronomy. Nor does evolution fit what we see on earth. There has never been a species which changed into another species. A dog never becomes a cat. All you see on earth is adaptability within a species showing the beauty of God's design. God created a wolf and in the wolf are 300 some types of dog. You can breed for big, small, furry, not so furry, that's adaptability within a species, but there's only one species wolf. God made the animals to have young after their own kind. Simple observation tells you what the bible says is true. Species are unique. A dog has never become a cat. A whale doesn't become a skunk. But if you don't want to believe in a God creating animals, you have to create a theory of how to get dogs and cats and whales and skunks from something other than God and you come up with wrong theories like evolution. But rather than prove evolution, science is showing evolution is a wrong theory."

Noah considered if he wanted to skip the deeper astronomy details. In a room of engineers who dealt with space and could do the math regarding gravity and power and flight like an elementary school student could give the ABC's it was always intimidating to discuss this subject from memory rather than from his notes. This group would understand the math involved considerably better than he would. He looked at the time. They still had an hour before a decision would be made regarding the launch. For Emily's sake, he took the harder path.

"A smart astronomer looking at data from the moon, planets, stars and galaxies says 'this universe is young'. He's not taking the word of the bible for it, he's simply using observations which tell him the universe can't be old, there's a moon nearby, blue stars, spiral galaxies, clean rings around Saturn, comets. It's not a hard conclusion to reach because the evidence is all around him. An astronomer who doesn't want to go against conventional wisdom strains to push what he sees and measures into those models requiring billions of years. He's using not the data but assumptions to reach his conclusion. Its like the conventional wisdom the world was flat when smart people looked at the data and said, no, the earth is round. The truth is the earth is round. It just took a long time for scientists to admit their answers were based on wrong assumptions and fix their error. There is comfort in being one of the crowd. But the fact is the crowd is often wrong.

"Time and space being bent by gravity, relativity itself, is odd but true. Einstein discovered something brilliant about God's design of this universe. But Einstein, not believing in a God or the bible, can find truth and at the same time also make flawed assumptions.

"In the footnote of his paper on relativity Einstein suggests the speed of light might be asynchronous rather than synchronous. There was no experiment he could think of which could answer the question of which the universe is using – synchronous or asynchronous. The speed of light can only be measured as a round trip there and back. It's a convention to say there are 12 inches in a foot. Likewise, its a convention to say the speed of light is the same in all directions. If everyone agreed the speed of light is infinite C toward you and 1/2 C moving away from you – asynchronous speed – everyone would also get the same answers to the math.

"Had Einstein realized the bible could answer his question he would have looked for evidence there and found the answer to his question. The day stars were created their light was upon the earth. It's the more intuitive answer. When we see things is when they happened – that's asynchronous speed of light. Einstein chose the wrong convention of synchronous speed to use in his relativity paper and footnoted that the choice he was making might be the wrong one. It was.

"Because astronomers try to keep Einstein's choice of convention rather than just say, 'what we see in the universe tells us this universe is young and that tells us Einstein chose the wrong convention for the speed of light,' astronomers instead come up with all kinds of wrong answers as they try to date the universe. They conclude the universe is billions of years old. They create the big bang theory trying to explain how stars and galaxies exist. They theorize the earth formed out of debris from exploding stars. All of which are wrong answers." Noah was grateful to have the deep math finished. Several nods around the group had confirmed he was at least explaining the options correctly.

"If you go with the footnote in Einstein's relativity paper, his math matches up with the bible's description of light," Emily said, looking for confirmation. "We can see galaxies on the other side of the universe. The light of those galaxies is shining on the earth and the earth and universe is only 6,146 years old. So the correct answer for the speed of light has to be asynchronous. The light of those galaxies has been seen from earth since day four of creation."

"Yes," Noah confirmed. "It's visible astronomy which says the bible is right about this being a young universe with an asynchronous speed of light. It's also less obvious facts. I'll give you two. There's matter in the physical world but not anti-matter. Why? God didn't create any. He could have, the math allows for it and under man's theories of how matter evolved the math even predicts anti-matter should be there. But it's not there. God simply chose not to make it. Probably because He doesn't like the idea of his creation annihilating itself.

"There is also a measurable uniform background temperature in all directions of the universe. It messes up the Big Bang Theory to the point they have to have the universe expanding at different rates at different times so they can get heat to transfer from one point of the universe to another. The bible answers that observed fact easily. On day one of creation, God said 'let there be light' and light is a wave form which by definition is also heat. Light exists throughout all of universe and is being measured in all directions in a uniform amount. I'll also mention God said let there be light before there was a source of light as we think of a sun. On day one there was light, on day four there was a sun – a thermonuclear burning mass of hydrogen and other basic elements hanging out in space at just the precise distance to keep us warm on earth but not fry us to a crisp. God likes math. The sun being at that precise distance from earth is not an accident."

Emily smiled. "I agree God likes math as physics and chemistry are both full of elegant math equations. And I agree you just made some more good points about what we observe and don't observe."

Noah wasn't surprised by her initial response. Emily hadn't thought the universe and earth were particularly young when this conversation started, that had been obvious in her reaction to his answers. He was curious how she'd sort out this matter for herself. Some people he spoke with would take the bible as accurate and from that point go figure out why man's time estimates were so off. Most would start with the data he offered, conclude from their own study of that data the earth and universe were indeed young, then looked at the bible dates and realized they could agree with them. Some would simply dismiss this conversation. But very few who looked for themselves at the basic data stayed with an old universe and earth. They might agree the earth and universe were young and yet deny God was involved, but the age question itself was pretty easy to tip by some simple observations.

"Talk to me about the earth. You've got some evidence related to its age as well?" Emily asked, curious. Those in the group echoed her request. Noah found that interest helpful, if only because he'd get a fair hearing on the facts.

"I do. The earth is old, its just 6,146 years old, not millions of years old. The geology of rocks and the earth surface itself points toward this being a planet which experienced a global flood 4,490 years ago.

"The bible says the earth was made from water and that the earth surface, the earth crust, rested atop water. When the global flood happened, the bible says the fountains of the deep burst open, that underground water burst above ground, and rains also came down from the heavens upon the earth without pause for 40 days. There was so much water released that even the tallest mountain peak on the earth was covered by feet of water. Every man and animal not in Noah's ark died. Then over a period of 150 days the waters receded. God caused a wind to blow upon the earth to dry it out – likely what we think of today as the jet streams that circle the earth. The waters receded into the oceans and formed inland lakes and evaporated into the atmosphere. What the majority of that water didn't do was flow back down under the earth crust. If a global flood as the bible described happened, there are some predictable things we should be able to observe. I'll give you several.

"There should be evidence of water from below the earth crust breaking out to above it. I'll come back to that point in a bit.

"Water flows according to gravity and it can flow fast, flowing over and cutting through obstacles with force. Today, just watching the weather channel, you can see vehicles shoved around, houses taken off foundations, trees slammed into bridges – all by fast moving water. Given that, think about the land during the flood. The first twenty days of rain would destabilize every hillside and mountainside and send mud and trees and debris flowing down into valleys. New rivers would form with rushing waters rolling boulders like they were pebbles. It's not going to be clear water, its muddy water, filled with ripped apart trees, plants, soil and anything dead, its carrying everything that can be moved along with it downhill.

"Think about the oceans. When you use a garden hose to add water to a fish pond it causes all the settled debris at the bottom to get stirred up and the water turns cloudy. Now magnify that scale. There would be enormous volumes of sand and decaying ocean life churning up from the ocean floors as the seas rapidly fill to double their depth. That loose silt-like material measures feet thick in some parts of the ocean floor. Imagine all that matter stirred up. The ocean waters are also going to be cloudy with debris.

"Over 40 days the waters rise higher than the tallest mountains. You would have ocean waters flowing over continents. One easy prediction, marine life and ocean debris should be found in the middle of continents all around the globe.

"At the end of 40 days the fountains of the deep close and the rain stops falling. As the waters finally stop churning all the debris the waters are carrying with them would begin to settle out and drop down. Massive sediment layers would build up, not inches deep but feet deep. And that sediment layer would be laying down all around the globe in the same time period.

"You should have a massive amount of fossils being formed as all the dead men and animals on earth are being buried quickly by that sediment. Within 150 days everything has died and then been buried by sediment – that's the definition of fossils forming on a massive scale. And again, it would be happening all around the globe in the same time period.

"Those sediment layers are going to get pushed around as the waters recede, mounded up in low lying areas and blown off higher elevations toward lower ones. They are soft and pliable saturated layers of dirt and rock and sand that will form mostly limestone rock as they dry out and harden. The receding waters will be cutting canyons and ravines through all those sediment layers of loose material. We've seen how fast water from a burst dam can cut new ravines – it's measured in hours and days. You'll see huge features in the earth's landscape cut out quickly."

Noah paused there and turned from the water effects to mention one of the ground effects which would also be going on. "The earth was covered with water for 150 days then the waters began to recede. You saturate ground with water for that long its like a liquefied bog and it moves with gravity like a fluid. As the waters recede and the ground begins to dry out gravity is taking over defining the landscape in more pronounced ways. Saturated ground moves in predictable ways, you would see things like slabs of rock that slide, not just rock slides. You would see ground movements that are localized but require unique circumstances that flood conditions would create. Those are some of the obvious predictions of what you'd see if a global flood had happened. Make sense?"

"Those seem obvious," Emily agreed and several others concurred.

"Okay. So go wide scale and look at the earth. What do you see?" Noah offered as a rhetorical question, then filled in some details. "For one thing, you quickly find out there is a lot of data to work with. Those exploring for oil and water and minerals have drilled and extracted cores of earth from all around the globe. Curious scientists have drilled and extracted many more cores of earth to fill in location data. You can study layers of the earth just like you study tree rings. It's basic science. Quartz rock in America is quartz rock in Australia. A fossil of a clam, its still a fossil of a clam no matter the continent where it is found. You simply record the depths when various types of clay and rock and fossils show up and you can build global maps of the earth layers.

"What you see in the earth cores is consistent. You see a fossil layer that suddenly appears in the earth depths. There is nothing much below it and suddenly every kind of marine and mammal and plant is there. It's world wide. You find marine life fossils in the middle of continents far from salt-water oceans. You find sediment layers of varying depths, generally thicker in lower elevations, but existing worldwide laid down at the same time period.

"You find vast fields of oil around the earth. Oil is simply a decaying bio-mass. The large oil fields points to a massive volume of vegetation and a large number of animals being buried between layers of sediment without their flesh decaying off first. It wasn't bones which were buried, but mostly intact animals. You find oil that is not tar. Oil ages. To find fresh oil that hasn't degraded into tar it has to be relatively young geologically speaking. The oil in those massive fields is about 4,500 years old, right as predicted by the flood date.

"There's also ample evidence above ground. You can drive through mountain passes cut through the rock and look at rock layers that have been folded while they were still wet pliable sediment layers. They weren't yet solid rock, they were sand and water and mud and debris being shoved around and compressed and folded by gravity and water as they slid into their final positions.

"There are vast plateaus in the American west showing the rapid shifting of miles of rock by gravity. A huge moving slab of rock leaves behind a friction layer of glass as it moves at upwards of 90 miles per hour. The rock moves as one slab because its resting on a thin compressed layer of water. You can find that friction black glass like a fingerprint layer in all parts of the globe.

"Take the grand canyon. It's not that the assumption water cut the grand canyon which is wrong. It's that people assume it took a long time. What it took was a massive amount of water moving at speed through layers of limestone.

"Small rivers and streams, tributaries, look like arrow feathers pointing to the lake or major river they are flowing into. When you look at the tributaries feeding into the Colorado river, some are pointing unexpected directions like they are carved backwards, showing they were once feeding into lakes that no longer exists. The Colorado plateau shows evidence of once having a couple massive lakes. When those lakes drained it wasn't a gentle event. You can see the result, they cut the grand canyon. Glacier lakes drained quickly and cut the grand canyon in a matter of weeks to months. The badlands are similar water and wind features of soft sediment rock being carved away. Most of the land features we see today around the globe point to the flood and its after effects. They are local features, some hundreds of miles in size, but localized evidence. What shows the scale of the flood is the fact those same basic features of fossils, folded rocks, marine life in unexpected places, are spotted all around the globe."

Noah paused there to accept the cold drink Gina brought him as she joined them. "Thanks." He checked the time and what was happening in mission control. He didn't want to step on an announcement about the launch. Kelly and Jim were having a conversation in mission control, but both were holding plates of food having a late dinner.

"Tell her the best part," Gina suggested, having heard him discuss this topic before and knowing the subject he liked to leave until the end.

Noah judged there was time to finish the topic, so he took Gina's advice. "There's even more striking evidence of the global flood if you go to the macro scale. The continents separated. The earth crust was resting upon a body of water and when that deep water burst upwards it ripped into pieces the land mass floating on it. You can put the continents back together like a jigsaw puzzle because they were once together. The continental drift we measure today in inches per year and think it's a huge movement, during those 150 days the land masses were being moved hundreds of miles apart as they were simply floating islands of stuff resting atop a layer of fast moving water."

"The continents were like lily pads on a pond?" Emily asked, trying to picture it, "one land mass was broken into pieces that then floated apart?"

"That's a good analogy of it."

"What you're describing would take a lot of force. Is there evidence for where that water from below the earth crust broke through?"

"There is. And its pretty spectacular evidence, too. The earth is like a ball that's been crushed inward on the Pacific side while the Atlantic side is still puckering upward blowing out a water kiss. It's a bad analogy but a perfect description of what the satellite data looks like. The fountains of the deep burst open on the Atlantic side of the globe sending water under high pressure shooting out. There is a huge mountain range running the length of the Atlantic Ocean and that land is still rising. That entire side of the globe looks like a nice long seam.

"The Pacific side looks the opposite. When water within the earth burst forth on the Atlantic side it caused the Pacific side to crush inward, sucked down into the vacuum. When a ping pong ball is crushed on one side, or when a basketball is deflated and collapses inward, the collapsed section forms all these curves and inflection points. What we call the pacific-rim of fire, those volcanoes around the Pacific Ocean, are showing the curves and inflection points of a continent size mass that collapsed in. All that land mass is liquefying in the intense heat nearer to the earth's core and coming back up the sides of the ocean bowl as melted rock.

"We think the volcanoes we see on earth now are pretty active. After the flood there were volcanic eruptions happening every week and month and year. The earth was settling and hot magma rock was flowing up to the surface, islands were being formed, major mountain ranges were being shaped across continents. Without the water layer under the earth's crust acting as a buffer, magma was flowing up to the surface in explosive fashion.

"Those volcanoes actually caused an ice age after the flood. All that volcano activity put so much ash into the air it blocked sunlight and thus heat, the atmosphere was saturated with humidity, you had winter after winter of heavy snow falls without enough summer sun to melt all that snow. The ice cores taken from glaciers and the earth ground cores both show layers of repeated volcanic ash. During an ice age you had ice bridges forming connecting the land masses back together that let men and animals flow out to all the continents. Noah's descendents and the animals had time to flow out from the middle east to repopulate all the earth. As volcanoes becomes quieter, the air clears and you begin to get a warmer climate, those ice bridges melt. The bible agrees with an ice age, it just says it began about 4,500 years ago after the global flood and it lasted a few hundred years."

Noah returned to her original question. "It's not that the data is wrong, we can see the rocks and the volcano ash and the sediment layers and the fossils and the oil and the evidence of an ice age. But if you don't think global flood and you try to explain what you see, you come up with ideas like the earth being millions of years old. You try to match up with evolution theories which need millions of years for there to be animals. You fit what you see into the theory you have. Your time scales end up in strange places that make no sense.

"What's even more remarkable is that the bible warns these are the three errors men will make in their science of the earth – they will deny there is a creator, they will deny a flood occurred and they make the basic wrong assumption that things have happened at the same rate going back in time.

First of all you must understand this, that scoffers will come in the last days with scoffing, following their own passions and saying, "Where is the promise of his coming?

For ever since the fathers fell asleep, all things have continued as they were from the beginning of creation." They deliberately ignore this fact, that by the word of God heavens existed long ago, and an earth formed out of water and by means of water, through which the world that then existed was deluged with water and perished. But by the same word the heavens and earth that now exist have been stored up for fire, being kept until the day of judgment and destruction of ungodly men. 2 Peter 3:3-7

"The bursting open of waters from within the earth, the global flood, the ice age that followed, the glaciers retreating, glacier lakes draining off – most landscapes worldwide are evidence of that one event and its aftermath. The evidence isn't rare or hidden, its everywhere you look. God created the earth 6,146 years ago, the earth flooded 4,490 years ago, and the ice age followed for a few hundred years." Noah ended his answer to her question there.

"I like that picture of earth's history because its logical," Emily remarked. "Especially the oil not having turned into tar. It's chemistry, that reaction. And predictable."

"Some more simple chemistry proofs the earth is young?" Noah offered. "Look at helium. The earth has rocks that pre-date Noah's flood which are still rich with helium. If the earth was old, those oldest rocks on earth would have no helium left in them because helium decays. Look at carbon-14. You know how fast carbon-14 decays. Make the whole earth carbon-14 and tell me how many years pass before there is no carbon-14 left on earth. It's like X million years. Now make the earth only 10 percent carbon-14, only 5 percent, and run the calculations again. The closer you get to the actual percentages of carbon-14 present on earth the younger the math says the earth has to be. You can find carbon-14 inside diamonds brought up from a mile below the earth surface. They still have carbon-14 in them because they are just not that old."

Emily nodded. "You've convinced me about one

general theme, Noah. This is easy science. The logical effects of a flood, dating oil, the decay rate of carbon-14, the location of the moon, how fast blue stars burn out, its all simple calculations. I don't understand why old earth and universe theories have persisted."

"Peer pressure," Noah replied, for that answer was simple. "Observational science is good science – see, watch, test, repeat – that's reliable and sound science. 'Historical' science is not true science. It's not observable, nor repeatable, so it is by definition a faith based theory.

"The bible is accurate history – the creation sequence, the young age of the universe and earth, the global flood. I can prove it in the sense I can show you lots of evidence the universe and earth are young and that the earth experienced a global flood. God created the heavens and earth 6,146 years ago. He created things with a 'working maturity' – Adam walked around, the sun was at the right distance from the earth, galaxies looked like galaxies. You have to accept that statement by faith. It can't be proven.

"Man can't figure out how to have a young earth and universe. That's the crux of this discussion. Man's theories on earth's history require vast time scales. They are based on assumptions that the geological record does not support; millions of years; evolution changing one species into another one, there wasn't a global flood. Theories about the universe have similar inconsistencies and require even larger time scales. You can either let the evidence convince you man's theories are wrong and the bible is accurate, you can just ignore the inconsistencies, or you can say its impossible to know and not let reason and logic take you to an answer.

"This is such a big fight because what you have is satan arguing against God by proxy, using mankind's science as his voice. If you can discount the first page of the bible you can argue the entire book isn't the truth it claims to be. 'In the beginning God created the heavens and the earth' – satan is focused on destroying the first words of the bible. But if you let the evidence convince you the earth is young and there was a flood, now you have a major question to consider. If the first pages of the book are accurate, what do you do with the last pages talking about judgment and everything in between? The bible says you are judged based on do you believe what is written and obey what it says.

"Satan wants science to take people away from God, but he overplays his hand, for the truth in science actually takes you directly to God's account. Satan simply waves his hands around with bad theories and then says 'hey, don't look too close, because its complicated and you won't be able to figure it out' when in fact anyone who actually looks at the topic realizes present day 'historical science' is a deception so obvious a child can see its wrong. Those standing in darkness with a vested interest in being the experts keep saying everything is old, evolution is the way it is, not realizing they are 'the emperor with no clothes on' and the children are starting to laugh at the foolishness they are spouted. Romans 3:7b says 'God's truthfulness abounds to his glory'. You can fool people with deception only up until the point they begin asking questions. Whereas truth holds up to rigorous inquiry."

"That's a very useful description of why this is so intensely fought over. Other areas of science overturn wrong assumptions easily and quickly and move on building new science, its how we're taught to think about problems. What is repeatable in this science and what hasn't been well understood yet? Yet this area has been like quicksand with its assumptions," Emily remarked.

Noah smiled. "Correct the wrong assumptions and you can do some really fascinating science. It's like knowing the world is round, while your fellow scientists think it is flat. Who will make discoveries which will stand the test of the next thousand years? It's not going to be the scientists who keep insisting wrong assumptions are right. Christianity has absolute truth written down for people to read. Believe it and you can leapfrog over a lot of errors others are making because you can look up the answer. It simply takes courage. You can be popular, or you can be right, but its rare that you can be both."

Emily smiled at that remark.

Noah offered his favorite point about creation. "Why do men call this planet 'earth'? Why that word? Why don't we call this planet 'george'? Why do men call the light 'day' and the darkness 'night'? Why those words? Why are men called 'men'? Why don't we say we are 'bricks'?

"Our language itself shows we are a created place and people. In the creation account in Genesis 1, God called the light Day. God called the darkness Night. God called the firmament Heaven. God called the dry land earth. God called the gathered waters Seas.

"How we think about ourselves and the world we inhabit, our language itself, is part of creation. The names of who we are and what is around us is are part of our created heritage. Some names came from God and some from Adam when God asked him to name things, but by day six of creation, trees were named trees and fish were named fish, and mankind was named man. When we talk about physical things we are talking about God's creation with the names He gave to creation. To argue God didn't create the earth while calling it 'earth' is to be blind to your own words. You just confirmed God created the earth because you used the name God called it. If God didn't create the earth you would have had no word 'earth' to say, as that name would not have been spoken. We would have decided to call it the equivalent of 'george'.

Ever since the creation of the world his [God's] invisible nature, namely, his eternal power and deity, has been clearly perceived in the things that have been made. (Romans 1:20a)

"The way we think about our world, our language, our perception of creation, is evidence all this was created by God. Why do we have a calendar? The concept of day makes sense with light and darkness happening every 24 hours, but why do we have years? Why is it called a 'year'? Why is a year twelve months? Why don't we have a 'brad' that is 3 months? 'And God said, "Let there be lights in the firmament of the heavens to separate the day from the night; and let them be for signs and for seasons and for days and years' (Genesis 1:14) Creation is God's voice speaking to mankind. Even if you never hear the gospel, you've already seen and heard God."

"I love that, Noah." Emily turned to the group listening in. "What do you think about this topic, Gina?" she asked, opening the conversation up to others.

"This universe and earth is too orderly to be random chance. Just looking around says there is a God involved. What we see is beautiful and symmetrical. Make that realization, and its easy to believe the creation account. Why wouldn't an account in the bible be accurate? God knew what He did in creation and He wrote it down. It reads simplified, God didn't tell us about DNA or the equation for gravity, but what God wrote down is accurate and points us toward that science. I trust the dates Noah rattles off from memory. I've read those genealogies and they makes my eyes cross, but the lists are there in the bible and its possible to calculate from them the dates for historical events.

"The math I do on major topics from solar weather to sonar rests upon mostly simple equations. You can almost see God having fun creating formulas simple enough for mankind to figure out. God wanted mankind to be able to sort out the equation for gravity and find the law of lift and calculate how to send a rocket to the moon. God never changes the rules. We can figure out an equation and keep using that same equation across the centuries.

"And to Noah's prior point - light, sound and heat are all the same basic science and math. They are all wave forms. And they are interchangeable in nature. I can use sound waves to create intense heat and bursts of light. We've had the speed of light convention wrong for decades. Which means we've also got sound and heat misunderstood. It suggests there are still some powerful new discoveries to be made in those areas. Things that would generate commercial value very quickly given how much of today's world is built around satellites and electronics. I play around with that math when I'm not busy on other questions because I know one of these days I'm going to stumble into something really fascinating," Gina mentioned.

Emily laughed. "You would find that kind of brain puzzle a hobby."

"It's like being told 'fish in this pond, there's a whale in there.' I love a good set-up in science."

Chimes began to sound from mission control. Their conversation stopped and people immediately turned their attention that direction.

Kelly came on over the intercom. "Winds have finally died down to acceptable levels. The launch clock will be restarting in two minutes."

Cheers erupted from those in the room.

"I was expecting an abort. This is fantastic!" Emily said.

Engineers began streaming back in from all corners of the building. There wasn't a bad seat in the house for watching a launch but there was a scramble in the room to refill drinks, grab a slice of celebration cake and move around chairs to face center on the video wall.

Kelly switched the speakers over to launch control in Florida. On the video wall they watched launch control personnel going about their tasks. They listened in as the launch sequence resumed.

"Winds?"

"We are a go."

"Recovery?"

"We're a go."

"Tracking?"

"Go."

The various personnel within launch control cleared the launch as the clock ticked down the minutes. When the launch clock was at two minutes Mark Bishop took a seat and made it official. "We are go for launch." He turned the key at his station setting the launch in motion.

It was hard waiting the final minute. Noah looked to mission control where Kelly and Jim were watching both monitors and the video wall, looking more calm than he would expect. Beside him, Emily was nervous, he could see it in both her face and posture. Gina was somewhere in between. The final countdown commenced from Florida.

"Ten seconds.

"Five seconds.

"Three.

"Two.

"One."

Explosives spiraled around the base of the rocket in rapid succession, the noise so loud through the speakers it felt like a compression wave hitting him. Snapped by the powerful force of physics, the rocket began to lift and spin.

"We have successful ignition."

The roar of the ignited fuel nearly drowned out that announcement.

The rocket rose and cleared the tower. Cheers broke out around the room. The rocket climbed into the sky leaving a glittering trail of fire in its wake.

"Tracking?"

"Course is good."

"Imaging?"

"We're reading nominal blue burn. We're good on elevation."

Noah knew from prior launches too much blue meant winds were tipping the rocket and the denser rocket fuels woven into the rocket were burning faster on the tipped side to compensate. If that condition persisted, the rocket wouldn't make the launch calculated height before it burned out. The imaging cameras were showing shades of red and yellow and pale blue within the burning tail flowing behind the rocket. Watching a Bishop Bottle Rocket fly – it was a breathtaking sight. "That is incredibly beautiful," Noah said simply, wanting to offer something to both Emily and Gina. Their science had accomplished something spectacular.

Emily simply nodded, rather than try to give him words.

"I never get tired of watching this sight," Gina agreed with a smile.

The camera image of the rocket became smaller and smaller until it was barely visible.

"Tracking?"

"Elevation and flight are in the cone."

On the video wall, Mark Bishop turned. "Six minutes until rocket burnout. Chicago, its all yours."

"We've got it, Launch," Kelly replied. "Thank you, Mark."

The wall video changed from Launch Control in Florida to the tracking software. The rocket flight cone was in green climbing away from the earth. The satellite they were after was tracing a purple orbit line. As the six minutes expired, the green cone slowed and consolidated back to a point in space. Tracking radar had locked onto the signal from the supply box atop the rocket. The supply box would automatically detach from the rocket body when the altimeter inside began to fall rather than rise. The rocket body left after the burn would be only about the size of a small barrel. What was left that hadn't burned during the launch would fall back to earth, incinerating those last remnants as it did so.

"That looks good," Gina judged, "nearly pinpoint perfect."

"Elevation is good," Emily agreed. "And there's separation from the rocket body, so we're at maximum height and now beginning to orbit."

"Houston, how do you read it?" Kelly inquired.

"We've got your box. Calculations are coming in now." A quiet half minute passed. "Chicago, we compute 78 hours 19 minutes to satellite intercept."

"Thank you, Houston."

"Okay. Mission on," Jim Bishop announced with satisfaction from mission control. "Let's go catch our satellite."

With a lot of hand slaps the group began to disperse.

"You can breathe now, Emily," Noah suggested with a smile.

"Working on it," she replied with a laugh. "In 82 hours," she calculated, "I'm going to be working to help fix a 70 million dollar satellite. I think I may want to hold my breath until that is over. Jim forgot to tell me what the in-between hours were going to be like."

"For the next three days its just gravity and time and some pre-game nerves," Gina agreed.

"Which bot are you on, Gina?"

"I'm bot 3 for this repair. I'm doing a gyroscope replacement."

"Talk me through a satellite capture. I haven't been around to see one of those," Noah asked.

"Over the next three days gravity will pull the supply box within the orbit path of the satellite. We're moving faster than the satellite right now so we're catching up to it as we both orbit the earth," Gina explained. "We are coming down from a slightly higher orbit so the satellite will be below us. Jim will let the supply box line flow out like a long anchor and simply let the line drift so it settled across the satellite, either across its body or a solar panel. A bot will scurry down the line and grab hold of the satellite and then pull the supply box and satellite together. If that easy capture fails, there are three-prong grappling hooks that can be trailed out or even magnetic sink weights. It's kind of hard to miss catching a bus in space. We can use the stabilizing rockets on the satellite if necessary to close the distance or the orientation. Once capture is complete, then the rest of the repair bots unfold and we get to work."

"When repairs are finished, the supply box with those repair bots falls back to earth and burns up on re-entry?" Noah asked, confirming what he'd heard before.

"A sad but necessary part of the sequence. We don't

want to be adding to the floating space junk up there," Gina replied.

Noah was glad he had seen the launch. It had been a good night. "Emily, I predict those repairs are going to go smoothly. Is it going to bother you to have spectators?"

"I'm going to be so focused on the job an elephant could walk behind me and I'd have to ask later, what elephant?"

Noah laughed at her remark. "Then I may come to be moral support since I don't have class on Friday."

"Emily? Gina?" Kelly called. "Come sign the launch card."

"Back in a minute, Noah."

It was tradition to sign the launch card if you had a hand in the rocket launch. There would be a satellite photo with signatures for those who helped plan and execute the repairs if that also was successful.

Noah turned his attention to practical matters. He gathered up plates and glasses to help with the cleanup. The foil trays of food had been collapsed down and the dinner remnants put into the refrigerator. The last of the cake he boxed for Grace to take with her. Angel had stayed awake for the launch but she was going to be a very sleepy girl come tomorrow.

"Noah."

"Thanks, Emily." He accepted the plastic cups she had collected to add to the recycling bag he was tying.

"I wanted to say again thanks for the birthday gift."

"You're welcome. I like shopping for gifts." He knew she'd be leaving for home shortly and it seemed like the right time to ask the question. "My brother makes a really good cheeseburger and onion rings. Friday, after the satellite repairs, would you like to join me for a celebration meal at his restaurant?"

"That sounds wonderful."

"It's a plan, then."

Rather than move away, she leaned against the table. "The conversation on creation was incredible and not at all what I was expecting. For not being a science type, you're pretty good at remembering dates and details."

"This topic is always a Q/A favorite. Students think science proves the bible is false. I like rattling people's thinking about that." He offered her the box of extra cookies. "How are you going to handle the next 80 some hours?"

"Watch a movie marathon of chick-flicks and the Star-Wars saga. I've already got them stacked up on my coffee table ready to go. My birthday plans are clothes shopping and dinner out with girlfriends, my version of a tradition going back now a decade. I'll be here bright and early Friday, well rested and ready to go. The only request from Jim was to avoid more than the normal level of caffeine so you aren't unusually jittery."

At his inquiring look she explained that last remark. "The bot motions are controlled by basic keystroke taps and a sophisticated form of a gaming console. We'll do the practice maze Friday morning just to limber up and then it will be show time. Nothing gets done in a hurry Friday. Satellite capture happens about 7 a.m. then pictures are taken and if everything looks okay to begin we'll open the first panel of the satellite around 10 a.m. The repairs are sequenced in a methodical fashion. There are two pause points in the sequence where the repairs could be suspended and the satellite buttoned up for a day or longer if it would be smart to finish the work after a rest break. Some satellite repairs are four hours, most have lasted six, some have been ten hours over a couple days. And all that is something you already know."

"I like listening to you talk about it," he replied mildly. He'd seen footage of several of the repairs as they replayed the videos to learn from each mission how to better approach the next satellite repair. Getting a conversation onto subjects where Emily was comfortable doing the talking was something he would like to see happen more often. Talking about BSR and what was going on here was a good conversation in that regard. "We'll both enjoy Friday."

Emily smiled. "I'll see you then, Noah." She headed home.

Noah thought the launch party had gone better than he had hoped. Helping clarify her science background and the bible's creation story hadn't been on his agenda, but it had obviously been on God's. It had likely been one of the more significant dilemmas Emily was wrestling with in the background of her mind. Faith rested on a personal God and what He had done and what He had written about what He had done. Creation and the flood were part of the foundations the bible discussed, with the statement 'In the beginning God...' a cornerstone. Being certain of that truth from the first word mattered. "Thanks for tonight, Lord." He felt an answering peace. This had been a good night on many levels. And it was time he headed home himself. He said goodnight to Gina and the others and headed out.

13

Emily spun the appetizer plate around to the olive loaf bread, having forgotten how good it was here. The restaurant was as crowded as it had been a year ago. And it was loud enough you had to want to be heard to have a conversation. But the food was good and the location convenient for those she wanted to invite. When her happy birthday balloons inevitably floated to the ceiling they would join others already there. Emily rather liked the tradition of the place. This round table in the back corner could seat eight comfortably and had been the place she'd seen in her last year's birthday, too. Tonight's party had been going on for three hours and most of her guests were now on the dance floor, husbands having been invited to join the party after the first two hours.

"So what's going on with you and Noah? You two were pretty tight at the launch party," Gina asked.

"We're becoming friends. I like asking him questions about God." Emily risked trying Gina's choice of sauce for the hot wings.

"That's all?"

"Mostly. I've spent a few hours in his company, Gina. Don't push."

"You like listening to him."

"He's a nice guy. And if we're hanging out together this same time next year you can ask me the question behind your question. Right now, he's simply part of my summer quest. I want to get to know God better and Noah is a useful guy to be around. I'm learning a lot without having to climb that learning curve on my own." And she wanted to change the conversation because this was Gina and she liked to tunnel into subjects. "Are you going to come over and watch a movie with me tonight?"

Gina's husband Mark was still in Florida finishing up the after-launch reports and wouldn't be back in Chicago until tomorrow mid-afternoon. The stack of birthday gifts on the table leaned heavily toward movies and books as Emily had put out a suggestion list of those she would like and didn't yet have. She was wearing several other gifts. By tradition she went clothes shopping on her birthday with whomever wanted to join her on that expedition.

"I see a couple features in that stack I missed at the theater. I'm game."

"We need to pick up ice cream. I finished the mint chip last night watching Tom Hanks and Meg Ryan."

"That's an easy enough stop. Still nervous about Friday?"

Emily shook her head. "Too blitzed on movies and ice cream to think about it. You?"

"I'm okay. Kind of. It's my fifth satellite repairs so I should be good at this waiting." Gina laughed. "I'm glad you invited me to your birthday. I needed a night like this."

"So did I." Emily offered something she'd been considering the last couple weeks. "When you married Mark, moved back to Chicago, got involved with BSR, were you looking out in time to a year like this one? I did the move from Austin to Chicago, the rocket work and the new job. It never really dawned on me that we were starting something which would make years like this routine. You fix a satellite, then you go fix the next one. It becomes a backdrop to life. The science I'm working on changed to fireworks then working on a battery. It's like a big constant mosaic."

Gina smiled. "I went from mapping the ocean floor back to sonar work, to a rocket design, to modeling the upper atmosphere, to studying the sun. What I create is being used in the real world – maybe that's the best part of science – when you can look around and see what is happening because of your work. In an unexpected way, marriage is like that. Building a life with Mark. We've now got all these shared experiences. We look around and its history we've built together. But I wasn't particularly thinking ahead about any of it. Life has just flowed in interesting ways. It is wonderful watching that rocket fly, but its also history. 'Okay, I've figured out that puzzle, what's next?' I'm not geared to enjoy resting in the past."

"Thank you," Emily replied. "I've already begun to wonder what's going to be next for me. The battery design is passing all the stress tests I've come up with thus far. By the end of the summer its going to be ready to patent and I'll let others take it from there. What comes next is already starting to be the question in the back of my mind."

"Anything catching your interest? Any glimmers of what might be coming?"

"Nothing yet." Emily finished her Iced tea. "Do you think its going to be Austin and a job offer that God has in mind for me?"

Gina considered it. "I've been praying its not, but maybe. Or it's a new avenue opening up. You're going to be wealthy. Maybe its something with science on a bigger scale."

"That thought just scares me," Emily admitted.

Gina laughed. "It took cash to build BSR. If you have a dream come to mind, you're young enough, and soon going to be rich enough, to explore it. You should think about that, Emily."

"I don't think I'm cut out to be a boss of a lot of people. Setting department goals and guidelines, that's more administration to make life flow smoother in my own field. I'm a peer given final decision making authority, but not so much a boss."

"Something is going to come together by end of summer," Gina predicted. "God gives us seasons in our lives and yours will be ready for a new one after this sabbatical."

Emily was appreciating more each day the value of this sabbatical. "I am glad I've put so much time into bible questions. I hadn't realized how many I was actively hoping to get sorted out until I started tackling the list with Noah. It's nice being able to have a deep conversation about God and it not be considered weird that you're interested in the topic."

"Noah likes to talk about God. The fact you're asking questions and want to hear his answers and you aren't bringing skepticism to the subject – you're like a breath of fresh air to him. It's why he gives you those long answers packed with all kinds of details. You're letting him show you a treasure he's found. He loves that. You may not agree with details he's offering, but you listen well."

"It's honor," Emily replied simply. "I haven't put years of thinking and talking to God into these topics. Noah has. The least I can do is honor what he's done and listen attentively. He makes sense, how he explains his answers. They're for the most part brilliant. The Holy Spirit wants to teach me and part of learning is to absorb information and then sort it out. The Holy Spirit will clarify where what Noah said was incomplete or where I didn't grasp a point." Emily thought a minute and shrugged. "I like school. This is like a sabbatical Ph.D. course in bible. It's actually my definition of having fun."

Gina laughed. "That's another reason we're friends. A subject to explore is our definition of having a good time."

Emily sliced herself another piece of the birthday cake. "I'm going to make reservations for here again next year." She waved her fork. "I'm traveling again after we get this satellite fixed. I'm thinking a nice long road trip next. Just meander through the mountains. Get scared out of my mind when I have to drive those switchbacks – going down is much worse than going up."

"I've been on a few of those drives," Gina said.

"So tell me more about trips you and Mark have taken and I'll accumulate some ideas on where to go."

Emily listened as Gina offered some travel highlights. She was looking forward to the coming year more than she was interested in looking back on the past. It was good to have milestone days like this to close out a year in her life. Friday was a satellite repair, then a road trip and July 4th would be looming immediately before her. That was a day she did not want to think about yet. She pulled out a pen and made a sketch on the back of a birthday card envelope of the locations Gina mentioned. She was heading a thousand miles away once the satellite repair was done and wasn't coming back until she'd put a lot of miles on a rental car.

What she really wanted was more time to think and more time with God, to do something where they could start a conversation and if it lasted for five or six hours it wasn't going to be interrupted. Noah had given her a lot to think about. And she wanted to talk to God about what was next, what came after this sabbatical was over. What she should be working on. God was the one who had the plan for her life and knew what suited her. She had wanted to know God better when this sabbatical began. She could feel that quest beginning to change its focus into the thought she wanted to know herself better in relationship to God, what God wanted in her life next. She knew change was coming. She just wanted to be able to step into that change confident she was walking the plan God had in mind for her.

"We need more raspberry tea," Trish mentioned as she came back to the table and picked up her glass.

Emily grinned at the remark and nodded toward the pitcher. "Already ahead of you. Gina was proactive. You and Kevin look good out there. The dance competition this year is going to be even better than last year."

"We've been practicing."

Trish turned to consider her husband on the dance floor giving Kelly an impromptu lesson. "I can't believe Jim Bishop doesn't already have a ring on Kelly's finger."

"This year," Gina predicted. "He doesn't want to be married if he's heading to space on a rocket and capsule of our design as he doesn't want to risk leaving behind a space widow. We'll knock that idea out of his head eventually. Kelly is being remarkably patient with him."

"He does have a point."

"He takes more risk driving in Chicago traffic," Emily replied, having done the math on that question with Gina one day when they were discussing the topic. "He's in traffic more often versus a one time rocket launch with its inherit risks. It turns out space is safer for him."

Trish laughed. "So what about you, Emily? No talk about a guy around the birthday table this year? I was hoping a name gets mentioned."

"Gina already asked. Maybe next year there's a guy."

"Seriously?"

Emily shrugged. "Liking a guy is a far stretch from dating a guy, but yeah, maybe. I'm enjoying getting to know a guy. Ask me next year."

"I can do that."

Her life was going to be different by next year, of that Emily was certain. Her income would be different, maybe her job as well. That she'd be dating again after so many years of not doing so was in the mix, either here or back in Austin. Her rest was in the fact God could see what she could not. He'd help her figure it out.

It was turning out to be a very nice birthday. She couldn't think of one major thing which had gone wrong in the prior year. She wondered if that was going to become the norm for the future. God liked to bless her. She turned the stack of books and videos to better see the titles. Her immediate future was clear. Watch some more movies, repair a satellite, take another trip west with some good books to read during the flights and late at night at the hotels. That would get her to the Fourth of July and yet another new chapter of her life becoming public.

"Emily, we talked our ballerina into doing a dance. Come and watch," Linda called.

Emily turned toward the dance floor where five-year-old Kimberly was giving instructions to her dad on the proper way to spin her. She slid from the booth to get a better view. Every birthday there was something which became the memory of it. Watching Kimberly dance would be this years highlight. The child was charming. Emily didn't often think about having a daughter of her own, but there were a few girls around in her life which made her pause to consider it. Kimberly was one of them. The girl twirled and danced and leaped with grace and the crowd clapped in delight as she gave a final bow.

"I want to enjoy life like she does, Dad. She's having fun. That's what I want this coming year," Emily said softly, making her final birthday wish. She went to award the little girl with a flower from her birthday bouquet.

*

14

Friday at Bishop Space Repair, Inc was quieter for the satellite repair than on launch day. There were more engineers around. The mood was relaxed but focused. Casual conversations weren't happening. Emily wished she'd thought to bring in a seat cushion. The office chair was comfortable, but after four hours she could use more comfort than it provided. She had a backup engineer who would take her place when she needed a few minutes break to use the restroom, walk around, but she didn't want to step away for minor discomforts and potentially miss something. She's assumed the satellite repairs would be intense, but hadn't been in the right ballpark for what the actual day felt like. This was a major job. Noah was probably around somewhere. She hadn't turned to see. She hadn't more than glanced away from the video wall since she sat down.

Her bot was in tile nineteen on the video wall. She was seeing what her bot's cameras were seeing. There were four cameras she could move around to give her perspectives on her surroundings and the other bots. Every practice session with her repair bot had been like this live session so far, except this was the first time she'd unfolded her bot and found herself looking down at earth passing by below in all its beauty.

Her cameras were now arrayed to give her a look above and around where her bot was presently perched on the side of the satellite. She was scanning for anything floating which would need grabbed.

Gina on bot 3 was presently on the center screen slowly maneuvering a new gyroscope into place. When it came time for her own task, her bot would be on that center screen.

So far the only object to catch had been a piece of insulation that floated out when the failed gyroscope was removed. Emily was surprised how rapidly time was passing. They were over three hours into the repairs. Moving the panel, unpacking the supply box, transporting replacement parts, so far she had always been one of two or one of three bots working as a group. If her grip wasn't perfect or a movement was a bit slow, those working with her had been able to compensate so there was no risk to the task.

Emily flexed her hands trying to take tension out of her somewhat stiff fingers. Bot 6 had moved in to close the gyroscope panel.

"Bot 7, are you ready?" Jim asked.

"I'm ready."

"You'll be up next."

She took a deep breath and let it out and waited.

Jim switched her bot to the center screen. "Bot 7, you're clear to begin."

Emily carefully started on her sequence. She sent her bot forward to the lip of the removed satellite side panel and peered inside. The wiring bundle on the screen looked identical to the practice bundle she had worked with. Magnified ten times in size it was huge. It was floating nearly vertical to the frame rather than being draped down by gravity as she had experienced on the practice mockup. "No shadows," Emily whispered to herself. She crawled her bot inside the satellite and stepped underneath the harness and let it rest across the back of her bot. She pivoted two arms to close above it forming a loose ring around the bundle. She set to work opening the connector. When she had the corner clips open she grasped each corner of the connector and started the rocking motion Kelly had taught her. The connector refused to move. "Come on," Emily whispered. She stopped the bot movements and studied the situation. She adjusted the cameras to zoom in on the connector. The clips were free. She turned and moved one of the cameras to study the wiring bundle. It wasn't pulling up putting unexpected stress on the connector. She turned the camera back to the connector. It had simply aged into being stuck. And it was plastic, so there was a limited amount of grip and tug she could apply without damaging it.

"Shadows," Jim cautioned softly.

She quickly moved back the camera causing the shadow to the lower wiring bundle.

"I think I have to tug on it."

"I agree."

She extended a bot arm and took hold of the connector as close to the center as she could, gently set the grip. She lifted. The pause while the command transmitted felt like an eternity. Nothing happened. She tugged again. The connector slid up and out. Emily exhaled with relief.

"Wiring is free." The bundle began to float up. It stopped as it encountered her encircling bot arms. The problem now was she had to back the bundle out when she wasn't really holding it. The bundle was floating loosely above her. She used a bot arm to tap the connector back toward her and the wiring bundle sailed back much faster than she had expected. Because there wasn't much slack in the bundle, it folded back on itself as Jim had predicted it might and she quickly tossed up two bot arms to act like a closing gate.

"Wiring harness is contained." It hadn't been elegant, but she had it.

Now all she had to do was get the body of her bot out of the way without changing the bot arm positions relative to the wiring harness. 'No shadows," Emily whispered to herself as a reminder again and began the slow process of adjusting her bot. She could make it go as flat as a pancake if necessary. She would like to get back to the lip of the panel if possible and be fully out of bot 8's way when he brought in the new antenna. She realized the wiring wasn't going to let her pivot that far, so she went with her next best option and slowly configured into a flat pancake, forming a protective floor to the wiring bundle. If Bot 8 had a problem maneuvering the antenna, he would bump into her bot rather than the wiring harness. "That looks like what's possible."

"I can work with that," the engineer driving bot 8 agreed.

Emily locked the grip arms so her bot became part of the satellite frame. "Bot 7 is locked."

"Nicely done, Emily," Jim remarked. "Bot 8, are you ready?"

"I'm ready."

Jim switched bot 8 to the center screen. "Bot 8, you're clear to begin."

Her bot switched back to tile nineteen on the video wall. Emily felt stress roll off. She'd done it. In about forty-five minutes she would be reversing that maneuver, taking hold of the connector, pulling the wiring harness straight and pushing the connector back snugly into place. The connector clips would do most of that work, she would just need to get the alignment right. In difficulty level, about 75 percent of her task was done. Then it would be back to the job of watching for floating objects until the repairs were finished. The last task on her list was both the fun and final one, a walk back along the supply line to the supply box to fold her bot back into its slot and put it to sleep.

Emily wanted to look over her shoulder to see if Noah was watching, but looking away risked missing something happening she needed to know. So she took it as highly probable he had been watching as her robot took the center screen. She was glad they had lunch plans, she wanted to share this day with him. She'd likely make him sit through a blow by blow of what it had been like, but he was a good enough friend to let her and simply smile at the rendering.

She'd been glad for the tradition, of it being a girl's night out, for why she hadn't invited him to her birthday party. But she was equally glad they had lunch plans to share part of this day together. It mattered to her. Gina had already mentioned Noah would be at the July 4th gathering. There were social reasons to hang out with him without it appearing like she was trying to create the situations. Lunch today had been his idea. And while her bot was inside a 70 million dollar satellite's guts, it was not a time to be thinking about why she wanted to see Noah this summer in more casual social settings. Emily put her focus back on what was happening in space.

The video wall had a fascinating array of views from the various bot cameras, many of them of the earth passing by below. The satellite was fully in view including its internal guts. This was the kind of day that was a lifetime memory. Emily was determined to absorb as much of this experience as she could.

A satellite repair was simple. It was a sequence of simple tasks, slowly done, but for decades satellites like this one had been written off because it wasn't affordable to get into space to do the repairs. There was going to be a lot of money made by BSR over the next decade because Gina, being curious, had made a model of a rocket form which could self-correct its flight and then figured out how to build it.

Every time a Bishop Bottle Rocket launched, it was also using some of her chemistry handiwork. The fireworks, now the battery design, she was doing Gina's kind of practical science too. She'd never thought of herself as anything other than a teacher. What her future was going to be, what she wanted it to be, was probably something she hadn't anticipated yet. Wasn't that an interesting question to ponder before God as this sabbatical continued to unfold? Where was God taking her? Emily was intensely curious about what was ahead of her in the coming years. She was seeing what scientific knowledge could build and do. And there was no question about it, this was an awesome outcome.

****

Noah held the door for Emily at Cherry's, his brother's restaurant, grateful the day had been a success. He declined with a smile and slight shake of his head the waitress who turned to come seat them and instead directed

Emily toward two empty bar stools at the curved end of the counter. His brother set down the milkshake glass he was drying and came down the long counter to greet them.

"Frank, this is Emily Worth, the chemistry professor I've mentioned."

"Sure." He offered his hand across the counter.

Emily accepted with a smile. "I've heard a lot about you Frank and its all good. I'd like the best cheeseburger you've ever created and a side order of onion rings. I'm starved."

Frank grinned. "I can meet that expectation. I hear the satellite repair was a success."

"I had the wiring harness to deal with. Stubborn connections, tricky movements, tight spaces. I crushed it."

Frank laughed.

"I don't think I'll ever volunteer again, given the stress of the last six hours, but I played my role to perfection. The satellite is now buttoned up and is going through all its checkout sequence before being boosted back up to its working orbital height later tonight."

"That deserves a good meal. Give me a few minutes and you can judge its perfection. Noah?"

"I'd like a Rueben and onion rings. And make it two cherry milkshakes; she needs to experience the namesake for this place."

"Coming up."

Frank headed back toward the kitchen.

Emily swiveled on her stool to look around the restaurant.

Noah glanced around, trying to see it as she would. The thirty tables were about a quarter full given the off hour between lunch and dinner. The tables were dressed with white tablecloths, had rolling padded chairs. The tables were adorned with bright red flower vases having a couple fresh roses in each. One of the departing guests was slipping a rose into a provided sleeve.

"Frank encourages guests to take a flower home?" Emily asked.

Noah nodded. "It's become the most profitable part of
the business as this place is never lacking a steady stream
of dating couples. Customers will talk about the first
pressed rose they have memorializing a meal here. This is a
casual restaurant for the menu, but Frank has always liked
the touches that say the occasion for the meal is something
special. This long barstool counter is a deliberate
counterbalance to that vibe, so guys doing construction
work don't think this isn't their lunch spot too."

The young man who came out to bus the table picked
up dishes, the flower vase, folded the tablecloth into fourths
and whisked it away. A fresh tablecloth, silverware, fresh
flowers for the vase, were set out. The process took him
under two minutes. He was humming along with the music
playing as he worked. Noah recognized him as one of
Frank's new hires. His brother had a habit of finding those
wanting to open a restaurant of their own, hiring them on as
an apprentice, taking them through all the paces of the
business over a couple years, then sending them off in pairs
to go make that dream happen.

"A lot of this business flourishes by the barter system.
The florist on the block supplies the flowers, the laundry
business washes around two hundred tablecloths each
night, the corner bakery and shop supplies the bakery fresh
bread and the chocolate mints. In return Frank caters events
for them and feeds employees and at the end of each
quarter the businesses square up whomever still owes the
others. The bakery brings early traffic to the block, this
restaurant an evening crowd, the florist benefits by
proximity. It works."

Emily nodded. "I like the kind of settled in
neighborhood feel this place has."

Frank brought them two milkshakes. "Cherry's is our
signature milkshake. You love it, you don't, no hard
feelings. We make them by hand, heavy on the cherries,
because you'll remember us. Foods up in about seven
minutes."

"Thanks, Frank." Emily accepted the tall milkshake

with delight.

Noah waited for her first taste and her smile, then turned their conversation to practical questions. "Now that this big day is past, are you going to take off and travel again?"

"I'm going to head out for about ten days and do a road trip starting in Idaho. Gina and I sketched out a route on the back of a birthday card envelope, its basically mountains and more mountains. I'll be back here for the July 4th celebrations."

"That will be another big day in your life."

"Huge in so many ways." Emily picked up a long spoon and dipped out cherries to eat. There were fresh red cherries and black cherries and a bunch of maraschino cherries blended into the vanilla ice cream and milk. "I'll be glad when the Fourth is over just to know we got through the first year of 3-D printed fireworks without encountering any unexpected problems. They are safer to manufacture and ignite than traditional shells but they are still fireworks. One good point is they are only available for purchase by licensed firework companies. The public can't buy them because the explosive content is to high. These aren't small scale fireworks."

"That's in your favor. You're dealing with people who have dealt with the more dangerous shells and they'll treat these fireworks with the same caution."

"That's the hope. And let's change the subject."

He grinned. "Okay. Choose a topic."

"Does your brain ever get tired of me asking you questions?"

"No. I'm not ready to ask you chemistry ones yet. I've got the chemistry books you teach from, I've even opened them, but it's a subject which requires more three-dimensional spatial thinking than I realized. Elements stack together, fold over each other, how they arrange themselves can be as important as what they are. Not to mention an atom itself is behaving like a miniature solar system inside."

Emily looked impressed with that remark, so he hadn't said something entirely funny. "Proteins, organic chemistry, cells in a body, they are mostly geometric puzzles, what can pass in and out, what is attracted and sticks, what gets gummed up and how. I don't do much with that side of the field. I mostly work with how atoms interact with one another, how elements respond to heat and cold, who mixes and plays well with others, what elements are aloof and self contained."

"Elements have personalities," Noah realized with a grin.

"And colors," Emily replied with an answering smile, "depending on how excited they get when heated. There are elements which are helpful to other elements. There are elements which sort of rule their surroundings. There are some which are skittish and don't like to mix. I like most the elements that help other elements do something neat. And I like the elements that burn easily, that get excited and throw off a lot of heat and color."

"Someday we'll have a chemistry conversation so I can just listen to you, or better yet, we'll have a day in your lab and you can just show me some things you find fascinating."

"You'd have a good time," Emily predicted.

Frank brought out two plates. "I'm thinking Emily, you'll want to declare this the best cheeseburger you've ever had when you are finished. But love it, hate it, no hard feelings. I had a good time crafting it for you."

Emily scanned her plate and smiled. "I appreciate your skills already." The cheeseburger was being crowded on the plate by the onion rings.

Noah hoped she enjoyed it as much as he'd predicted. Frank hadn't gotten fancy on the cheeseburger, the bun was lightly grilled, the hamburger was seared thin with a crisp edge, stacked two high, melted cheese atop both, the basics for condiments, sliced dill pickle, mustard and ketchup. But Noah knew from experience it was better than about any other cheeseburger in the city. Frank ground his own hamburger every morning and had been perfecting his shaker of seasonings for a decade. The onion rings were Frank's own batter mix and stacked into a mini-mountain.

Emily took her first bite of the cheeseburger, realized what she was in for, and gave Frank a smile that suited his brother just fine.

"Enjoy it." Frank said with a grin.

"I'm planning to," Emily promised.

Noah picked up his Reuben sandwich. His brother had been equally generous building it. Their conversation paused for the food.

This was the kind of place where you came for a casual meal and a conversation. When it was time to consider it a date, you simply shifted the atmosphere a bit by where you sat. Noah could envision a few years of meals being shared with Emily here. The fact his brother loved to cook had always been part of his life. Now that fact was paying dividends of another nature. Inviting Emily to a casual meal here wasn't going to be a hard sell.

"Why haven't I heard about this place before now?"

Noah smiled at Emily's question. "Frank prefers the neighborhood couple and the grandparents, the local families, so he doesn't advertise much around campus. But I bring those in my world at the university over for a meal and conversation often enough its becoming known as a good place to have lunch."

"I didn't eat this morning because of the nervous tension. We worked over the lunch hour. Now I'm enjoying the best cheeseburger ever created. Today was worth it."

Noah laughed.

Emily eventually reached for the milkshake. "That was incredible."

Noah slid over his plate of onion rings to share the last few as she finished hers.

"I'm glad you enjoyed it."

She ate one of his onion rings.

"Ready to crash?"

"I'm going to head home and probably sleep for

twelve hours, but I'm not ready to do that yet. Too much is still running around in my mind. We opened up a 70 million dollar satellite and fixed it without breaking it. That relief is tangible." She glanced around. "Would you mind if we just took a table and talked for awhile?"

"My day is free. Like mushrooms?"

"Sure."

"Frank, would you fix us a basket of mushrooms? We'll be at table seven."

Emily smiled at his choice. "My favorite number today, nice."

He picked up his milkshake and she brought hers. Noah held the chair for her at a table by the wall. Sledding penguins, Frank's version of a whimsical print, got a second look from Emily before she sat down. "That's not photo-shopped."

"It's a zoo photo, one of twelve from a promotional calendar."

"The penguins look like they were having fun."

"I bought the print for Frank because I thought the same. This is one of the family tables; kids like the image."

"I can see why."

Noah considered what to say as he took a seat. If he let her offer a topic he'd be talking for a while and despite his earlier comment he would like to avoid doing that today. "Tell me about Austin."

"What do you want to know?"

"Whatever comes to your mind. I just want to hear about it through your history."

"Tired of talking?"

"You've absorbed enough stuff today. You like the city. You're still a bit homesick. Talk to me about why."

"Okay." Emily thought about it, then nodded. "Austin has a population of around a million. It's spread out more than Chicago. It sits like a beautiful gem in the middle of the state, Fort Worth and Dallas are to its north, Houston is south and east, San Antonio south and west. The Colorado River runs through the center of the city. Austin is the capital of Texas and has a big Texas mindset. The University of Texas does football there in a big way. That's the tourist guide answer.

"Lady Bird Lake is near downtown Austin. There are 10 miles of hiking and biking trails around it. Franklin's BBQ in Austin has frequently been voted the best barbeque in the state. Brisket, pork ribs, pulled pork, you can't beat the food that's available. Austin has a vibrant art and music culture, a year round outdoor culture. You can watch one and a half million bats at dusk depart from under the Congress Avenue Bridge for their nightly mosquito feast. Can get a breakfast taco on the way to work. Find local music and food and outdoor spaces to enjoy an evening.

"What I think about with Austin is the people, socializing, not the drinking college parties, but the spending two or three hours with friends without a rush to the evening. Lingering together at a restaurant, an outdoor table, chatting. Meeting at Lady Bird Lake with a blanket and a food truck carryout and a cold drink to watch the evening sunset. The flowers are spectacular and the views gorgeous. I had a life that was urban city but I could also have nature in every day without much effort. In Chicago its hard to ever feel like I'm out of the city. Chicago's option is to look at Lake Michigan. It's the congestion of traffic. The winters are horrible. I loved Austin weather even when it was hot for long stretches.

"If I wanted to get away, I could spend three day weekends in Houston. I could easily enjoy the Gulf, its sandy beaches and warm water. I could go out on a boat with friends. It's not Chicago and Lake Michigan. Seafood there is fresh and delicious and easy to find. You could live in Austin, vacation elsewhere and still never leave the state of Texas. People simply think with optimism because its mostly sunny all the time and that rubs off on people," Emily mentioned.

Noah laughed at that point but thought she was probably right about the sunshine. Winters in Chicago were a trial in their duration.

A basket of mushrooms was delivered to their table by a smiling waitress. "They're just out, so eat gingerly for the first few minutes."

Emily took the advice seriously and sliced one open on her side plate to let steam out before she ate it. "Hot but really good," she decided.

Noah ate one with caution, already knowing they were going to be delicious. They weren't out of a frozen bag, Frank dumped fresh mushrooms into batter when an order was made.

Some questions had come to mind about Austin as she gave that general picture, but he didn't ask them. The best tactic with Emily was to simply see where she wanted to take a subject. If she would move toward her personal past or stay with general memories. Either were useful to him. She wasn't dating someone else, but she was attached elsewhere, and it was to a place. Austin and her history with that city was something Noah wanted to understand for a lot of reasons.

Emily finished another mushroom. "I moved to Austin to go to college. Austin University is a smaller cousin to the University of Texas. My grandmother on my mother's side had moved to Austin two years before and my parents liked the idea of having family in the area if she needed help. I could have stayed in Chicago but I wanted to spread my wings away from my parents.

"My grandparents would go to Texas in the winter months, leave Chicago in October and come back in March. They would typically rent a condo or an apartment and explore different cities. They loved it in Texas. After my grandfather died, my grandmother sold their Chicago home and bought a home in Austin. She'd made good friends in Austin. It was easier on her than living alone in the house she'd shared with her husband for decades.

"I knew I wanted to study chemistry and probably teach it. I had applied to five colleges. Austin University offered me a full scholarship, room and board, tuition. About the only cost I had for college was the plane ticket. I had applied for a chemistry and teaching double major and been selected to receive financial assistance under both programs.

"My grandmother showed me the Austin she loved, the small restaurants, the art galleries. We would walk together every Saturday morning. Those two hours were priceless to both of us. I had someone to love, family, a break from a heavy study load. She was someone I could talk with about life whose perspective was wise and laughter filled at the same time. My grandmother was full of joy. I know now where that joy she had came from. The topic of Jesus would become a regular part of our conversation in the later years of those walks. She had become a Christian in her 60s and after her husband died that side of her life simply blossomed.

"We were pals, my grandmother and I. I truly miss her. She passed away in her sleep just after her 75th birthday. She'd been writing me a letter, she was in the habit of doing that and then handing it to me when we'd walk. It was on her nightstand. I have treasured having those last thoughts from her about mostly silly things, a joke she'd heard. A thanks for a blouse I'd bought her. A memory she had from when I'd been 15 and we'd made pies together. My grandmother was the anchor I had left for family. My parents had been killed in a car accident on a foggy night in Austin a couple years before. Leaving Austin for Chicago, giving me space to let those family memories settle, was one of God's many recent gifts to me."

Noah understood that comment. "A new place can remove the triggers that otherwise persist in stirring up the memories."

Emily nodded. "When Gina made her offer to help with the rocket design, there wasn't even a hesitation about saying yes. I was grateful to God for arranging it. God knew what I most needed and it was to leave Austin for awhile."

She ate another mushroom, wiped her fingers with a

napkin. "My parents were both teachers. Daniel and Caroline Worth."

Noah realized he knew the names. "Philosophy and Sociology. They co-wrote the book The Art of Society."

Emily nodded. "They were pretty famous in their professional lives. They were frequent guest lecturers, conference speakers, would teach together on occasion. They poured their lives into teaching students how to think about society and its challenges.

"They viewed peace in society as being achievable around four pillars – equal opportunities, sharing of resources, good administration, compassion. My parents thought religion was an outdated way of thinking about life and they considered religion to be an unwelcome source of tension in society. They believed science precluded the need for a God. They thought society should be doing what churches talked about doing, but rarely did. The Art of Society was more than a book for them. It was a way they wanted to shape the communities they were in.

"My parents had settled in Austin to work on a project together under the auspices of Texas University. 'The Art of Society in Texas. How the various voices of its population are shaping the state of Texas.' It was going to be their next book together. They were considering leaving teaching behind to write and research full time. This was going to be a trial run of what that might look like. They came south because I wasn't returning to Chicago. I had settled in teaching at Austin University and loved the job. I was able to have eighteen months with them nearby, enjoying their company, before their car accident.

"My parents were empathetic listeners, they could draw people out and they were rigorous in their methodologies. They took great care that what people said was accurately recorded and modeled. Their datasets on people and their patterns of relating within family and community are some of the richest legacies they've left behind. Its how they thought about that gathered information which gives me pause as their daughter. They had a detached way of thinking about people which was inherent in the type and scale of the work they were doing. I understood that. They weren't judging people so much as they were simply blind to what was in the data. They were not able to see the value in what other people were shaping their lives around. Particularly when it came to religious life. There was a 'we can be better if only you'll come to our way of thinking about society' sort of plea in their writing. They couldn't see that religion was actually offering people that peace they were searching to find.

"They were good people without Jesus, wanting to live moral and ethical lives, wanting to contribute to society and leave the world a better place. They weren't cruel people, weren't evil, they were good citizens who cared about their world. They simply thought all the solutions society needed would come from within. People cooperating with each other would do what was right and life would improve for everyone. There was no afterlife in their way of thinking. You lived and enjoyed life and you died. It was better to live life doing good because you would live at peace with people and enjoy more of your life than if you lived life being as selfish and evil as you wanted. All that brought you was the wrath of everyone around you and your life would be miserable. Even when you thought you were winning the fight to do whatever you desired, you were still in a fight.

"It was a strange world to grow up in looking back on it. One where there was a commitment and zeal to finding answers for society but with no basis to understanding evil. Why society wasn't ever going to be able to be good. Without a God able to make people good, the 'Art of Society' would always be a hopeful image but never a reality."

Noah found listening to Emily talk about her parents both fascinating and also incredibly sad. She didn't have parents who had been open to Jesus and the implications of that meant Emily lived with a great deal of grief deeper than just mourning their death.

Emily paused the conversation there and simply changed the subject. "NASA Houston has an active partnership with all the Texas Universities. I did my Ph.D. on solid rocket fuel chemistry. They had a vast library of data going back to the Apollo days and with the end of the space shuttle program a lot of the knowledge base with people was disappearing. I wanted to talk with people in my field of study like my parents did. To blend what they had taught me into my life doing chemistry. I worked with rocket fuels because the power those elements could produce fascinated me.

"That's how I met Jim Bishop. I interviewed him as an astronaut who had done a significant amount of chemistry while in space. Mostly I simply let Jim tell his story about falling in love with space and what it had allowed him to do. What he still dreamed about doing now that the space shuttle was being retired and this career he loved was going away.

"Jim said his sister-in-law had some questions about rocket fuel. It's how I met Gina. She was asking some fascinating questions and I was deep in this archive of useful information. We bonded quickly on a shared topic of interest and became really good friends. Gina is smart in a way I had never encountered before. She loves large datasets and what she can learn from them. Her large dataset models are intense. I looked at what she was doing and what my parents had spent their lives doing and wished I had the skills to merge those two streams of my life together. With my parents I'd seen the large datasets of 'soft data'. With Gina the value of 'hard data.' I still wonder sometimes what I can do in chemistry, if there's a dataset of that sort to work with."

She stopped there and Noah elected to avoid most of the topics she'd offered. "Tell me about your teaching, Emily. I know you are good at it. That interest originally came from your parents?"

She nodded. "Teaching was both my double major, my parents desire for me, and what I loved doing nearly as much as chemistry. I was offered the job teaching at Austin University during my Ph.D. work. The chemistry professor I was working under as a Teaching Assistant got a promotion and he had the clout to put my name forward as his replacement. I stepped behind the podium of my first class – 47 first year chemistry students – and it was so much more joy than I had ever thought it would be. I loved every minute of it. Trying to remember names, teaching for twenty minutes, asking them questions, listening to how they had learned what I presented, teaching another concept, asking more questions. It was interactive and it was fun and students actually learned. I didn't want to ever do anything else. I had found my niche.

"Seven years at Austin University taught me *how* to teach chemistry. When a student shows up with a question now there is a vast lexicon of explanations that have helped other students I can draw upon. Teaching chemistry is much easier for me today than it was in my third year of teaching or even my sixth. I've learned the recipe that gives a good outcome. 'Talk about chemistry in these ways and in this sequence and they'll pick up what you're saying'. I know how students learn chemistry. I've now interacted with around two thousand of them going back to the days I was one of those students.

"What I didn't have time for at Austin University was the research I had so enjoyed during my Ph.D. years. I had lost the segment of my life that was me in a chemistry lab just enjoying what I could figure out. I'd do a little of that of an evening when the papers were graded and the last student question was handled, but I couldn't focus there.

"Gina pulled some strings to get me the interview with Chicago University. I'm a really good fit for what this position is, but it was a friend opening the door for me which put it together. The job is broader. There are four chemistry professors on staff to share the teaching. I have more student interactions here than I did at Austin University. I have more research time to pursue questions which interest me."

"Why choose chemistry, Emily?" He'd been wanting to ask that simple question ever since he met her.

"I was fascinated with science from an early age. 'What's it made of?' was my favorite question as a child. My first chemistry set was in fourth grade and you would have thought my parents had bought me the moon. I was overjoyed. I taught myself chemistry from books I took from the library. I could draw the atom and its parts and recite all the elements in order by the time I was a junior in high school. I was doing it for my own enjoyment. I wanted to teach because of my parents. I wanted to teach chemistry because that was my passion since I was a child. God had given me something unique to focus on and I discovered what it was when I was very young."

"I'm glad for you. It makes life smoother when you don't spend a decade in the wrong track, doing something that isn't the passion of your heart."

"Chemistry was my fit." Emily relaxed back in her chair. "Your initial question about Austin, and why I'm still sort of homesick. What I miss most about Austin – my life was full of people. Classmates I went to college with who live in the area. Fellow teachers. Neighbors I was close with. My grandmother. There were thirty people I'd consider friends rather than casual associates, many of them single. There wasn't a lack of gatherings in my life, food and events defined my social calendar. Later on, the campus church added another rich layer of people to my life.

"In Chicago – I have couples who are good friends. Gina and Mark. Charlotte and Bryce. Ann and Paul. I have God who is my best friend. I have grad students who I spend time with teaching at a deeper level. I have hours in the lab doing research. I have more open space in my life. God drastically changed my life when he opened the door to return to Chicago. So I guess I'm curious, Noah. What do you see when I describe all that history?"

"God calls you away from good in order to give you a greater good. God called you to Himself."

"Really? That's an interesting way to put it."

"It's not that unusual an arc in a Christian's life. Do you mind if I lay a foundation for a moment?" He was reverting back to describing something but he thought it would be helpful to her.

"Sure. It will be nice to have you do the talking while I finish the mushrooms. These are really good."

"They are and you were hungry." Noah sketched a picture for her. "In the parable about the seed and the types of soil, Jesus mentions four types of people. Those who hear the word, but don't grab hold of it, so satan immediately steals it. Those who hear the word and receive it with joy, but they don't have a root in themselves. They grow tall and fast but then wind hits and the plant falls over. Their root is not in themselves but in what others think, so they can't stand up when those around them reject this interest in Jesus they have. The third type are those who hear the word but 'the cares of the world, and the delight in riches, and the desire for other things, enter in and choke the word, and it proves unfruitful' (Mark 4:19).

"Cares of the world tend to center around family, health, what needs done, it can be anything related to life. The delight in riches – you put in extra time at work because you'll enjoy the bonus you earn, you plan the vacation trip, you focus on getting ready for retirement, you plan a career path and work toward what you want to have. The desire for other things can simply be the ballgame you want to watch, the television series you keep up with, the friends gathering because its Friday night and that's what you do. You're not doing evil, you're just busy with things other than God. The Word and God have a part of your life and you would say they matter to you, but without realizing it your thoughts, words, and actions – they are mostly about cares you have, your job, your future plans, things you want to do. In percentage terms the word and God are getting 10 percent of your focus during a week? 15 percent? The word can't produce fruit because all its growth is spent holding ground against the significantly higher percentage of your life choking it. What typically happens is the word looses ground. You need more sleep so the bible reading and prayer drop off your daily calendar. The vacation takes priority over being at church. You have to work to meet project deadlines so you drop out of the weekly bible study. The 10 percent is now down to 5 percent.

"God prunes us by removing what is choking the word and time with Him. Growth comes from time alone with God and His word. There's no substitute for that time. And we either cooperate with God when He prunes us or we can resist Him. We either let the word gain ground in our lives or we grow cold toward God.

"What I see in your history is the fingerprints of God at work. You heard the word about Jesus from your grandmother and received it and held on to it despite the conflict that caused with your parents beliefs. You made the decision to become a Christian and follow Jesus. You obeyed when God moved you away from what was comfortable in Austin. You pressed into Him with the open space that had been created in your life. Rather than build a life in Chicago that was busy with other desires, you choose time with God. The word and God they are probably 30 percent of your week now? Double what it was in Austin?" Noah asked.

"At least that," Emily guessed.

"God could have eased you out of that busyness in Austin, but my sense is He wanted to give you some things he could only do here in Chicago. He did three things at the same time. He gave you distance from the loss of family which helped with the grief. He gave you space for more of Him. And He gave you an open door to do chemistry for your own enjoyment. He added to teaching chemistry in a way that actually created more space for you to be with Him and also let you enjoy more of what he created you to do.

"The fourth type of soil in the parable is those who hear the word and accept it and bear fruit. God requires us to orient our lives to Him first. We accept and obey his words to us. From that posture God can use us in all kinds of ways. God bears fruit through us. That's a really good thing for it takes the pressure off our lives. The Holy Spirit is our Helper and Guide. He's faithful in making sure we are at the right place at the right time to bear the fruit God desires to produce. Some fruit needs us to be at a specific place and time – if I wasn't doing this job at this university I would be missing an assignment on my life. Other fruit is opportunity fruit – you're available to God so when someone in your vicinity needs a question answered, needs resources, needs healed, God will use you as His Ambassador. You'll fulfill your assignment simply by being obedient to what the Holy Spirit directs you to do. Your part is obedience, God's part is the outcome, the result."

Emily thought about it. "Do you think God would ever call me back to Austin? There's a position at Austin University that's coming open, the Dean of the Chemistry department is retiring. I know my name is on the list they are considering."

"You love Austin, you still miss it."

"I do."

"Then yes, it would be like Him. Our lives are full of seasons. To take you out of Austin for a season, add into you, and then send you back there as the Dean of the Chemistry department would be very much in line with God's way of working. We are blessed as his children. One way we are blessed is God makes us the head and not the tail. 'I know the plans I have for you, says the LORD, plans for welfare and not for evil, to give you a future and a hope.' (Jeremiah 29:11b) God has plans to prosper us that involve resources, people, work we enjoy, places to live, kingdom assignments to fulfill.

"When your desire is for God as the focus of your heart, God can safely add all kinds of things to your life. You won't let anything knock Him out of center priority. For your own sake, He has to get you to desire the relationship with Him more than other stuff. So he strips stuff off, he prunes your life, so that in that vacuum you find God and realize He was what you were actually longing for. You fall in love with Him and now he can safely add things back to your life.

"When we are obedient to God's voice we will walk the journey God has planned for us. Or we can refuse that voice, disobey His directions and spend an entire lifetime in a wrong career and wrong city doing the wrong tasks. God will still love us, but we'll have no lasting fruit to show for ours lives.

"Isaiah 14 says the Lord has sworn, 'as I have planned, so shall it be, as I have purposed, so shall it stand.' The kingdom of God is expanding around the earth. We're either helping God by being obedient or we've taking ourselves out of being useful by doing our own thing. God respects our free will. If we miss our assignments, what God does is try to get our attention so we turn back on course. If we continue to disobey, God simply gives our assignment to someone else to complete. He'll still use us to produce opportunity fruit – there are always people we can love in Jesus' name, but we'll have missed the larger call on our life.

"Austin may be the place God plans to plant you again. When we pursue God, one way God leads is by directing our heart. We have peace in our heart when a decision is in line with God's direction. When we have a desire in our heart that persists, its because God is showing us something about our future. The path God has for you probably still involves Austin. That desire in your heart is like a clue, its showing you God isn't finished with the Austin chapter of your life. There's more God either wants to show you or do that is related to Austin. It could be remaining in your heart because you'll be returning to live there."

"Am I to be doing anything with that? Should I be planning an Austin trip this summer?" Emily asked.

"Ask the Holy Spirit. Unless he says do something,

just wait," Noah recommended. "God talks about things which are one year in our future and those which are fifty years off. It sounds much the same in the language He uses because God thinks in thousands of years. He's just talking to us about our lives so we have a sense of what our picture is. God surprises us on the timing and how things come about, but rarely does He surprise us on the picture. You knew as a child 'I like science, I'm a chemist.' I knew as a child that people misunderstood God and that made me sad. I wanted to fix that. I could see God smile when I said that was what I wanted to do with my life. He had instilled in me to see something that I would have a lifelong passion to do. I grew up wanting to help people see who God really is and love Him. God did the same for you with chemistry."

"That's a good picture of what happened."

"Trust God, Emily. He knows you, the person deep inside. He designed everything about you and knows what will give you joy. He leads you to those places in life because He loves you."

Noah saw her get caught off guard by a yawn and had to grin. "You're finally reaching the end of your energy. I wondered how long you would be able to go."

"I feel like I just hit a brick wall," Emily admitted. "The good meal and the milkshake probably contributed too."

Noah pointed to the roses on the table. "Pink or White? You need a flower to hallmark your first successful satellite repair."

"Pink."

He slipped the stem into a cardboard sleeve so she wouldn't touch a thorn. "If you want to press your flower, you pull the flower down into the cardboard sleeve and place it between two heavy books for a couple months."

"That's a handy sleeve." Emily accepted the rose.

Noah pushed back his chair. "Let's get you back to your car and on the way home." Her car was still parked at BSR and that was only a short drive from here.

Noah lifted a hand in thanks to Frank as they walked

to the door. He got a grin in reply and a wave of the towel being used to dry a glass. He'd catch up with Frank later. His brother had watched a two hour conversation happen and hadn't interrupted. That it had been going on two hours didn't surprise Noah, but it had clearly shifted Frank's perception of what was going on. There would be a lot more questions asked about Emily over the next meal Frank fixed him.

It had been a day that Noah hoped would become the pattern for the rest of the summer, one filled with conversations which filled in for him a perspective on her life and let him better see who Emily was. There would be a good deal to talk about tonight as he walked with God and reflected on what he had learned. She was much more in transition than he had realized. She might have been teaching at Chicago University for the last three years but Chicago wasn't a settled home for her yet.

*

15

Noah didn't know what to expect when it came to a Fourth of July party the Bishop's were hosting at BSR both inside the building and out, with part of the parking lot roped off for the event. What he encountered was his childhood. There were kids bike races and water balloon tosses and even some face painting getting done. The expectation of a hundred plus for the food was probably in the ballpark. He wandered back outside at dusk to take a seat on one of the many picnic tables. It was good food – brats, hot dogs, hamburgers, pulled-pork, steak for those who preferred it. Potato salad both hot and cold, watermelon, strawberries, cake, ice cream – all his childhood favorites. There were kids running around, a couple dogs in the mix, a few babies who were getting smiled over by everyone passing by. The person who wasn't here was Emily. Gina had said Emily was on her way, but Noah was beginning to think she was going to hide until it was over.

Tonight her fireworks would be public for the first time nationwide. Emily had done three television interviews in the last week on the national morning shows. Only one highlight had been released. The firework called Bubbles which looked very much like a child blowing a stream of bubbles. Firework companies were hyping what was coming, inviting the viewing public to participate and vote in top ten lists for their favorite new designs. Being able to now 3-D print the fireworks and launch rocket was being promoted as transformative. For once Noah suspected the hype was underselling what was going to be seen tonight.

From this parking lot they would have an unobstructed view down Clayton Avenue for the local firework display over the carillon scheduled for eight p.m. The city of Chicago fireworks from Navy Pier on Lake Michigan were scheduled for nine p.m. The two story high video wall inside would be showing those Chicago fireworks on scale. They had a camera on the roof of this building to see if they could get the Lake Michigan fireworks directly. If not, they would bring in the local television feed. After Chicago, they would switch the video wall to the live fireworks in Los Angeles. After that would be the Washington D.C. fireworks being taped now. The first fireworks this crowd should see were those live and in person. It was going to be a full evening of fireworks. The center of the attention should be here enjoying the excitement rather than hiding out. The fading sunset indicated the start time was approaching.

Gina joined him, licking a vanilla ice cream cone. The Bishop family had gone all in for their Fourth of July celebration. Her husband Mark was overseeing the roof camera and video wall. Bryce was handling the grill. Jim had appointed himself in charge of events and kids entertainment. They were treating friends and family and those involved at BSR to a fun filled perfect day.

"Should I go over to Emily's place and coax her out of hiding?"

Gina smiled. "I already dispatched Charlotte and Ann. It's the pressure of what if some fireworks had a production problem and you get a color blob in the sky rather than a pretty display, coupled with all the basic unknowns of an event this size. Tonight is like a rocket launch party times a couple hundred thousand in volume. There's not a community firework display in the country that won't have at least one or two of this new type of firework in their presentation. How's the camera setup?"

Noah checked the video camera position on the tripod. He wanted the best view of the sky for the carillon fireworks he could get to add to the video montage being assembled. "It looks good."

"I appreciate your help with this."

"I'm enjoying it. There's about an hour of footage of kids, dogs, babies, and food taken with the handheld camera for you to work with thus far. I'll easily have a couple hours more of crowd reactions by the end of the evening. Tony will have equal that or more, his teenage sons have been doing a great job helping us out."

The carillon bells began to ring out a melody, the musical part of the evening beginning. When the music ended and the deep bell chimed out eight o'clock the fireworks would begin. Individuals and families began streaming out of the BSR building to find perches on the picnic tables, some carrying out folding chairs, others choosing to stand to watch the show.

"Here Emily comes now," Gina said with faint relief.

Noah turned to see her weaving through the gathering crowd, sharing smiles, a couple words, but not stopping. Emily took a seat on the picnic table beside him. "Sorry I'm late. I was distracting myself finishing up some research work."

One of the engineers passing by handed her a cold iced coffee. "Thanks."

"What would you like for food? It's a full spread in there," Noah offered, calculating he had time to bring a plate for her.

"I'm passing on food for now. I feel as fidgety as a child before a pageant begins. No use pushing my nervous stomach with a loaded hotdog."

He smiled. "I'd say some nerves are warranted."

"How are you doing Gina?" Emily asked.

Gina held up the last of her ice cream. "I'm stress eating. I know the little rocket design is solid, it has only a fraction of the complexity of the big rocket. But we're about to see a couple hundred thousand of them fly all in one evening. It's both exciting and terrifying at the same time."

Emily laughed. "Oh, I echo those words."

Noah tugged the roll of hard candy mints from his shirt pocket and held it out. Orange was at the end. "Don't decline a gift. Orange is good for you."

Emily accepted it with a smile. Noah offered Gina the blueberry one next in the roll, then took the lemon yellow for himself and pocketed the roll of mints. Talking was better than not when it came to helping pass time, so Noah pushed what they were nervous about into words hoping to tame its size. "Talk to me about tonight, Emily, what you expect to see."

"That's the problem. I don't know what to expect we will see. I've only seen a few of the designs the various firework manufacturers have created, like Bubbles. There are around two hundred which are being released this first year. There is a qualification process which confirms a design meets all the required safety parameters before a firework can be sold – height above the ground, size, density, duration of glitter – the falling fire elements – it's an extensive independent review. A manufacturer also has to have a minimum of 1,000 of the design 3-D printed before it can be put on sale and limit sales to one per venue to prevent instant price gauging while only that initial inventory of the design is available."

"You were thinking ahead."

"We tried. Bryce did a wonderful job constructing the licensing details. We wanted it to be a fair process. Designs are unique to a manufacturer only during the year of release. Manufactures are free to then sell their designs to one another or to do the work to copy designs and create their own versions. It's our hope manufacturers will refine the best designs so they become industry standard products."

He could hear the building nerves in her voice even as she offered him those details, so Noah diverted to another the subject entirely, not sure she'd be willing to follow the shift. "How was the trip West?" He hadn't seen her since the satellite repair, though he'd heard via Gina she'd arrived back in town.

"Incredible. I drove about eight hundred miles, most all of it in the mountains."

"What do you enjoy about the mountains the most?"

"The fact they are absolutely huge. The fact there are these really beautiful lakes at high elevations which are so clear they are pristine gems. The rivers and the waterfalls. Oh my, Noah, the waterfalls were spectacular. There was a heavy snow melt and more rain than normal this year. The waterfalls are in full splendor. About half the known waterfalls, the smaller ones, are normally dry. I got to see waterfalls that are only flowing with water on average once every five years. There would be this cliff with seven different waterfalls cascading down. And what was really amazing to realize? God thinks all of that is normal. When He wanted to create something, He comes up with mountains and waterfalls. No offense to architects who design buildings, but nothing man has built comes close to the beauty of a mountain waterfall."

Noah laughed. "I think you've probably got a picture or two to show me."

"Maybe a few hundred," Emily admitted. "But even projecting those photos onto that two-story video wall inside won't make the scenes come alive enough. You really need to travel and see the West, Noah, you'd love it."

"I spent two summers doing just that," he replied, encapsulating his final high school years. "I worked as a ranch hand for a month, worked on an Indian reservation for a month, tried my hand at water rafting as a guide's helper. I wanted adventure and my dad was willing to let me swing for the fences for what that looked like. I had enough outdoors over two summers to last the next decade of concentration on college studies."

"Why haven't you mentioned that before?"

"You'd have asked if I had pictures and I'm mostly this tall thin good looking kid with a smile on his face doing something goofy when the photo got snapped."

A musical crescendo filled the night and then faded off, saving him from having to explain further. The eight o'clock bell began to sound. "Here we go." Noah picked up the handheld video camera for the crowd reaction shots and looked around to place where the kids were sitting. He wanted their reactions in particular.

"Don't film me," Gina requested instantly.

"Nor me," Emily insisted in tandem.

"Both of you relax, you're not on candid camera tonight," he reassured.

The first firework burst into the air. A huge glittering red circle filled the sky. It was beautiful but something he had seen before. "This view is excellent." The firework was high above the trees and aligned down Clayton Avenue.

The next firework painted a bursting white oval.

"That's a traditional one, too," Gina said softly. "I saw the sequence script. Two new ones are next."

"I can't watch," Emily groaned and covered her eyes.

Noah laughed and rubbed her back with his free hand.

A rainbow painted in the sky with vivid color bands. "Wow!" Noah nearly dropped the camera. The crowd around them gasped and spontaneous applause broke out.

Emily risked a peek between her fingers and dropped her hands as the color glittered down. "Oh, wow, indeed."

It had no more than faded from the sky then the next appeared. A double rainbow, higher and wider. "The colors are incredible," Noah said, amazed.

"That's the best part of the chemistry she did," Gina answered, having to raise her voice to be heard over the crowd's delight. "Emily created a full color pallet for designers to use. They never had that before."

A series of traditional fireworks followed.

A traditional circle appeared but now filled with hundreds of colors. The crowd reaction to it was the strongest so far.

"Oh, that's gorgeous." Emily said, enjoying the display more than anyone else here.

"Those glitter tails are like color icicles on a Christmas tree," Gina decided.

Bubbles appeared blowing outward in different colors. Noah was delighted with the kids reaction to it.

A Smiley Face painted in the sky in bright yellow. Spontaneous laughter erupted.

"That is going to be one of my top favorites," Noah predicted.

A series of traditional fireworks were launched. The local show lasted fifteen minutes. As it reached its finale a series of percussion shells boomed out and the sky filled with an amazing display of solid colored circles the size of plates.

"That one is called Candy Dots," Emily said with joy.

"I can see why." As they finally faded out, Noah closed the video. "I'm astonished, Emily."

"Your phone is going to be ringing off the hook wanting interviews," Gina predicted.

"The university is already geared up to handle the calls. They'll be doing the bulk of the interviews for me." She slipped off the picnic table perch. "That went really well." Her relief at being able to say that was obvious.

People began to stream over to offer Emily their congratulations. Noah stepped out of the way. He secured the camera and tripod and video taken. He'd set up the camera inside to capture crowd shots as they watched the video wall. He used his phone and took one photo of Emily smiling, surrounded by people, for his own sake. This was her night and he was glad he'd been able to share it with her. He caught a second one of Gina laughing as her husband Mark lifted her up off her feet. That there would be a lot to celebrate tonight was an understatement.

****

They had a good camera feed from the roof for the coming Chicago Fireworks. The crowd was assembling inside to watch the video wall. Noah took another wedge of the seedless watermelon to enjoy. It was excellent when this cold. The melons were being kept in a kids wading pool ice water bath until they were cut. Emily joined him. She had picked up a short cluster of the grapes but still not filled a plate. He was going to make sure before this evening was over that she had something more substantial to eat.

"Noah, would you do me a favor? Hang around

tonight? I mean afterwards?"

He looked at her curious, for her voice was unexpectedly serious. "I can do that."

"Thanks."

Mark had brought out office chairs and pointed Emily toward one at the back of the gathering crowd. With the video wall scale no one was going to be blocking the view. "Sit. Enjoy. Its going to be fine."

Emily smiled and went where directed.

The local television station audio was on the speakers and the station telecast was an inset on the video wall. The festivities at Navy Pier had been going on all day with live music and a food street festival. The Mayor's remarks were just ending.

Chicago's Fourth of July celebration began as the sky lit up with red white and blue bursts and the music swelled for the Star Spangled Banner. With the scale of the video wall it was like being in both surround sound and surround view. The choreographers for the firework show were taking full advantage of the scale they had to work with. Instead of one Smiley Face, five filled the sky.

The music changed to a serious Chicago Blue's tune and an instant later a series of C's spread across the horizon in the Chicago Cubs color of blue. The sight was met with laughter.

The sky suddenly filled with emeralds and rubies appearing almost solid in form. "Jewels," Emily said with delight, naming the firework design. "I'd heard they'd come up with solid forms – the Candy Dots were the first – but had only heard about this one."

The choreography of music and colorful blasts wove together traditional fireworks and new ones in seamless fashion for twenty-five minutes. Hundreds of Candy Dots filled the sky from horizon to horizon. A new one that looked like trees growing upward filled the sky with fire branches expanding toward the moon. Squares painted which blinked from color to color. As the show drew to a close, the letter 'I' appeared, the letter made up by three separate blasts of simple lines, so well coordinated they were nearly perfect in spatial relationship to each other. LOVE spelled out next with the E at the end made up of four separate blasts of simple lines, the crowd cheering as the final line properly painted. Then the sky filled with C's and the crowd roared its delight. Ten large balls filled with a hundred colors each saturated the sky to end the Chicago show.

Emily, clapping along with the rest of the crowd, rendered her own verdict. "Nice."

"Washington D.C. and Los Angeles are next."

"Bring them on," she replied with a smile, no longer sounding or looking nervous.

The video wall changed over to the Los Angeles live telecast in progress. A glittering sky of traditional firework circles were fading out as the National Anthem concluded. The following ten seconds of silence was broken by the swelling of opening music and the sudden popping of colorful star bursts as the music took on a strong beat. More rapid bursts of color, shaping a mountain of them, like a towering mound of popcorn began to fill the sky, persisting, not fading out. As it grew and grew in boldness and brightness Emily began to laugh. "Oh, they are spending a lot of money to saturate that much air space but its beautiful; that is the definition of gorgeous." The effect ended with a clap of thunder and a burst of white in the center of the kaleidoscope of colors which pushed the colors out in concentric shimmering circles to the cheers of the watching crowd.

"The sky looks like a snowball just struck a pallet of wet rich oil paints," Noah remarked, lowering the camera capturing the crowd in the room's reaction to enjoy the final fading image of it.

"That's a great description," Emily replied, smiling.

A soft baby lullaby began for the music and a trio of overlapping blankets of lace appeared in the sky so bright and yet thin in their lines it appeared to be tangible thread. Noah loved it. Big and bold was beautiful. So was soft and simple.

For the next two hours Noah simply absorbed the evening, the fireworks from LA, the recorded ones from earlier in Washington D.C, the crowd reactions, along with those of Emily and Gina and the Bishop family. He walked around with the camera as the fireworks shifted from Los Angeles to Washington D.C. wanting to make the memory footage of this evening for Emily as rich as possible.

Washington D.C. ended its program by framing the Washington Monument on all sides with towers of red white and blue. The ability to project solid forms had captured the designers imaginations this first year and been used in very creative ways. Noah thought the color columns would make his own top ten list. There were so many beautiful firework patterns he had never seen before he had lost count and would have to use the video to help him remember them all.

As the applause for the evening filled the spacious room, Jim stepped up on the platform normally used to move around the satellite mockups.

"Thanks for coming everyone. It's been a breathtaking unveiling of Emily's fireworks and as successful an evening as we had hoped. We have one last event to conclude tonight." He turned his attention to the star of the evening. "Emily, we've been talking as a Bishop family how to commemorate this very special night and we've decided you should have a gift chosen specially for you. Mark, if you would do the honors." He pointed to the back wall.

The oversized warehouse door at the back of the building lifted and headlights came on. A car drove slowly into the building.

Emily watched, stunned. "No way." It came into the lights proper and Emily began laughing. "Gina, what did you guys manage to do?" It was an old Lincoln town car.

"We like old memories as much as you do. We found it in Wisconsin, owned by a gentleman who appreciated a good story."

"You actually found my first car."

"We did indeed."

"Emily," Mark said with a smile from the platform, "it's not expensive nor does it look particularly attractive, but it's a reminder of your former life in Chicago. As life inevitably now gets bigger and busier, you can step back in time and remember when life was simple."

"It is absolutely perfect," Emily replied, delighted. "My grandmother owned it, gave me the keys when I got my license at 16, I drove it around Chicago until I left for college and had to leave it behind to be sold. I loved this car."

Bryce stepped out of the drivers side door and held up the keys for her.

"I got through this entire night and now you're making me want to cry."

She hugged Bryce and accepted the keys. "Thank you, everyone. So very much."

*

16

Noah wrote the date and time on the video card sleeve for
Gina. The live telecast on the video wall was now replaying
highlights of the new fireworks. He paused to watch the
Candy Dots again.

"This was a spectacular evening, Emily."

She was carrying a plate with two loaded hot dogs and
some coleslaw. She was finally relaxing. "I think so, too.
My science is novel and groundbreaking, but it's the tool
for other's creativity. I just gave them a color pallet and
software to work with, the chemical methods for the 3-D
printer to create what they envisioned. They have exceeded
what I envisioned could be brought together within this
first year."

She took a seat on a folding chair and picked up her
fork to sample the coleslaw. "I'm thinking I need some
practice in my old car when its daylight out to make sure I
remember its dimensions before I drive city streets at night.
Ann was going to give me a lift home but would you mind
if I ask you to do that instead? I've got a question I'd like to
ask you."

"Sure, I can give you a lift whenever you're ready to
go."

"Once I finish this plate so I'm no longer famished I'll
be ready to go. It's been quite a night."

"That it has. Tell Jim to give you those driving
lessons. He'll enjoy it."

She considered the car and laughed. "I may do just
that. It's a great gift."

They left BSR together twenty minutes later. "Head to
the university. I'll give you street directions as we get to
my neighborhood. I'm on Nolan Drive."

"Easy enough." It was humid enough out that he
turned the air conditioning on high and then turned down
the radio volume. The parking lot had emptied but for a

half a dozen cars. He pulled around the roped off section flagged for the kids bike races and out onto the quiet side street, stopped at the stoplight, then turned south to the university.

"My question is rather personal."

Noah glanced over, noting the serious tone in her voice again. "Ask anything. If its too personal I'll simply decline to answer."

He saw Emily smile in the indirect light of a street light. "Not that personal. I don't know what I'm going to do with the money. It's been coming in since the patent licensing, but the bulk of it will get computed in about 120 days when the window for returns for any unused fireworks closes. It's going to be a lot, Noah. And its going to keep coming in year after year while these patents are a viable foundation to what is being manufactured."

She wanted to ask him a question about money. He hadn't expected that. "What do you want to do with it?"

"Act wisely."

"God gives wisdom to anyone who asks, freely and in abundance."

"I've asked Him. And Bryce has been giving me some good advice. But I thought you might have some unique insights to offer. Would you talk to me about how you manage your money?"

"I don't mind the subject." Noah thought about what might help her and decided it was a brief enough conversation he might as well give her the full picture. "My money management for my life is very simple. I get paid once a month by the university in salary and have various speaking honorariums. I give twenty percent to God as money comes in. I put into savings the equivalent of one paycheck a year. I pay the bills for the lifestyle I've chosen for myself. And the rest I invest in the kingdom of God.

"The house is paid off, I have no debts. I have the house, car and lifestyle I want for myself. It's a lifestyle that balances the amount of stuff I have to maintain with what I enjoy doing with my time. The cost of that lifestyle hasn't really changed much in the last ten years.

"I keep my savings plan simple. I keep a year of cash in a savings account and the rest invested in a low-fee stock index fund. Rising bull markets endure for a decade and bear markets go swiftly down. You can spot those huge waves on a long-term stock market chart. If its more than six years since a bull market started, I let my cash build up in my savings account. Otherwise I buy the stock index fund as extra cash comes in every month.

"I have a maximum amount I will save. When my investments and cash hit that amount, I give 20 percent of my investments away and let it build up again. I've been hitting that maximum amount frequently these last few years. That's mostly it. I don't have a complicated financial life. The annuity is my only retirement type investment and that's as much for proof of my age as income in future years."

"I'm still resolving what to do with my inheritance from my parents and grandmother. How do you decide how much savings you need?"

"You trust God and ask Him for a number. There will be peace in your heart with that number. My maximum savings level use to be higher than it is now. I talk about it with God every few years and adjust the level. I've realized giving into the kingdom of God is its own form of saving account. God says 'he who is kind to the poor lends to the Lord'. God will return it when I need something. I don't require as much in my own accounts when the reason it is not in my account is I have deployed it into kingdom uses."

"That's a good perspective."

"My brother has chosen land as his primary investment for the long term. He likes to buy land around growing towns with a population of about seventy thousand. He goes out ten miles and looks for farmland or timber, something with no house on the property, but maybe a stream. He leases the land to area farmers or sets it aside for wildlife under a land use agreement with the government. The land will generate enough cash flow to cover the tax bill plus a few percentage points of return. In fifty years, a hundred years, most of that land will have found commercial or residential use. The profit will come when he sells it. He jokes about his land being his inheritance gift to me when he dies young at the age of one-hundred. Frank sees what I do in the scripture regarding eternal life but is content with the idea his life is going to be fully lived by the time he's a hundred, he'll have done whatever God has prepared for him by then and he'll be ready to go to heaven. I admire that pragmatic view about life, that the best part of it is heaven so why would you want to stick around earth a day long than necessary? Frank looks forward to being called home. While I look at it the opposite way, the most fun is being able to stay on earth as a witness to the good news until Jesus come."

Emily smiled. "I can see that about Frank. I enjoyed meeting him."

"He's the kind of brother everyone should have. Solid, dependable, good to talk with."

Noah thought about the decisions she would need to make and offered his best advice. "Treat the inheritance, this new source of cash, as a pivot point, Emily. God likes to build things. Jesus is building his church. God created everything we see. God has built the new city Jerusalem which is presently in heaven. Let God help you build your life. Dream with God. He'll have been working in your heart with some ideas as the money isn't a surprise to him. Vacations, travel, things you desire to do. Don't be afraid to deploy that extra cash, or let it build toward something God will direct you towards."

"Thanks. Take a right at this next light," Emily directed, "then at the stop sign a left on Nolan Drive."

Noah nodded and clicked on the right turn signal.

"Audio bibles," Emily mentioned. "Half the world's population can't read, so audio versions of the bible in different languages is a major recent interest. The poor in the world, the conflict zones, refugees, they remain a constant interest. My grandmother had a heart for missions and I picked it up from her."

"There's your plan coming together. If you need permission from someone to simply give the money away, Emily, let me be that voice. Give as you purpose in your heart to give, for God loves a cheerful giver. If He wants you to keep a certain amount, God will tell you to hold onto it.

"Giving to God is a safe plan for resources. He's not going to frown on you giving away stored up cash. Just ask him, can I give this money away? If he says yes, cheerfully give it and don't worry about the future resources. They will be there when needed. He's a really big God. Trust Him to have your back."

"Thanks for that, Noah."

"Sure." He liked the look of her neighborhood, it was older than he had expected, narrow lots with mostly two story homes with full front porches, older trees lining the sidewalk.

"The house with the light on the flag."

He pulled into her driveway.

Emily unbuckled her seatbelt. "Can you come in for a few minutes?"

He was surprised by the question but nodded and turned off the car, unclipped his own seatbelt and stepped out. The night wasn't particularly quiet, there were still fireworks going off sporadically in the surrounding neighborhood.

The house was a basic two story with white siding and a colorful house number painted on the mailbox. Emily unlocked her front door and opened it, turned on lights. A long entry hall flanked stairs going upstairs. Noah could see through to a dining room and guessed the kitchen was along the back of the house. A living room was to their left. Emily slipped off her shoes but shook her head when he moved to do the same. "It's simply habit."

The interior had been remodeled to be much more current than the outside of the house. The rugs on the hardwood floors were bold southern colors. The wooden bench in the entry way, the cowboy boots beside her tennis shoes, the cowboy hat on the hook beside an umbrella were evidence of another life.

The entryway was hung with photos. Here were the photos from Austin and personal things of family. A few of the photos were of Chicago and her childhood, a snowman and proud little girl beside it, the lake when it was crashing with ice. "Your family?"

"My parents on the left, my grandmother on the right. Can I interest you in something cold to drink? I'm pretty well stocked."

He studied photos then followed her back to the kitchen. "Would you happen to have lemonade? It's a Fourth of July tradition."

"We share that tradition. I've got a pitcher that's cold."

The kitchen was neat, a towel by the sink, a vase of flowers on the counter. Coffee was set out to start in the morning. There were green leafy plants in pots by the window he guessed to be herbs. She was old school with cookbooks arranged by subject by the flour and sugar canisters. His birthday gift to her was beside the counter top grill and showed use, the salt levels had dropped in two of the test tubes.

Papers across the dining room table, books stacked on the table beside the couch in the living room, a collection of movies on the floor by a tossed pillow – she lived in these rooms. He realized she collected pottery. There was a Texas feel to the home without it being overly obvious. It felt like Emily's place. It was good to see her home. "No pets?"

She got down glasses from a cabinet for them both. "I'm unpredictable in my schedule and feel it wouldn't be fair to a pet. I had both cats and dogs growing up. My parents traveled enough it was easy to plead them into the idea I should have both to keep me company while they were away."

Noah smiled at that memory she offered. "I'm a dog

guy. I like Irish Setters, border collies. The last dog I had was a black border collie mix named Elizabeth. She loved the couch in my office, both at home and on campus. I miss her. I still find myself glancing up from my desk thinking I'll see her asleep on the couch. I haven't replaced her yet but its getting to be time. I think its going to be back to another Irish Setter."

Emily handed him the filled glass. "I can see you with a dog who loves to walk."

She pulled out a chair at the dining room table and stacked papers out of the way.

"Your research?" he asked, curious, pulling out a chair to her left.

"Yes. I'd like to show you something." She picked up an object from the ceramic bowl on the table and offered it.

He studied it with interest, not sure what to make of the chubby disk of polished bronze with little fan shaped metal wings.

"What is it?"

"A new type of battery. What if you could recharge a battery using heat?"

He instantly grinned. "Oh, that's a fascinating question."

"I've been stress testing the design and its passing every test. I've had it in my refrigerator for the last couple days. That's actually why I was late to the gathering tonight. I was recording the test data on it as a distraction from the coming fireworks."

She plugged the battery into an older model phone and turned it on. "That money question I asked you is probably more involved than it appears on the surface. The fireworks are one scale, a new type of battery, it's on a vastly different scale."

"You're nervous about being rich," he realized.

"I find I really am."

"Bryce can help you. He and Charlotte are handling a lot of personal wealth. Lean on him."

"I've been talking to him about the basic structure of

what to do. He's offered to share the research they do on charities if I'd find that information helpful."

"Good. It will be useful to you."

"I guess my question is – why is God making me this rich?"

Noah smiled. "Now that's a good question. A simple answer from scripture, 'you will be made rich in every way for great generosity.' (2 Corinthians 9:11) You glorify God when you further the good news about Jesus. You glorify God when you help out Christians and all others. Generosity results in thanksgiving being offered to God.

"My best advice? Don't worry about it, Emily. Simply ask God what to do with the money as it comes in. He's got a plan in mind. If He tells you to buy something, buy it, if he tells you to sell something, sell it. If he tells you to give something, give it. God will be as involved as you desire Him to be in giving guidance on what to do."

"That sounds so simple. Do you ever think about being rich?"

"I already am. God gave me all things with Jesus."

"You know what I mean."

"I know what you mean. Sure, I have on occasion. Money is described as being the least thing in the kingdom. When you're faithful with the least, God will give you more – more money as well as more of what are the truly important things in life. So I can tell you this money is a test. God wants to know if your heart will stay on Him or will you get distracted by money. The lack of money, the excess of money – what happens to our hearts under both conditions is what God wants us to see about ourselves.

"When we fear lack, we think money is more faithful than God to supply our needs.

"When we fear abundance, we are mostly thinking about how people will view us for having money. Who will envy us. Which friends won't feel comfortable around us because now we have more options than they do. Who will judge us as being too rich and holding onto excess. People always think those with money should be doing philanthropic good deeds with it. All of that is what other people think. The fear of man drives so much of our thinking. God can only test how our heart handles being wealthy by providing abundance. God will often tell us to do something simply to show how much we are letting the fear of man actually drive our decision. If we fear having a surplus, God will ask us to save a dollar amount that makes us feel too rich. If we hesitate to give, he'll ask us to give a sacrificial size gift. Money is a teaching tool for God." Noah drank good lemonade. "What do you think about the idea of being rich?"

"I'm going to enjoy it," Emily replied.

"A smart answer." Noah leaned in his thoughts toward the Holy Spirit looking for insights into what Emily needed tonight. She was being blessed by God, that much was obvious.

"Money is a neutral thing. It's neither good nor bad. Its like a brick, you can build with it or throw it through a window. The hand that holds it is what matters. You can't serve God and Mammon. Mammon is the name for the evil spirit which loves to rest on money, a spirit tied very closely to the devil himself. That's why the love of money is the root of all evil. If you aren't worshipping and depending on God, money is your solution to all your problems and wants and desires. The love of what money can do for you is actually worship of the evil spirit that is resting on that money.

"Held by someone who loves God, money is a powerful tool to build the kingdom. Held by someone who is shaky in their relationship with God, money is a powerful other lover, something to have an affair with while you still call yourself married to God.

"The spirit of mammon wants you to depend on money rather than depend on God. That's the thing you have to guard against in your heart. Who are you trusting? If you're trusting God and managing His money, you're on solid ground. If a problem comes up and you feel relief because you have enough money on hand to solve it, before you feel relief that you have God with you to solve it, you've got something going wrong in your heart. God doesn't give you money to cause you to fail in life. But it is a test. Can you handle money? Pass this test and God knows He can trust you with the more important things in the kingdom. Most Christians never pass this money test and so stay at the entry to the kingdom of God.

"How do you handle fame? You'll be tasting more and more of that one too. People will want your time and attention for what you've accomplished. How do you handle that admiration and acclaim? Are you able to reflect that glory back to God and not get tangled up with pride? You can trust God to take you into success. God's walking with you to help you. What he's actually showing you is what is in your heart so if there's a problem you can realize it and let Him help you fix it.

The blessing of the LORD makes rich, and he adds no sorrow with it. (Proverbs 10:22)

"The word sorrow in that verse means heavy labor, there is no toil, heavy labor, sweat with God's blessings, it comes as a gift. You enjoy your life and what He gives you to do and riches show up that are from Him."

He finished the lemonade and glanced at the time. "You need to wrap up this day and crash for about ten hours of sleep." He pushed back his chair as he said it so the conversation wouldn't continue tonight. "I want to hear more about your battery and how that design developed, but we can do that as part of an evening walk. You'll be doing most of the talking on the walk. We'll both find that a refreshing swap."

"I'd like to talk to you about the discovery. It has been intense these last couple years, the rocket work, the fireworks, now the battery design. Sometimes its hard to keep my breath its been happening so fast."

"Then that's what we'll talk about, Emily. The pace of life and how to keep up with God when He's moving at this speed. It's not a constant about life, there are seasons, and you're in a fast one right now."

"I am indeed feeling like life is moving fast." She walked with him to the front door.

The whistle of a bottle rocket and sharp pop reminded him the night was going to stay noisy for at least another couple hours. "Why don't you call me tomorrow and we'll decide on something to do – I'll take you horseback riding, we can walk through the art museum, something to change up the pace and talk in another environment. I've got class Thursday morning and I leave Friday afternoon at four heading to Tennessee. Otherwise my schedule is free."

"I'll call you," Emily agreed. "It was a good night."

"A great night," Noah corrected as he stepped onto the walk. "You should relax and enjoy the fact its over."

Emily laughed and waved goodnight.

*

17

Noah's phone chimed with a text as he passed the university administration building. "walking tonight? want company?"

It was a good text to receive. "Thanks, Jesus," he said softly, for the opportunity to spend time with Emily was welcome. He sent a text back and changed course to meet her.

In the four weeks since the Fourth of July festivities, their friendship had found a more solid footing. They were still mostly talking about questions she had, but there were personal matters coming into the conversations more often. They'd been horseback riding, walked through the art museum, shared cotton candy at the fair night the university hosted. Emily had been out of town nearly as often as he was, traveling with her time to see more of the Rockies, while he'd been attending conferences where he was presenting sessions. And she's been particularly busy in the lab lately, often working late on the battery stress testing. There hadn't been much truly open time in their schedules.

For their walk tonight Noah changed directions and took Emily on the path toward the student housing. Several sculpture pieces crafted by artist alumni, some in metal, some in stone, were displayed along the path, many now having been dressed by students with a scarf or shirt or hat, in an endless variety of creativity of their own. They were a type of collective student voice and Noah liked seeing the changes as a semester progressed. A dozen pair of sunglasses now adorned the metal sculpture of a tree, someone had crafted a poodle out of wire and the patriot statue was now walking his dog.

Emily had brought two shaved ice fruit slushies from her lab for them. The drink was delicious but way colder than he expected. Noah felt like his teeth were beginning to freeze. "What would you like to talk about tonight?"

"Is there anything left on the list we haven't talked about yet?"

"There's always a few more topics to explore. It's the nice thing about God. You never get to the end of the good news. How about a simple starting point. What have you been thinking about lately?"

"Two-thirds of my sabbatical has passed. I've been thinking a lot about that. I can tell I'm different. I wasn't expecting that. The peace is much more intense. It's more than a feeling. My life, my thoughts, I'm simply more peaceful inside."

"God is the God of Peace. The more you talk with God, the more peaceful your life becomes. You've been spending a summer mostly talking with Him. Even your travel has been about finding places to enjoy what God has created and just appreciate Him."

"The travel has been amazing. It's like God is arranging both the places He wants me to see and the perfect day I should arrive there. I haven't planned it, I've just gone, and its been better than anything I could have arranged myself. Without realizing it, I was letting God become my travel coordinator this summer. I've loved it."

Noah smiled. "I've seen the pictures. God likes that travel time with you. It's been the two of you on an adventure together."

"That's a perfect way to describe it," Emily agreed. "I've been enjoying that time with God this summer. And its been nice to have time to read scripture in larger blocks so I can think about it as a whole. I go through a book now, Romans, Hebrews, John, and I'm aware I'm beginning to hear what's being said in a richer way."

"The living active word is building into you understanding. Your chemistry experience is a good model. You learned chemistry when you were a child and then more completely as a student and now as you teach it, you grasp it at an even deeper level. Some parts of chemistry have become yours. You see in your mind what you're thinking about and can do things within chemistry without effort. The Holy Spirit, God in us, teaches us the word of God to that level over time. We come to know the word, then understand it, then grasp it deeply so its internal to how you think. God is the God of Peace, God loves you, those are tangible things we learn and experience. You hang out with God by talking with him, by reading what He's written, by praising him, by speaking in tongues letting your spirit talk with God. It's all good. It's all helpful to you. The fact you chose to make God the priority of your time during your sabbatical – that delights God."

"Thanks for that, Noah. I didn't do it expecting to get this in return. I didn't know what to expect. I just wanted to get to know Him. I wanted to get questions answered and know about Him, but mostly I just wanted to get to know Him. I think I am."

"What's He thinking right now?" Noah asked, curious if she'd be confident enough to hear His voice in a situation like this.

Emily walked quietly for a bit. "He thinks it's a nice evening to walk. And that someone finally dressed the metal turtle in suitable colors."

Noah glanced ahead on the path. The parachute fabric dome over the metal turtle's back was the colors of a bright rainbow.

"He says that the rainbow will always be His no matter how satan likes to steal his colors and make it a symbol for what is perverse."

Noah was startled by that comment, but then not. "You hear Him well, Emily. That sounds like God's voice."

"The more we talk, the more I can tell his voice from other thoughts. It's weird how God does that. I couldn't explain to someone how that happens but I'm experiencing it."

"It's how we're created, we are designed to hear God's voice."

At the statue of two dancers Noah took the path that circled around to the student union. There was free popcorn available at all hours and he could use something salty to munch on.

"Do you have a topic you want to talk about?" Emily asked him.

Noah thought about it. "More of a suggestion. I'm scheduled to speak in Fort Worth, Texas on Thursday evening, August 16th. Why don't you fly down with me, we'll spend a couple days in Austin afterwards and you can introduce me to good barbeque."

"That's an unexpected offer."

"It would be good for you to see Austin and talk about it with someone who doesn't have history there. You go and you see what memories come to the surface and if you want to talk about them, we will. Otherwise we'll just eat good barbeque and I can see firsthand the places you talk about with such fondness. No agenda, just whatever's helpful to you."

"You would do that with me?"

"Sure. I think the only reason you haven't been back is that you don't want to do it alone. And its been steady in me the last few weeks, the thought that it would be useful to you to go back and just see what God has in mind to show you. Maybe He hasn't nudged you about it because He was trying first to nudge me to go along. Think about it for a few days. If there's peace about the idea, I'll make the travel arrangements. We'd fly out in the early afternoon of August 16th for Fort Worth, spend Friday and Saturday in Austin, fly back on the 19th."

"I'll let you know by the end of the week."

Noah nodded toward the student union so they could stop for popcorn. When they had full paper sleeves loaded with buttery and salty popcorn, they headed back to the center of campus.

"What else have you been thinking about, Noah? What's the topic you've been exploring the most?"

"Praise."

"Really?" Emily looked over, curious. "For a class or personally? What have you discovered?"

"Everything in my line of work is personal, I tend to

teach from what I'm learning." Noah considered how to put together what he'd been thinking about. "To express admiration, to glorify, to worship – praise lives in that intersecting circle of ways we honor God. God's been connecting some thought about praise and what is happening as we do so. The Revised Standard Version renders Psalm 22:3, talking about God, 'thou art holy, enthroned on the praises of Israel.' The King James Version renders it, 'thou art holy, O thou that inhabitest the praises of Israel.'

"Praise links us with God's presence as King. God inhabits praise. And praise is verbal. I've realized one of the reasons so much happens in church gatherings – healings, insights, breakthroughs – during times we are praising God is because we are calling upon God to be manifest in our midst as King.

"God is spirit and God is truth. He doesn't need our cooperation to be wherever He desires to be. But God created our free will and honors it. God comes as King where He is invited and welcome. If we don't stop and welcome Him to a meeting, we can have a meeting called church and never have God's presence manifest. He's waiting for us to invite Him.

"A gathering honoring God is focused on him. For example, 'God, you are good, loving, faithful and worthy of all our praise. You are an awesome King. We honor you as our God. We now sing *Amazing Grace* because what you've done for us is truly that – amazing.' And after the song, its ' Holy Spirit, please come and minister to us now as you desire. This gathering and time is for your agenda, not ours.' Then we sing *Worship the Lord, Power in the Blood, Worthy is God*. Those songs, those words, those expressions of praise – it's the difference between the rest of the time being a man led gathering and a God led one. People find out they were healed while singing, prayers are said in unity and connection with the Father, the preacher speaks with clarity and boldness – it's because we stopped and came *to Him*. We didn't come to a random gathering.

We came together, *to Him*, and welcomed and invited Him
to come *to us*."

Emily thought about it. "It's very much Psalm 100:4.
'Enter his gates with thanksgiving, and his courts with
praise!' We come into His presence with thanksgiving and
praise. So the inverse is also happening. He comes into our
presence when we thank and praise Him. One is happening
in unseen heaven, one on visible earth, but both are
occurring simultaneously."

Noah nodded. "Praise is the missing link most people
have overlooked. They sing with distracted thoughts, they
can't wait for the song time to be over, so the service can
get on to more important business. When it's that opening
praise that is the key to everything that matters. If they
sincerely praise God, God shows up to them and to the
others gathered. God then handles everything for us so that
we walk out of his presence no longer in need. God is our
righteousness, our peace, our healer, our deliverer, our
provider, our Shepherd. It should catch our attention when
we gather and do not begin by inviting Him with
thanksgiving and praise to be our enthroned King.

"Laying aside our agenda is different than not having
orderly meetings with a plan for the gathering. The
planning is done by asking the King before the meeting,
what do you want on the agenda? Who do you want leading
the worship? Who do you want speaking? Those who lead
are under His leadership.

"You can tell when someone has written their own
agenda without consulting God. They don't start the
meeting with thanksgiving, praise, or worship. They say a
prayer asking God to bless their plans and then start
presenting their plans. You can have a plan done in his
name that has God's hand nowhere on it. God's plans and
agenda have room for God. They aren't just thing done in
his name. Praise matters. Do we recognize the King and do
we invite him into our gatherings? I've seen more healings
this summer than I have in the last four years because of
one simply change. When I'm speaking, the songs

immediately before I step on stage will be: *God is Good* and *Come, Holy Spirit*. The one who is singing them the deepest from the heart is going to be me, every time."

"Thanks for that, Noah."

"I'm not very eloquent in describing it yet. God wants me to understand praise, so that's what we've been focused on recently." He tugged out extra napkins he had picked up with the popcorn and offered her a couple as they'd both gone heavy on the melted butter and salt. "How is the battery work going?"

"Very well. I had my second meeting with Bryce to talk through the plans for when I show it to the university. He's been working on the business side of it, researching the industry and what the licensing might look like. Bryce is to business like Gina is to science. He simply understands it. He's been very helpful to have involved."

"He's a good guy."

"You've been friends with him for a long time."

Noah nodded. "He's the guy I do life with most other than Frank. If I'm not hearing clearly from God what to do in a situation, Bryce is often who God uses to speak into the matter for me. We share a passion for teaching about Jesus, so we're helpful to each other in practical ways, with books and resources and ideas."

"Did that friendship change when he married Charlotte?"

"Sure. It's good for him to be married. He's happy in a deep way. We don't see each other as often as we once did but we probably talk as often. Friendships adapt."

"I was thinking I'd like to also get Charlotte a gift as a thank you for the time Bryce has been investing to help me. Would you have any suggestions?"

"She needs a new chair for her art studio, one like Mark has at BSR, with all those adjustable levers. She was commenting on it on the fourth. I don't think she's followed through getting one yet."

"That's practical and perfect." Emily handed him her popcorn so she could pull out her phone and make a note of it.

The Physical Sciences Building was ahead of them.
"Going to work more tonight?"

"Another hour or two. Where are you off to this
weekend?"

"Tennessee to speak at a men's gathering. It's a late
addition to my summer calendar."

"I hope it's a good gathering. I'll let you know about
Texas before you go." She took back her nearly empty
popcorn sleeve. "Thanks for the walk."

"I hope that wasn't your dinner."

She laughed but didn't deny it. "I'll order in
something later, or stop on the way home. Safe travel,
Noah."

"See you, Emily."

She disappeared into the building and he walked on
toward his car. They weren't such intense conversations
any more but they were just as valuable to him. When he
didn't see her, he missed her. If he had his choice, he'd
spend his life with her. He had a date planned for the two of
them, to see if she wanted to change what this was from a
friendship to exploring something more in a formal way.
He just knew the value of time. They needed more casual
time together first. He wasn't sure what kind of answer he
would get from her. And until he had a better sense of that,
walks like this one were all good first steps.

18

The curriculum for the two new courses he had been working on this summer was nearly complete. Noah closed the binder with the latest iterations of study notes he would use as handouts, pleased with the progress. He had a two p.m. appointment to talk with a graduate student about his thesis topic and a five p.m. dinner meeting with Jason and Connie to talk about the concert tour Jason was planning for next year. He was making some introductions for them with pastors he knew in the cities they were targeting. He had a trip to Texas with Emily coming up, she'd taken him up on his invitation, and then a final exam to write for his summer class. He kept his life organized out of necessity but this year was going smoother than most.

His office phone rang. Emily was calling from her university extension.

"Hey, Emily." They'd shared breakfast at the faculty club a few hours ago. She had her fourth meeting with Bryce scheduled for this evening and was planning to meet with the university staff to officially reveal the existence of her battery design the final week of August. So far the people she'd told about the battery and those who had seen it numbered less than five. By early September, the whole world was likely to know about it. Noah could predict the University would have a public press conference to announce the patent filing and her discovery of a new type of battery as soon as it could be scheduled. It would be good publicity for the start of the fall semester.

"I just got a call from Austin University. They'd like me to come down and meet with the President. I told them I had plans to be in Austin on the 17th so we made the appointment for that afternoon."

Their upcoming trip to Austin just took on an entirely different light. "God was planning ahead the details for you." She was getting a job offer to take her a thousand miles away. And on that thought Noah stopped his emotions until after this phone call was concluded.

"I wasn't expecting the call."

He leaned back in his chair and had to smile. "They would be overlooking someone major if they didn't offer you the job, Emily."

"They're making the call because of the firework success."

"Probably. You were a teacher there for seven years, they know your skill in the classroom and with students. Now they've seen what else you are capable of accomplishing and they want to see what's possible."

"It feels like I just got jarred hard by God. I know this has been out there since the sabbatical started, but I wasn't seriously thinking about this being a possible avenue. I figured they would have made their decision by now, not still be interviewing candidates."

"Go and listen," Noah advised. "This is the kind of thing God uses to change your course or solidify your present location or just show you new avenues to think about. It's a good thing, Emily. God has something in mind for you."

"He's doing something. You were first I wanted to call. Next up is Gina. She's been actively praying they wouldn't invite me for an interview I think, so I'm going to be adding some stress to her day."

"You've been long distance friends before. You two will make your friendship work whatever happens. So will you and I. Don't fret about it. Just keep an open mind."

"Thanks, Noah."

He hung up the phone after the call ended and let himself feel the emotions. "She's moving God? Really? Austin University would be blundering if they didn't offer her the job." He let himself feel that intense disappointment for about a minute and then intentionally stopped his train of thought. Capturing every thought to obedience to Christ meant not getting disappointed when a turn appeared in life that wasn't to his liking. He couldn't see what God did and knew that. He had to trust it, he had to or life became about what only he could see. "Okay. Whatever you have planned, God, that's what I'm going to choose to be comfortable with. If this is the job Emily needs, then I want them to offer it to her."

It was the absolutely wrong prayer for where his emotions were but the right one for where his relationship with God had to remain. Trust didn't show itself until the circumstance cost him something.

If she needed to be in Austin, he'd help with that transition however he could. Distance was hard on a relationship trying to find its footing but it wasn't insurmountable. He was living a very long time. And he was determined to let God sort out what that future looked like for him. He'd been thinking about marriage. That was a major change in his own thinking. Emily was going through a few major changes of her own. Topics that hadn't been present for either of them at the first of the summer were being stirred up. This was just another step in something already going on.

Noah saw one silver lining. At least this would force their relationship onto more solid ground. Nothing happened with distance involved that was not intentional. If he needed to travel to Texas because she was there he had plenty of airline miles in his travel account to spend on the tickets. They would figure this out. The peace about one thing was steady. God had introduced him to Emily to start this summer. Noah didn't plan to end the summer by saying goodbye.

****

Noah unlocked the trunk of his car. Emily had one mid-size suitcase and her purse. "You pack light."

"Habit. If I need something, I'll buy it there."

He had a garment bag and suitcase, his briefcase and a carry-on bag. It was standard for any trip, refined down from long experience regarding what he might need when speaking. He added her luggage to his. Emily had been flying frequently this summer so O'Hare wasn't going to be new to her but Noah wasn't sure how much she enjoyed the experience of flying. She'd talk about her trips but not much about the journey west itself. "Our flight leaves at three. Once we check-in and get through security, we'll likely have an hour of time to fill. The frequent flyer lounge has comfortable seating or we can plane watch, there's good viewing of the runways from the taxiway restaurant."

"Either suits me. I'm tagging along with you. That's the definition of relaxed travel."

"In that case, I'll show you some of my O'Hare airport favorite spots and introduce you to some people who work there. I've been coming and going from O'Hare for years. It's like any established community of people. I've gotten to know some people I see on a regular basis."

On the drive to the airport, since he wasn't sure if Emily was looking forward to Austin or feeling tentative about it, he chose to avoid the subject entirely. Instead, he asked about her meeting with Bryce, catching up with her on what he had recommended.

"The university side of this looks like it will be much like the fireworks patent. It's the licensing that is unique. I'm patenting a battery type, the chemistry and physics of it, but every manufacturer is going to use what I've done as a starting point for their own designs, a power company may build a huge version of my jelly donut, while a laptop designer may need a long tube variation. It's heat and the solid to liquid to solid again sequence with magnetic fields involved which is the science. The rest is packaging."

"For the fireworks, you're being paid based on the numbers manufactured. Will this be similar?"

"I get so much per battery manufactured, or an annual licensing fee – Bryce has some ideas in mind along those lines. It's initially going to be a development license so companies can explore what they want to do regarding trying to bring something to market. Whoever can get to market first with a battery for your phone that doesn't need recharged is going to seize a good deal of market share from its later competitors. As I'm already walking around with a stable prototype of what they will be refining and taking through the certification and manufacturing process. Bryce is thinking three years for the first batteries to reach market.

"The fireworks have a licensing manager, someone who handles the annual accounting and worldwide certifications. There was a worldwide industry of about a hundred companies which make up the bulk of all firework manufacturing, which made it a manageable client universe to work with. For the fireworks, I was seeking patent protection in several countries with that protection based on the US patent.

"The battery is a similar process, only magnified. This will need a team of people involved in the licensing management simply because of the scale of how many businesses are going to find the patent useful. There are companies who can handle a worldwide patent filing. From the day I file for the US patent until the paperwork process gets completed around the world, we're realistically talking five years. Manufacturers will be working under a patent pending arrangement in most territories."

"When these batteries begin to appear, there won't be a person in the world who doesn't want your battery in their phone or laptop. No more charging a battery? That's revolutionary."

"Hence Bryce's question about how I want to handle things long term. Gina runs her designs primarily through the Navy and government contracts, the first one she commercialized was the rocket done within BSR. As she has more ideas she might want to commercialize, BSR is there as a company which can help her manage them. Bryce wants to know if I want to go to a similar arrangement.

"Right now I develop ideas under a research contract with the university. I use their facilities, resources and time to explore ideas and they get a percentage of any licensing fees from what I patent or otherwise market. Bryce wants to know if I want to set up a company through which I can flow whatever designs I come up with in the future.

"The teaching side of my contract is annual and covers a fall, spring and summer session. The research contract renews every three years, so the university can change my status from tenured research professor back to tenured professor based on their assessment of how much I'm costing them versus what I'm producing in research value. Given the firework patents, it's a formality it would be renewed, but that existing research contract ends this month. Which is why I wanted to finalize the battery package and present it to the university by the end of August just to put a bow on the work done to date. It leaves a clear slate for what the future should look like."

Noah had been around the university long enough he understood the research designation and how it operated as well as anyone who actually was a research professor. "What's your cap arrangement with the university? Five times your expenses?"

"Yes. After that their percentage of the licensing fees drops to five percent in perpetuity."

"As most research doesn't have significant commercial value that contract is in general terms a fair deal. They came out very well with the fireworks. They're going to make a fortune with this battery."

"I don't mind benefiting the university. I've always viewed it as they opened the door and I found something. I could have spent their resources and found nothing."

"You would be wise to simply request an extension of your existing research contract until the end of the year and give yourself time to weigh options. That takes the time pressure off the decision. You'll have ample goodwill with the university to come up with a new agreement which accommodates what you want the future to look like."

"If you were in my place, what would you do, Noah?"

The airport exit was half a mile ahead. "It's an interesting decision. Let me come back to that question when we're at our next lull in this journey." Unsaid was the very real possibility it would be a moot point if she was offered and accepted the Austin University job, though she'd have to come to some similar arrangement with that university regarding future research. He just didn't know what their starting offer for that arrangement might be.

He glanced left and smiled. "Look up. We're about to have a jumbo jet come across us with enough engine wash this car is going to rock." The winds were calm today and air traffic control was bringing flights in east to west taking advantage of the lake as geography for the holding pattern.

The car rocked as the plane passed overhead, the noise loud enough to pause any conversation. Moments later it landed on the runway they could see a corner of around the highway exit sign.

"Okay, that was really cool!"

Noah laughed. "We'll do some plane watching while we're here. They aren't as elegant as a rocket launch but watching a plane that size lift into the air never gets old."

****

He'd booked them first class seats. He liked a comfortable flight when he was speaking the same evening. "The window seat is yours unless you prefer otherwise. Chicago to Texas is a pretty flight as the Mississippi river is below us for much of the flight."

"Thanks." Emily took the window seat.

He stored his carry-on bag and settled in. First class was about half full. People were streaming into business class behind them, mostly business people with a few families in the mix, this particular plane configuration had no economy class seating. They would be at least thirty minutes loading and going through the pre-flight instructions and then sitting on the taxi-way before they would be cleared for takeoff. Emily had mentioned she hadn't flown first class before, but after a few minutes of exploring she'd found all the differences worth noting. The seats were more comfortable and there was more leg room and the in-flight personal video screens had a movie selection list.

Noah resumed their conversation from earlier just to finish the topic before they were in the air. "Your fireworks and the battery are going to generate the cash flow to let you work where you would like on chemistry questions. The question is more – do you still want to teach? There are private chemistry roles. Major labs. Do you have any desire to set up your own business like BSR, to have your own lab and people you choose to hire?

"If you want to teach and research and let others manage what you create, the present arrangement is fundamentally working. You're subcontracting out the patent filing and licensing management to companies which specialize in that work. The university research contract can have a sunset clause added to eliminate the in perpetuity nature of it and be capped by a maximum lifetime payout amount on discoveries. You can negotiate having those clauses made retroactive to the firework and battery patents as a condition for renewing your research contract with the university. You'll have to be more generous in the terms than might otherwise be necessary, but there's an agreeable answer that gets that done. It's more a matter of what you want Emily. This is the window of time you get to decide those fundamental questions."

"I've always thought of myself as a teacher. It seems odd to think about taking on a different role."

"You've always answered that question of who am I with 'I'm a scientist' and 'I'm a chemist.' How much does 'I'm a teacher' sit as a core value of who you are? You love teaching because that's your connection to your parents. You enjoy it. But in God's plan for you there is a close fit and there is a perfect fit. You might be in the ring outside the bull's-eye rather than dead center. The season of life for teaching may have a duration to it and God will call you away from it at some point to spend more time just thinking about chemistry."

"How do you find out those answers?"

"Ask God. Put the questions to Him. He mostly waits until we ask before He answers life questions of that scale."

"I've been talking to God about the future quite a bit but I probably haven't put those basic questions to him in a formal way."

"Do that over the next few weeks and just see what settles in your heart with peace. If there's a major change ahead the one thing you don't want to do is not take the step because of the comfort you have with the present. When God says 'go that way' the smart thing to do is by faith take that risk."

Emily nodded. "That's good advice."

The flight attendants began the basic safety instructions. They pulled away from the gate and the plane began to taxi.

The pilot came on over the speakers. "We're fifth in line for departure so we'll be in the air shortly. Weather in Fort Worth is 91 degrees and sunny. We expect clear skies and favorable winds for the flight and anticipate landing a few minutes early. On behalf of the airline, I'd like to thank you for flying with us."

The plane came to a gentle stop. Out the window Noah could see the plane at the front of the queue turning onto the runway.

"Talk to me about tonight. What's the protocol involved? What are you speaking about?" Emily asked.

She was just a bit nervous about flying, that was interesting. He gave her the distraction she'd requested. "The kingdom of God," he replied. "We'll be met at the airport. Hotel accommodations are within walking distance of the church, its situated within what I'd describe as a rebuilt neighborhood. I'm expecting there will be about 700 in attendance. The program begins at 7 p.m. I'll speak for about thirty minutes then have about forty minutes of Q/A's. After that we'll open it up to a ministry time of prayer and worship. These evenings can run late. Don't feel obligated to stay until I'm free. It can easily be midnight or later before I say goodnight and return to the hotel."

Their conversation paused as the plane turned onto the runway and the engines began to rev up. Emily turned toward the window to watch the ground begin to speed by. Noah felt the nose of the plane come up and there was a sudden weight against his chest pushing him into the seat as the aircraft climbed for altitude.

Emily laughed softly. "Oh, I love the rush of liftoff."

"That's one way to describe it." The plane banked hard to the south to clear the airport airspace. Within a couple minutes the excitement was over and the flight leveled and began a slow climb to cruising altitude. The fasten seatbelt sign turned off.

"I don't like the moments before we get enough speed to liftoff, but flying itself is fun." Emily picked up the conversation where they had left off. "Is there anything in particular you'd like me to do tonight?"

"Smile at my two jokes."

"I can do that for you. I can nod in agreement at appropriate times too."

Noah smiled at her good humor. He was very aware this was the first time Emily would be seeing him speak to a group. She had sat in on two of his classes this summer so she'd seen him with students. But she hadn't been at an event where he was the invited speaker. He didn't want to impress her so much as he simply wanted to show her what it was he did with most of his weekends. This part of his life was very different than the university life he lead. "I'm going to let you enjoy the scenery of the flight and catch a brief nap. It's habit. Evenings like this take a lot of energy. I've learned to simply rest going into them and let the Holy Spirit have space to give me any last minute instructions I need."

"That works for me," Emily agreed. "Do you want anything when they bring around refreshments?"

"Pepsi and whatever chips they have, pretzels are my fallback."

"Okay."

Noah rested his head back against the headrest and closed his eyes, content with how this day had unfolded thus far. It was nice having someone traveling with him. Normally he was politely conversing with a stranger for the first twenty minutes of a flight, then trying not be rude as he tuned them out and took a nap. He turned his thoughts to this evening. 700 people were expected to be in attendance tonight. 'God, what's on your heart for them tonight?' He'd learned to trust God that when speaking, they were working in partnership. He asked the question and simply listened during the flight.

*

19

The words from the songs, *God is Good*, and *Come, Holy Spirit* were still lingering in Noah's mind as he stepped to the podium, more relaxed than normal as he approached a presentation. This one had already been fully turned over to God and the outcome was in God's hands.

"Thank you for that welcome, Peter. It's always an honor to be invited to speak to the congregation you lead. Every time we are together, its as brothers. I hope to honor that friendship tonight with words of encouragement and perspective on a topic we both treasure, the kingdom of God."

Noah didn't bother to try to find Emily in the crowd for the stage lights were bright and somewhat in his eyes. He'd left Emily with Peter's wife, Olivia, the two having bonded over talk of barbeque and Texas football, so she was in good hands and likely now seated somewhere toward the front of the auditorium. The air conditioning had been set to chill the room down in anticipation of this crowd, but under the stage lights he was going to be sweating through his suit jacket before the presentation was over. The house was packed so attendance was closer to eight hundred. It was already a good evening, for God had brought people together to hear the message.

"I'd like to begin tonight by asking you a question. Do you know your King? If you are comfortable calling yourself a Christian, a follower of Jesus, do you know your King?" Noah settled into the topic he had offered in various ways for now a decade.

"As Christians we love Jesus. We come to church to worship God. We desire to obey God and live good lives. But all too often we think in terms of our present life living in a democracy, that obedience is something we chose to do, or occasionally not do, depending on what God has asked of us. We are free people. We love God, but we retain our independence and the right to make up our mind as life unfolds for what we are going to do in any particular situation. As Christians, do we want to choose well and do what God would find right? Yes. But tonight I want to point out a problem in our thinking. We consider our life with God to be an ongoing choice, rather than a one time decision of the heart.

"We are not living in a democracy. The kingdom of God is a King's rule. Your thoughts on will you obey or not – even if you choose obedience – that habit isn't honoring to God. And it is dangerous to you as a Christian. You have not understood you are now a citizen of a kingdom.

"A kingdom has a King and the citizens he rules and the place he rules over. This earth is the Lord's and the fullness of it is his. Jesus has been made King of all heaven and earth. He rules today. All those who have chosen to love Jesus are his citizens.

"Do you know your King?

"Do you desire to obey Jesus because He is your King?

"That is where you must stand as a Christian. I do not retain the choice to disobey. I have laid down my self will. I obey Jesus because He is my King. It is a permanent choice of my heart. Whatever He says, I will do, because He is my King. I am a citizen in His Kingdom. Whether I understand his reasons or his timing or why I have been asked to do something rather than another does not concern me. I have presented myself as a living sacrifice to God. I no longer consider the choice to disobey. A kingdom has only one ruler – the King."

Noah paused there and reached for the water bottle he had brought with him to the podium. He'd flipped the message order and begun with the challenge of obedience, rather than end with it. The crowd was listening but there wasn't a lightness to the atmosphere anymore, God had landed a rebuke to a few people. It had probably been needed, it always was, but it made being the presenter a difficult task.

"Think about this matter of kingdom from another perspective. It exists. It's all around you. Whether you like the fact Jesus is ruling heaven and earth doesn't affect the fact He is. Your opinion in a kingdom has no bearing on the laws, decrees, will or desires of the King. And this kingdom is timeless. Jesus will reign as King forever. That's not good, unless we have a good King. If we do, then that is very good news indeed.

"I'm here tonight to remind you we have a good King. There is no King in all of history who compares to Jesus. He is kind, righteous, loving, and good in every aspect of his rule. He is a trustworthy and faithful King. He takes responsibility for the wellbeing of all his citizens. He sees us and loves us in a very personal way.

"Jesus is like His Father.

"There is a day coming when Jesus will remove all wickedness and causes of sin from his kingdom. It's why we strive so hard to present to everyone the good news that Jesus died on a cross to pay the penalty for every man's sin. Salvation is free. It's already been paid for. But all too often we shorten the message of grace, present following Jesus as a way to avoid hell and attain heaven, but we leave off his full title. To accept Jesus is to accept a King. To accept Jesus is to step into a kingdom.

"As a citizen of the kingdom of God we are now born from above and are no longer of the world. We carry the title Ambassador.

"While he was on earth, Jesus modeled what he is asking of us as his citizens. Jesus was sent by God. Jesus was God's Ambassador to us. Jesus lived in perfect obedience to the one who had sent him. 'I have not spoken on my own authority. The Father who sent me has himself given me commandment what to say and what to speak.' (John 12:49b) Jesus was faithful and true to the one who sent him.

"Jesus is a King. His kingdom is not a democracy. To be a useful citizen, you need to do what he assigns with a willing and cheerful heart, working to the best of your

ability. He's testing the quality of your work. He's testing
your obedience. He's testing your attitude.

"When the King asks you to speak to someone about a
matter, do so as instructed without adding your own
thoughts. He's testing if will you say more than He told you
to say.

"The reason our King Jesus tests us is because he
desires to reward us. He loves to elevate his people, to give
us more and greater responsibilities and assignments to
carry out representing his kingdom. He calls us
Ambassadors. Let us be faithful as Jesus was faithful.

"Do you honor other citizens of the kingdom? Are you
as kind as your King? As loving as your King? Do you do
what you say you will? The King is looking for those
whose words match up with their actions. Are you making
yourself useful to the King?

"When you are serving with a humble heart your
brothers and sisters in the kingdom it is the King, God
himself, who is watching you. There is nothing you do
which goes unnoticed. That is a good thing. Jesus promises
us rewards for what we have done on earth which will last
for eternity. But we must choose. We must lay down
deciding if we will obey our King and settle it in our hearts
once for all that kingdom living means obedience to the
King, always, with a cheerful and willing attitude. To do
less is to dishonor our King."

Noah began to shift to the close of his message only to
have the Holy Spirit check him and bring him back to the
opening point again. In obedience, Noah returned to hit the
opening point more forcefully.

"To obey because we've concluded we agree with an
instruction is to place ourselves above our King. To think
we know better than King Jesus what is the right thing to
do and the right timing to do it is sin. To place ourselves
above our King in our thinking is to be as satan himself,
who desired to set his throne on high, to make himself like
the Most High. Obedience as citizens of the kingdom of
God is for our own protection, it is our only defense against

what caused satan to fall and Adam to fall. We must accept
we have a King. To question our King's rule is to step back
into lawlessness. To reject Him is to choose death. So I ask
you again tonight, Do you know your King?"

He didn't need the notes for this message but turned
the pages on the podium to let his words have time to sink
into people's thoughts.

"What is the King's business? Righteousness. People.
Honor.

"Jesus is God. That is why we trust him as our King.
Jesus knows all about life on earth. He has been tempted in
every way and yet never sinned. Jesus is the first fully good
man to ever walk the earth. That's our King. He is
righteous from his heart. There is liberty in the choice to
follow him, to obey always.

"God is big. Bigger than the universe. God is also
small. God became small enough to fit inside Mary's belly.
God is with you. God's spirit abides in you. God says come
apart from the world, sanctify yourself, be holy as I am
holy, not because He's trying to take away your fun but
because he's trying to give you what true life really is. The
God of the universe has come to you. He wants a
relationship with you. He will never leave you nor forsake
you. You will have to walk by faith and risk obedience to
find out just how truly good Jesus is. The only way to know
is to taste and see.

"So answer his call, take him up on his invitation.
Don't stiff arm him. Don't grieve him by thinking you
know better than him. Let Jesus rule your life. He is with
you in every situation and knows every detail of what is
happening better than you. Trust your King. Be fearless
around people. Honor your King. Value your King and his
kingdom over what the world may think or say.

"Be with people. Don't be with people with an
agenda. Be kind. Be nice. When a topic comes to mind, go
with it. Let God help you love people. Don't over think
ahead of time what to say. You'll say what's on your mind
rather than let God guide the conversation from your heart.

Tell your story of life with the King when someone asks.

"The King's assignment to you will be filled with actions focused on loving your neighbors. Let the King set your agenda and your timing and your plans. He knows what people around you need. As a practical example, honor a child because he loved Jesus. Take him for ice cream because he likes ice cream. Take him to a ballgame. Not with an agenda to teach him something about God. Simply honor the fact he is your brother in Christ and you'll spend eternity with him. So treat him as family now. Young or old, we are family and citizens of one kingdom. That's what it means to love one another.

"Your King invites you to his table, to listen to his wisdom, hear his instructions and receive honor and rewards, both in this lifetime and the age to come." Noah picked his bible. "Your King would like to talk with you. King Jesus bears the name The Word of God. Ask where to read and when a book and chapter comes to mind, start reading with a listening ear. Come every morning. Your life will show the results. On earth as it is in heaven. That's what King Jesus will bring to your life today if you listen and obey. Citizens of the kingdom, I ask you a final time tonight, do you know your King? Whatever you must change in your life to do so, make those changes. Make it your priority to get to know your King."

Noah chose to end the message there. The worship leader took the podium as applause that fell between polite and accepting of the message rose from the congregation. Noah noted it but had long since learned to not response to it as the value on what he'd accomplished. He returned to his seat on the left side of the stage.

His mic now off as the music began, Noah leaned toward Peter to be heard, "tougher than I had planned," he said, not in apology, but in recognition of what had happened.

Peter shook his head and leaned over in like manner to reply. "You were speaking to people I can name. They weren't listening to that word from me. If they're still resisting what was said after this, God's likely to have to put pressure directly on some hard hearts."

Noah sincerely hoped his message had been heard. Free now to scan the crowd, he looked across the gathering. He spotted Emily just off the center aisle. It was the first time they'd been in a worship service together. He'd deliberately not changed his Sunday morning routine to join her at Lake Christian Church and their travel schedules hadn't left a Friday night open for them to attend a Jason Lasting concert together. She appeared to genuinely like to sing which was good to discover.

Peter accepted a note from one of his staff, scanned it and nodded. He leaned over. "I have two special requests this evening. I've got a blind lady I'd like for you to pray for during the ministry time, her name is Catherine. She believes, her sister doesn't. And I'd like you to spend five minutes talking with a young man named Brad Lewis. I'm not saying more by way of introduction or reason why. It should be obvious and I don't want to color your opinion."

Noah nodded, neither request that unusual from Peter.

Peter rose as the Worship leader brought the fifth song to a close and moved to the podium. "Thank you for offering that heartfelt praise to God, it's a beautiful sound in this packed house. Would the elders and staff please come to the front to pray for people during this next ministry time. Thank you. We're going to stand as a congregation and continue to sing and worship together. As we do so, would those desiring prayer come forward using the center aisle, that way people can return to their seats by the outside aisles. For those who have children in children's worship who would like to bring them into the auditorium for this part of the service, please feel free to do so. For those who need to depart at this time, I wish to thank you for attending this evening's program and I hope to see you again on Sunday."

As the congregation stood, Noah left the stage and walked over to join Emily. "There's going to be a crowd at the front as people come forward for prayer. I've been asked to join them as one praying for people. Peter is going to stand with me to make introductions to people. You're welcome to move around the auditorium, come stand with me, or head back to the hotel, its going to be a casual evening from here on. Just let Olivia know if you can't get to me."

Because the music was beginning for the next song Emily didn't try to give more than an answering nod and a smile. The center aisle was already filling with people. Noah moved to join Peter.

****

The auditorium was loud with music and song, overlapping conversations, the worship leader doing a good job guiding the five hundred or so people still present in worship. The prayer lines were still long after the first hour.

"This is MaryAnn and her husband Gary, her son Joel," Peter said in introduction. The woman was blind from the way she used her husband's arm for guidance and was looking slightly left of where he stood.

Because Peter had added no qualifiers to the introduction, Noah knew the woman had been a believer for some time and approached their conversation accordingly. "Hi, MaryAnn. I'm Noah. May I take your right hand?" She offered her hand and he took it in both of his so she had a sense of where he stood. "What would you like Jesus to do for you tonight?"

"I want my sight back. I want to see my family."

"Jesus has opened a lot of blind eyes and he loves that request. I want you to close your eyes and let me do the praying. If your thoughts want to find words, I want you to dwell on the phrase Jesus loves me. Are you okay with that?"

"Yes."

"I'd also like you to leave your eyes closed even after I've prayed until I give you instruction to open them. Are you good with that too?"

"Yes."

"Jesus, this is my sister in the faith, MaryAnn. She would like her sight back tonight. We are in agreement for this request. I now speak to this affliction and its cause in your name Jesus. Spirit of blindness come out of MaryAnn right now, in Jesus' name. Eyes, be open and see clearly, in Jesus' name. Thank you for healing her eyes, God, by the power of your Holy Spirit. Thank you for blessing her, Father. Receive your sight, MaryAnn." He lightly squeezed her hand as he concluded the prayer. "Leave your eyes closed for now. In your imagination let yourself see yourself with sight. See yourself doing what you want to do because you can see. When you feel peace in your heart, you feel yourself relax, like a dove settles down and rests, then open your eyes. We've all the time in the world, just dwell on the phrase Jesus loves me and let the peace in your heart rule in this matter. The Holy Spirit will let you know when to open your eyes. All is finished."

She nodded and remained with her eyes closed for a minute before cautiously opening them. He'd seen so many blind eyes open he knew the answer before he asked. "What do you see now, MaryAnn?"

"You."

He grinned. "You should look at someone better than me." He turned her gently toward her husband and son. "Meet Gary and Joel."

"Oh."

The tears streaming down her face were going to make it hard for her to see but they were perfect tears.

"Did her eyes really just open?" Emily leaned in to whisper, startled.

"You haven't seen blind eyes open before, have you?"

"No."

"Cool, isn't it?"

"Oh, yeah."

"Welcome to the kingdom, Emily."

As spectacular as the miracle was it wasn't the first one this evening, nor would it likely be the last. Noah was still waiting for Catherine to come forward for prayer. On the other side of the auditorium deafness had been dealt with. A child with club feet was now walking normally. They had watched a woman suffering from a stroke regain clear speech and a gentleman walking with a cane be able to stand straight for the first time in a decade. Faith was steady in this church that God healed and they were seeing it happen.

Noah thought it a safe enough environment to simply throw Emily in the deep end. "Why don't you pray for the next person?"

"Me? I might mess it up."

"You can't. Jesus is a good King. You learn by doing with him. Just dwell in your thoughts on Jesus loves me and Jesus loves the person in front of me. Then do and say what comes to mind. It works every time."

"Let me watch some more first."

He grinned. "Jesus, tell Emily to have courage before the night is done to heal the sick."

She struck his ribs with her elbow in mild protest of him having said a prayer that put her in the corner like that. Noah smiled and simply gave her the basic instructions he did everyone he taught. "If it's a demon, tell it to leave. If its made of dust and water, tell it what to do. If you're not sure which needs done, do both. You are under the authority of King Jesus and with authority in Jesus' name. Heal the sick is a standing command of the kingdom of God. There is no sickness in heaven. Command it to be on earth as it is in heaven."

"That's what you're doing?"

"Yes. Start with a child. They expect what you say to happen. God won't leave you in the lurch. Just listen and follow the instructions the Holy Spirit gives you. Faith is the courage to act. So step out and act."

****

Emily watched as Noah prayed for Catherine, watched

as a woman blind since birth saw for the first time. His prayer was similar to before with an added command this time for her eyes to be created new and to open for the first time. The sister beside Catherine let out more of a moan and shriek than a cry of joy, not sure of what to think of what was happening. The delight and wonder on Catherine's face couldn't be masked. She had never seen before. She had to feel a face to connect what she was seeing with what she had learned by hearing and touch only. The kingdom of God was delivering the blind tonight. Emily realized tears were tracing down her own cheeks and dashed them away.

A tug on her pant leg had Emily looking down.

"I want to see like she does," a child protested. She was maybe six, holding a white cane, her other hand securely in the hand of a man who was probably her grandfather.

Emily knelt down before she realized she was moving and immediately felt off balance. Was she suppose to help in this situation or get Noah's attention? He was still involved in a conversation with Catherine and her sister. The child had some vision because she was clearly frustrated by what she was seeing happen, that it wasn't her. "I'm Emily."

"Kayla. I can't see out of this eye because a horse kicked me," she tapped the right side of her face, "and the other one is fuzzy. I want to see like she does."

"I could pray for you."

"You can pray as well as he can? Cause everybody on that side of the room can't help me."

Emily felt her confidence land in the mud. Of course this child had been prayed for many times. Noah had said find some courage and pray for a child. Kayla clearly expected Jesus to heal her. Into that mixed reality she had a choice. "I can pray for you like Noah can. Trust me."

The child looked hard at her face and then nodded. She held up her cane to her grandfather. "I won't need this anymore."

Emily grinned and held out her hand. "May I hold your hand, Kayla?"

The child's hand felt sticky and warm but it was comfortable too.

"I want you to close your eyes and think Jesus loves me and I'll do the praying. Okay with that?"

Kayla nodded and closed her eyes.

"Jesus, this is Kayla. She wants to see like Catherine does. I want that for her too. I now speak to her eyes in your name Jesus. Eyes, be open, in Jesus' name. Amen." She waiting ten seconds. "Now open your eyes. Can you see anything? Is there any change you are noticing?"

Kayla slapped her hand over her good eye to try just her blind one.

"Nothing."

"Jesus has opened your eyes. Someone is stealing your sight and they must go. Let me pray again." Emily took Kayla's hand. "Spirit of blindness, come out of my sister Kayla right now, in Jesus' name."

"It feels funny."

"Yeah?"

"Someone is tickling my eyelashes."

Emily said the only thing which came to mind. "Close your eyes, count to ten then open your eyes."

The child obediently did so.

When she reached ten she opened her eyes and immediately grinned. "I can see you like a real face!" She danced around to see her parents. "Hi, mom! Daddy!" She giggled. "Your beard is really white grandpa."

It took a minute to corral Kayla into standing still so Emily could ask her questions. "Hand over your left eye, how many fingers am I holding up?"

The child promptly complied. "Two," she giggled.

"Hand over your right eye, what am I holding?"

"A tootsie roll."

Emily offered it.

"Do you have one I can give Jesus too?"

Emily tugged another one from her pocket.

Emily glanced over and realized Noah was watching their conversation. She figured he deserved one too and dug out another one. That had been way easier than she thought. She wanted to do it again and looked back in the line of people coming to be prayed for hoping there was someone else blind. She stood and realized Noah was grinning, aware of what she had been thinking. He'd been hiding the fun he'd been having all summer. Oh, she had questions for him now.

****

They walked back to the hotel just after midnight.

"This is what you do on trips. You heal people."

Noah unwrapped the tootsie roll she had given him, not having had a free moment to do so earlier. "Yes. People can heal themselves by knowing the word of God, they just haven't grasped that yet, so Jesus lets me help people and to teach others how to do it too. Blindness is sort of my thing. I haven't ever had blind eyes not open at least partially. It's what makes it easier to handle any other need. God loves to heal people. I'm just putting that in words for people with the confidence that what I say is what is going to happen."

"It's been a couple hours since I saw Kayla's eyes open and its still mostly wonder that God let me pray for her. It's not like I chose her. She came tugging on me. She had more faith God wanted to heal her eyesight than I did."

"She can see because you two cooperated with each other. She wanted the gift of healed eyes and she was willing to listen to what you said and do it by faith. You were Jesus' delegated authority in her life. By following your instructions, what she was doing was following what Jesus was asking her to do. All Jesus needed was that open door of faith and obedience to get her healing to her."

"I'm glad you pushed me."

"How many people did you pray for after Kayla?" he asked, curious.

"Eleven."

"You didn't see another visible miracle tonight."

"Nothing significant, no."

"Why the difference?"

Emily looked at him, puzzled.

"What did you observe? There's no right or wrong answer, just give me what you noticed."

"The eleven were all adults. Most had several things they wanted prayer for. I was a lot less certain what to pray. It was arthritis and knee problems and the effects from a stroke, things like that."

"'In Jesus' name, I command life reign in this body.' Or a variation, 'In Jesus' name, I abolish death in this person. I command them be filled with life.' You're looking for something powerful enough to shatter whatever the ailment is. Life can do it. Life is the source of health."

"That's useful."

"Many of those you prayed for tonight will show they are healed in a few days if they stay thanking God for healing them, rather than begin grumbling that they weren't healed. Life and death are in the power of the tongue. People don't realize most of the time the problem is simply what they are saying. 'God, thank you for giving life to my mortal body. I am blessed with health.' – if you would say that and mean it every morning and night and anytime in between when something hurts, its amazing how much health you would walk in. Life is what heals us. God gives us life, we have to agree so we can walk full of life. Healing isn't complicated, it just takes steady simple childlike faith that God has given us life."

"How'd you learn to pray for people to heal them?"

"Practice. Desire to be useful to God. The constant request as I would look around a crowd, 'Is there someone here we can heal?' God wants to heal everyone. He knows who is receptive to his help on any particular night. Jesus would teach, preach about the kingdom of God, and then heal people. He was basically saying 'I'm the Messiah you've been waiting for, I'm him, the kingdom of God is here, now let me show you what the kingdom of God looks like.' And he'd promptly heal everyone who came to him of every disease. What he wants us to do as his Ambassadors is straightforward – heal the sick, raise the dead, cast out demons, cleanse lepers, and tell people about the kingdom of God. We're to do the works Jesus did. The Father releases healing for someone through us, just as he did through Jesus. The courage to step out and speak is faith."

"When did you see your first miracle of blind eyes open?"

"I was 28. I was praying for people after a service in Detroit. She was an elderly lady who loved to play the piano, still did so by memory even though she couldn't see the keys or the sheet music. I said a long and wandering prayer, but pretty much have it memorized now because I wrote it down afterwards.

"'Deloris, I don't know what's wrong with your eyes, but Jesus does. So Jesus, I ask in your name for you to heal her eyes right now so she can see the piano and read music again. I speak to this mountain of blindness and I declare Jesus took this blindness away when he became a curse on our behalf. Blindness is listed as a curse of the law and it has been completely taken away. My sister is under the grace of God and is blessed with good eyesight. Deloris will see right now in Jesus' name. Amen.'

"Her sight was fuzzy when she opened her eyes but it had improved so she sat down at the piano and started in on praise music and her eyesight just kept getting clearer until she was telling people to get her the small print bible so she could read out of Leviticus and prove she could see it. We had a good time that evening, celebrating. She kissed my forehead when the evening was done and declared I was a good young Christian man and I should go do that for some more blind folks. And I wisely said I will."

"I love that, Noah."

"Her blessing is probably why the blind keep seeing. Every time I pray for blind eyes I'm remembering Deloris."

"I'll be remembering Kayla for a lifetime," Emily agreed. "You're as popular a speaker as my parents. I recognized the general feel of the day. The reception committee waiting to greet you, the pre-selected group to take you to dinner, the way you were introduced to the audience. They offered well-deserved honor. How are you handling the fame?"

Noah smiled. "With kid gloves."

"You were sort of mobbed once MaryAnn received her eyesight."

Noah nodded. "The man of God coming as a special guest, blind eyes opening, people assume I have something special to offer. What was happening was much more simple. They showed me honor. And God blessed them for it. If they would show Peter the same honor each Sunday, they would be healed when he prays for them. God's delegated authority in a church is the elders and pastor, an enormous amount of anointing rests upon them because of the roles they are in. God will bless those who honor authority, its why he commands children to honor their parents, honor is something we are to learn to do from a very young age because it carries with it a blessing. Jesus couldn't heal people in his home town of Nazareth, not because the power of God wasn't present with him to heal, but because they showed him no honor. They rejected who he was, the Messiah, and thus rejected the Holy Spirit with him. Jesus marveled at their unbelief. They didn't receive him as the Christ, the Anointed One, so they were not blessed by his presence. Their lack of honor blocked their ability to receive a blessing from him."

"Is that why you're not known around the university as someone who prays and heals people?"

Noah debated how to answer her. "Around the university I handle matters differently. I tell those who experience a healing not to tell others what has occurred. They are free to suggest someone come see me, that I'll pray for whatever ailment is going on to be healed. But I ask them not to share the fact they themselves were healed when I prayed for them."

"Why?"

"Someone who wants Jesus to heal them will receive the suggestion, 'have Professor Shepherd pray for you', and will take it to heart and track me down. They're Kayla, ready to be healed. My prayer is already mostly answered because they have faith, they just need help with some knowledge of how to pray or what to ask. Jesus heals people. I'm useful to him. But someone needs to want to be healed. If its out there that I can heal cancer, people are thinking there's something about me that is special and are looking at me rather than Jesus. Nothing is going to happen. When I'm traveling like this, people are coming forward wanting to be healed, the expectations and faith are high so healings can happen. When I speak in Jesus' name its being received. They expect my prayers to work. They don't realize Peter could have prayed and healed them two months ago if they would come forward with that same expectation and faith."

"It's not the messenger, it's the person coming to receive."

"Yes. You have the same faith the Apostle Peter did. The same anointing. Peter walked along and people got healed when his shadow passed over them. You have the same faith Paul did. The same anointing. When they sent a sweat band Paul wore to someone who was sick, the person was healed. Why? People saw Peter and Paul as carrying something from God and expected to be healed. They had faith to receive from them. With you, with me, we pass sick people all the time and nothing happens. No one expects to touch us and get healed, so they don't. If I pray for you and you expect my prayer to yield a result it will. If you don't think my prayer will do anything, it won't. I'm showing faith in Jesus by praying for you. You're showing faith in Jesus by expecting to receive healing. I can't be your faith and you can't be mine. But when we are in agreement with what we ask, God has a free open door to give us what we've asked. God wants to heal. He simply needs faith expressed by people so he can."

"I want to hang around more when you're praying with people and just watch what is going on because I'd love to be steadily doing what I saw you doing."

"You're welcome too. Connie August, she's doing much the same thing. Her words are different, but it's the same basic action. Tell a demon to leave. Tell things made of dust and water – our bodies – what to do. Speak in Jesus' name, his authority. Expect what you say to happen. That's how you do anything in the kingdom. You speak what is to happen and expect it to be done. The Holy Spirit, God, causes it to happen. You speak to a sycamore tree and it obeys you. Creation itself will obey your words because you are a child of God."

They were standing outside talking rather than enter the hotel, so Noah turned the topic to something he wanted to know to end this evening. "Do I dare risk asking how I did with the message?"

"You give a nice talk. It's like a simplified summary of what you've been trying to help me understand this summer only said with more bluntness. I noticed there were no jokes though. I loved the worship service which followed as you were praying for people."

"I noticed you like to sing."

"It's sort of my language, music. I enjoy it."

"The Holy Spirit reordered the message for tonight on the flight down. He cut out about a third, including the jokes. It wasn't the tone he wanted for the evening."

"Does that happen often?"

Noah thought about it. "It happens more now than it did in prior years. I've got a lot of material I'm comfortable with so I think the Holy Spirit changes messages around depending on the people who will be in the crowd."

Noah held the hotel lobby door for her. "It's a short flight to Austin. We can be there within the hour. Or we can stay overnight and leave here tomorrow morning."

"Let's head to Austin. I'm still awake."

Noah had hoped she would say that as he needed

another hour to unwind. Tonight had taken all the energy he had to give, but the replay in his mind wasn't going to settle until he'd thought back through what he needed to learn from tonight. There were always details he wanted to ask the Holy Spirit about, things to change, things to notice. He was doing these evenings for his own benefit as well as the crowd. To miss that debrief with God would be to miss the best part of the night personally.

*

20

They met in the lobby of the Austin Hotel at nine a.m. Emily looked like she had slept well and Noah relaxed at that fact. "So what's on the agenda for today? The plan for these two days is whatever you would like to do."

Emily promptly tugged out a list and Noah laughed. She was well prepared for that question.

"A breakfast taco, a drive past my parents home and my grandmother's place because I'm curious what's changed, then lunch with good barbeque. I'll take you to little Franklin's. It's a BBQ place owned by a cousin to those who run Franklin's BBQ. My meeting at the university is at four. We can explore the campus for a while around that. Then I'll take you to meet some college friends of mine at a local music festival, we'll find an outdoor table and some good Mexican food for dinner."

Noah thought it sounded perfect and said so.

Emily looked relieved at that approval. "Tomorrow I'd like to spend it at around Lady Bird Lake, feed some ducks, walk some trails, find a good food truck for a casual lunch. We can watch the bat exodus from under Congress Avenue Bridge at dusk if you'd like so you can say you've seen it."

"That's got an eerie and fascinating sound to it, so I'm game. I like these two days before they've even begun. I'll be able to say I've seen Austin." She was dressed for their day in Austin wearing jeans, boots, cowboy hat and lime green knit top. She looked comfortable. "Put in the mix its time I bought a decent pair of real boots and a cowboy hat. I want my version of memories for this trip."

"I know the place," Emily replied promptly, "just close your eyes to the price and let those on staff who know what they're doing make some recommendations."

"I can do that." He tugged out keys. "I've got us a car arranged. You're welcome to drive as you know the town's traffic better than I do."

"Sure." She accepted the keys he offered. "Would you like food truck or sit down restaurant for the breakfast taco?"

"I'll trust your choice."

"Then let's start with a walk around this block, I'll point out some landmarks and choose a place to eat."

They headed out of the hotel to start their day.

****

"That's my grandmother's home. The ranch with the long front porch and the red front door." Emily pulled to the side of the road across the street from it and just soaked in the sight. "The bushes along the porch were half that height when she lived here. We use to sit on that porch and swing on that glide rocker when it was too hot to want to walk on Saturday mornings. But most days we'd make the circuit down to get an iced coffee, then around to the neighborhood park. We'd sit for a bit and then come back here. She always had sweet tea fixed and either iced lemon cookies or sugar cookies with sprinkles on them. She made both for her husband every weekend and she refused to give up that tradition. I remember this place for the joy it gave her and that she gave to it. She'd put out lights at Christmas and there would be bunnies at Easter and chocolates for the neighborhood kids and for the Fourth of July it would look all red, white and blue with bunting around the porch and flags of all sizes. She was growing old but she was living younger every year. She liked life."

Emily smiled and put the car back in gear. "The place still looks like her, more plain than when she left it, but hers."

Emily left the neighborhood and circled southwest into what looked like an older section of Austin but more wealthy, larger yards, older trees, brick homes which had a more formal architecture, many with columns on the porch.

"That's my parents home, the one with the flag pole they added out front. It's nice to see the new owners kept that tradition."

The US flag and a Texas State flag were fluttering in the breeze. The house sat on an acre of land and had a sloping lawn with several shade trees. It was a statesman home with probably four bedrooms on the second floor, a formal living room and office on the main level. A kid's bike was in the drive and the side yard had a swing and climbing set next to what looked like a volleyball net.

"I'm glad its now a family with kids. I sold it to an older gentleman who's sister lived in the neighborhood."

"Where did you live, Emily?"

"Closer downtown, near the college. I'll show you this afternoon."

Noah thought she might pull to the side of the road and stop as she had done at her grandmother's home but after a slow drive by Emily chose to go on. "It is odd to be back here, to drive down familiar roads."

She left the neighborhood and pulled back onto the interstate. "I-35 makes this town easy to navigate as it goes straight through downtown. You're either east or west of I-35, then east or west of the river. The highlight of the day is ahead. Lunch and good BBQ."

"I'm looking forward to the experience."

"I'm sorry I haven't been particularly chatty today."

"I don't mind quiet. I've been watching you remember places as we drive by shops and restaurants and neighborhoods."

"Friends dot Austin, particularly around where my grandmother chose to live. You can still afford a home in some of these neighborhoods on a single person's salary."

She pointed to a corner. "That gas station? I pulled in to get gas one evening and the next thing I know a steer is looking in my driver's side window. He had horns that were about four feet tip to tip. He'd busted the lock on a cattle trailer. We stared at each other equally curious for about a minute and then he went back to eating the flowers along that boundary fence.

"The first rattlesnake I saw was two days later, curled

up on the concrete bench I normally chose to stop at on
Sunday mornings after I picked up bagels and a coffee.
Friends at the college laughed when I told those events as
adventures and promptly hauled me out of town the next
Saturday to a family ranch so I could get up close to a
hundred head of cattle, learn to ride a horse and experience
what an actual adventure was. The land of Texas can be
amazing for what is out there to find. I'd come back with
arrow heads and old musket balls and small skulls of
antelopes and foxes."

"You enjoyed those days."

"It was a break from studying and then from teaching.
And the treasures you would find made good conversation
starters with friends. I passed on my finds as white-elephant
gifts at Christmas parties."

Austin reminded Noah of most cities he had traveled
in, four lanes of traffic, shops, restaurants, auto dealerships,
the business districts with five and ten story businesses,
insurance firms, medical buildings, an abundance of banks.
There were more historical markers than most towns and
frequent signs pointing toward state government buildings.
When he occasionally caught sight of the winding Colorado
river, it reminded him of a narrower version of the
Mississippi river. There was more roll to the land in Austin
than he had been expecting.

As they neared downtown, Emily left the interstate,
drove a mile and turned onto a back road. "He can get away
with a hard to find location because his name is the reason
people hunt him down. It's the only way he can get enough
parking." She pulled into what looked to have once been a
metal scrap yard, the tall crane now fenced and padlocked
beside a metal heap that rivaled a two-story building. In the
center of the parking lot sat a permanently parked food
truck with hog size smokers lined up in a row. A large
circus tent provided shade and picnic tables for seating. The
surrounding parking lot could hold fifty cars and she had to
search to find an open space. "Welcome to Little Franklin's
BBQ."

The line of customers was long, but it moved swiftly. Twenty minutes later Noah was seated at a picnic table with a stack of napkins held down by one of fist sized rocks which dotted the tables, a tall Texas lemonade, and a platter of the house special. Emily had done the ordering. She hadn't needed to do much selling. The smoke from the kettles had been doing the sales job for her.

"What do you think?"

"Okay. This is simply falling apart good." He'd never tasted brisket this good before.

Emily laughed. "It's the wood they smoke it with, the time it sits in the heat, the recipe for the rub. Everything that Texas does with BBQ works because its big scale and not rushed. Good food takes time."

"You've convinced me."

He could honestly say he'd never really tasted BBQ before if this was a sample of what he'd been missing. "I can equate this experience to the first time I ate lobster in Maine. The menu was by the count, did you want two, four or six. Eating one was considered an appetizer. They were steaming the lobsters in a massive pile of seaweed alongside bags of oysters. I'd never tasted seafood that good before."

Emily grinned. "In Texas, it's considered good manners to go back for more."

"I'm thinking I should find room for half a slab of ribs."

She picked up another warm tortilla from the stack with her meal and layered in more pulled pork, rolled it. "I got spoiled by the food, Noah. I arrived on campus, a new place, new people, truly on my own for the first time and I went looking for something to eat mostly looking for comfort. I stopped at the first food truck I saw, which happened to be a Torchy's Tacos, and promptly fell in love with Mexican food and Austin. Here was outdoors that was close by, I could walk and enjoy good food and study this subject that had fascinated me my whole life."

"It became your home. Chicago had always been your

parents home. Austin was yours."

"That's a good description of what it feels like."

"Show me more of it, Emily. Those memories."

She nodded. "I will. Thanks for tagging along for a day like this."

"I'm enjoying it."

****

Austin University reminding him of a quiet community, mostly six-story brick buildings in an orderly square, tall trees, fountains, benches, a large outdoor table area that flowed out of the student campus center.

"I spent the majority of my seven years teaching and the student years before that calling that blue corner table with red chairs my favorite spot. It gets shade and a nice breeze on even the hottest days. Iced drinks are about all you find on campus. You have to have an orange smoothie at least once a week or you're letting down the Texas Orange football crowd.

"The Chemistry department is part of that corner building." Emily pointed it out.

They'd been walking on campus for half an hour now. Her meeting was in twenty-five minutes. She'd up-scaled her wardrobe to a lightweight jacket and dress slacks over a knit top for it. And she was nervous, Noah could hear it in her voice. "I'll meet you here. Go enjoy your meeting, Emily."

"Yeah. I wonder why I came, Noah. It's not like I'm wanting to have the past back. Just walking on campus I'm comparing here to Chicago. This was huge in my thinking when I was here and now it looks small."

He simply turned her toward the administration building they'd passed earlier. "Go to your meeting and listen. Ask good questions. You loved it here. That's still true."

"I may be an hour or more."

"I'll be here."

She nodded and left him.

Noah glanced up. 'Don't ask me to pray what I want to pray. Just give her a good meeting please." There was a bookstore on campus that had looked worth exploring. Noah headed back that direction.

He was drinking an orange smoothie and had another set beside him when Emily returned an hour and a half later. He offered it as she joined him. "How did the meeting go?"

"Good. There are three names on the short list and I'm one of them. They'll let me know by the end of the month their decision."

"Want to talk about it?"

"No. Mostly because I haven't decided if I want the job or not."

He didn't want to talk about the topic either. "Anyone around campus you want to say hi to while we're here?"

"You don't mind?"

"Of course not."

"There are a couple people. Belinda in the registrars office. Sharon teaches English, I can see what her class schedule is. Others are meeting us tonight at the music festival."

Noah walked with her, met her friends, heard more stories about her life on campus. Now that the meeting was over and Emily wasn't feeling pressured by it, she was more easily reminiscing. Austin University didn't have the character the Chicago University did. There were no sculptures along a walk path, no sports stadium, no student housing on campus. But the students they passed reminded him of those he taught. He liked the fact the university was small and felt contained. This had been a very good place for Emily to study and learn to teach chemistry. She was thriving at the bigger University but this place had substance of a different kind to offer her. If she stepped back in as dean of chemistry she would be able to shape her life here to bring in more of what she was doing in Chicago.

They walked the campus for an hour then headed out. Emily slowed the car as they came to an intersection a mile away from campus. "That's my home, the building on the east corner. I had the top floor condo that faces west."

"Really?" That caught him off guard. He'd been expecting her to have a house in one of the nearby neighborhoods.

"It has the best view in practically the whole city because it looked along the Colorado river without the statehouse or other high rises obstructing the view. I wanted to live near work. I was building my life around my career. It wasn't a conscious thing, but looking back that's what I was doing. Even being high up, it was what I wanted. In Chicago I use to dream about the place I would have and it was some apartment about twenty or thirty stories up that would be above the city congestion."

"You carried that dream here."

Emily nodded. "Transplanted it. That condo I truly do miss. It was a beautiful home, spacious for one. The sunsets were incredible with that open view."

"I admit, Chicago can't easily replace that home."

"I didn't even try. When I arrived in Chicago I bought an older place that was a good price in a nice neighborhood figuring I'd live there five years and move on. The most I've done to the place is paint and buy some furniture."

That evening, they walked from the hotel to the music festival, met up with four of her friends, chose a Mexican restaurant for dinner, and didn't return to the hotel until after ten p.m.

"You got a fair amount of sun today." Emily remarked as they waited for the elevator in the hotel lobby.

He could feel it. "So did you."

"Tomorrow will be shady outdoors," she promised. "Want to meet in the lobby again, same time?"

"That works." They were on different floors of the hotel, both in suites. Noah had one piece of advice to offer given what he had observed today. "Don't think too hard about this day, Emily. Just watch some television or read a book and get some sleep. The thinking about what this is can happen later."

"I'll try to do just that," she promised. Two elevators opened for the lobby and they parted ways with a final goodnight.

****

Lady Bird Lake glistened in the mid-morning light through the leaves of the trees as Emily took the east branch of the trail without needing to check the map she'd picked up. "I'm glad I walk every day," Noah mentioned. "There's more hill to this terrain than you would expect for Texas."

"It's not all flat country," she agreed. She slowed their hike two minutes later. "This is one of my favorite overlook points."

She'd chosen one with a view of a rockslide that had created a cove in the lake where the ducks were congregating. Noah counted twelve there now, swimming around. The two picnic tables were empty. "This works for me."

He set the sack he carried on a table, lunch bought from a food truck in the parking lot, and walked over to the fenced edge to look down, curious to see if they were standing on an undercut ledge. He was relieved to see a solid sloping river bank below them.

Emily lifted the foil around the lid of her plate. "Austin is two halves of a place built around nature in the middle. I know the river is why the town originally built up the way it did, so much of its life and commerce was the flow of goods along the Colorado River. But the city kept nature as its heart even when the roads to Houston and Dallas and San Antonio changed its need for the river. This is the capital of Texas and Texas has a love for the land. I think that's why I'm so comfortable being here. I get around nature and its like my soul unpacks from the crowds and concrete that is otherwise life."

"I need to add a Texas flag to those boots and cowboy hat to take home with me," Noah decided.

"They're easy to find here; the hotel gift shop probably has several sizes."

"What did you do with the project your parents were working on about Texas?" he asked, curious, as he returned to the table and unwrapped plastic silverware and napkins.

"They had a good friend who researched with them occasionally who was willing to take over the project. The book is coming out next year."

"I'm glad its being finished."

They ate quietly, enjoying the view, Noah grateful to simply sit and relax after what the last two days had been.

"Think you could handle more barbeque for dinner?"

"I'm loving the food," he replied with a smile.

Emily nodded. "I've got a favorite restaurant. I had a crush on the owner a long while ago. I've always loved his laugh, he's a gregarious guy about my age who never forgets my name nor my favorite dessert. I hear he's married now. I'd like to say hello while I'm here. He makes a onion blossom that reminds me of Frank's onion rings. The pork ribs and the beef ribs, you have to try both."

"I'm game. It's the first past crush you've mentioned."

"There was a guy I was dating who got more serious than me, who wanted to talk marriage. I wasn't ready. I was teaching, settling into what that career would be, I needed the open schedule – a lot of reasons that are mostly I hadn't fallen in love with him yet. I liked him, admired him, but wasn't ready to say I wanted forever. That was ten years ago."

Noah could understand it. "Life and the people around us move on. Some stick and become the friends we hold onto. Others were opportunities that for one reason or another didn't become a permanent connection. You acquired Jim Bishop as a friend, and through him, Gina. I met several of your friends last night at the music festival. Your life turned a different direction than theirs so the people are in flux again."

"Pretty much." Emily considered it. "I'm not as homesick as I thought I would be. This is a good place. Good memories. But I'm not dreading flying back to Chicago. I have a home there I'm comfortable with. Gina's friendship is valuable to me and its better in person than on the phone. I'm kind of in love with that office and its work table, my chemistry lab, and the students who come and go."

"Chicago has long winters and basically no nature. No gulf of Mexico, no parks like this," Noah pointed out.

"You liked Austin University."

Noah nodded. "I really did. My life has always been the bigger University. Smaller has its charms. It was substantially quieter. Just sitting at the table listening to the city around the campus, it wasn't as hectic. You had good history there for a reason. Your friends mirrored that. They have comfortable lives here in Austin. Coming back here wouldn't be a bad outcome if that happens."

"I didn't expect you to say that."

"I'm not wishing for it, but if God leads you back here, I'm wise enough to see it could be something He wants to do."

She thought quietly for a moment then straightened on the picnic table bench. "I'm changing the subject because I really don't know what to do about the future just yet. But I have been thinking about the past, particularly when I travel west. I'd like to have a very difficult conversation with you about my parents. I don't want to have it, but need to. It seems fitting, given we're here, to maybe tackle that today. Would you be willing to do that?"

He didn't want the conversation, particularly not today. "I thought you might one day. Are your parents buried here or in Chicago?"

"They're here."

"If you want to pay your respects, I'll be glad to give you your privacy."

"I'm not one for the gravesite memories and conversations but I would like to take by flowers to leave on my grandmother's headstone. She considered flowers a necessary gift. We'll do that later this afternoon, after the heat of the day breaks, if that's okay with you."

"Sure."

It was a hard subject. She'd likely need Kleenex and the best he had to offer was the extra napkins. It would turn the entire day black, the subject always did that. But to not have the conversation with her would be its own dilemma. She'd asked to talk about the hardest question, he had to honor that. Still neutral to the idea, he probed first for more understanding. "How do you want to approach talking about it?"

"There are four questions I would like to ask you. Hell is a real place? Who goes to eternal punishment? Are my parents in hell now? Is there any hope for them?"

He listened to those four questions, absorbed them and for her own sake hoped they could get through that conversation without so much pain it overwhelmed her. Right now really wasn't the time or place for it. He leaned hard against the Holy Spirit looking for the right words. "Those are very good questions. You've been thinking about this quite a bit."

"I need the truth, Noah. I already know its going to be hard. I need help sorting out what I know, what I fear, what the bible says that I may have misunderstood, to know the truth. Don't water down the details because you're trying not to hurt me. I'm already there. I need understanding and I'm too close to the subject to know what that is."

He nodded. "Let's take your questions in order then. We may need to break occasionally but by the time we leave flowers on your grandmother's grave we will have talked about all four. There's no use letting this conversation take any longer than it requires. I promise to share it as fully as I understand scriptures, but for both our sakes, lets only do this once. Will that work for you?"

Emily nodded. "Thank you."

There was no thanks to be offered for this subject, only the courage to have it, for him to talk about it and her to have the strength to listen. He looked around where they sat. It was good shade, comfortable, but it was also pretty and this topic wasn't. "Let's walk, Emily." He stood and gathered their lunch trash together, put it back in the sack. "There was a downhill trail you pointed out?"

"The second fork back meanders mostly downhill along the river and drops out on the road we drove in on. From there it's about half a mile walk back on a bike trail to the parking lot."

"Let's try it."

The trails around Lady Bird Lake were well packed ground, the occasional tree limb that had to be dodged, but there wasn't brush crowding the paths. For long stretches you could walk side by side. He walked with her and talked about the hardest subject of all.

"Your first question. Yes, hell is a real place. It's a lake of fire. Hell is where satan and the demons will be for eternity. It's where those who don't believe in Jesus will be sent. There is no goodness, no hope in hell. It's suffering that never ends.

"What scripture calls hades is the waiting place for those awaiting judgment who will be sentenced to hell. It's a horrible place of torment and heat and people are in agony, but it is not yet hell. You enter hell after you appear before the judgment seat of God. God is the judge. The word He's spoken tries you. It's very much a court of law as we think of one at the judgment. Books are open which give evidence about your life. The Lamb's Book of Life is opened. A verdict is given according to the word. A sentence is rendered. If your name is not in the Book of Life, you are cast into hell.

"Hell lasts for eternity. No one leaves hell. No one ever dies in hell. You will want to but you can't. It's a place, but not a life in terms of days and nights and places you go, you don't party in hell or climb in stature ruling over other people in hell. There is no life in hell. You're conscious, you know where you are, but you can't escape the place, you can't plan a way out of it, there is no relief."

Noah couldn't give her the rest of it. God has permitted a few people to see visions of hell and he wasn't beginning to do justice to what they had described. It was cries of agony, pain, tremendous fear. You burned alive so your flesh fell off but you could never die. You were in a literal lake of fire and couldn't get out. "I'm sorry for how hard this is."

Emily had turned pale but she swiftly shook her head. "Scriptures are that clear, I've read the passages."

"Would you like to stop?"

"No."

For his own sake, he inserted a brief aside. "The judgment seat of Christ is different. It's a distribution of rewards. It is a judge rewarding you based on what you did that was worthy of honor. As I understand scripture, only sinners appear before the judgment seat of God and only believers appear before the judgment seat of Christ."

Emily offered him a faint nod for that personal hope.

He waited until they were on the downhill path to continue. "Your second question: Who goes to eternal punishment? I can sum it up in a simple sentence. Those who refuse to let God make them good.

"God desires to save everyone. God desires no one to perish. But God is a righteous God and sin can't be in his presence. So to be with God, we've got to become as clean and as righteous as God. We can't become righteous by our own efforts. So God makes us righteous and changes our thinking and cleans up our behavior as an act of grace. God makes righteous those who have faith in what Jesus has done at the cross on our behalf.

"You can know you are saved by looking at your life. God is doing this changing within us to show our new righteousness and He is relentless. He doesn't stop until we are completely conformed to Jesus. Your life will show proof you've either been changed or you haven't been. The reason the Son of God appeared was to destroy (undo) the works of the devil. To destroy sin. No one born of God commits sin; for God's nature abides in him, and he cannot sin because he is born of God. (1 John 3:9) Those who belong to Christ Jesus have crucified the flesh with its passions and desires. (Galatians 5:24b) It's John writing, 'Little children, let no one deceive you. He who does right is righteous, as he [Jesus] is righteous.' (1 John 3:7) A Christian will show by their deeds they have been changed by God, that they are a new creation. We become ever more like Jesus in our thoughts, our words, our actions. Our lives will show we have accepted Jesus and have allowed God to change us. God always makes good a person who belongs to Jesus.

"Who goes to eternal punishment? Those who refuse to let God make them good. Hebrews 3:12 is a warning to believers. 'Take care, brethren, lest there be in any of you an evil, unbelieving heart, leading you to fall away from the living God.' It's a warning written to brothers in Christ. There are going to be many in hell who thought they were Christians. They misunderstood what a Christian is. A Christian is one who has given his life to God, is walking with the Holy Spirit, and is being changed to be like Christ. A Christian is one who stays firm in that faith decision to follow Jesus all their life.

"You can have an encounter with God in your youth and can later turn back to the world, your life shows no change, and while you are still calling yourself Christian, you have deceived yourself. Your faith is dead, you have no works showing you've been changed inside, and you will go to eternal destruction, you will be in hell. God will not cast you out but scripture says you can walk away. You have free will. If you accept Jesus you walk with him and are changed. God always makes righteous those He lives in. You will see the changes as you look at your life. You will have evidence of your salvation. But if you accept Jesus and then walk away, you have rejected Jesus. Your direction in life shows your heart. Those who turn back will not enter heaven.

For it is impossible to restore again to repentance those who have once been enlightened, who have tasted the

Immortality

heavenly gift, and have become partakers of the Holy Spirit, and have tasted the goodness of the word of God and the powers of the age to come, if they then commit apostasy, since they crucify the Son of God on their own account and hold him up to contempt. Hebrews 6:4-6

For if we sin deliberately after receiving the knowledge of the truth, there no longer remains a sacrifice for sins, but a fearful prospect of judgment, and a fury of fire which will consume the adversaries. A man who has violated the law of Moses dies without mercy at the testimony of two or three witnesses. How much worse punishment do you think will be deserved by the man who has spurned the Son of God, and profaned the blood of the covenant by which he was sanctified, and outraged the Spirit of grace? For we know him who said, "Vengeance is mine, I will repay." And again, "The Lord will judge his people." It is a fearful thing to fall into the hands of the living God. Hebrews 10:26-31

"God describes many times in scripture the attributes of what we can see happening in our lives so we will be able to judge accurately our condition.

"A person with a righteous mind and proper conduct are those who: have received grace, belong to Jesus, are saints, God's Beloved, there is obedience of faith, they acknowledge God, honor God (give him tithes and offerings), give thanks to God, hold to the truth about God, worship God, show repentance, seek God, display a fear of God (they hate lawlessness and love righteousness) and are humble in their heart. They are people who know peace.

"A person with a base mind, improper conduct and without God are known by numerous outward warning signs: they are gossips, slanderers, liars, insolent, haughty, boastful, inventors of evil, disobedient to parents, they have dishonorable sexual passions - women with women and men with men. They are foolish, faithless, heartless, ruthless, filled with wickedness and evil, murder, strife and malice. They covet and they envy. They do not acknowledge God, do not honor God, they worship and serve created things rather than God, they are haters of God, they have hard and impenitent hearts, by their wickedness they suppress the truth, their mouths are full of curses and bitterness, the venom of asps is under their lips, there is no fear of God before their eyes, they do not seek God, their feet are swift to shed blood, their paths are ruin and misery, the way of peace they do not know. They know God's decree that those who do such things deserve to die, they not only do them but approve those who practice them. We know that the judgment of God rightly falls upon those who do such things. (Romans 2:2)

"Feeling emotions over your sins, sadness or sorrow, having a fear of judgment, a fear of going to hell, can lead you to repentance. But those emotions are not themselves repentance. Repentance is a change in direction. Repentance is a turn to God, to his grace, and a decision to make Jesus your Lord, Savior and King. A true repentance and belief in Jesus will always produce fruit. If you are still acting unrighteous than all you had was an emotional experience. You did not repent. You did not turn. You only felt sorrow and fear and said words hoping those words would get you out of your trouble with God."

Noah paused at a curve in the path to hold a tree limb back for Emily. His many years of evening walks had all been on level ground. He liked walking downhill. It was practically without effort. Of the four questions she had asked, this was the only one he could answer without causing as much pain, so for his own sake he chose to remain on the topic to show her the full picture of it.

"What most people don't realize, even Christians, is that obedience isn't a rule book. Obedience isn't a new form of the law. The law is righteous and separates accurately good from evil – this is good, this is evil, you did right, you did wrong. But obedience to law is not what God is calling us to as Christians. We have died to sin and we have died to the law. We are under grace. Yet under grace God calls us to the same level of perfect obedience He did when we were under the law. We are called to the obedience that exists perfectly within the grace of relationship.

"Obedience is personal. It's the sign a relationship exists. I don't have to ask why Jesus wants me to do something. We have a relationship. It's a close relationship, a personal one, I love Jesus and I know Jesus loves me. When Jesus asks me to do something, I'm delighted and I go promptly to do what he asked. I love Jesus trusting me with things I can do for him. Sometimes Jesus explains why he wants me to do something, sometimes he simply wakes me up and says "go…" and I get up and go do what he asked. I don't need the why when I know him. If Jesus asks me to do an inconvenient thing its because he trusts me to do something he needs done. I have the same freedom with Jesus. When I ask him to do something for me, I don't have to wonder if Jesus is going to do it for me. We're friends. He doesn't mind me inconveniencing him. When I need Jesus to do something for me I ask him. That's the freedom of our relationship. That's friendship. It's also how the kingdom functions. We talk to each other. I am obedient to Jesus because he's my friend, but also because he's my King. He has authority over all heaven and all earth. I honor Him because he's worthy of all honor.

"In the same way, I obey God the Father because He's God and He's also my Dad. I love Him. I show the fact I love Him by doing whatever He asks me to do. I don't grumble about it or get put out by it or wonder why he's given me this to do rather than give it to someone else. I simply go do it with a willing and cheerful heart. I love my Dad. When He asks me to do something I willingly undertake it. That's a relationship which is at peace. Because I know I can come to my Father and God will give me whatever I come and ask of Him. God trusts me. And I trust Him. Obedience is the expression of trust.

"There are always degrees of maturity but within every Christian the heart faith for salvation is always present and focused toward Jesus. A Christian is one who is walking in newness of life, one who is being transformed into the image of Jesus.

"Jesus warns his disciples, "Not every one who says to me, `Lord, Lord,' shall enter the kingdom of heaven, but he who does the will of my Father who is in heaven. On that day many will say to me, `Lord, Lord, did we not prophesy in your name, and cast out demons in your name, and do many mighty works in your name?' And then will I declare to them, `I never knew you; depart from me, you evildoers.' (Matthew 7:21-23)

"On that day *many...* it's sobering, that word. *Many.* They thought they were in good standing with God because they understood the authority and power in Jesus' name and did might works in his name. But they had no relationship with Jesus. They were not listening to his voice. They were not walking in obedience to Jesus and God the Father. They were doing what they decided to do, running their own show, living by self-will. Jesus was not their Lord. They were acting in religious ways but with a heart that was lawless. They were not in submission to Jesus as their King. Jesus will use them to free others for He is a compassionate God, but he will judge them lawless and send them to hell. They are the wolves in sheep's clothing that live among the church family, looking good on the outside but they are doing their own will. You can do good deeds and be judged to be sinning. Your good works don't matter. Your heart attitude to Jesus is everything. A proud heart is an evil heart.

"Jesus is talking to the church when he warns, 'And because wickedness is multiplied, most men's love will grow cold.' (Matthew 24:12). Most men's love will grow cold. Not a few, not a minority, *most*. It is sobering these warnings from Jesus because they are addressed to people who think they are following him and are in good standing with him. Lawlessness will arise within society and within the church. People grow cold toward God, toward obedience to Him. You'll look good on the outside as a

Christian, be there on Sunday morning, say the right words, have the pedigree of faith, be baptized as a child. 'I'm a Christian, I've been attending church for thirty years' but its outward show. There's no heart passion for Jesus, no relationship with him as a person. You've learned the language and the appearance but God isn't mocked. Jesus isn't your Lord or King. You rule your own life and make your own decisions without Jesus involved. You spend your life thinking everything is fine, you're going to heaven, and realize too late you are going to hell because you didn't love Jesus. Apostasy, this turning away from God, is of the heart.

"We who are following Jesus need to be asking the Holy Spirit – is my love for Jesus hot? is my passion for my God strong? We need to be hearing from the Spirit of Truth how God sees us now, while it is possible to repent and correct our actions where we are off course. Heaven is a wonderful place. The path there is by grace. But its not to be taken lightly this walk with God, the transformation process God takes us through to change us. We bail out and don't even realize we've done so. He who endures to the end shall be saved. There is a steady, permanent 'Jesus is my Lord and Savior' set of our heart and our thoughts. Our words and actions constantly press in closer to Jesus in love. This self-will idea of what we should do as Christians is a contradiction. There are no self-willed Christians. There are only those who have laid down their lives and submitted to Jesus. He tells us what to do and we obey him."

"You're going back to the core of your conversation in Fort Worth. Do you know your King?"

Noah nodded. "Without saying it in so many words, I'm worried about the church, we've become complacent, our love grows cold, and we are walking away from this relationship with God we had when we first got to know him. What we understood about salvation and the kingdom was very little in the beginning but we did see Jesus. As the years go by we seem to learn more but know him less, we don't value Jesus like we did. We don't know him. When Jesus is forced to tell many on that last day, 'I never knew you', he's going to say it with great sadness. People who thought they were Christians will discover they were living self-fashioned religious lives full of self-pride about their righteous lifestyle compared to others, not realizing until that day that they never got to know their King – Jesus. Deception is a dangerous thing because you can deceive yourself and not realize you're standing in darkness. Only light can show you the truth.

"I don't want anyone to be left behind on the day of the rapture of the church. But in the parable of the ten virgins coming to meet the bridegroom, only five of them are ready and receive entry to the marriage supper. The women in the parable are a type both for individual Christians and for local churches. They all thought they were ready, but five didn't have oil, the picture of the Holy Spirit, which they needed in their lives so they would be ready for the bridegroom. Going after God, after the Holy Spirit, its our protection, its how we stay ready. Half the women in Jesus' parable were not ready when the Lord returned. *Half.* Can you imagine the dismay, what its going to be like, when half the churches, half those who called themselves Christian, aren't part of the rapture?

"Jesus had tough words for the seven churches in Revelation. He wasn't pleased with them. He was correcting what was wrong, giving instruction on what to do, he wanted them to overcome and be with him but he wasn't lowering the standard he expected from them. God makes people good, but we have to let him. That's a word for the church and for individuals. God isn't pleased when we don't live by faith, abiding in the word, letting the Holy Spirit work in us, changing us to be good.

"But of that day and hour no one knows, not even the angels of heaven, nor the Son, but the Father only. As were the days of Noah, so will be the coming of the Son of man. For as in those days before the flood they were eating and drinking, marrying and giving in marriage, until the day when Noah entered the ark, and they did not know until the flood came and swept them all away, so will be the coming of the Son of man. Then two men will be in the field; one is taken and one is left. Two women will be grinding at the mill; one is taken and one is left. Watch therefore, for you do not know on what day your Lord is coming. Matthew 24:36-42

They were nearing the end of the trail, Noah could hear traffic ahead of them.

"We take a right on the bike trail just ahead," Emily said. "It will take us back to the parking lot."

The bike path was asphalt smooth and wide enough for four bikes to be passing each other. Noah could see a couple walking about three hundred yards ahead of them and two bike riders approaching. It was a path where you needed to stay aware of your surroundings but otherwise was an upgrade for the comfort of the walk as there were no tree limbs to occasionally dodge.

He didn't want to move on to her third question and he had only a couple last things to offer on the present topic, so concluded with them. "You often hear it said that God gave us free will so we can love God. That if there wasn't a choice not to love him, there couldn't be authentic love. That's true. But it's a side benefit of why God gave us free will, not the reason he gave it to us. Free will is one of the ways we are made in the likeness and image of God. God has free will. So we get free will too.

"God is only good. It's his nature. But it's his nature because that is His free will choice. God has chosen to be good. God wants children. That's why He created this world. A child has the characteristics of his Father. We see that in Jesus. Jesus is good like his Father. An adopted child of God is someone who chooses to let God make them good. We become part of the family of God. Who goes to destruction? Someone who refuses to let God make them good.

"We have a free will choice to be like God or not. That's what people miss. Christianity is not a decision to obey or not. It's a decision do we want to be like God or not. God changes Christians to be like Himself. From glory to glory we are transformed to be like Jesus.

"Do we want to be like God or not – do we want to rule a kingdom, have God's nature, have authority in our words, be a son of God? That's what Christianity actually is.

"If people would think about what was being offered there would be no one who wasn't a Christian. Who wouldn't want to rule a kingdom, have God's good nature, have authority in our words, be a son of God? Only someone who is blinded by darkness and can't see what God is offering them.

"People don't accept the good news because they can't believe it's true. That's basically the entire problem. Doing evil seems like more fun than this process of being transformed into a child of God. Talk about taking the immediate gratification instead of the taking the real prize of everything! You can end up in a lake of fire for eternity or become a person made entirely good who is ruling a kingdom alongside God for eternity. It's not a hard choice.

"Another way to answer the question who goes to eternal punishment is by the categories scriptures describe. There are six.

the unrighteous – those who do not accept Jesus.

those living unrighteous – the idolater, the impure man, those who indulge in the lust of defiling passion and despise authority – they may have the name Christian but they no longer show evidence of repentance; they have turned back to the world.

those who commit apostasy – apostasy means abandonment of a prior loyalty; renunciation of faith, a defector; they hold Christ up to contempt on their own account; they have trampled on the blood of Jesus.

the cursed – those who do not do good to people in need; there is no fruit of righteous.

the wicked servant – one who is not doing his assignment from the Master, who is hanging out with the drunken, who is abusing those servants who are being faithful; there is no faithfulness.

the worthless, wicked, slothful servant – one who is afraid and does nothing for his Master with what he has been given, money in particular.

ungodly sinners – worldly people devoid of the Spirit; the cowardly, the faithless, the polluted; scoffers, following their own ungodly passions; any one who practices abomination; sorcerers and fornicators and murderers and idolaters; every one who loves and practices falsehood; all liars; those who indulge in the lust of defiling passion and despise authority; these are grumblers, malcontents, following their own passions, loud-mouthed boasters, flattering people to gain advantage.; they have eyes full of adultery, insatiable for sin; they have hearts trained in greed.

"We need to look at that list as Christians just to check our own hearts and see if we are deceiving ourselves. God doesn't want anyone to perish. If you've got a problem going on the Holy Spirit is going to convict you if you will let him. Jesus is full of grace and truth. It's truth that says 'you're in trouble, you need to accept me as your Savior and King and let me change you.'"

"Behavior matters," Emily summed up.

Noah nodded. "Over time, it's the evidence of our salvation. God is good. Good conduct is a reflection of the fact we are being made good. Is isn't a sin free life God requires of a Christian, Jesus blood will cleanse us from sins we commit, but God requires a heart that remains focused on Him. David commits adultery and murder, it's a horrible pair of sins, yet when confronted by Nathan, David's eyes are opened to what he had done and his immediate reaction is 'I have sinned against you, God'. His heart was still toward God. His conduct was deplorable, but he had genuine repentance in his heart and he was forgiven by God.

"That's why God is so relentless with his children. When we sin, we know we've blown it. If we respond with godly repentance, God can forgive us and fix us. But if we harden our heart and keep walking in sin, we stop turning back to God. Sin can progressively take us out and we won't even notice we've walked away from God. Any sin in dangerous. But sin that becomes an attitude of the heart will send us to hell. Those who are in heaven are those who let God make them good. It's grace and truth, faith and works. God will do all the heavy lifting for us but unless we truly accept Jesus and follow him, we're fools. Who doesn't enter heaven – the foolish, faithless, liars, gossips – scripture's lists of warnings doesn't just say murderers."

Noah looked at the angle of the sun as they came to the parking lot. He needed a break and so did she. "Let's go find cold drinks and flowers for your grandmother's grave and just let this topic rest for an hour. We'll finish it, but after a break."

Emily nodded her acceptance of that. "I do appreciate the conversation, Noah, as hard as it is, I've needed to have it for some time."

"I know you have. I've been braced for this day since our first conversation."

****

Humidity was rising. Noah felt it in the way his shirt now stuck to his back. Emily set the flowers she carried on the grave of her parents and grandmother, the three lying in rest together under one family headstone. Beloved grandmother. Beloved parents. Emily had honored them well. The cemetery was quiet, peaceful, beautiful in a way with all the granite stones and it was sad. Incredibly sad.

Noah offered Emily the water bottle he had brought when she stepped back after a couple minutes.

"My last two questions: Are my parents in hell now? Is there any hope for them? You don't have to answer that first one, Noah. My parents never accepted Jesus. My parents are in Hades right now, they'll be judged by God and sent to hell. And oh, that knowledge hurts. But that second question, Noah, I have to ask. Is there any hope for them?"

It was the question Noah dreaded most. "I can't offer you hope, Emily, but I can offer you an observation. We are told only those who are called by God are able to respond to the good news about Jesus. And God knows how painful it is to be without your family. In Acts the references to households being saved is prevalent. The indication is when you believe, you and your household – everyone in your family – are also given the call to believe in Jesus. Every individual makes their own decision about Jesus, but we are assured all in our household will receive that call.

"When your grandmother believed in God, everyone in her family received the call to know Jesus. That's likely why you were able to hear and responded to the good news. That same call would have rested upon your parents. You can be assured your parents were both called to know Jesus and that call is powerful. Did they have a change of heart about God in the last days or hours or moments before their death? Only God knows.

"The word says God desires no man to perish. After the flood in Noah's day, God limited mankind to 120 years for his Spirit to wrestle with them to decide for God. But He did give mankind 120 years.

Then the LORD said, "My Spirit will not contend with humans forever, for they are mortal; their days will be a hundred and twenty years." (Genesis 6:3 NIV)

"I don't think mankind can change their decision about Jesus after they die. I think that's why God told Christians to raise the dead when someone dies early so they would have that full 120 years to get their decision right, because God was thinking about those who were going to perish unless they were rescued by a Christian.

Jesus gave Christians the authority to raise the dead. No one was there when your parents were killed to pray to raise them from the dead, so that help wasn't offered to them.

"God will honor a person's free will. If they have rejected Jesus there isn't hope. Even though they were deceived and it was the wrong decision, it was still their choice. And that answer is so painful to deal with I've thought long and hard searching to see if there is any hint of hope left. It's very thin, but there is a glimmer of something in the bible that says maybe God's mercy can still reach them. I do know if God in Christ can find a way to show mercy to your parents without violating what his Word says, God will find it.

"If satan who has the power of death kills a person who doesn't believe in God before they have lived a 120 years, they have left earth early and been denied the 120 years for the Holy Spirit to bring them to conviction and repentance. We know the final day of judgment makes our decision about Jesus permanent for eternity. We are left with a slim glimmer of hope that God could find a way to show mercy to those in hades who rejected him but hadn't lived 120 years yet when satan took their life. We don't know that answer.

"Jesus holds the keys of death and hades. You don't hold keys unless you plan to open a door. Jesus paid for the sins of the whole world. Could Jesus make a case to his Father based on the fact this person didn't have 120 years on earth, Jesus paid for their sins with his death, and this person now in hades having realized their horrific decision wants to call on Jesus as savior – on that basis could Jesus save them and take a person out of hades? It's so narrow as to be non-existent, but I could come up with a just argument that might be acceptable to God the Father. That is why I want to say there is a glimmer of hope for those of us who have lost loved ones who didn't believe. God forgave the sins of everyone in the world at the price of his own Son. Your parents were fully forgiven by God. They

simply didn't accept that forgiveness through Jesus before
they died. If there is a way for those who haven't lived a
120 years before they die to still accept Jesus, God can find
it. We're told by Jude to save some by snatching them out
of the fire. Out of the fire means they are in the fire.
There's my sliver of hope. One verse and the knowledge of
God's love. Maybe someone who didn't live 120 years can
still call on Jesus and be saved out of hades.

But you, beloved, build yourselves up on your most
holy faith; pray in the Holy Spirit; keep yourselves in the
love of God; wait for the mercy of our Lord Jesus Christ
unto eternal life. And convince some, who doubt; save
some, by snatching them out of the fire; on some have
mercy with fear, hating even the garment spotted by the
flesh. Jude 1:20-23

"We can ask Jesus. If there is a way to save their lives,
God would find it if asked. That we can do for them,
Emily."

"Would you pray with me for that?"

"Yes." Noah took her hand, thought a minute and then
offered, "Jesus, your father and ours is incredibly merciful
to mankind. God doesn't want Emily's parents to perish. If
there is any way Emily's parents can be given the right to
call upon your name as their savior because they didn't live
120 years and you said 'you and your household would be
saved' to Emily's grandmother and to Emily, I ask you to
use the keys you hold Jesus to open the door of hades and
for you to give Emily's parents and those in similar place
as theirs the good news you at the cross forgave their sins. I
ask that you let them be able to freely call upon your name
and live, for them to be with you today, forgiven of their
sins. I ask because you are a great and merciful God full of
grace and truth and if there is any way to answer this
prayer, you will find it Jesus. Thank you. Amen."

Emily squeezed his hand. "Thanks, Noah."

"He will if its possible, Emily. That's the only sliver

of hope I can offer."

"It's more than I had. This grief is crushing Noah. That's my family." She wiped at tears freely flowing.

"I wish I had known them. I wish I had those memories to share with you."

"They were good, my parents; they just weren't saved." Emily struggled with the tears and nodded toward the car. "Let's leave this place."

"Sure."

Noah had accepted the car keys when they bought the flowers. He drove now, from the cemetery and into downtown Austin, just to give Emily time to quietly grieve. He had a very big and wonderful and loving God. And in a very long search for hope he'd come up with one verse to offer. Only God knew the final answer to Emily's last two questions.

"Don't look so sad."

He glanced over to Emily and she offered an attempt at a smile. "It's okay. The day was what I needed Noah. Sometimes you simply need to face hard things. You didn't pull back from the truth but you said it from your heart. You can't make hard things easy. Only God can help carry this weight."

"I know. But I can share the sadness."

Emily looked at the setting sun. "Take a left at the next light. Let's go watch like a million and a half bats swarm into the sky. If nothing else I'll shriek enough in startled surprise its going to take my mind off this entire conversation. You can park along Congress Avenue Bridge and watch them leave at dusk. The bats live under the bridge."

Noah agreed the sight was going to change what they were thinking about and that suited him. He took a left at the light. After this, he'd talk her into going back to the music festival for an hour or just walk Austin's downtown district. The only bright point of today was the agreement to only have that conversation once.

*

21

"The flight back to Chicago is a private flight," Noah mentioned as they unloaded luggage from the rental car the next day shortly after noon. "Ann tapped a favor from a friend. We're heading to private terminal C to meet up with our pilot."

"Really? That is going to be exciting."

"I've enjoyed this businessman's plane before. It's going to exceed anything you think of as first class and be a very nice way to end this trip."

Emily laughed. "All of it has been an adventure, Noah. I like tagging along with you."

Thirty minutes they were enjoying all it meant.

One of the many comforts of the plane's configuration was being able to sit facing each other with a table between them for drinks, papers and laptops if you desired to do some work. The businessman who owned the plane had taken out seats and configured the cabin to be his office in the air. It suited Noah just fine. He draped his suit jacket over the back of the chair and settled in with a cold drink and small bag of potato chips. "You sure you don't want something to eat?"

"I'm heading to Frank's place when we land for a Reuben Sandwich, coleslaw and fries. I eat now, I'll insult him by not arriving hungry."

Noah chuckled at the way she said it, but thought it suited matters. She'd been figuring out his brother as well as him over the course of the summer. That was a good thing. "I'll join you for that sandwich. It's tradition to stop in and see him after I get back from a trip."

The plane began to taxi. Noah checked his seat belt and watched out the windows with Emily as they turned onto a runway and rapidly began to accelerate. The pressure he felt on his chest was different than the airliner, the ascent and turn were both more gradual. In seven minutes the takeoff was over, the city below them was fading in size and a few clouds were skimming by the wings at the same altitude as they were traveling. The seatbelt fasten light turned off.

"That was nice." Emily nudged off her shoes and swiveled her chair around. "Feel like having one of our conversations or do you want to just veg out?"

"It's about a three hour flight. We can do both. What's your question?"

"I'd like to go back to our initial Monday night conversation with a personal question."

That surprised him. "Sure." It had been now ten or eleven weeks and they hadn't been back to it in a formal way.

"I don't want a husband who dies early."

"Oh." He couldn't stop the start of a smile. She'd taken his point to heart.

"I like you. So could we date and see where a relationship might go? I can't promise I can get over my aversion to snow, but I like what I know about you."

"I'd like that Emily."

"Yeah?"

"I told Frank that first Tuesday I had possibly met my future wife. I've been smitten for a while."

She blinked at that mild remark. "Why haven't you asked me on a date then?"

"I'm a planner. I bought two tickets to the lunar eclipse dinner and viewing at the planetarium thinking it would make a nice first date. I wanted to see Texas first and why you were homesick, to know if Chicago was even a viable answer for you so I didn't approach the topic the wrong way. So would you like to go to dinner and see the lunar eclipse with me as our first official date?"

"I really would."

"It's a date then, hopefully the first of many."

"I'm fine with stacking the next several months with dates. If Jesus is coming soon and we decide to end up getting married, I'd like to enjoy that season of my life before he arrives."

Noah laughed but he nodded. "You'll find me enjoying the challenge of coming up with interesting places we can go together this fall."

"Thank you. And I'm tabling that topic for now." She raised the footrest on her seat. "Talk to me about the subject most on your mind lately. Hopefully it's a long topic. As much as I wanted to ask that personal question and your answer just delighted me, I can't stay thinking about personal matters for three hours of this flight without saying something idiotic. So do me a favor and talk for awhile about something else."

He understood her desire to move off personal matters for the rest of the trip; he'd like to avoid saying something he'd decide later was miss-timed too. The subject most on his mind lately other than her... "Most recently, that would be the fact we are heirs of God," Noah replied.

"Really? Talk to me about what you've discovered."

Her reply was one of the reasons he was falling in love with her. It wasn't polite interest, it was genuine interest. He could talk with her about anything and she sincerely liked to listen.

"Eternal means always, means now. The gift of eternal life God gives us – it has already begun. Yet most people are waiting until they get to heaven or Jesus returns to have eternal life. There is a similar error happening regarding the promised eternal inheritance. The promised eternal inheritance God gives us – its now – it has already begun." He settled into a topic that had him fascinated.

"Scripture says Jesus is the heir of all things. 'In many and various ways God spoke of old to our fathers by the prophets; but in these last days he has spoken to us by a Son, whom he appointed the heir of all things, through whom also he created the world.' (Hebrews 1:1-2)

"In Luke 10:22a Jesus remarks, 'All things have been delivered to me by my Father'. And John tells us why. 'the Father loves the Son, and has given all things into his hand.' (John 3:35)

"As believers, we are heirs of God and fellow heirs

with Christ. We are also heirs of all things. 'For you did not receive the spirit of slavery to fall back into fear, but you have received the spirit of sonship. When we cry, "Abba! Father!" it is the Spirit himself bearing witness with our spirit that we are children of God, and if children, then heirs, heirs of God and fellow heirs with Christ, provided we suffer with him in order that we may also be glorified with him.' (Romans 8:15-17) And 'He who did not spare his own Son but gave him up for us all, will he not also give us all things with him?' (Romans 8:32)

"Jesus has died, the new covenant is in effect, and it is the new covenant which gives us this inheritance. It became available in A.D. 33 and when we become a child of God the inheritance is released to us through Jesus. We inherit all things; we literally inherit the world. 'The promise to Abraham and his descendants, that they should inherit the world, did not come through the law but through the righteousness of faith.' (Romans 4:13)

he [Jesus] is the mediator of a new covenant, so that those who are called may receive the promised eternal inheritance, since a death has occurred which redeems them from the transgressions under the first covenant. For where a will is involved, the death of the one who made it must be established. For a will takes effect only at death, since it is not in force as long as the one who made it is alive. (Hebrews 9:15b-17)

Whatever your task, work heartily, as serving the Lord and not men, knowing that from the Lord you will receive the inheritance as your reward; you are serving the Lord Christ. (Colossians 3:23-24)

For all things are yours, whether Paul or Apol'los or Cephas or the world or life or death or the present or the future, all are yours; and you are Christ's; and Christ is God's. ... What have you that you did not receive? If then you received it, why do you boast as if it were not a gift?

Already you are filled! Already you have become rich! Without us you have become kings! And would that you did reign, so that we might share the rule with you! (1 Corinthians 3:21b-23, 4:7b-8)

"God gave Jesus all things. Jesus then dies to put the new covenant in effect. His death made us righteous and allowed God to give us all things with Jesus. We are now heirs of God and fellow heirs with Christ. Jesus is now the mediator distributing the inheritance. The Holy Spirit helps us understand what our inheritance is and acquire possession of it. We hear the good news about our inheritance, believe it, ask and thus receive our inheritance.

we who first hoped in Christ have been destined and appointed to live for the praise of his glory. In him you also, who have heard the word of truth, the gospel of your salvation, and have believed in him, were sealed with the promised Holy Spirit, which is the guarantee of our inheritance until we acquire possession of it, to the praise of his glory. (Ephesians 1:12-14)

When the Spirit of truth comes, he will guide you into all the truth; for he will not speak on his own authority, but whatever he hears he will speak, and he will declare to you the things that are to come. He will glorify me, for he will take what is mine and declare it to you. All that the Father has is mine; therefore I said that he will take what is mine and declare it to you. (John 16:13-15)

"It is by our cooperation with the Holy Spirit we acquire, we receive our inheritance. It comes from Jesus to us by way of the Holy Spirit. The Holy Spirit glorifies Jesus by taking the 'all things' which have been given to Jesus and declaring (speaking) those 'all things' to us. The Holy Spirit is declaring (speaking) tangible things into your possession. That's how God works. He speaks and what he says becomes visible in the physical world. It parallels the

Old Testament passage in Isaiah:

> "Behold, the former things have come to pass,
> and new things I now declare;
> before they spring forth
> I tell you of them."
> (Isaiah 42:9)

"We receive this inheritance by grace, not by our works. Everything that God has He has given to his children – to Jesus and to us. God made us his heirs. God gave us all things with his Son Jesus. The gift happened in A.D. 33. If we don't accept all that is in our inheritance, if we don't have faith in the word, the Holy Spirit is unable to declare it, unable to give it to us. We receive our inheritance by faith. If we receive only forgiveness of sins and righteousness, the gift of heaven, but don't receive 'all things' we live in poverty here on earth that God never intended for his children."

"I love that explanation, Noah. God gave Jesus all things because Jesus was his first-born Son, and as more children come into the family, Jesus turns and shares all things with us by the Holy Spirit. All God's children are his equal heirs. He gave Jesus honor as the first-born son, Jesus will always be the King of Kings, but God then gave us all equally the inheritance of what was His."

Noah nodded. "The Lord's prayer, 'Thy kingdom come, they will be done, on earth as it is in heaven.' Jesus would like us to realize the earth is our inheritance and its by the kingdom which He rules that we are able to enjoy all things on earth now."

"The more you describe the kingdom of God and what God has given us, the more amazing life becomes Noah. I am startled how much I'm seeing for the first time even after four years of joy looking around. All this was still out there. How much more treasure is in the scriptures to find?"

Noah simply smiled. "One of the nice things about God? There is always more. I haven't stopped treasure hunting because I keep finding more treasures every time I go looking. That's why Jesus says abide in the word. He wasn't saying study for study sake, he was saying 'you're standing on a field of treasures. Dig! You'll love what you find!'"

Emily laughed. "Yeah. That's how its felt this summer. Even the trips west, the mountains. I've never encountered anything like it before. God's been arranging the trips just to show me stuff he has made. He's proud of it. He likes his creation. That beauty fits God, and the scale of it. That's my Dad's handiwork."

Noah understood what she was finding. "Sometimes God shows us his nature by telling us about it, other times he says 'go out and look up at the stars. I made everything you see. That's me working. Now let's talk about your problems because I'm really big and I can handle them for you.' His creation is his reassurance to us. Every morning the sun comes up. Plants thrive and multiply. Seasons always come. There is immense glory in creation and its reflecting God. His steadfast love can be seen as well as heard in his Word."

"I've got one more trip planned for the summer, the tourist kind of stop in Yellowstone to see the geysers and the hot springs, the chemist in me is fascinated by what is bubbling up from inside the earth. I think what I most want to share with God on the trips is an appreciation for what He's made. To go and see nature is to honor the one who created it. Just as reading the scriptures is honoring Him for writing them."

"That's a good perspective, Emily. My sense of it, looking at the pictures you bring back, hearing the stories, God is enjoying this travel as much as you are."

"I like to think so. The world is part of our inheritance. Is that why Jesus comes back and rules from Jerusalem? The earth was created for Jesus as much as any of us? God knew Jesus would come as the Son of Man from the foundation of the world."

Noah smiled. "You just spotted another treasure in

scripture. Yes. Jesus loves this earth. It was created for him as much as any one else, as he is the second Adam, the Son of Man. The new heavens and the new earth, they may be literal new physical creations, or they may be new as in refreshed, restored, new in the sense they are restored to their glory. Scripture implies this earth will be swept clean with fire.

"We know the earth exists after the wedding of Jesus and his bride the church for we see the new city of Jerusalem coming out of heaven to earth. In eternity the earth may be like the center of government for the universe. God may have put ideas of space, what we try to envision with Star Trek and Star Wars, into our nature because they are clues of what eternity is like. We know angels come and go from earth now. Jesus comes and goes from earth to heaven and back to earth. I suspect we will be doing the same."

Emily thought about that and nodded. "I have a different related question. Jesus in heaven receives a scroll and starts to undo the seals of that scroll. The scroll is written on the front and back. God wrote that scroll. What do you think is written on it? Revelation ends before Jesus begins to read it. He's only opened it. Do you think God wrote down the details of eternity? God likes to write things down then do them, that's his nature, his way of acting. First he speaks and tells us what is going to happen, then he does it. Is the scroll Jesus is holding God's words about our future?"

"It's a fascinating question. It could be the history of what he's done for mankind, a personal diary of sorts, 'Emily asked me today for this and this is what I say in reply' and we get to hear our story with God from his perspective. Or the scroll may be a letter to Jesus, a Father's words to his Son, for Jesus will rule the heavens and earth as King for eternity. It could be a love letter of sorts, blessing Jesus and his bride. Those words have been sealed up for the day the heavens and earth are restored to righteousness. Maybe there are some blessings so beautiful they can only be spoken when all is righteous again."

Emily smiled. "I love that image. It leaves me longing for the day I hear what else God has written."

"Was that far enough off the personal as a topic?"

Emily laughed. "We managed to get pretty far. I've needed this time Noah, these conversations, the perspective this summer has brought to the picture of my life. I could have had another normal summer teaching classes, being available to students, and I would have missed days like this."

"When did the idea for a sabbatical start getting traction in you such that you decided to take one?"

"Christmas week last year. I was opening gifts alone but wasn't alone, I was aware Jesus was hanging out with me enjoying the day. There was Christmas music on, I'd fixed cookies, had a meal planned for what I would make for dinner. I had the sense 'I want more of this'. It wasn't my thought, it was Jesus' thought, because I said aloud, 'I do, too'. And so I looked at the calendar and asked 'how about this summer?' and the peace in my heart was instant. It was the best decision I could have made. I love how this sabbatical evolved. It's been perfect."

"You said yes. That's often the key to the best gifts God wants to bring us. I've enjoyed the summer of conversations too." He was grateful she'd made this trip with him. The assurance Emily was looking at this relationship as being something which lasted beyond the summer was very good news indeed. If the job offer went to another, this trip would have accomplished what it needed, given Emily closure. If the job was offered to her, the decision she made would determine the pace of their relationship. Maybe God needed to give her time and opening a door back to Austin was the way to slow this relationship down to the right speed going forward. Noah was no longer concerned. He'd seen Austin. It felt like a good place for Emily. If God took her back there, it would be for a good reason.

It would be a busy couple weeks from here as the

month ended. He had class finals. She had a battery
presentation to make to the university. At least his travel
was done for the month. Life was turning remarkably good.
He was dating again. Frank was going to laugh and say it
was about time. Noah smiled at the thought. It was time his
brother found someone special too.

22

Noah met up with Emily on campus Thursday evening to walk to dinner, an unofficial date, to keep their first official one the evening of the lunar eclipse.

"Your final class went well?" Emily asked, curious.

Noah nodded. "It's a good group of students. Everyone leaves with a decent grade. I give take home finals because I want them to give me essay format answers. It makes writing the test questions challenging as I'm looking to avoid questions similar to prior classes to remove the temptation for any plagiarism but that works with my subject matter. Based on the final conversations we had in class I would judge three student's changed their minds from unbelief to believe in Jesus and another twenty shifted how they thought about the bible to now believe it is a book of true saying. The rest pretty much hardened into the belief they came in with."

"That seems like a good outcome."

"Those who were open to changing their minds did," Noah assessed. "I would teach the course even if I was unable to change any one's mind, because they would then have no reason to fault God for not having told them the truth. But it makes it easier on me to be able to see fruit from a class even this early. I keep a list of all the students who have attended one of my classes and pray over that list weekly. It's one reason I enjoy stopping by the alumni events. I often find myself saying hello to a former student and discover they've become a Christian as the years have passed."

"You have more tangible kingdom work than I do. I'm one of those who gets to water the good news on occasion. Students who are hanging around inevitably realized I'm a Christian because I'm asking God questions all the time. Some ask me questions about God and what I believe. But it's a byproduct of people being around me. I rarely start those conversations. Maybe I should."

"If the Holy Spirit says talk about God, you do so. Otherwise you be yourself. When someone has a headache, your instinct is simply to say, 'can I pray for you that it goes away? God likes to heal headaches.' You live being a Christian. That's mostly what being salt and light in the world means. You live faithful to your God and what He would do in situations and you act like him. You're God's daughter. You're going to act like Him because of it. Our actions and our words are mostly family things. We are this way because of who our Father is, who our old brother Jesus is. We're just one of their family."

Emily smiled at that picture. "I admit, I'm looking forward to the fall semester and teaching again. I've missed not having students. I wanted a sabbatical break from teaching and what it showed me is that I love teaching. I don't want to give that part of my life up even though I will soon have the ability to so do financially if I desired to drop teaching from my life."

"You answered part of your question about what's next. Teaching is part of it."

"It's who I am. At least for this season in my life."

"That's a good realization to have. So you've heard about my day. How has yours been? Ready for the battery presentation tomorrow?"

"I practiced it through with Gina again this morning. It's mostly show-and-tell, you open the phone and show the battery and then walk through a binder of information about it reading the highlights. Everything the university will need is there. I do the science conversation, then Bryce will do the second half of the presentation on the licensing configurations which make sense, the companies we've chosen for the patent filing and the licensing management. The university business office then starts working through how they want to publicize the research. These meetings happen all the time, its just rare to be presenting something with this kind of commercial potential. Ideally, once I hand that paperwork off, I'm mostly hands off for the process.

I've done all the refinement I want to do on the science and design. Other chemists and engineers will take my work and begin adding their own. This part of the process is more Bryce's expertise, he'll be the one to actually hire the patent and licensing companies and do that coordination. Bryce is willing to handle those for me on the same terms he suggested for the fireworks patents and licensing. I'm to make a donation to the charity of his choice."

"You can't beat those terms. Bryce likes business, Emily, its how he's wired. Helping with this kind of work is like offering him a piece of cake. It's fun for him. Like you enjoy chemistry and I enjoy talking about God, Bryce thrives in business matters. You giving to a charity makes sense as he doesn't need the income himself."

"Without Bryce, the fun part of science gets drowned by the not-so-fun complexity of the business which follows. From my position, Bryce was as big a gift from God to my life as the fireworks and the battery ideas themselves have become."

"Any additional thoughts about the money and what you want to do with it?"

"It's coming every year for the foreseeable future. I want to chose about twenty charities to invest in every year for the next decade. And I want to establish a handful of fellowship grants for the chemistry department to help a few Ph.D. students have time to study without the constant financial pressure. I'd like to do the same for your department if you think that would be wise."

"It would be a nice gift, Emily. Students would appreciate that help."

"I benefited from those kind of gifts as a student and I'd like to pass on that practical help."

"Decisions are getting settled in your thinking, that's a good way to end your sabbatical."

They walked in quiet for a half a block. "Going to tell me the rest of it?" Noah asked, curious. "God's been steady all afternoon with the simple words 'it's settled'. I've been having to nail my feet to the floor not to come over and ask what's happened."

"I got a call from the President of Austin University. It was a good conversation. They want to know if I'll say yes if offered the position."

Noah accepted that news with a better reaction than he had the first time he'd heard she'd received a call from them. "A wise question on their part. If they offer you the job and you decline, they don't want to offer it to the next person and if asked, have to say that person was their second choice."

Regardless of her decision, it wasn't going to end this relationship. He thought Austin would be a nice place for her and the job somewhere she would thrive. "Which way are you leaning?"

"I don't want the job. I have no desire to return to Austin. The desire of my heart flipped like a switch from yes to no before the conversation had even finished. I asked him to give me 48 hours and I'll call him back. I'll give God those hours to confirm that should be my answer. But its settled in my heart, Noah. I didn't have to make the decision. God made it for me. I didn't have to wrestle through what was best for me versus best for us and this relationship. Here, Chicago, is best for me professionally and for us."

Noah listened to how she said it and simply nodded. "Okay." God had been telling him all afternoon it was settled. It was. "Just so you know, I would have leaned toward you telling Austin University yes. I liked the campus and the city. It's a good opportunity for you. And we would have made it work for us."

"I think its no because I saw the city and the campus in a different way. I saw them as a step backwards. They were smaller than my world that I've found here. And I'm starting to spread my wings and like the possibilities of here. Not only because of us and the fact your family is here. If I was in Austin I'd rarely get to see Frank and you together. Here I can ask a science question and around me within walking distance are subject matter experts to help me. I like this place. To teach here and research here, that life works for me.

"At the end of the meeting tomorrow I'll mention that I would like to have Bryce talk with them about the research contract I work under which expires in a few days. Unknown to me, Gina has been thinking about this research question too, and has been putting together another reason I might want to stay in Chicago rather than go back to Austin. If Bryce is able to negotiate research terms with the University that fit me, great, if not, there is a chemistry company in the start up complex an alumni of the college has built. Gina knows him. I can do research in his lab if I like and take the university out of the equation. I'll teach here and research there. It's only a twenty minute walk from my lab and office on campus."

"The complex on fourth street, where some of the medical start-up companies are housed?" Noah asked, recalling what he knew about the start up complex.

"That's the place. He's in the south building extension, the single story addition, that wing was built specifically to handle chemistry labs. His company is hired on a project basis to answer questions other businesses have, some are industrial in nature, they need an adhesive that handles high temperatures, a new lubricant, a better cat litter, some are basic chemistry – a company needs a specialized chemical refined, a museum needs an independent analysis of a paint or patina analyzed.

"I can use their lab for whatever science I like. He'll expense me the chemicals I use. If I create or do something which generates an income, then I pitch in on the lab costs based on the hours I used the lab. Basically, rent is free, unless you can afford to pay it from your profits. But what I develop is mine. If I want to hire students to work with me there, he would put them on his company payroll. I would become basically a stand-alone company within his company."

"It's the university system and their business office as your resource or you do the work directly using an outside lab space. You've already got contacts with patent and licensing companies, would need to add a law firm, CPA, publicity, to the mix. Any science you come up with would flow through that same pipeline."

"It's about half created already. I think I prefer the convenience of the university system but there is the possibility of going independent now if that's what makes sense."

"The nice thing is, you can simple turn to Jesus and say here's where I'm at. What should I do? He's a good shepherd for a reason. He figures these steps out for you."

"For which I am ever grateful."

They were trying out the London Pub which had opened near the campus; the sound of laughter and enticing smell of shepherd's pie met them as they stepped inside. It was crowded with college students which spoke to both the good prices and good food. "Booth or table?"

"Let's try a booth," Emily replied.

Noah chose one toward the quieter side of the room. This constituted a date as he had offered the invitation and would be paying for the meal but he didn't want this evening to step on the actual first date he had planned for the lunar eclipse. That night he would make an event, this one was about having her company and enjoying the conversation wherever it happened to flow. The nice thing about the summer was the gradual ramp it had given this relationship. They weren't in a hurry to end up somewhere. They both needed that in their lives.

When their meal had arrived, Emily mentioned, "I had a dream last night. It felt like a dream God gave me."

"Tell me about it," Noah invited.

"I saw the earth, not buildings and cities and roads and seas, but rather earth as an expanse of ground stretching as far as the eye could see. It was gray out, like the moments before dawn. There were people silently rising, standing, a vast multitude. Everything was in silence, stillness, waiting. And I had the thought, 'they don't know who they are. They don't know they are sons and daughters of God!'

"Rising from the earth were the sons and daughters of God, standing there with no sense of their identity at the start of a new day. Then here one, there another, they began looking down to resume labor rather than looking up to their father. They were returning to be natural man. They don't know they are sons of glory. Then I woke up, with a heartbreaking sadness in me."

Noah was startled by the vividness of what she described. He leaned against the Holy Spirit in his thoughts, wanting to understand the dream, for the unusual nature of it did sound like a dream from God. He smiled as a thought came to mind. Of course.

"Jesus is 'bringing many sons to glory'," Noah commented. "Your dream is a picture of Hebrews 2. Only the people in your dream didn't realize they were now free of bondage." He quoted the scripture that had come to mind.

But we see Jesus, who for a little while was made lower than the angels, crowned with glory and honor because of the suffering of death, so that by the grace of God he might taste death for every one. For it was fitting that he, for whom and by whom all things exist, in bringing many sons to glory, should make the pioneer of their salvation perfect through suffering. For he who sanctifies and those who are sanctified have all one origin. That is why he is not ashamed to call them brethren, saying, "I will proclaim thy name to my brethren, in the midst of the congregation I will praise thee." And again, "I will put my trust in him." And again, "Here am I, and the children God has given me." Since therefore the children share in flesh and blood, he himself likewise partook of the same nature, that through death he might destroy him who has the power of death, that is, the devil, and deliver all those who through fear of death were subject to lifelong bondage. (Hebrews 2:9-15)

"Thank you. That's what I was seeing. The children of

God, glory was theirs and they didn't know it. They weren't looking up. They were returning to labor, to life as it had been, not as it was now."

"There's hope, Emily. Because God won't leave his children without the knowledge of who they really are. It will come. And people will begin to look up."

"I wish it happened faster."

Noah smiled. "In four years he's taken you from unbelief to knowing some of the best treasures in the scriptures. I'd say what God is doing with you is a good example of what He'd like to do with everyone. You were hungry, Emily. You wanted to find God. And when you sought him out with all your heart, you found him."

"He likes to be found," Emily replied.

Noah laughed. "He does indeed."

"I'm glad I found you this summer. Wherever this," she gestured with her fork between the two of them, "goes, it's been nice. I was in need of a friend like you."

"I'd say that sentiment was mutual. I like the fact you let me talk about God and go on and on…."

Emily laughed. "You forget I like to learn. When you're talking, I'm piling up connections between stuff I had already learned and what I hadn't put together yet. Dad's got this really spectacular kingdom he's given me and I want to walk around in all of it. I'm greedy to see what it all looks like. So God gave me you to help fill in that answer.

"What you don't realize, Noah, is that I'm really learning your story as you talk about subjects. Your journey through life is being laid out as clearly as mine. You just found God at a young age and have been enjoying the kingdom longer. Mine has been chemistry and different places, different discoveries, yours has been one place, one subject, growing very deep roots into what God has done for you. You're like one of those oaks of righteousness God talks about, planted beside living waters just growing and growing. You've never needed to be elsewhere to grow."

Noah thought about it, back to his student days. Emily

was right. God had planted him early and given him the desire to stay put and just learn, to share what he was finding, to talk about God with those who would listen. "It's nice, having God plan our lives."

"I've learned He even gives good directions on where to eat. This meal is delicious. I'm thinking strawberry shortcake for dessert."

The dessert menu was six pictures on the card over the condiment holder and hard to miss, he'd been eyeing it too. "I'm going to go with the mud pie," Noah mentioned, the layers of chocolate appealing to him. 'Something about the name suits a guy."

Emily laughed. "This makes a good end to the semester, Noah. We should make it a tradition."

"I like that idea. We'll consider it our first."

****

Emily thought for a minute, then filled in the email text.

Noah, for the last few months I've been creating a list of what God has highlighted to me in the scriptures so I can see who I am. It's become the theme of what God wanted to accomplish with this sabbatical. You've sent me good material to read this summer. This is my contribution in return, with thanks for a good summer of conversations. Emily

P.S. I've been thinking a lot about righteousness lately (see the scripture list also attached). I'd like to talk about that topic next.

Emily sent the email with its two attached documents to Noah's university account and settled back in her office chair. The final days of her sabbatical were flowing out in anti-climatic fashion, but that was fine. She was dating a good guy, they were engaged in conversations about God which were benefiting them both and her life was peaceful.

It was a good ending. The battery presentation had gone well and its further progress was now being overseen by Bryce. She'd probably cook out a steak for her dinner tonight and then call Noah after the late evening news. He was presenting at a conference in Michigan tomorrow and had flown out earlier in the afternoon to meet with the sponsors this evening.

She'd made one decision over the summer that would continue on. She wouldn't go back to a life without hours of time spent with God of a morning. It was too valuable to her. Her first class this fall began at eleven, most were in the afternoons, and that schedule was going to be ideal.

The best wine took time to create. She was understanding things at the end of the summer that she had only begun to think about when the summer began. The continued outcome she wanted with God was going to come because of the steady day-by-day press into Him. The intimate knowing Him, the growth she needed, wasn't going to happen with intense hot days followed by busy weeks where she was passing by Him with only quick conversations. She wanted the substance of what she had tasted this summer, she wanted God, she wanted *Him*.

The valuable wine was still ahead of her, the insights and knowledge and revelation of God went much deeper. She had tasted the first of the good wine, the first of the goodness she could put into words, but the riches of it? The depths of what God had to offer? He had barely begun to reveal those to her. She had a choice, to figure out how to pursue Him for more, or let the busyness of life intrude back into her pursuit of God and choke it for time. She'd made her decision. Whatever it took – she was going after God first.

A relationship with Noah was forming in the midst of this life too. "I want you God, whatever the cost. And I want whatever you have planned for me with Noah, too." She said it aloud because the decision had been made in her heart and she wanted it on record with God. "Now I need you to show me what that looks like as I return to a life teaching students and doing research."

She instinctively knew time with people would be a priority with God, what he was giving her was received so she could share it on, but it might look very different in how that time was arranged. God would figure it out for her.

It had been a good summer. One whose value was only now becoming clear. Taking a sabbatical and hanging out with God had been the best decision of her life. Her step of faith had been met by God's goodness. She had given Him her time and attention and He had given her back peace and joy and a guy who truly liked her. It had been a very solid exchange. "Loving you, God, is simply nice." She gathered up the pages on the printer and headed downstairs to spend an hour with God stretched out reading through whatever book in the bible he suggested, eager to see what their conversation would be about. Life was good. Eternal. It was never going to end. And she was beginning for the first time to truly live its fullness. The reality of that was God's goodness to her. She had never felt more blessed than she did now.

[If you would like to read Emily's two documents please turn to page 373 in the extra section.]

****

Noah heard his phone chime as he walked into the hotel. He'd set his university account to forward emails from Emily. He pulled out his phone as the elevator took him to the fifteenth floor. The nice thing about technology was being connected while in different cities. He smiled as he read her note. It had indeed been a good summer of conversations. Righteousness was a great subject. He wondered if Emily understood what he'd come to realize. Their relationship was being born out of conversations. If he had the desire of his heart they would be talking together every day for the rest of eternity. It was nice falling in love.

He pocketed his phone rather than send a text reply. He liked to hear her voice and he should be free early enough to call her and have an hour conversation tonight.

He entered his hotel room and put the gift he had purchased beside his briefcase. He knew she liked conversations, it was time to find out if she also liked gifts. Because he had in mind more than a few he would like to give her. He'd been making a list on the flight.

He was speaking tomorrow on the goodness of God. He was experiencing it right now. God had been very good to him this summer. To both of them. He'd never felt more blessed than he did now.

EXTRA'S

the following pages include the full conversations between Noah and Emily on topics

&

notes sent between Noah and Emily

*

7 continued

Noah typically walked alone of an evening. It was nice walking with Emily. "Had enough for now?" he asked, opening the door so she could choose a lighter subject for the remainder of their walk.

Emily laughed. "My big puzzle just got solved. My eternal life has already begun. I'd love to listen to more, even if I have to ask you questions later. I've been wrestling with this puzzle for a long time and I want to enjoy this moment to the fullest."

Noah adored her for that bubbling joy. He considered the possible directions to go. "Okay. A couple more observations then."

He took Emily back to the foundation of the exchange. "Jesus comes to the cross perfect. His whole being is righteous and he is fully under the authority of God. There is no corruption in him. Jesus has never sinned and there is no death or disease in him. Even his act of going to the cross is out of obedience to the Father – 'not my will, but yours be done'. On that Friday Jesus takes our place. God puts on Jesus all the bad in us and gives us all the good in Jesus. Jesus bears our sins, our diseases, our infirmities and pains. Jesus experiences death on our behalf. The exchange is total. It's pure love pouring out pure grace upon us.

"We come to God in bad shape, corrupted by sin and death. We have a dead spirit. We have a soul with a sin nature, a self-will which is disobedient to God, we are slaves to sin and under the authority of satan. We have a body which is perishing, corrupt with disease and being destroyed by death, for death came into the world through sin.

"We hear the good news about Jesus. We repent (we change the way we think, we desire to no longer be a sinner), we call on Jesus to save us, to be our Savior. We identify with what Jesus did for us at the cross by being baptized. During our baptism, we die. The scriptures say we are crucified with Christ. It's past tense, its a total death. We are buried with Christ. Our sinful nature of flesh is circumcised (cut away) from us by God Himself. Nothing of that sinful nature remains in us when God is done. We have literally died to sin. It was that sin nature which brought spiritual and physical death to us. When we rise out of the water of baptism we are raised a child of God, righteous, with God's own nature abiding in us. We are no longer sinners, but saints. The corruption in the world is no longer part of us. We are no longer of the world. There is no more death in us, only life. We have been ransomed from the kingdom of darkness by the precious blood of Jesus and translated into the kingdom of light by God the Father. We have been placed into Jesus' kingdom.

"'you have died, and your life is hid with Christ in God.' (Colossians 3:3b) That's the good news of what just happened in one sentence.

"We exit the resurrection of baptism born-again from above. We are a new creation, a new kind of being that did not exist before. We have a new living spirit, able again to hear the voice of God. We have a new soul that has been made righteous, God has given us a new heart and God has written his laws on our hearts and minds so we desire to do the Father's will, to say like Jesus – 'not my will but yours, Father'. And we have a new living body, one no longer subject to satan's rule, one no longer subject to disease or death. Instead, our body is now the dwelling place, the temple, of God. The Holy Spirit, God, living in us now displays the life of Jesus in our mortal bodies. We have put on Christ Jesus. We are a saint; as completely clean and righteous as Jesus Himself. We are like him in every way but one, we don't yet have a heavenly body. When Jesus returns for the church we will see him as he is now and in the twinkle of an eye we will be changed to be like him as we rise to meet him in the air. The mortal will be swallowed up by immortality. We will have our heavenly bodies.

"People struggle with are we saved when we repent and call upon Jesus to be our Savior or are we saved when we are baptized (immersed) in water. The answer is yes. Both are necessary. We need three things – an alive spirit, a soul set free of sin and a body that is now under the rule of Jesus. Jesus says in John 3:5b, 'unless one is born of water and the Spirit, he cannot enter the kingdom of God.' Entering the kingdom of God requires both repentance, calling upon Jesus to be our Savior by faith and baptism (immersion) in water. We can't be a Christian without a new spirit and we can't walk in righteousness without the sin nature being cut away from us. Our spirit comes alive when we cry out to Jesus with faith. So faith is necessary. Obedience is also equally necessary, for baptism cuts away our sin nature. We die to sin. This struggle with the old nature ends when we die in baptism. God sets us free. Believe and be baptized, words and action, complete us being born-again a new creation.

"Jesus is our Savior (he has redeemed us from sin), Jesus is our Lord (Lord means owner – he purchased us with his blood), and Jesus is Our King (our ruler – we obey him). Hebrews 5:9b says 'he [Jesus] became the source of eternal salvation to all who obey him' Obedience is a requirement of salvation. Faith without works is dead. Faith plus works gives you salvation. Without faith *and* obedience you will not enter heaven. Obedience is like the mirror that shows you what happened on the inside of you. When you repent and have faith in Jesus as your Savior you are changed on the inside and your outside actions will show what happened on the inside. If you aren't obeying Jesus, what you had was an emotional experience that you were a sinner going to hell, but you never repented of your sin, turned to Jesus, and accepted Jesus as your Savior, Lord, and King. You just wanted to avoid the bad outcome of hell. You didn't want to follow and obey Jesus. You didn't want Jesus to rule you. The presence or absence of obedience shows what happened in your heart. Your obedience is confirmation your salvation happened. Your obedience or lack thereof will show you if you are saved.

"A new Christian is a babe in Christ. He's been made perfect, but he's a perfect baby. He may not know or understand much scripture and he hasn't practiced living in this new nature walking with the Holy Spirit. He matures and shows himself to be a Christian who does not sin as he puts off the habits of the old man that is not him anymore. It's a process but it doesn't need to be a long one. God abides in us now. God's gift to us is Himself. That's the most remarkable fact of all in our new creation.

"God reveals seven names for Himself in the Old Testament. God's names are beautiful and they are expressions of who He is. They are also expressions of what God abiding in us will mean for us. I AM your righteous. I AM your peace. I AM your healer. I AM your provider. I AM your good shepherd. I AM your victory. I AM always present to you. We are radically changed by salvation and baptism because God Himself is now dwelling within us. A disciple lives his life listening to Jesus' voice and doing what Jesus says. He's your Lord, your King, your Savior. You're righteous now. You're a saint. When you walk with the Holy Spirit, are led by the Holy Spirit, you will automatically and without effort show your new nature. It's not hard to be who you are. A mature Christian looks like Jesus." He chose to end the topic there.

"I love that image, Noah. It's like a boy who looks like his father. You can see it in the mannerisms, the hair and eyes, the build, a child is soon recognized because the traits from his father are his from birth. Christians are born-again of God and we now have God's nature."

"That's the most powerful part of baptism," Noah agreed. "The old is gone, the new has come. All things are now of God. He's the one within us empowering this new life we live. Our part is to let go of the old thinking, to walk with the Holy Spirit, so we will show the new and different life we have been given by grace."

"You just put together a lot of scriptures easily," Emily mentioned. "I knew a lot happened when I believed and was baptized. I've been collecting notes and verses on the topic, but it really helps seeing it put together like you just did. At the time I knew I was a sinner and needed a savior and Jesus was the Son of God, the guy I needed. That's why I was baptized. Then I realized all this 'more' is in the bible – we have eternal life that has already begun, we are healed, we are a new creation. It's mind blowing, Noah. No wonder my last four years have felt like standing under a waterfall of good gifts. All this goodness has been pouring over me and I was mostly clueless when I walked into being a Christian. I just didn't want God to be mad at me and send me to hell, so I said yes when asked if I wanted Jesus to be my Savior, if I wanted to follow him. I didn't know at the time I was getting all this, too."

Noah knew the sensation she was feeling. "The men and women with Jesus, they didn't know much when their journey started either, Jesus just gave them an invitation to 'follow me' and they were wise enough to do so. They found all these gifts waiting for them, too. God is good, Emily. He loves you. You became His daughter when you accepted Jesus. It's like stepping into a mansion and realizing your new Dad is the one everyone calls God and your eyes start opening to how amazing your new Father is. Because that's what just happened. God is now your Father. He knows your name. He talks with you and listens to you. He loves you with a passion beyond words. Jesus is now your older brother and your King. Being a Christian is a good experience. A fact satan tries to distort and ridicule any way he can in culture, for all he has left is deception. Those who say yes to following Jesus quickly realize just how amazing and abundant the life is Jesus freely gives us. Laying down life as we would direct it for the life Jesus gives us is the best deal in the world. Knowing the Father and Jesus, being friends with them, nothing else comes close to that joy."

"I love that description. Do you have a verse list that would include what you just shared?"

"Sure; I'll send it to you. You like to read, so I'll fill

your inbox over the summer with resources you might find helpful. You can wave a white flag of surrender when you reach the point you're drowning in too much to read and I'll pause until you ask for more."

Emily laughed. "I know you're being serious about that white flag but test me; I like to learn."

Noah felt the Holy Spirit underline her simple remark, I like to learn, and realized it was probably the most revealing comment she'd made about herself thus far. There was her heart and why the Holy Spirit had been revealing His treasures to her. Emily sincerely liked to learn. Okay. That would be the guiding line for their summer of conversations. Noah would accept the challenge to pour out truth to the point she was satisfied. It wasn't the first time he'd been given an assignment related to a specific individual but it was unusual how this one had evolved. "I promise to be strategic with what I send so it's a fair test. If you give me an occasional 'more like this one' I'll learn your preferences for what you find helpful."

"I can do that."

He and Emily were on the far side of the track so even if they called the evening finished now they would be walking back to the gate exit and then back to the Physical Sciences Building. They had a few more minutes together. Noah decided to turn their conversation to one of the most revealing comments Jesus had made about himself. "Do you remember the story about Lazarus?"

"He's one of the people Jesus raised from the dead," Emily replied. "His sisters were – their names both start with M."

"Martha and Mary."

"Thanks. I'm remembering the right account."

"Lazarus gets sick and dies. By the time Jesus arrives at the village of Bethany, Lazarus has been in the tomb for four days. When he arrives, Jesus makes a very interesting statement about himself. Jesus says to Martha, 'I am the resurrection and the life', literally 'I am the rising again, and the life' as the Young's Literal Translation renders the

Greek. Jesus then tells Martha two facts and asks her a question, 'he who believes in me, though he die, yet shall he live, and whoever lives and believes in me shall never die. Do you believe this?' It's John 11:25-26.

"I love that passage because it tells us something very important about Jesus. He makes two I am statements about himself. I am the resurrection. I am the life. Then he makes two statements showing what 'I am the resurrection' and what 'I am the life' look like.

"Take the first statement. 'I am the resurrection.' And what it looks like – 'he who believes in me, though he die, yet shall he live.' We see that with Lazarus. Lazarus believed in Jesus, believed Jesus was the Messiah, believed Jesus was the Savior sent to save the world. But Jesus hasn't died on the cross yet. Jesus can only give Lazarus life by external means, by showing up at his grave and commanding death to let Lazarus go. "Lazarus, come out!" and the dead man walks out of the tomb after being dead four days. Jesus has authority to raise him from death back to life. That is the first half of the statement Jesus makes. I am the resurrection. Jesus then proves it by raising Lazarus from the dead.

"Now take the second statement. 'I am the life.' And what it looks like – 'whoever lives and believes in me shall never die.' After Jesus dies on the cross and rises again, we are able to be born again from above, we are able to become children of God. Jesus – the life – can now abide in us. Christians are living in the second half of Jesus' statement to Martha. Jesus' question is addressed to us. 'whoever lives and believes in me shall never die. Do you believe this?' Christians have life in us now that is eternal life. It's a present tense now life that never ends. We shall never die. Jesus' question is directly to us – 'whoever lives and believes in me shall never die. Do you believe this?'

"Jesus spent three years of ministry trying to get us to hear and believe what he was saying. He wasn't hiding truth, he was stating it in the clearest and simplest terms he could. 'I am the life. Whoever lives and believes in me shall never die.' You have to be a child to hear what Jesus says and not read right over it. To not think, 'we die first, then we live and never die.' Satan loves to add words to what Jesus said and change what we think. We've watched so much death, both real and fictional through the entertainment of television and movies, we have been inoculated to the fact there isn't death in God, that what we are seeing with death is only satan's handiwork. Death came into the world through sin. Jesus completely dealt with sin and abolished death. That's the good news. We struggle to hear and accept truth. Satan isn't afraid of you reading the bible, he's afraid of you reading it like a child and hearing what it actually says. Jesus has abolished death and brought life and immortality to light through the good news. 2 Timothy 1:10b means what it says.

"Another favorite phrase of Jesus is, 'He who has ears to hear, let him hear.' We often listen, but don't hear, because we add words which change what Jesus said.

"Jesus is the Passover Lamb of God. His death, his blood, put away the sins of the whole world. In Egypt, the blood of the Passover lamb on the doorpost caused the angel of death to pass over the households of Israel – it was a picture of the blood of Jesus which now causes death to pass over us. The Old Testament is a picture, a shadow, of the substance that is ours with Jesus. Because Jesus' blood was shed for us, because we are covered with Jesus' blood when we call on him as our Savior, death now passes over us. We have passed out of death into life.

"If we think our life is like Lazarus' life – we believe in Jesus, we get sick and die, then Jesus comes and raises us from the dead to be with him in heaven – that will be our experience. We are living on the wrong side of the cross in our thinking. We live a Lazarus life because it is easier to get sick and die and accept that fact, comfort ourselves that we will be with Jesus after we die, then live differently than everyone else around us does and simply not die. We let what we see with our eyes around us override the truth Jesus is telling us. Faith in the truth would set us free of a

Lazarus life.

"The truth is we have eternal life now, we are healed and we never die. We have Jesus – the life – abiding in us now. We are in this world, but not of it. We are already a new creation. We died during baptism. We'll never die again. We can live on earth until Jesus comes again and simply rise to meet him in the air, putting on our immortal heavenly body in the twinkle of an eye. Paraphrasing 1 Thessalonians.5:23-24, it is the God of peace Himself who now keeps our spirit, soul and body sound and blameless. Jesus' statement – 'whoever lives and believes in me shall never die. Do you believe this?' – is our finished good news."

"It's beautiful news," Emily decided.

Noah laughed at her tone. "You're going to enjoy every day of it," he predicted easily.

Emily pointed to the stands and took a stadium seat. "How long have you understood this, Noah? That our eternal life has already begun? That death is not part of a Christian's life?"

He took a seat near hers, surprised she was silently asking for a longer conversation, but welcoming it, for the topic needed the time and it was a pleasant night to be outside. "In full view understood it? About a decade. My question, my puzzle was slightly different than yours, but it led to the same treasure.

"The sermon on the mount is a conversation Jesus had with his disciples. Matthew 5 begins with, 'Seeing the crowds, he [Jesus] went up on the mountain, and when he sat down his disciples came to him.' It's important to know these are disciples he is teaching, not the general crowd, although the crowds were around.

"In the sermon on the mount there is a verse where Jesus tells his disciples, "Enter by the narrow gate; for the gate is wide and the way is easy, that leads to destruction, and those who enter by it are many. For the gate is narrow and the way is hard, that leads to life, and those who find it are few." (Matthew 7:13-14)

"Jesus says those who find life are few. But Revelation says those who come out of the great tribulation, who find salvation, are 'a great multitude which no man could number.'

After this I looked, and behold, a great multitude which no man could number, from every nation, from all tribes and peoples and tongues, standing before the throne and before the Lamb, clothed in white robes, with palm branches in their hands, and crying out with a loud voice, "Salvation belongs to our God who sits upon the throne, and to the Lamb!" Revelation 7:8-10

"I was trying to puzzle out which verse I wasn't understanding. A 'few' and 'a great multitude' are vastly different answers. Jesus in John's gospel describes himself as being the door for the sheep, so its likely the narrow gate reference is also to Jesus Himself. Then I realized the sermon on the mount was Jesus talking to his disciples who already believed in him. Jesus was telling his disciples something important about finding life. I began to trail the word life through the New Testament and that's when I found 1 John 5 and God's testimony about His Son. God has given us eternal life and that life is in His Son. The verse is present tense. We have eternal life now, it's already begun. 'by his wounds you have been healed'. I realized we are healed by Jesus – the life – abiding in us. It came together for me from there.

"Jesus tells us the gate is narrow and the way is hard that leads to life. It's two stages, we enter the narrow gate (we accept Jesus as our Savior and receive salvation) and then we find life (we realize our eternal life has already begun so we live and do not die). Jesus with the sermon on the mount was talking to his disciples about how to live – how to conduct their inward thought life, how to conduct their outward religious life and how to obey his words so they would build their lives on rock, on a firm foundation that would not be shaken by the storms that came into their lives. Entering the narrow gate and walking the hard path that leads to life is what Jesus desired all his disciples to walk.

"As I've thought about that, I've come to describe the hard path that leads to life by seven things: Believing in Jesus as our Savior. Abiding in the word and believing it means what it says. Walking with the Spirit. Not being conformed to the world. Living under grace without condemnation. Realizing a Christian now has a divine righteous nature that does not sin. And last, but actually first, the overarching priority to love God and love our neighbor with everything we are. The primary feature of the narrow gate and the way to life is the decision to walk as Jesus walked, following him, conforming our lives to scripture and not the world. The world dies. Christians live."

"That's a helpful list," Emily remarked, noting down the items on her phone

Noah gave her a moment and then finished the thought. "It's not only individuals, its also the church corporately which finds life. Jesus says in Matthew 16:18b, 'I will build my church, and the powers of death shall not prevail against it.' The King James translation renders the Greek, 'I will build my church; and the gates of hell shall not prevail against it.' Other translations phrase it, 'I will build my church; and the gates of hades shall not prevail against it.' Jesus was being literal.

"Hades and hell are names for the resting place of the wicked dead. Gates are the entry way into a place. In bible times the rulers of a town would sit at the town gate and render verdicts on disputes among the people, would witness land sales, confirm business dealings. When this verse says the gates will not prevail it is speaking of the rulers of the place. The rulers and powers of death, hell, hades – satan and demons, the angel of death – will not prevail against the church, the people of God. 'I will build my church, and the rulers of the wicked dead shall not prevail against it.' The church walks in abundant life; death isn't part of our story."

"That's a powerful verse," Emily agreed.

She slapped her arm where a mosquito had landed. Noah knew where there was one others would be. He rose, figuring it was better to walk while they talked, than sit. Emily rose with him and followed him.

As they exited the track and turned toward the stadium gate, Noah mentioned another relevant point. "How long we remain on earth is Jesus' decision. Our story is now governed by the plan God has for our individual lives. There's an interesting conversation recorded in John chapter 21. After Jesus' resurrection, when Peter and Jesus are walking along the beach, Jesus tells Peter he will die a martyr and Peter turns, sees John and asks Jesus 'what about John?' Jesus makes a fascinating statement in reply.

Jesus said to him [Peter], "If it is my will that he [John] remain until I come, what is that to you? Follow me!" The saying spread abroad among the brethren that this disciple was not to die; yet Jesus did not say to him that he was not to die, but, "If it is my will that he remain until I come, what is that to you?" John 21:22-23

"There will be those of us who will finish the works God has prepared for us to do, to whom Jesus will say, 'its not my will for you to remain on earth until I return'. So we will take our last breath on earth and next in heaven. Moses was a type of this in the Old Testament. God told him today you'll die, so he climbed a mountain at age 120 and looked at the promised land, his eyesight was good, he was in good health, he simply took his last breath on earth and next one in heaven. It's said in the letter of Jude that the archangel Michael disputed with the devil about the body of Moses, so we know his body remained behind.

"Think of it like stepping through a doorway. We are on earth one moment and we are in God's presence the next. We aren't aware of that last breath, thinking that we want to take another breath and can't do so. Our spirit leaves our body and then our body stops breathing because a body without a spirit is dead. It's not death we experience. It's more like a 'goodbye, I'm done here, so I'm stepping into heaven (literally paradise) now.' The medical examiner doing our autopsy can't find a cause for why we stopped breathing as our bodies are in perfect health.

"Some Christians are martyred, some go to heaven because their work on earth is done and they leave their bodies behind, and it's possible that some Christians are translated like Enoch and Elijah and are taken to heaven with their bodies. It's said of Enoch that 'he walked habitually with God, and he was not, for God took him.'

"Jesus' decision about who he wants to remain on earth until he returns appears to be mostly a practical matter, if you look at how he handled his own situation. After his resurrection Jesus' was on earth another forty days and he chose to show himself only to his followers, not the world at large who didn't believe in him. Jesus didn't stand in front of Pilate as the resurrected King and say, 'I'm alive. Believe in me'. God values faith. We don't need faith to believe Jesus is alive when we see Jesus alive.

"Seeing a 2,000-year-old first century believer leading the communion service would be one step away from seeing Jesus leading that service. So I think there was a season early in Church history where Jesus said to those who understood they had eternal life now that it was not his will that they remain on earth until he returned and so they passed from earth to heaven in accordance with Jesus' will for their lives. I think we're in a different season now, when Jesus desires to answer yes to Christians who want to remain on the earth until he returns for his church, but only a few now have faith in eternal life and think to ask Jesus to do so. It's counter-intuitive, but I think many will hear the good news eternal life is already ours, it has already begun, and reject that good news because there isn't a 400-year-old believer standing here on earth as proof and Jesus intentionally created just that box. We've become people who only believe what we see. We've forgotten how to have faith in the Word and accept what it says. I think we're actually in a season now where Jesus would like the majority of the church to remain alive until he comes, but not many have faith to do so."

He unlocked the stadium gate, let Emily pass through, then relocked it behind them.

"I can see that, Noah. The decision Jesus has to make. He wants faith, he's given us life, and he enjoys our company. Even for those who have faith in life, there's a point at which Jesus' will for us is 'come up here. You've done a good job on earth. Come be with me in heaven.'"

Noah nodded his agreement. "It's Jesus' words, 'Father, I desire that they also, whom thou hast given me, may be with me where I am, to behold my glory which thou hast given me in thy love for me before the foundation of the world.' (John 17:24) We're friends. He wants us with him and Jesus is currently ruling earth from heaven."

The night was pleasant and the flower gardens by the conservatory were close by. The bike path would bring them back to the Physical Sciences Building by a more scenic path. Noah turned onto it with Emily.

"There is a reason God is so emphatic in his command to us that we are to be constantly in the Word, thinking about it, pondering it, talking about it and getting it into our hearts. The Word of God is living and active, powerful and perfect. It produces what it says.

"We are babes in Christ when we begin our journey and the Holy Spirit reveals truth as we walk with Him. Connie August, in those audios on healing I mentioned, does a wonderful job trying to get people to first base, to see that all mankind can live to be 120 years old, believers and non-believers alike. She hasn't yet taken the next step and realized that age-limit itself has been obliterated for Christians. Yet she heals the sick and raises the dead with confident faith, for she knows God has given all mankind 120 years. That's what partial knowledge of the truth can do. I find that incredibly reassuring. Connie has fully grasped that Jesus has healed us and given us life by what He did at the cross and from that faith she has both healed the sick and raised the dead. To the degree she has grasped the good news, it is powerfully able to work. She'll spend her lifetime being useful to God even if she never sees any more of the truth than she does now. Truth is powerful. And it builds on itself the more truth you see."

Noah reached for a way to sum up the good news he was talking about. "The good news of the gospel seems well suited for those who have a childlike heart. If you see Jesus is your Savior and call on his name, are baptized, your sins are forgiven and you have moved from death to life, you have escaped judgment and hell, you have moved into the kingdom of Jesus. If you see Jesus has healed you by his life abiding in you, take communion with faith, you live without disease. If you see God has given you life and that you always have that life, you realize you have eternal life now and you do not die when you reach a certain age, you continue living until Jesus returns for his church. You might be martyred, you might be translated, you might be told by Jesus it is not his will that you remain on earth until he returns, but satan will not take your life by disease or death. Jesus is your ruling Lord. Even if you draw the tough straw and are martyred for believing in Jesus, God honors that faithfulness with a reward in heaven only given to those martyred. God sees our life and wants good for us, always. God gave us a great salvation through Jesus. The more you see Jesus and what he did for you the better your life here on earth becomes."

"Why aren't people walking around astonished and amazed at what Christianity is?" Emily asked, curious. "How come this isn't simply the best news ever shared that everyone wants?"

Noah loved her question. "There are periods in church history where this good news was that vibrant in its effects on society. In Acts it was said of Christians, the 'men who have turned the world upside down have come here also'. The problem today is that Christianity gets clouded by its messengers. People see a mix of our lack of knowledge, our unbelief, rather than simply see Jesus and the good news. We look too much like the world and not enough like the Christians we are. Believers have been starving their lives of time in the Word and so don't know the scope of the good news. The Holy Spirit loves to teach us, but we must choose to be present with Him, listening and learning the scriptures.

"Many Christians actually still see themselves as sinners rather than saints. They spend their lifetime battling sin, not realizing, or having forgotten, that they are dead to sin. You have to read the Word and know what Jesus did for you for the truth to set you free. We are saints, not sinners. We are told to abstain from evil, to not engage in that fight. We are told to walk with the Spirit, to always do the positive, and that by doing so we will never fulfill the negative. A Christian no longer sins precisely because we are walking according to our new nature. That new nature is of God. We walk in righteousness. It's not that we are trying not to sin, its that we are dead to sin. It's 1 John 3:9 – 'No one born of God commits sin; for God's nature abides in him, and he cannot sin because he is born of God.' We no longer sin because we are no longer walking in the old nature of the flesh. We are walking now in the spirit.

"When something is dead, it gives no reaction or response. You can poke it, yell at it, hold up what use to appeal – and it just lays there. That's how completely God has solved the problem of sin for us. When we walk with the Spirit we won't have to struggle not to sin. Sin can do anything it wants to try to get our attention and we will give no reaction or response because we're dead to it. God freely gives us abundant grace, His empowerment to live a righteous life. We just have to set our heart on Jesus and walk with him. God will do the rest for us. So the first problem going on is a perception problem. As a man thinks in his heart, so is he. (Proverbs 23:7 KJV) Too many Christians see themselves as sinners and live struggling with sin when that's not who they are. They are saints.

"The second problem going on is mostly a timing one. Many Christians are waiting for heaven or for the rapture – Jesus' return for the church – so they can be healed, have eternal life and start living in the kingdom of God. Christians get the time period wrong for what has occurred and that throws off what they expect to happen on earth today.

"The kingdom of God is already here. It arrived with Jesus. Jesus is the King of the Kingdom of God. His ministry began with the proclamation 'the time is fulfilled, and the kingdom of God is at hand; repent (change your way of thinking) and believe in the good news.' You could reach out your hand and touch Jesus, the King.

"Jesus was healing the sick, casting out demons and raising the dead because the kingdom of God was now on earth ruling over and destroying the works of the devil. It was by the Holy Spirit Jesus was doing the works of the kingdom. The Holy Spirit is the one who fulfils the King's words. Jesus sent his disciples out to share that same good news. 'Whenever you enter a town and they receive you, eat what is set before you; heal the sick in it and say to them, 'The kingdom of God has come near to you.' (Luke 10:8-9).

"At the cross satan was tossed out as ruler of the world. When Jesus enters Jerusalem on the way to the cross, he declared, 'Now is the judgment of this world, now shall the ruler of this world be cast out'. (John 12:31) When Jesus died on the cross, Jesus died to pay the penalty for sin for all mankind, not just those who would choose to believe in him. Satan was using man's sin as his legal right to rule the earth. With all sin atoned for by Jesus, God promptly cast satan out, turned to his Son and rewarded Jesus' obedience. Jesus was given authority over the entire world. Matthew 28:18b-19a says after the resurrection, 'Jesus came and said to them, 'All authority in heaven and on earth has been given to me. Go therefore and make disciples....'

"The only one ruling earth right now is Jesus. Satan has no authority over any of mankind. God was so pleased with his son's obedience, God gave him rule over both earth *and* heaven. Jesus received his rule in A.D. 33. His rule is not beginning sometime in the future, it has already begun. Every principality and power, every angel and demon, every man, in heaven, earth and under the earth, are under Jesus' rule. Jesus is the crowned King of heaven and earth with all authority over both realms now. His authority is total.

"Jesus is choosing to reign from heaven during the church age. Jesus is seated at the right hand of God. Jesus is carrying out the Father's will on earth today just as he did while he walked on the earth. Jesus has given to his church kingdom rule. It's an absolute rule in Jesus' name. The church is the body of Christ; Jesus is the head of the church. Right now the devil, demons and men who reject Jesus are still running around causing havoc on earth; the wicked still delight to do evil. But the Church has authority over everything satan is trying to do and the power in Jesus' name to stop what is not in accord with righteousness. One reason God left our defeated adversary on earth is so the church can learn how to reign and use power. What we speak in Jesus' name happens. We learn how to rule by ruling. It's very much a hands on assignment.

"We have been given authority – the right to speak in Jesus' name. We are his Ambassadors speaking in accordance with the Kingdom of God we represent. We have been given power. Jesus said 'you shall receive power when the Holy Spirit comes upon you' (Acts 1:8). Jesus describes it as 'you are clothed with power from on high.' (Luke 24:49) Those who are baptized have 'put on Christ'. Think of it like a garment. We now have God with us and dwelling in us. When we speak in the name of Jesus we are speaking according to that 'put on Christ' mantle. We speak with the authority and with the power which Jesus has given to us.

"Moses carried a rod that represented his authority. It was called the rod of God. By the word of God Moses used that authority given to him. He held out his rod over the Red Sea and the sea parted so the children of Israel could cross on dry land. (Exodus 14). Moses represents the law. Elijah carried a mantle. It represented the Holy Spirit of God resting upon him. He took off his mantle, struck the Jordan river, and the river parted so Elijah could walk across on dry land. (2 Kings 2:8) Elijah represents the prophets. Both had authority from God which released the power of God. God's Word (the rod) and the Holy Spirit (the mantle). When Moses and Elijah acted using their authority, the power of God was released over the problem they were dealing with. That's why at the Red Sea the Lord told Moses to stop praying and instead go use his authority. The Lord had already given Moses what he needed to solve the problem. Authority speaks by word ('go, your son will live') and by action (lay hands on the sick and they will recover). Power fulfills what authority commands happen. Authority and power are both gifts from God.

"Jesus was a man just like us when he walked on earth. Jesus had to be commissioned and empowered by God to do the works of God. Jesus says of himself in Luke 4:18, quoting Isaiah, 'The Spirit of the Lord is upon me, because he has anointed me to…' and then he describes the five works he will do. Anointed means 'rubbed on like ointment, smeared on.' Jesus was like Elijah, his commissioning was by the Holy Spirit. Jesus received the Holy Spirit coming upon him after he came out of the water at his baptism and was praying. (Luke 3:21-22) And Jesus' commissioning was like Moses. Jesus spoke the word from the authority of the Father.

"We are given the same Holy Spirit as a gift in the same way Jesus received him. Jesus is the one who baptizes us with the Holy Spirit after our water baptism. We are anointed with the Holy Spirit and given power just as Jesus was so we may do the works Jesus did. All the works come from the Father. They are done on earth by the power of

God. God gave Jesus authority and power (Acts 10:38) and Jesus has now given that same authority and power to us, his disciples.

"'you have been anointed by the Holy One.' (1 John 2:20b) 'the anointing which you received from him abides in you, and you have no need that any one should teach you; as his anointing teaches you about everything, and is true,' (1 John 2:27b) The Holy One is Jesus. The anointing is the Holy Spirit, the Spirit of Truth.

"The disciples were already experiencing this coming authority the church would have even before the cross. Luke 10:17-20 'The seventy [disciples] returned with joy, saying, "Lord, even the demons are subject to us in your name!" And he [Jesus] said to them, "I saw Satan fall like lightning from heaven. Behold, I have given you authority to tread upon serpents and scorpions, and over all the power of the enemy; and nothing shall hurt you. Nevertheless do not rejoice in this, that the spirits are subject to you; but rejoice that your names are written in heaven."' Serpents and scorpions are biblical references to demons. Christians have the authority to cast out demons, heal disease, open blind eyes, raise the dead, to do the same works Jesus' did. That rule is not someday in the future, that authority and power are ours as a church today. In heaven there will be no one sick to heal. In heaven there will be no one who needs freed of a demon. This is the church age where we are commissioned by Jesus to do the works on earth which he did. If we believe the Word, we will speak in Jesus' name and use that authority and power we have been given.

"Truly, truly, I say to you, he who believes in me will also do the works that I do; and greater works than these will he do, because I go to the Father. Whatever you ask in my name, I will do it, that the Father may be glorified in the Son; if you ask anything in my name, I will do it." (John 14:12-14)

"This church age will end soon. Jesus will return to earth to rule from the city of Jerusalem. It will be easy to see the Kingdom of God after all evil is removed. Today is called the day of salvation – the period of time people can chose to be saved. God is showing mercy to mankind with this time. Jesus paid a very high price to save every individual. If Jesus had his desire, everyone would be saved, everyone would accept God's grace. But God has given mankind free will and will honor each man's decision about His Son. The time to make that decision to follow Jesus is right now, why the choice is available." Noah chose to pause what was a very involved topic there.

Emily thought about it and nodded. "I see why you say it's a timing problem, Noah. If you don't know you have been given the authority to rule, you won't do so. Jesus, reigning in heaven, has assignments for us to do, but what the King wants done isn't happening on earth because we're not acting in his name. Jesus can either act through other means, or wait on us. And he mostly waits, because he told us to act in his name."

"Jesus doesn't remove authority or power once he gives it," Noah agreed. "The local church is to be teaching Christians how to reign – how to walk with God, listen to His voice and then speak with authority in Jesus' name. When the local church drops that mandate, Christians don't know what they are commissioned to do, nor understand how to carry it out. A King rules by speaking. Our words in Jesus' name have power. All that happens here on earth, in nations, cities, businesses and families can be governed by righteousness if Christians would speak with authority what Jesus is directing them to do. Ruling isn't hard, but it's a different way of operating then what we see in the world around us."

They came to the Physical Sciences Building but rather than take the steps to the building, Emily took a seat on the half-wall by the metal sculpture of the earth globe. "Would you finish that thought? You understand the kingdom better than I do."

"Sure." Noah leaned back against the empty bike rack and relaxed. This was one of his favorite subjects. "Scripture says Christians are literally children of light. (Ephesians 5:8) God the Father has already translated us into the kingdom of his Son. We are now standing in the bright light of God's kingdom under the rule of a very good King Jesus. We are not in darkness. We just perceive darkness by what our natural eyes see happening in the world around us by those who do evil and we reach the wrong conclusion, thinking we are still living in the kingdom of darkness with satan still having authority over the world. The scriptures tell us something very different is true. Colossians 2:15 says 'He [God] disarmed the principalities and powers and made a public example of them, triumphing over them in him [Jesus].' Satan and the demons have already been disarmed and triumphed over. Our enemy is defeated. The battle is already finished. When we submit to God and resist the devil, the Word says satan and his demons literally *flee* from us. This isn't even a fight anymore. Satan prowls around looking for someone to devour – looking for someone who will let themselves be deceived, so satan can resume his assault to kill, steal and destroy their life. Only those who are letting themselves be deceived, who are choosing fear, are dealing with that darkness. Satan has no weapons, no authority, no power. He can only lie to those who don't know the truth. When we are afraid of the devil, or something he can do, we are putting our faith in the wrong person. He who is in us (God) is greater than he who is in the world. God laughs at satan and wicked men who think they are greater than He is. (Psalm 59:8, Psalm 2:4, Psalm 37:13)

"Most Christians don't realize when Jesus cried from the cross 'It is finished' just how finished the matter really was. God Himself was announcing the redemption of mankind and the destruction of the kingdom of satan. Both happened in A.D. 33. This fight with satan and the enemy is over. The kingdom of God has come. Jesus reigns today over all of heaven and earth. It's ours now if we will simply

express what is righteous in Jesus' name and rule. The
kingdom is invisible to our natural eyes but invisible does
not mean not present. Our heavenly bodies will have eyes
able to see it. We live by faith in the church age, believing
what the word says, because it says it. We know the
kingdom of God is true and present because the one who
can see it has described it to us.

"The kingdom of God is here. The kingdom of God is
ours now. 'Fear not little children, it is the Father's good
pleasure to give you the kingdom.' (Luke 12:32) You have
to know that in order to live in it. If you think the kingdom
is a future reality that comes after you die, you will spend a
miserable life on earth lacking what Jesus actually gave
you. You lack it because you don't know the truth. God's
lament hasn't changed: 'my people perish for lack of
knowledge' (Hosea 4:6). The Hebrew word for knowledge
used in the verse is one of intimacy, of knowing the word
and the person who spoke it. The biggest tragedy in the
world is Christians lacking knowledge of the Word and not
walking in deep friendship with God. We've been given a
kingdom. And it's a very nice kingdom! It's full of power
and authority and provision. Jesus has given us his name,
think of it as his signet ring, we go in Jesus' authority. We
speak as Jesus' Ambassadors and wield the power of God
against darkness. The Holy Spirit, God Himself, is with us.
We are co-laborers with Christ establishing his kingdom of
earth. It's a job assignment for today.

"Similarly, our primary resurrection is not when Jesus
returns for the church. Our primary resurrection has already
happened at our baptism. We have come to fullness of life
in Christ. Colossians 2:17b says 'the substance belongs to
Christ.' Once we have Christ, we have the substance of
what God promised to us. Righteousness. Life. Health.
Peace. The kingdom. God gave us all things with Jesus.

"The good news is wonderfully good news. We have
been born-again from above. We are now in this world but
not of it. We are healed, past tense. Jesus has abolished
death, past tense. We have been translated from the

kingdom of darkness into the kingdom of the light, the kingdom of Jesus. That, too, is already done. Psalms 103:5 mentions God even restores our youth. God has given us eternal life and that life is in His Son. Jesus has abolished death and brought life and immortality to light through the good news. When you see that, believe that, you cease conforming to the world and instead live and never die."

"I'll say again – Wow."

Noah laughed. "Grace is beautiful. That was the Son of God who died for us – Jesus' death was a vast overpayment for all the sins of the world and for all these extraordinary gifts God is offering. We don't need to bring anything to the table but a willing heart to receive freely from God. Jesus has abundantly paid for all these gifts God would like to give us. We should eagerly be desiring all of what salvation is. Deliverance. Provision. Health. Life. Righteousness. Salvation is free. Take it. All of it. Eagerly. Joyfully. With laughter. It's a really good free gift that was overpaid for by Jesus. He went abundantly overboard and went out and bought everything for us. Here! Take it! If you don't, I have nowhere to put it all!"

Emily laughed. "Jesus is the image of his Father, so it's the Father who is this lavishly generous too."

Noah was glad she had seen that truth. "He is indeed. We grow up in a world surrounded by people worried about having enough, with a poverty mentality about life, always stressed about the future – we've lived so long under the kingdom of darkness it is hard to shake that old nature mindset. Will our health last? Will our resources be sufficient? Will things turn out okay? That's not our reality anymore. God is good and His kingdom is filled with abundance. The Father is lavishly abundant in everything He does. When God says let me through Jesus save you, deliver you, give you health and life and abundance, He does it to a scale that is according to His riches in glory. God gives us as vast gifts and treasures. God loves us. He wants to pour all His goodness out upon us now on earth. We just have to let Him."

Emily smiled as she thought about it. "I think God desires to do so much good to me there isn't going to be enough years in my life on earth for Him to fit it all in. Since becoming a Christian it has been one open door of abundance after another. And I didn't deserve any of this. God just decided to love me. All I did was respond to the good news Jesus loves me. That's basically all I've brought to God. I changed my mind about Jesus. God didn't even hold all those years I was rejecting Jesus against me. He just said welcome home and threw a party in my honor in heaven and promptly dumped a waterfall of blessings on top of me here on earth." She laughed as she finished that thought. "Oh, God is indeed good."

Noah felt something inside himself relax as she said those words. She really had found the heart of God and understood it. She had accepted God's goodness. And God was able to bless her because of it. "He loves you, Emily, because you're His. You belong to Him. Love is an incredible reality. It propels a God of all power and righteousness and majesty to come and die Himself in order to rescue you and save you and help you. The lavish good that God now wants to pour out upon you because you're his daughter will take Him all of eternity to accomplish. The last chapters of Revelation describing what eternity is like for us are breathtaking. Salvation is a very good gift from a very good God. And it starts on earth the day we receive Jesus."

The moon was high in the sky, casting shadows through the trees. "I don't want to even guess how long we have been talking," Noah remarked, aware this hadn't been the walk he had asked her to take or that she had expected when she said yes. It had to be after ten p.m. now.

"I don't mind evenings like this," Emily replied. "I like conversations. I envy you, Noah, that calendar time you've had in the bible. I want to enjoy the full good news. I want to live the life Jesus died to give me. I'm greedy in a good sense. I have a lot and want more. I want God's full goodness. Sometimes our conversations will be like Gina trying to explain the thermodynamics of a tilting rocket to me, where I listen entranced, enjoying every minute of the explanation, then have to ask the most basic questions regarding the physics when she's done. I know enough to do the chemistry for that rocket, so I can be brilliant in some lanes depending upon what I have been thinking about in-depth. I have been thinking about the scriptures. I can keep up better than you might think."

Noah smiled at her last remark. "The Holy Spirit has already been handing you treasures, Emily. God shows no partiality, He gives treasures to anyone who will be curious and come seek them out. You'll be digging up ones I haven't found yet and sharing them with me and I shall enjoy that immensely, too."

"Did we just become friends?" Emily asked him, curious.

"Yes."

"Then I'll be nosey. You've bought a life insurance annuity, haven't you?"

He grinned. "A modest one. I figure they will start balking at the payouts around the time I'm 130, which is why there is a rider added putting my fingerprints and DNA profile on file as proof of identity. The annuity will be income for me and a way to generate some independent press coverage on how old I am. I figure around age 150 people will really start listening when I say God dwelling in me is keeping me healthy and alive.

"I've asked Jesus to let me remain until he returns for his church and I believe I'll receive that desire of my heart. I like to teach and it's a profession which will remain useful. I think Jesus returns for his church soon, like right now, given the number of leading signs already fulfilled, but if it isn't for another 1,000 years I'm comfortable being known for eternity as the oldest man to have ever lived on the earth. I think about that sometimes, when the evenings are quiet. I travel and speak more than I otherwise might because I think the calendar is very short and I want to make the most of every opportunity to talk about Jesus. I save a bit differently as compounding for 200 years makes decisions easier if the calendar runs long. And for practical reasons I don't want a wife who is going to die at 85 when my life expectancy is until Jesus returns for his church. I figure when I'm 150 I'll look around for a lady who is also 150 and easily spot who else believed Jesus meant literally what he said."

Emily started to say something, but stopped herself before she made the remark, shook her head to indicate she wasn't going to comment. Noah smiled as he could make an educated guess on what she hadn't said. "I joke about this, the implications of living into the hundreds of years, but at the same time I know it's the most serious matter God will require of me, what do I believe about Jesus, the word of God and what it says. God desires every man to be saved and to come to the full knowledge of the truth. I'm willing to be a child and read what Jesus says to mean what he says, to look foolish in the eyes of others. God says He has given me eternal life and that life is in His Son. Jesus abides in me. I have eternal life now. I can accept that means exactly what it says."

"I get that, the seriousness of it and the lighter side too," Emily remarked. "I was going to say it must make for some fascinating decisions. Both in practical terms, what place to buy and live, what improvements to make of what quality, and in serious decisions, like the value of writing a book, knowing it could be income for a hundred years, or the importance of a conversation with a student, knowing it might be the last conversation you have before Jesus returns. Timescales shift the relative value of so many decisions. You're living both very short and very long when you are balancing the immediacy of Jesus' possible return against the length of eternal life. It strikes me as being a fun challenge. Though until you mentioned the implications for a marriage, I hadn't spotted that knot. A believer and unbeliever don't match up for obvious reasons. But two believers with different assumptions about health and longevity of life – that would be a type of similar stress. This gets complex in a lot of ways the more you think about it."

"I'm comfortable being single for a lot of reasons, but that complication is one of the reasons I haven't married," Noah agreed. "I'm content letting Jesus sort it out for me."

He thought for a moment, then offered the thought that drove most of his own decisions. "It is appointed for men to die once and after that comes judgment," he said, going back to her initial point. "That verse is powerful. It's both a warning to mankind and a hidden clue to God's planned rescue. The lake of fire was created for the devil and his angels, it was never designed for mankind. That lake of fire is called the second death. That's why scripture says God appointed men to die once rather than twice. In God's plan, all of mankind were intended to be saved by Jesus. God planned from the foundation of the world that Jesus would die for all mankind, that Jesus would be the one to experience death and judgment on our behalf. Our baptism into Christ's death at our water baptism would be our one and only death and our way out of judgment. We accept Jesus and pass out of death into life. Jesus came to be the Savior of the entire world. That's the saddest part of our history. God rescued us from our sin. God says 'My Son died on your behalf, trust him as your Savior' and many of mankind will refuse to accept the gift.

"People don't realize God will honor their free will. Men and women who reject Jesus will be judged to be lawless and suffer the second death, they will be cast into the lake of fire with the devil and the fallen angels.

"An equally horrifying realization? People's rejection of salvation may have taken them five seconds. 'No, I don't want to listen to anything about Jesus'. They've just repeated that five second snap decision one too many times and their time to change their answer ran out. In the United States information about Jesus is everywhere – internet, television, bookstores, neighborhood churches, bibles are abundant and available free. People use their freedom to click past the preachers on television, decline invitations to church, change the conversation when a neighbor or co-worker mentions Jesus. But using your free will to be free of listening to anything about Jesus during your lifetime means you are choosing hell for your eternity. Judgment Day has one question – did you accept my Son Jesus as your Savior? God will honor your free will. It's scary how many well meaning good people have blindly closed their eyes to thinking about God, never pausing to realize good people don't go to heaven, only saved people do. People live rushed busy lives thinking earth continues on as they see it around them when in fact this world is rushing toward its ending and many are heading toward hell because they are not considering the only decision that actually matters in this world – who is Jesus. It's the only decision that changes eternity."

Noah paused because Emily had just visibly winced.

"That was me, Noah," Emily said. "If it were not for my grandmother, I could have easily been one of those too busy people. I didn't have a Jesus connection until she brought him into my life. I'd declined opportunities and thought nothing of doing so, religion and Jesus weren't in my priority list, though I had begun to shift my thinking to believe there was a God – chemistry is too beautiful for there not to be – but I hadn't taken that thought and done anything with it yet of my own volition. I'd never voluntarily listened to a sermon that I can recall. I lived in Texas, the heart of the bible belt, where not having church ties was somewhat unusual and Jesus was mentioned in casual conversations. I heard prayers and saw those around me who did prioritize their lives around a religious faith, but I was choosing to let it pass by me. I was blind to what I was doing, the implications of that repeated decision I was making. And it was casually made for the most part. A fact which makes me shudder today."

Noah understood that emotion. "I'm incredibly grateful you listened when your grandmother wanted to talk about Jesus. Angels rejoice every time someone accepts Jesus. Because those in heaven understand the implications, that someone's life was just saved from hell. There is no one Jesus would not like to reach; the question is, will we let Jesus reach us? Because time is running out.

"How time ends is a popular question. We know Jesus returns to earth. And we know on the Day of Judgment God will remove all causes of sin and evildoers from the kingdom of God. Men will be judged on that final day by one question. Have they accepted and followed Jesus as their Savior, Lord, and King. Are their names in the Book of Life. Those who haven't will be thrown into the lake of fire and spend eternity in hell.

"The scriptures talk about other events – the time of the Gentiles, the great tribulation, the antichrist, the war of Armageddon. The order of events is debated as well as which are literal events versus symbolic descriptions of events which are happening now.

"I personally believe God has a plan for Israel which is separate from that of the church. I believe that a remnant, if not all, of the Jewish people will accept Jesus as their Messiah in the final days. I take that from Romans 11:25-28. I believe the church will do enormous good as the light of the world. We will see nations become peaceful with the majority of their citizens following Jesus. I believe as time nears its end that the church will be removed from the earth to allow the antichrist and evil to again dominate the world. Christians will rise to meet Jesus in the air and will go with him into heaven – what is called the rapture – we will escape the trouble that is to come upon the earth. (1 Thessalonians 4:15-17, Luke 17:34-35) Then seven years of tribulation happens on the earth and includes a great war against Israel. That tribulation period ends when Jesus returns with the saints (the church) to rescue his people Israel and to rule from Jerusalem.

"Scripture gives no leading signs for the rapture, the return of Jesus for his church. It's described as coming as a thief in the night. But we are told several leading signs of Jesus' second coming to reign from Jerusalem. And those who are watching can see all those signs being checked off.

Israel has become a nation again. Jerusalem is under Israel's authority again. The time of the Gentiles has been fulfilled. Within a generation of those signs happening, Jesus returns to earth to rule from Jerusalem. Israel became a nation in 1948 and Jerusalem returned to Israel's authority in 1967, during the six-day war. 70 to 100 years is a typical generation. The very last days are happening right now. I believe we are on the verge of seeing nations turn to God in a new massive revival that will be worldwide. Muslims and Hindus will find Jesus. China will become a Christian nation. The populations of Europe and the Americas will return to God and again follow Jesus.

"1 Corinthians 15:25b-26 says '[Christ] must reign until he has put all his enemies under his feet. The last enemy to be destroyed is death.' Jesus reigns today through his church. How are his enemies put under Jesus' feet? By the Holy Spirit revealing truth to the church. We are seated with Jesus, what is under his feet is also under ours. Death is destroyed, made null and void, as Christians realize we have eternal life now, that our life has already begun. It is the words of Jesus – 'whoever lives and believes in me shall never die. Do you believe this?' bearing fruit. The angel of death is the last enemy thrown into the lake of fire. But death will have been conquered by the church before then. Christ is our victory over death. Jesus has abolished death. It's past tense finished. The church simply has to believe and display what Jesus has already done.

"That's why the question you were puzzling over 'why do Christians die? It's illogical' was another confirmation to me of what's happening right now. The Holy Spirit had already unwrapped the treasure for you that eternal means always, means now. Christians already have eternal life. The Holy Spirit is putting that final enemy beneath Jesus' feet right now by showing the church Jesus has already abolished death. You are a living example of that fact. And that is one of the very last markers before Jesus' return to earth. And if the second coming is very close, that means the rapture of the church is very, very close."

"You were actually surprised the rapture didn't happen today." Emily realized, startled.

Noah smiled. "The Holy Spirit was persistent all afternoon that you hadn't mentioned the question you were thinking about the most and when you said this evening what it was – let me say I'm surprised we are still talking, that our conversation wasn't interrupted by Jesus' return."

"Okay, that certainly spiked my adrenalin a bit."

Noah laughed. "Jesus' repeats his statement 'I am coming soon' three times in Revelation, in 3:11, 22:7 and 22:12. That certainly gets my attention. Jesus never lies. Soon is a powerful word. The word cousins for soon are 'rapidly, shortly, quickly, almost immediately, in next to no time'. Jesus said soon about 2,000 years ago, so whatever time period he implied has been colored in to nearly the final dot in the timeline. Jesus repeatedly warned the rapture of the church will come like a thief in the night. '[you] must be ready; for the Son of man is coming at an hour you do not expect.' (Matthew 24:44). The second coming in so close you can practically reach out and touch it. I think Jesus' return for his church is moments away, a right now event.

"The easy days to hear the good news and become a Christian are drawing to a close. Yet the world is mostly too busy to have time to listen to that good news. And I'm going to end this conversation here before I roll right into another topic and time turns into tomorrow on us."

Emily laughed at his humorous tone. "You like this conversation, I can hear both the depth of how much you've thought about it and your urgency about its implications. It was very helpful, Noah. It's hard to put into words how much I appreciate everything you shared tonight. I have conversations about God, but not many at this level and I could feel so many gaps in what I knew being filled in. Not much of what you said was new to me, but it was ordered and thus it helped clear my view. It takes the good news I knew and shifts it from being a hope for the future to being a faith for something in the present. I get to experience God's full goodness being mine now. I love that."

"I do, too," Noah comfortably agreed.

"Do you mind me asking – do you talk about this kind of thing much with friends like Gina?"

"Sure, I do on occasion. You can take in the bottom line and simply accept it and not need to think through all the reasons and whys that get you there. Gina is healthy and knows the why is Jesus – the life – abiding in her. She knows God has given her eternal life. Has she thought about the implications of living past a hundred? Probably not. She doesn't need to right now. She's got a busy life thinking about other things. My job is to ponder scripture and share it broadly, hers is to ponder science and make discoveries and talk about God with those in her world. We are both doing what God desires of us."

"I agree with that busy life Gina has. In general, do many believe you?"

Noah smiled. "Jesus told a parable that described one in four people believing the good news he was sharing to the point they were able to accept it, understand it and bear fruit. Jesus was a perfect teacher. So I take the long view on this subject. If someone doesn't believe the good news I'm sharing today, they may tomorrow. I know when I'm age 150 and take the stage looking young, most of my message will be preached before I even open my mouth.

"The Holy Spirit is a wise teacher of the good news. I try not to jump ahead of where he is working with someone. An individual may first need to hear that God does not lie. Or that a Christian can live righteously and not sin. That God has healed them of disease by Jesus at the cross as part of his salvation gift to us. The topic of eternal life is part of a whole. Those that are seeking treasures find this one, as it is one of the primary treasures of scripture. Jesus has abolished death and brought to light life and immortality through the good news. The kingdom of God is very good news indeed."

"It is. And I admit, it feels strange tonight, anticipating I'm going to be on earth when Jesus returns for the church. If not, it will be because I have finished everything God prepared for me to do on earth – and since we've known each other only four years I imagine there are many years of things prepared for me to do. It makes chemistry and my present research project rather minor in importance."

"Not to God," Noah replied. "He made us for his own enjoyment and glory and God likes hanging around a chemistry lab with you."

Emily smiled. "Thanks for saying that. I feel that all the time, as I make discoveries and understand the science, I feel God's pleasure in sharing with me what He created."

"He's enjoying that time with you. In three years on campus Emily, you have interacted with a different population of faculty, students and university staff than I have on the same campus – God needs us both where we are. You're a light in the world now. You don't have to work at being that. You shine wherever you are. A Christian's life is simple. You abide in the word, you make time for people and you enjoy walking with God. God bears fruit through you. You are a branch. You don't have to try to be one. It's who you are. Branches are leafy, taking in sunlight – the word of God. Branches let sap – the Holy Spirit – flow through them. Branches rub against other branches – we talk to each other. Branches bear fruit – what God does through us produces something good for other people to enjoy. That's most of our lives. We treat people as though they are Jesus standing in front of us and show them love. We love God and love those around us. Those who love know God. You can do that while being a great chemistry professor. When it is time to change something in our lives, the geography, profession, how we spend blocks of our time, God is good about making that clear."

"Thanks for that, too." Emily slid off the half-wall. "Would you do me a favor, Noah? Would you lean against the Holy Spirit for help and give me a final verse or two, maybe even prophesy again to end this evening? I'm curious how that works and I loved being on the receiving end this morning."

Noah leaned in his thoughts for a moment and smiled. "I already know the two verses for they end most presentations I make when I travel. They are from Peter's letters. The first, 'set your hope fully upon the grace that is coming to you at the revelation of Jesus Christ.' (1 Peter 1:13b) And the second one is similar, 'grow in the grace and knowledge of our Lord and Savior Jesus Christ.' (2 Peter 3:18a) The knowledge, the revelation, of Jesus and what he did brings us a steady stream of treasures."

Emily made a note of those scriptures and his comment on her phone. "What a perfect way to wrap up tonight. I've enjoyed this, Noah."

"It was a nice start to my summer as well," Noah assured her, wondering casually if he had just met his future wife.

****

"Okay, God, that was simply incredibly fun." Emily didn't know how else to begin the conversation with Him. The night she had figured out with God's help how to unzip chemical chains of solid rocket fuel like they were Lego blocks held together by a zipper, the breakthrough discovery that had made 3-D printing Gina's rocket design possible, that night had felt like this one. She was feeling bubbling joy and fatigue in equal measure.

She hadn't had that much fun talking about God in years, not since her grandmother had passed away. The conversation with Noah tonight had been excellent. One of her study topics for the summer had just taken on shape. Immortality. The Holy Spirit had walked Noah down the same truth a decade ago, she was standing not on new ground, but on truth he'd been exploring for years. She'd been right in realizing eternal meant always, meant now, that eternal life had already begun. She wanted to understand all that meant in depth.

"I have so missed these conversations, God, being able to talk about you in more than a surface way. Thank you for the two conversations with Noah which you arranged for today. I don't know how you could have crafted a more enjoyable gift for me. You saw the unspoken need in my heart and just piled on love by filling it up. The topic is excellent – I love my eternal life! – but it was the conversation itself that mattered even more. It was deep and it was about you and I wasn't having to wonder if I was thinking about something the wrong way – you just took over and flew that conversation in a bunch of directions pouring information about the good news all over me." She laughed. "Oh, that felt good, God. Like stepping into air conditioning on a sweltering summer day, like the smell of brownies coming out of the oven or the smell of a rose in a bouquet of them. It was perfect.

"You just blessed me in a magnificent way and from the sound of it you were setting up this evening for most of the day, prompting Noah to come find me to ask about the question I was pondering but hadn't asked him. It mattered that much to you, God? That we talk about this in-depth tonight? Is it because you are coming tomorrow for your church and wanted me to have this question answered before then? I imagine there are all kinds of items on your very last list that you want to get done."

She tried to imagine what it must be like to be God, the details He would want to wrap up on the day before Jesus' return. There were billions of people on His mind and He was seeing each person individually. Just the thought of it reminded her how big God was. There would be details big and small and He would handle each and every one of them perfectly. That thought was equally reassuring. "Thanks, God, sincerely. I want to enjoy life with you. Every detail you have thought about for me, for however long I have with you here on earth before your return, I want all of it. Wherever you plan to take these conversations with Noah, thanks in advance. They are going to be a highlight of my summer."

She tugged out her car keys, well satisfied with her day and ready to be home, to call this day complete. There was no more bandwidth in her left to fill, that was how complete God had made his gifts to her. He had exceeded everything she could have thought of for the first day of her vacation. "I love that about you," she mentioned, knowing God knew her thoughts. If God was going to do this for her entire summer it was going to be an overwhelmingly good sabbatical. "Thank you, Dad." She could feel his answering pleasure. It was obvious He had enjoyed tonight's conversation as much as she had. She drove home experiencing joy and fatigue and the comfort of being well and fully and perfectly loved.

****

There was an email from Noah in her university account the next morning. He had sent it just after midnight. She hadn't been the only one up late last night pondering their conversation.

I enjoyed our conversation, Emily. You might find these verses helpful. Noah.

She sent the attached document to the printer and read the brief note again. She hoped his comment was an indication Noah wasn't going to inwardly wince the next time she showed up at his office door. She had taken forty minutes of his time on their first conversation and the second one had exploded into more than two hours. Could they even have a twenty minute conversation given the type of questions she had for him? She didn't want to wear out her welcome. She was at a loss to know how to proceed. "Jesus, when should I go see Noah again and what should I ask him?" She asked the question aloud and trusted she would get good directions in reply.

Maybe this turned into an evening walk with Noah

364 Immortality

once a week and that was its boundaries. That could work given the topics on her list. Jesus would figure it out for her. Right now she had a verse list to study so she was current with what Noah had given her before she saw him again and then work to do testing a battery. She moved the post-it note 'pay bills' to the center of the monitor as a reminder for tomorrow, picked up the document from Noah off the printer and headed downstairs. She wanted to spend the morning with God.

Her favorite place to hang out with Him was the living room where the sun drenched in the east windows. She liked to stretch out on the floor with her bible and a ream of paper to make notes and enjoy her Father's company. She liked reading the words He had written to her with the Holy Spirit pausing her to point out interesting things. God loved her. And He loved talking with her. One of the reasons she had so looked forward to this summer break was the fact she could hang out with God for as long as she desired of a morning without a class to teach to interrupt their conversations. She planned to make this the pattern of her summer, spending the first part of her day hanging out with God. She wanted a much deeper friendship with God by the end of this summer. The best way to develop a friendship was to spend time together and that part of the equation she could do. God would meet her as she sought Him.

****

Noah's Note

sin came into the world through one man [Adam] and death through sin, and so death spread to all men because all men sinned Romans 5:12b

by one man's disobedience [Adam's] many were made sinners Romans 5:19a

death reigned through that one man [Adam]

Romans 5:17a

one man's act of righteousness [Jesus'] leads to acquittal and life for all men. Romans 5:18b

by one man's obedience [Jesus'] many will be made righteous. Romans 5:19b

those who receive the abundance of grace and the free gift of righteousness [will] reign in life through the one man Jesus Christ.   Romans 5:17b

when Christ had offered for all time a single sacrifice for sins, he sat down at the right hand of God, then to wait until his enemies should be made a stool for his feet. For by a single offering he has perfected for all time those who are sanctified. And the Holy Spirit also bears witness to us; for after saying, "This is the covenant that I will make with them after those days, says the Lord: I will put my laws on their hearts, and write them on their minds," then he adds, "I will remember their sins and their misdeeds no more." Hebrews 10:12b-17

He [Jesus] himself bore our sins in his body on the tree, that we might die to sin and live to righteousness. By his wounds you have been healed. 1 Peter 2:24

if any one is in Christ, he is a new creation; the old has passed away, behold, the new has come. All this is from God, who through Christ reconciled us to himself
2 Corinthians 5:17b-18a

you have died, and your life is hid with Christ in God. Colossians 3:3b

You have been born anew, not of perishable seed but of imperishable, through the living and abiding word of God, 1 Peter 1:23

you were ransomed . . . with the precious blood of Christ
1 Peter 1:18a,19a

For God has not destined us for wrath, but to obtain
salvation through our Lord Jesus Christ, who died for us so
that whether we wake [live] or sleep [die] we might live
with him. 1 Thessalonians 5:9-10

[God] is the source of your life in Christ Jesus, whom God
made our wisdom, our righteousness and sanctification and
redemption; 1 Corinthians 1:30

He [God] destined us in love to be his sons through Jesus
Christ Ephesians 1:5a

now that faith has come, we are no longer under a
custodian [the law]; for in Christ Jesus you are all sons of
God, through faith. For as many of you as were baptized
into Christ have put on Christ. Galatians 3:25b-27

those who belong to Christ Jesus have crucified the flesh
with its passions and desires. Galatians 5:24b

Do you not know that all of us who have been baptized into
Christ Jesus were baptized into his death? We know that
our old self was crucified with him [Jesus] so that the sinful
body might be destroyed, and we might no longer be
enslaved to sin. For he who has died is freed from sin.
Romans 6:3,6-7

you have put off the old nature with its practices and have
put on the new nature, ... Put on then, as God's chosen
ones, holy and beloved, compassion, kindness, lowliness,
meekness, and patience, forbearing one another and, if one
has a complaint against another, forgiving each other; as
the Lord has forgiven you, so you also must forgive. And
above all these put on love, which binds everything

together in perfect harmony. Colossians 3:9b,10a,12-14

I [Jesus] have come as light into the world, that whoever believes in me may not remain in darkness. John 12:46

He [God] has delivered us from the dominion of darkness and transferred us to the kingdom of his beloved Son, in whom we have redemption, the forgiveness of sins. Colossians 1:13-14

for once you were darkness, but now you are light in the Lord; walk as children of light Ephesians 5:8

you are all sons of light   1 Thessalonians 5:5a

As therefore you received Christ Jesus the Lord, so live in him, rooted and built up in him and established in the faith, just as you were taught, abounding in thanksgiving. See to it that no one makes a prey of you by philosophy and empty deceit, according to human tradition, according to the elemental spirits of the universe, and not according to Christ. For in him the whole fulness of deity dwells bodily, and you have come to fulness of life in him, who is the head of all rule and authority. In him also you were circumcised with a circumcision made without hands, by putting off the body of flesh in the circumcision of Christ; and you were buried with him in baptism, in which you were also raised with him through faith in the working of God, who raised him from the dead. And you, who were dead in trespasses and the uncircumcision of your flesh, God made alive together with him, having forgiven us all our trespasses, having canceled the bond which stood against us with its legal demands; this he set aside, nailing it to the cross. He disarmed the principalities and powers and made a public example of them, triumphing over them in him. Colossians.2:6-15

[God] raised him [Jesus] from the dead and made him sit at

his right hand in the heavenly places, far above all rule and authority and power and dominion, and above every name that is named, not only in this age but also in that which is to come; and he has put all things under his feet and has made him the head over all things for the church, which is his body Ephesians 1:20b-23a

God, who is rich in mercy, out of the great love with which he loved us, even when we were dead through our trespasses, made us alive together with Christ (by grace you have been saved), and raised us up with him, and made us sit with him in the heavenly places in Christ Jesus, Ephesians 2:4b-6

the law of the Spirit of life in Christ Jesus has set me free from the law of sin and death. Romans 8:2b

if we have died with Christ, we believe that we shall also live with him. For we know that Christ being raised from the dead will never die again; death no longer has dominion over him. Romans 6:8b-9

He [Jesus] is the head of the body, the church; he is the beginning, the first-born from the dead, that in everything he might be pre-eminent. Colossians 1:18

[you] belong to another, to him [Jesus] who has been raised from the dead in order that we may bear fruit for God. Romans 7:4b

For by grace you have been saved through faith; and this is not your own doing, it is the gift of God – not because of works, lest any man should boast. For we are his [God's] workmanship, created in Christ Jesus for good works, which God prepared beforehand, that we should walk in them. Ephesians 2:8-10

He who does not believe God has made him a liar, because

he has not believed in the testimony that God has borne to his Son. And this is the testimony, that God gave us eternal life, and this life is in his Son. He who has the Son has life; he who has not the Son of God has not life. I write this to you who believe in the name of the Son of God, that you may know that you have eternal life. 1 John 5:10b-13

beholding the glory of the Lord, [we] are being changed into his likeness from one degree of glory to another; for this comes from the Lord who is the Spirit.
2 Corinthians 3:18b

No one born of God commits sin; for God's nature abides in him, and he cannot sin because he is born of God.
1 John 3:9

It is the spirit that gives life, the flesh is of no avail; the words that I [Jesus] have spoken to you are spirit and life. John 6:63

Do not be deceived; God is not mocked, for whatever a man sows, that he will also reap. For he who sows to his own flesh will from the flesh reap corruption; but he who sows to the Spirit will from the Spirit reap eternal life. Galatians 6:7-8

the Spirit gives life   2 Corinthians 3:6b

For we are the temple of the living God; as God said, "I will live in them and move among them, and I will be their God, and they shall be my people. 2 Corinthians 6:16b

Beloved, we are God's children now; it does not yet appear what we shall be, but we know that when he [Jesus] appears we shall be like him, for we shall see him as he is. And every one who thus hopes in him purifies himself as he is pure. 1 John 3:2-3

For while we are still in this tent [this earthly body made of dust], we sigh with anxiety; not that we would be unclothed, but that we would be further clothed [with our heavenly body], so that what is mortal may be swallowed up by life. He who has prepared us for this very thing is God, who has given us the Spirit as a guarantee. So we are always of good courage; we know that while we are at home in the body [made of dust] we are away from the Lord [who is in heaven], for we walk by faith, not by sight. We are of good courage, and we would rather be away from the body and at home with the Lord. So whether we are at home or away, we make it our aim to please him. For we must all appear before the judgment seat of Christ, so that each one may receive good or evil, according to what he has done in the body.   2 Corinthians 5:4-10

Our commonwealth is in heaven, and from it we await a Savior, the Lord Jesus Christ, who will change our lowly body to be like his glorious body, by the power which enables him even to subject all things to himself. Philippians 3:20b-21

Jesus came into Galilee, preaching the gospel of God, and saying, "The time is fulfilled, and the kingdom of God is at hand; repent, and believe in the gospel." Mark 1:14a-15

the kingdom of God has come with power. Mark.9:1b

Jesus said … "whoever is ashamed of me and of my words in this adulterous and sinful generation, of him will the Son of man also be ashamed, when he comes in the glory of his Father with the holy angels." Mark 8:38a

Establish your hearts, for the coming of the Lord is at hand. James 5:8b

For this we declare to you by the word of the Lord, that we who are alive, who are left until the coming of the Lord,

shall not precede those who have fallen asleep. For the Lord himself will descend from heaven with a cry of command, with the archangel's call, and with the sound of the trumpet of God. And the dead in Christ will rise first; then we who are alive, who are left, shall be caught up together with them in the clouds to meet the Lord in the air; and so we shall always be with the Lord.
1 Thessalonians 4:15-17

as to the times and the seasons... you yourselves know well that the day of the Lord will come like a thief in the night. When people say, "There is peace and security," then sudden destruction will come upon them... and there will be no escape. 1 Thessalonians 5:1a,2b,3a,3b

*

22 continued

Emily's Note #1

<u>Who I am</u>
I am now a child of God.
I am a saint!
I am God's Beloved!
The righteousness of God is mine!
I no longer fall short of the glory of God!
I have been acquitted and given life by the grace of God.
I belong to Christ in order that I may bear fruit for God.

<u>My new name</u>
I was baptized into the name of God the Father, God the Son, and God the Holy Spirit.
I am now a child of God.
God is my Righteousness
God is my Peace
God is my Shepherd / Guide
God is my Healer / Physician
God is my Provider / Source
God is my Victory
God is Ever Present
This is He who dwells in me.

<u>Foundations</u>
- Jesus loved me and gave himself for me. (see Galatians 2:20)
- Christ died for my sins in accordance with the scriptures, (see 1 Corinthians 15:3)
- Christ was raised on the third day in accordance with the scriptures, (see 1 Corinthians 15:4)
- I receive the Holy Spirit by hearing with faith (see Galatians 3:2)
- the Holy Spirit helps me in me weakness (see Romans 8:26)

- the Holy Spirit intercedes for the saints (me!) according to the will of God (see Romans 8:27)
- Christ is in me and my spirit is alive because of righteousness (see Romans 8:10)
- this mind is mine in Christ Jesus – I look to the interest of others and I count others better than myself (see Philippians 2:3-5)
- In Christ Jesus I am a daughter of God, through faith, (see Galatians 3:26)
- the Father has delivered me from the dominion of darkness and transferred me to the kingdom of his beloved Son, (see Colossians 1:13)
- I glorify God by the generosity of my contribution for saints and for all others (see 2 Corinthians 9:13)
- God is my supply. I always have enough of everything and I provide in abundance for every good work. (see 2 Corinthians 9:8)
- I am made rich in every way for great generosity (see 2 Corinthians 9:11)
- I am a partaker of God's grace (see Philippians 1:7)
- I have died (see Colossians 1:3)
- I have been crucified with Christ (see Galatians 2:20)
- I have been raised with Christ (see Colossians 3:1)
- Jesus – 'Because I live, you will live also.' (see John 14:19)
- In Jesus the whole fullness of deity dwells bodily (see Colossians 2:9)
- I have come to fullness of life in Jesus (see Colossians 2:10)
- I want to be filled with the fruits of righteousness which come through Jesus Christ to the glory and praise of God. (see Philippians 1:9-11)
- I want my love to abound more and more, with knowledge and all discernment, so that I may approve what is excellent, and may be pure and blameless for the day of Christ (see Philippians 1:9-11)
- God works miracles for me and around me by the hearing with faith (see Galatians 3:5)
- I say to this sycamine tree, `Be rooted up, and be planted in

the sea,' and **it** obeys me. (see Luke 17:6)

- by the Spirit of God I cast out demons (see Matthew 12:28)
- Women of faith are the daughters of Abraham (see Galatians 3:7)
- The promises were made to Abraham and to Christ (see Galatians 3:16)
- A servant of Christ does not seek the favor of men, nor try to please men (see Galatians 1:10)
- the Spirit of God dwells in me, I am in the Spirit, I am not in the flesh (see Romans 8:9)
- to set the mind on the Spirit is life and peace. (see Romans 8:6)
- Whatever my task, I work heartily, for I am serving the Lord Christ (see Colossians 3:23-24)
- I am not carrying on a worldly war (see 2 Corinthians 10:3)
- the weapons of my warfare have divine power to destroy strongholds (see 2 Corinthians 10:4)
- I take every thought captive to obey Christ, (see 2 Corinthians 10:5)
- Confident in the Lord I am bold to speak the word of God without fear. (see Philippians 1:14)
- I work out my salvation with fear and trembling, for God is at work in me, both to will and to work for his good pleasure. (see Philippians 2:13)
- I do all things without grumbling or questioning so that I may be blameless and innocent, a child of God without blemish (see Philippians 2:14-15)
- I hope for what I do not see and I wait for it with patience. (see Romans 8:25)

Questions God asks me

Jesus said to her [Martha], "I am the resurrection and the life; he who believes in me, though he die, yet shall he live, and whoever lives and believes in me shall never die. Do you believe this?" (see John 11:25)

Why do you live as if you still belong to the world? Why do you submit to regulations, "Do not handle, Do not taste, Do not touch" (referring to things which all perish as they are used), according to human precepts and doctrines? (see Colossians 2:20-22)

****

Emily's Note #2

<u>Righteousness</u>

let him who glories glory in this, that he understands and knows me, that I am the LORD who practice steadfast love, justice, and righteousness in the earth; for in these things I delight, says the LORD." Jeremiah 9:24b

Noah was a righteous man, blameless in his generation; Noah walked with God. Genesis 6:9

After these things the word of the LORD came to Abram in a vision, "Fear not, Abram, I am your shield; your reward shall be very great." ... "...your own son shall be your heir." And he [the LORD] brought him [Abram] outside and said, "Look toward heaven, and number the stars, if you are able to number them." Then he said to him, "So shall your descendants be." And he [Abram] believed the LORD; and he [the LORD] reckoned it to him [Abram] as righteousness. Genesis 15:1,4b-6

For thou dost bless the righteous, O LORD;
thou dost cover him with favor as with a shield.
Psalm 5:12

For the LORD is righteous, he loves righteous deeds;
the upright shall behold his face.
Psalm 11:7

The LORD is my shepherd, I shall not want;
he makes me lie down in green pastures.

He leads me beside still waters;
he restores my soul.
He leads me in paths of righteousness
for his name's sake.
Psalm 23:1-3

the LORD upholds the righteous.
Psalm 37:17b

Let me hear what God the LORD will speak,
for he will speak peace to his people,
to his saints, to those who turn to him in their hearts.
Surely his salvation is at hand for those who fear him,
that glory may dwell in our land.
Steadfast love and faithfulness will meet;
righteousness and peace will kiss each other.
Faithfulness will spring up from the ground,
and righteousness will look down from the sky.
Yea, the LORD will give what is good,
and our land will yield its increase.
Psalm 85:8-12

Righteousness and justice are the foundation of thy throne;
steadfast love and faithfulness go before thee.
Blessed are the people who know the festal shout,
who walk, O LORD, in the light of thy countenance,
who exult in thy name all the day,
and extol thy righteousness.
For thou art the glory of their strength;
by thy favor our horn is exalted.
Psalm 89:14-17

Let thy priests be clothed with righteousness,
and let thy saints shout for joy.
Psalm 132:9

Surely the righteous shall give thanks to thy name;
the upright shall dwell in thy presence.   Psalm 140:13

righteousness delivers from death.
Proverbs 11:4b

The fruit of the righteous is a tree of life,
Proverbs 11:30a

And the effect of righteousness will be peace,
and the result of righteousness, quietness and trust for ever.
Isaiah 32:17

the LORD loves the righteous.
Psalm 146:8b

Further Study

Interested in learning more about the subjects discussed in this story? I highly recommend books by Derek Prince, Chad Norris, Jack R. Taylor, Andrew Wommack, Creflo Dollar, Bill Johnson, Robert Morris, Watchman Nee, Randy Clark, Reinhard Bonnke, Joseph Prince, and others, on the topics of the Kingdom of God, grace, healing and the Holy Spirit. Randy Clark DVDs on healing are very practical resources. I also highly recommend the deluxe edition DVDs by Darren Wilson, *Furious Love, Father of Lights, Finger of God, Holy Ghost and Holy Ghost Reborn*, (the deluxe editions have full interviews included in the extra DVD's, beyond the excerpts in the movies.) Visit wpfilms.tv to watch them online.

Author Biography

Dee Henderson is the author of numerous novels, including *An Unfinished Death, Taken, Unspoken* and the acclaimed O'MALLEY series. Several titles have appeared on the USA Today Bestseller list; *Full Disclosure* has also appeared on the New York Times Bestseller list. Her books have won or been nominated for several industry awards, such as the RITA Award, the Christy Award and the ECPA Gold Medallion. For more information, visit www.DeeHenderson.com

Contact information

The Author welcomes your feedback.

Dee Henderson
P.O. Box 13086
Springfield, IL 62791

dee@deehenderson.com
www.deehenderson.com

*

Books by Dee Henderson

<u>The Most Recent Release</u>
Immortality

<u>Companion Books (read one or the other)</u>
Healing is by Grace Alone (non-fiction)
An Unfinished Death (fiction)

<u>The O'Malley Series</u>
The Negotiator – Kate and Dave
The Guardian – Shari and Marcus
The Truth Seeker – Lisa and Quinn
The Protector – Cassie and Jack
The Healer – Rachel and Cole
The Rescuer – Meghan and Stephen
Danger in the Shadows (prequel - Dave's story)
Jennifer: An O'Malley Love Story (prequel –
Jennifer's backstory)

Full Disclosure – Ann and Paul Falcon
Unspoken – Charlotte and Bryce Bishop
Undetected – Gina and Mark Bishop
Taken – Shannon and Matthew Dane

<u>Evie Blackwell Stories</u>
Traces of Guilt
Threads of Suspicion

<u>Military Stories</u>
True Devotion
True Valor
True Honor

Various Other Titles
Kidnapped
The Witness
Before I Wake
The Marriage Wish
God's Gift

Short Stories
"Missing" in anthology Sins of the Past
"Betrayed" in anthology The Cost of Betrayal

Visit the website www.DeeHenderson.com
for additional book details.

Immortality

*

49301800R00211

Made in the USA
Columbia, SC
18 January 2019